Winner of
THE PULITZER PRIZE
THE NATIONAL BOOK CRITICS CIRCLE AWARD
THE ANISFIELD-WOLF BOOK AWARD
THE JOHN SARGENT, SR. FIRST NOVEL PRIZE

PRAISE FOR
THE BRIEF WONDROUS LIFE *of* OSCAR WAO

"The Dominican Republic [Díaz] portrays in *The Brief Wondrous Life of Oscar Wao* is a wild, beautiful, dangerous, and contradictory place, both hopelessly impoverished and impossibly rich . . . [a] weirdly wonderful novel. Díaz made us wait eleven years for this first novel and *boom!*—it's over just like that. It's not a bad gambit, to always leave your audience wanting more. So brief and wondrous, this life of Oscar. Wow."   —*The Washington Post Book World*

"A triumph of style and wit, moving along Oscar de León's story with cracking, down-low humor, and at times expertly stunning us with heart-stabbing sentences. . . . [It is] something exceedingly rare: a book in which a new America can recognize itself, but so can everyone else."   —*San Francisco Chronicle*

"In the imagination of many writers it is the untold stories that propel—those vibrant, colorful, magical, historical swirls of humanity that make up our knowing. Junot Díaz's wondrous first novel offers that and more, enchanting us with energetic poetry and offering us a splendid portrait of ordinary folks set against the extraordinarily cruel history of the Dominican Republic in the twentieth century."   —Edward P. Jones, author of *The Known World*

"Díaz's writing is unruly, manic, seductive. . . . In Díaz's landscape we are all the same, victims of a history and a present that don't just bleed together but stew. Often in hilarity. Mostly in heartbreak."   —*Esquire*

"Rich and vital . . . That Díaz accomplishes so much in his first novel is remarkable but not surprising. His short story collection of 1997, *Drown*, earned him stellar reviews; in the case of his first novel, the phrase 'eagerly awaited' is for once not hyperbole."

—*The Sunday Oregonian*

"Readers who have had to wait a decade for Díaz's first novel are now spectacularly rewarded." —*Booklist* (starred review)

"What carries the book is Díaz's voice, which is as distinct and energetic as it is multifarious. It's this voice that inspires whatever pleasure, pathos, and wonder we glean from Oscar Wao's short, yearning life." —*The Globe & Mail*

"Completely engrossing . . . Díaz makes you care so much about these characters that once you're done reading this novel, you'll miss them." —*Newport News Daily Press*

"Dark and exuberant . . . rich and playful . . . but mostly this fierce, funny, tragic book is just what a reader would have hoped for in a novel by Junot Díaz." —*Publishers Weekly*

continued . . .

Books by Junot Díaz

DROWN

THE BRIEF WONDROUS LIFE OF OSCAR WAO

THE BRIEF
WONDROUS LIFE
of
OSCAR WAO

JUNOT DÍAZ

RIVERHEAD BOOKS
New York

RIVERHEAD BOOKS
Published by the Penguin Group
Penguin Group (USA) Inc.
375 Hudson Street, New York, New York 10014, USA
Penguin Group (Canada), 90 Eglinton Avenue East, Suite 700, Toronto, Ontario M4P 2Y3, Canada (a division of Pearson Penguin Canada Inc.)
Penguin Books Ltd., 80 Strand, London WC2R 0RL, England
Penguin Group Ireland, 25 St. Stephen's Green, Dublin 2, Ireland (a division of Penguin Books Ltd.)
Penguin Group (Australia), 250 Camberwell Road, Camberwell, Victoria 3124, Australia (a division of Pearson Australia Group Pty. Ltd.)
Penguin Books India Pvt. Ltd., 11 Community Centre, Panchsheel Park, New Delhi—110 017, India
Penguin Group (NZ), 67 Apollo Drive, Rosedale, North Shore 0632, New Zealand (a division of Pearson New Zealand Ltd.)
Penguin Books (South Africa) (Pty.) Ltd., 24 Sturdee Avenue, Rosebank, Johannesburg 2196, South Africa

Penguin Books Ltd., Registered Offices: 80 Strand, London WC2R 0RL, England

This is a work of fiction. Names, characters, places, and incidents either are the product of the author's imagination or are used fictitiously and any resemblance to actual persons, living or dead, business establishments, events, or locales is completely coincidental. The publisher does not have any control over and does not assume any responsibility for author or third-party websites or their content.

THE BRIEF WONDROUS LIFE OF OSCAR WAO

A Berkley Book / published by arrangement with the author

PRINTING HISTORY
Riverhead hardcover edition: September 2007
Riverhead trade paperback edition: September 2008
Riverhead mass-market international edition: September 2008

Copyright © 2008 by Junot Díaz
Cover design © 2007 Rodrigo Corral

Portions of this book originally appeared in *The New Yorker*, in somewhat different form.

The author gratefully acknowledges permission to reprint lines from *The Schooner "Flight"* from *Collected Poems 1948–1984* by Derek Walcott. Copyright © 1986 by Derek Walcott. Reprinted by permission of Farrar, Straus and Giroux, LLC.

ISBN: 978-1-59448-359-2

RIVERHEAD®
Riverhead Books are published by the Penguin Group
Penguin Group (USA) Inc., 375 Hudson Street, New York, New York 10014.
RIVERHEAD is a registered trademark of Penguin Group (USA) Inc.
The RIVERHEAD logo is a trademark belonging to Penguin Group (USA) Inc.

PRINTED IN THE UNITED STATES OF AMERICA

10   9   8   7   6   5   4   3

Elizabeth de León

"Of what import are brief, nameless lives . . . to **Galactus**??"

Fantastic Four
Stan Lee and Jack Kirby
(Vol. 1, No. 49, April 1966)

Christ have mercy on all sleeping things!
From that dog rotting down Wrightson Road
to when I was a dog on these streets;
if loving these islands must be my load,
out of corruption my soul takes wings,
But they had started to poison my soul
with their big house, big car, big-time bohbohl,
coolie, nigger, Syrian, and French Creole,
so I leave it for them and their carnival—
I taking a sea-bath, I gone down the road.
I know these islands from Monos to Nassau,
a rusty head sailor with sea-green eyes
that they nickname Shabine, the patois for
any red nigger, and I, Shabine, saw
when these slums of empire was paradise.
I'm just a red nigger who love the sea,
I had a sound colonial education,
I have Dutch, nigger, and English in me,
and either I'm nobody, or I'm a nation.

DEREK WALCOTT

They say it came first from Africa, carried in the screams of the enslaved; that it was the death bane of the Tainos, uttered just as one world perished and another began; that it was a demon drawn into Creation through the nightmare door that was cracked open in the Antilles. *Fukú americanus,* or more colloquially, fukú—generally a curse or a doom of some kind; specifically the Curse and the Doom of the New World. Also called the fukú of the Admiral because the Admiral was both its midwife and one of its great European victims; despite "discovering" the New World the Admiral died miserable and syphilitic, hearing (dique) divine voices. In Santo Domingo, the Land He Loved Best (what Oscar, at the end, would call the Ground Zero of the New World), the Admiral's very name has become synonymous with both kinds of fukú, little and large; to say his name aloud or even to hear it is to invite calamity on the heads of you and yours.

No matter what its name or provenance, it is believed that the arrival of Europeans on Hispaniola unleashed the fukú on the world, and we've all been in the shit ever since. Santo Domingo might be fukú's Kilometer Zero, its port of entry, but we are all of us its children, whether we know it or not.

But the fukú ain't just ancient history, a ghost story from the past with no power to scare. In my parents' day the fukú was real as shit, something your everyday person could believe in. Everybody knew someone who'd been eaten by a fukú, just like everybody knew somebody who worked up in the Palacio. It was in the air, you could say, though, like all the most important things on the Island, not something folks really talked about. But in those elder days, fukú had it good; it even had a hypeman of sorts, a high priest, you could say. Our then dictator-for-life Rafael Leónidas Trujillo Molina.[1] No one knows whether Trujillo was the Curse's servant or its master, its agent or its principal, but it was clear he and it had an understanding, that them two was *tight*. It was believed,

1. For those of you who missed your mandatory two seconds of Dominican history: Trujillo, one of the twentieth century's most infamous dictators, ruled the Dominican Republic between 1930 and 1961 with an implacable ruthless brutality. A portly, sadistic, pig-eyed mulato who bleached his skin, wore platform shoes, and had a fondness for Napoleon-era haberdashery, Trujillo (also known as El Jefe, the Failed Cattle Thief, and Fuckface) came to control nearly every aspect of the DR's political, cultural, social, and economic life through a potent (and familiar) mixture of violence, intimidation, massacre, rape, co-optation, and terror; treated the country like it was a plantation and he was the master. At first glance, he was just your prototypical Latin American caudillo, but his power was terminal in ways that few historians or writers have ever truly captured or, I would argue, imagined. He was our Sauron, our Arawn, our Darkseid, our Once and Future Dictator, a personaje so outlandish, so perverse, so dreadful that not even a sci-fi writer could have made his ass up. Famous for

even in educated circles, that anyone who plotted against Trujillo would incur a fukú most powerful, down to the seventh generation and beyond. If you even thought a bad thing about Trujillo, *fuá*, a hurricane would sweep your family out to sea, *fuá*, a boulder would fall out of a clear sky and squash you, *fuá*, the shrimp you ate today was the cramp that killed you tomorrow. Which explains why everyone who tried to assassinate him always got done, why those dudes who finally did buck him down all died so horrifically. And what about fucking Kennedy? He was the one who green-lighted the assassination of Trujillo in 1961, who ordered the CIA to

changing ALL THE NAMES of ALL THE LANDMARKS in the Dominican Republic to honor himself (Pico Duarte became Pico Trujillo, and Santo Domingo de Guzmán, the first and oldest city in the New World, became Ciudad Trujillo); for making ill monopolies out of every slice of the national patrimony (which quickly made him one of the wealthiest men on the planet); for building one of the largest militaries in the hemisphere (dude had bomber wings, for fuck's sake); for fucking every hot girl in sight, even the wives of his subordinates, thousands upon thousands upon thousands of women; for expecting, no, *insisting* on absolute veneration from his pueblo (tellingly, the national slogan was "Dios y Trujillo"; for running the country like it was a Marine boot camp; for stripping friends and allies of their positions and properties for no reason at all; and for his almost *supernatural* abilities.

Outstanding accomplishments include: the 1937 genocide against the Haitian and Haitian-Dominican community; one of the longest, most damaging U.S.-backed dictatorships in the Western Hemisphere (and if we Latin types are skillful at anything it's tolerating U.S.-backed dictators, so you know this was a hard-earned victory, the chilenos and the argentinos are still appealing); the creation of the first modern kleptocracy (Trujillo was Mobutu before Mobutu was Mobutu); the systematic bribing of American senators; and, last but not least, the forging of the Dominican peoples into a modern state (did what his Marine trainers, during the Occupation, were unable to do).

deliver arms to the Island. Bad move, cap'n. For what Kennedy's intelligence experts failed to tell him was what every single Dominican, from the richest jabao in Mao to the poorest güey in El Buey, from the oldest anciano sanmacorisano to the littlest carajito in San Francisco, knew: that whoever killed Trujillo, their family would suffer a fukú so dreadful it would make the one that attached itself to the Admiral jojote in comparison. You want a final conclusive answer to the Warren Commission's question, Who killed JFK? Let me, your humble Watcher, reveal once and for all the God's Honest Truth: It wasn't the mob or LBJ or the ghost of Marilyn Fucking Monroe. It wasn't aliens or the KGB or a lone gunman. It wasn't the Hunt Brothers of Texas or Lee Harvey or the Trilateral Commission. It was Trujillo; it was the fukú. Where in coñazo do you think the so-called Curse of the Kennedys comes from?² How about Vietnam? Why do you think the greatest power in the world lost its first war to a Third World country like Vietnam? I mean, Negro, *please*. It might interest you that just as the U.S. was ramping up its involvement in Vietnam, LBJ launched an illegal invasion of the Dominican Republic (April 28, 1965). (Santo Domingo was Iraq before Iraq was Iraq.) A smashing military success for the U.S., and many of the same units and

2. Here's one for you conspiracy-minded fools: on the night that John Kennedy, Jr., and Carolyn Bessette and her sister Lauren went down in their Piper Saratoga, John-John's father's favorite domestic, Providencia Paredes, dominicana, was in Martha's Vineyard cooking up for John-John his favorite dish: chicharrón de pollo. But fukú always eats first and it eats alone.

intelligence teams that took part in the "democratization" of Santo Domingo were immediately shipped off to Saigon. What do you think these soldiers, technicians, and spooks carried with them, in their rucks, in their suitcases, in their shirt pockets, on the hair inside their nostrils, caked up around their shoes? Just a little gift from my people to America, a small repayment for an unjust war. That's right, folks. Fukú.

Which is why it's important to remember fukú doesn't always strike like lightning. Sometimes it works patiently, drowning a nigger by degrees, like with the Admiral or the U.S. in paddies outside of Saigon. Sometimes it's slow and sometimes it's fast. It's doom-ish in that way, makes it harder to put a finger on, to brace yourself against. But be assured: like Darkseid's Omega Effect, like Morgoth's bane, [3] no matter how many turns and digressions this shit might take, it always—and I mean always—gets its man.

Whether I believe in what many have described as the Great American Doom is not really the point. You live as long as I did in the heart of fukú country, you hear these kinds of tales all the time. Everybody in Santo Domingo has a fukú story

3. "I am the Elder King: Melkor, first and mightiest of all the Valar, who was before the world and made it. The shadow of my purpose lies upon Arda, and all that is in it bends slowly and surely to my will. But upon all whom you love my thought shall weigh as a cloud of Doom, and it shall bring them down into darkness and despair. Wherever they go, evil shall arise. Whenever they speak, their words shall bring ill counsel. Whatsoever they do shall turn against them. They shall die without hope, cursing both life and death."

knocking around in their family. I have a twelve-daughter uncle in the Cibao who believed that he'd been cursed by an old lover never to have male children. Fukú. I have a tía who believed she'd been denied happiness because she'd laughed at a rival's funeral. Fukú. My paternal abuelo believes that diaspora was Trujillo's payback to the pueblo that betrayed him. Fukú.

It's perfectly fine if you don't believe in these "superstitions." In fact, it's better than fine—it's perfect. Because no matter what you believe, fukú believes in you.

A couple weeks ago, while I was finishing this book, I posted the thread *fukú* on the DR1 forum, just out of curiosity. These days I'm nerdy like that. The talkback blew the fuck up. You should see how many responses I've gotten. They just keep coming in. And not just from Domos. The Puertorocks want to talk about fufus, and the Haitians have some shit just like it. There are a zillion of these fukú stories. Even my mother, who almost never talks about Santo Domingo, has started sharing hers with me.

As I'm sure you've guessed by now, I have a fukú story too. I wish I could say it was the best of the lot—fukú number one—but I can't. Mine ain't the scariest, the clearest, the most painful, or the most beautiful.

It just happens to be the one that's got its fingers around my throat.

I'm not entirely sure Oscar would have liked this designation. Fukú story. He was a hardcore sci-fi and fantasy man, believed that that was the kind of story we were all living in.

He'd ask: What more sci-fi than the Santo Domingo? What more fantasy than the Antilles?

But now that I know how it all turns out, I have to ask, in turn: What more fukú?

One final final note, Toto, before Kansas goes bye-bye: traditionally in Santo Domingo anytime you mentioned or overheard the Admiral's name or anytime a fukú reared its many heads there was only one way to prevent disaster from coiling around you, only one surefire counterspell that would keep you and your family safe. Not surprisingly, it was a word. A simple word (followed usually by a vigorous crossing of index fingers).

Zafa.

It used to be more popular in the old days, bigger, so to speak, in Macondo than in McOndo. There are people, though, like my tío Miguel in the Bronx who still zafa everything. He's old-school like that. If the Yanks commit an error in the late innings it's zafa; if somebody brings shells in from the beach it's zafa; if you serve a man parcha it's zafa. Twenty-four-hour zafa in the hope that the bad luck will not have had time to cohere. Even now as I write these words I wonder if this book ain't a zafa of sorts. My very own counterspell.

I

1

GhettoNerd at the
End of the World
1974–1987

THE GOLDEN AGE

Our hero was not one of those Dominican cats everybody's always going on about—he wasn't no home-run hitter or a fly bachatero, not a playboy with a million hots on his jock.

And except for one period early in his life, dude never had much luck with the females (how *very* un-Dominican of him).

He was seven then.

In those blessed days of his youth, Oscar was something of a Casanova. One of those preschool loverboys who was always trying to kiss the girls, always coming up behind them during a merengue and giving them the pelvic pump, the first nigger to learn the perrito and the one who danced it any chance he got. Because in those days he was (still) a "normal" Dominican boy raised in a "typical" Dominican family, his nascent pimp-liness was encouraged by blood and friends alike. During parties—and there were many many parties in those long-ago seventies days, before Washington Heights was Washington Heights, before the Bergenline became a straight shot of Spanish for almost a hundred blocks—some drunk relative inevitably pushed Oscar onto some little girl and then everyone would howl as boy and girl approximated the hip-motism of the adults.

You should have seen him, his mother sighed in her Last Days. He was our little Porfirio Rubirosa.[4]

All the other boys his age avoided the girls like they were a bad case of Captain Trips. Not Oscar. The little guy loved himself the females, had "girlfriends" galore. (He was a stout

---

4. In the forties and fifties, Porfirio Rubirosa—or Rubi, as he was known in the papers—was the third-most-famous Dominican in the world (first came the Failed Cattle Thief, and then the Cobra Woman herself, María Montez). A tall, debonair prettyboy whose "enormous phallus created havoc in Europe and North America," Rubirosa was the quintessential jet-setting car-racing polo-obsessed playboy, the Trujillato's "happy side" (for he was indeed one of Trujillo's best-known minions). A part-time former model and dashing man-about-town, Rubirosa famously married Trujillo's daughter Flor de Oro in 1932, and even though they were divorced five years later, in the Year of the Haitian Genocide, homeboy managed to re-main in El Jefe's good graces throughout the regime's long run. Unlike his ex-brother-in-law Ramfis (to whom he was frequently connected), Rubirosa seemed incapable of carrying out many murders; in 1935 he traveled to New York to deliver El Jefe's death sentence against the exile leader Angel Morales but fled before the botched assassination could take place. Rubi was the original Dominican Player, fucked all sorts of women—Barbara Hutton, Doris Duke (who happened to be the richest woman in the world), the French actress Danielle Darrieux, and Zsa Zsa Gabor—to name but a few. Like his pal Ramfis, Porfirio died in a car crash, in 1965, his twelve-cylinder Ferrari skidding off a road in the Bois de Boulogne. (Hard to overstate the role cars play in our narrative.)

kid, heading straight to fat, but his mother kept him nice in haircuts and clothes, and before the proportions of his head changed he'd had these lovely flashing eyes and these cute-ass cheeks, visible in all his pictures.) The girls—his sister Lola's friends, his mother's friends, even their neighbor, Mari Colón, a thirty-something postal employee who wore red on her lips and walked like she had a bell for an ass—all purportedly fell for him. Ese muchacho está bueno! (Did it hurt that he was earnest and clearly attention-deprived? Not at all!) In the DR during summer visits to his family digs in Baní he was the worst, would stand in front of Nena Inca's house and call out to passing women—Tú eres guapa! Tú eres guapa!—until a Seventh-day Adventist complained to his grandmother and she shut down the hit parade lickety-split. Muchacho del diablo! This is not a cabaret!

It truly was a Golden Age for Oscar, one that reached its apotheosis in the fall of his seventh year, when he had two little girlfriends at the same time, his first and only ménage à trois. With Maritza Chacón and Olga Polanco.

Maritza was Lola's friend. Long-haired and prissy and so pretty she could have played young Dejah Thoris. Olga, on the other hand, was no friend of the family. She lived in the house at the end of the block that his mother complained about because it was filled with puertoricans who were always hanging out on their porch drinking beer. (What, they couldn't have done that in Coamo? Oscar's mom asked crossly.) Olga had like ninety cousins, all who seemed to be named Hector or Luis or Wanda. And since her mother was una maldita borracha (to quote Oscar's mom), Olga smelled on some days of ass, which is why the kids took to calling her Mrs. Peabody.

Mrs. Peabody or not, Oscar liked how quiet she was, how she let him throw her to the ground and wrestle with her, the interest she showed in his *Star Trek* dolls. Maritza was just plain beautiful, no need for motivation there, always around too, and it was just a stroke of pure genius that convinced him to kick it to them both at once. At first he pretended that it was his number-one hero, Shazam, who wanted to date them. But after they agreed he dropped all pretense. It wasn't Shazam—it was Oscar.

Those were more innocent days, so their relationship amounted to standing close to each other at the bus stop, some undercover hand-holding, and twice kissing on the cheeks very seriously, first Maritza, then Olga, while they were hidden from the street by some bushes. (Look at that little macho, his mother's friends said. Que hombre.)

The threesome only lasted a single beautiful week. One day after school Maritza cornered Oscar behind the swing set and laid down the law, It's either her or *me*! Oscar held Maritza's hand and talked seriously and at great length about his love for her and reminded her that they had agreed to *share*, but Maritza wasn't having any of it. She had three older sisters, knew everything she needed to know about the possibilities of *sharing*. Don't talk to me no more unless you get rid of her! Maritza, with her chocolate skin and narrow eyes, already expressing the Ogún energy that she would chop at everybody with for the rest of her life. Oscar went home morose to his pre–Korean-sweatshop-era cartoons—to the *Herculoids* and *Space Ghost*. What's wrong with you? his mother asked. She was getting ready to go to her second job, the eczema on her hands looking like a messy meal that had set. When Oscar whimpered, Girls, Moms de León nearly exploded. Tú ta llorando por una muchacha? She hauled Oscar to his feet by his ear.

Mami, stop it, his sister cried, stop it!

She threw him to the floor. Dale un galletazo, she panted, then see if the little puta respects you.

If he'd been a different nigger he might have considered the galletazo. It wasn't just that he didn't have no kind of father to show him the masculine ropes, he simply lacked all aggressive and martial tendencies. (Unlike his sister, who fought boys and packs of morena girls who hated her thin nose and straightish hair.) Oscar had like a zero combat rating; even Olga and her toothpick arms could have stomped him silly. Aggression and intimidation out of the question. So he thought it over. Didn't take him long to decide. After all, Maritza was beautiful and Olga was not; Olga sometimes smelled like pee and Maritza did not. Maritza was allowed over their house and Olga was not. (A puertorican over here? his mother scoffed. Jamás!) His logic as close to the yes/no math of insects as a nigger could get. He broke up with Olga the following day on the playground, Maritza at his side, and how Olga had cried! Shaking like a rag in her hand-me-downs and in the shoes that were four sizes too big! Snots pouring out her nose and everything!

In later years, after he and Olga had both turned into overweight freaks, Oscar could not resist feeling the occasional flash of guilt when he saw Olga loping across a street or staring blankly out near the New York bus stop, couldn't stop himself from wondering how much his cold-as-balls breakup had contributed to her present fucked-upness. (Breaking up with her, he would remember, hadn't felt like anything; even when she started crying, he hadn't been moved. He'd said, No be a baby.)

What *had* hurt, however, was when Maritza dumped *him*. Monday after he'd fed Olga to the dogs he arrived at the bus stop with his beloved *Planet of the Apes* lunch box only to discover beautiful Maritza holding hands with butt-ugly Nelson Pardo. Nelson Pardo who looked like Chaka from *Land of the Lost*! Nelson Pardo who was so stupid he thought the moon was a stain that God had forgotten to clean. (He'll get to it soon, he assured his whole class.) Nelson Pardo who would become the neighborhood B&E expert before joining the Marines and losing eight toes in the First Gulf War. At first Oscar thought it a mistake; the sun was in his eyes, he'd not slept enough the night before. He stood next to them and admired his lunch box, how realistic and diabolical Dr. Zaius looked. But Maritza wouldn't even *smile* at him! Pretended he wasn't there. We should get married, she said to Nelson, and Nelson grinned moronically, turning up the street to look for the bus. Oscar had been too hurt to speak; he sat down on the curb and felt something overwhelming surge up from his chest, scared the shit out of him, and before he knew it he was crying; when his sister, Lola, walked over and asked him what was the matter he'd shaken his head. Look at the mariconcito, somebody snickered. Somebody else kicked his beloved lunch box and scratched it right across General Urko's face. When he got on the bus, still crying, the driver, a famously reformed PCP addict, had said, Christ, don't be a fucking *baby*.

How had the breakup affected Olga? What he really was asking was: *How had the breakup affected Oscar?*

It seemed to Oscar that from the moment Maritza dumped him—Shazam!—his life started going down the tubes. Over the next couple of years he grew fatter and fatter. Early adolescence hit him especially hard, scrambling his face into nothing you could call cute, splotching his skin with zits, making him self-conscious; and his interest—in Genres!—which nobody had said boo about before, suddenly became synonymous with being a loser with a capital L. Couldn't make friends for the life of him, too dorky, too shy, and (if the kids from his neighborhood are to be believed) too *weird* (had a habit of using big words he had memorized only the day before). He no longer went anywhere near the girls because at best they ignored him, at worst they shrieked and called him gordo asqueroso! He forgot the perrito, forgot the pride he felt when the women in the family had called him hombre. Did not kiss another girl for a long *long* time. As though almost everything he had in the girl department had burned up that one fucking week.

Not that his "girlfriends" fared much better. It seemed that whatever bad no-love karma hit Oscar hit them too. By seventh grade Olga had grown huge and scary, a troll gene in her somewhere, started drinking 151 straight out the bottle and was finally taken out of school because she had a habit of screaming *NATAS!* in the middle of homeroom. Even her breasts, when they finally emerged, were floppy and terrifying. Once on the bus Olga had called Oscar a *cake eater*, and he'd almost said, Look who's talking, puerca, but he was afraid that she would rear back and trample him; his cool-index, already low, couldn't have survived that kind of a paliza, would have put him on par with the handicapped kids and with Joe Locorotundo, who was famous for masturbating in public.

And the lovely Maritza Chacón? The hypotenuse of our triangle, how had she fared? Well, before you could say *Oh Mighty Isis*, Maritza blew up into the flyest guapa in Paterson, one of the Queens of New Peru. Since they stayed neighbors, Oscar saw her plenty, a ghetto Mary Jane, hair as black and lush as a thunderhead, probably the only Peruvian girl on the planet with pelo curlier than his sister's (he hadn't heard of Afro-Peruvians yet, or of a town called Chincha), body fine enough to make old men forget their infirmities, and from the sixth grade on dating men two, three times her age. (Maritza might not have been good at much—not sports, not school, not work—but she was good at men.) Did that mean she had avoided the curse—that she was happier than Oscar or Olga? That was doubtful. From what Oscar could see, Maritza was a girl who seemed to delight in getting slapped around by her boyfriends. Since it happened to her *all the time*. If a boy hit *me*, Lola said cockily, I would bite his *face*.

See Maritza: French-kissing on the front stoop of her house, getting in or out of some roughneck's ride, being pushed down onto the sidewalk. Oscar would watch the

French-kissing, the getting in and out, the pushing, all through his cheerless, sexless adolescence. What else could he do? His bedroom window looked out over the front of her house, and so he always peeped her while he was painting his D&D miniatures or reading the latest Stephen King. The only things that changed in those years were the models of the cars, the size of Maritza's ass, and the kind of music volting out the cars' speakers. First freestyle, then Ill Will–era hiphop, and, right at the very end, for just a little while, Héctor Lavoe and the boys.

He said hi to her almost every day, all upbeat and fauxhappy, and she said hi back, indifferently, but that was it. He didn't imagine that she remembered their kissing—but of course he could not forget.

THE MORONIC INFERNO

High school was Don Bosco Tech, and since Don Bosco Tech was an urban all-boys Catholic school packed to the strakes with a couple hundred insecure hyperactive adolescents, it was, for a fat sci-fi–reading nerd like Oscar, a source of endless anguish. For Oscar, high school was the equivalent of a medieval spectacle, like being put in the stocks and forced to endure the peltings and outrages of a mob of deranged halfwits, an experience from which he supposed he should have emerged a better person, but that's not really what happened—and if there were any lessons to be gleaned from the ordeal of those years he never quite figured out what they were. He walked into school every day like the fat lonely nerdy kid he was, and all he could think about was the day of his manumission, when he would at last be set free from its unending horror. Hey, Oscar, are there faggots on Mars?—Hey, Kazoo, catch *this*. The first time he heard the term *moronic inferno* he knew exactly where it was located and who were its inhabitants.

Sophomore year Oscar found himself weighing in at a whopping 245 (260 when he was depressed, which was often) and it had become clear to everybody, especially his family, that he'd become the neighborhood parigüayo.[5] Had none of the Higher Powers of your typical Dominican male, couldn't have pulled a girl if his life depended on it. Couldn't play sports for shit, or dominoes, was beyond uncoordinated, threw a ball like a girl. Had no knack for music or business or dance, no hustle, no rap, no G. And most damning of all: no

5. The pejorative *parigüayo*, Watchers agree, is a corruption of the English neologism "party watcher." The word came into common usage during the First American Occupation of the DR, which ran from 1916 to 1924. (You didn't know we were occupied twice in the twentieth century? Don't worry, when you have kids they won't know the U.S. occupied Iraq either.) During the First Occupation it was reported that members of the American Occupying Forces would often attend Dominican parties but instead of joining in the fun the Outlanders would simply stand at the edge of dances and *watch*. Which of course must have seemed like the craziest thing in the world. Who goes to a party to *watch*? Thereafter, the Marines were parigüayos—a word that in contemporary usage describes anybody who stands outside and watches while other people scoop up the girls. The kid who don't dance, who ain't got game, who lets people clown him—he's the parigüayo.

If you looked in the Dictionary of Dominican Things, the entry for *parigüayo* would include a wood carving of Oscar. It is a name that would haunt him for the rest of his life and that would lead him to another Watcher, the one who lamps on the Blue Side of the Moon.

looks. He wore his semikink hair in a Puerto Rican afro, rocked enormous Section 8 glasses—his "anti-pussy devices," Al and Miggs, his only friends, called them—sported an unappealing trace of mustache on his upper lip and possessed a pair of close-set eyes that made him look somewhat retarded. The Eyes of Mingus. (A comparison he made himself one day going through his mother's record collection; she was the only old-school dominicana he knew who had dated a moreno until Oscar's father put an end to that particular chapter of the All-African World Party.) You have the same eyes as your abuelo, his Nena Inca had told him on one of his visits to the DR, which should have been some comfort— who doesn't like resembling an ancestor?—except this particular ancestor had ended his days in prison.

Oscar had always been a young nerd—the kind of kid who read Tom Swift, who loved comic books and watched *Ultraman*—but by high school his commitment to the Genres had become absolute. Back when the rest of us were learning to play wallball and pitch quarters and drive our older brothers' cars and sneak dead soldiers from under our parents' eyes, he was gorging himself on a steady stream of Lovecraft, Wells, Burroughs, Howard, Alexander, Herbert, Asimov, Bova, and Heinlein, and even the Old Ones who were already beginning to fade—E. E. "Doc" Smith, Stapledon, and the guy who wrote all the Doc Savage books— moving hungrily from book to book, author to author, age to age. (It was his good fortune that the libraries of Paterson were so underfunded that they still kept a lot of the previous generation's nerdery in circulation.) You couldn't have torn him away from any movie or TV show or cartoon where there were monsters or spaceships or mutants or doomsday devices or destinies or magic or evil villains. In these pursuits alone Oscar showed the genius his grandmother insisted was part of the family patrimony. Could write in Elvish, could speak Chakobsa, could differentiate between a Slan, a Dorsai, and a Lensman in acute detail, knew more about the Marvel Universe than Stan Lee, and was a role-playing game fanatic. (If only he'd been good at videogames it would have been a slam dunk but despite owning an Atari and an Intellivision he didn't have the reflexes for it.) Perhaps if like me he'd been able to hide his otakuness maybe shit would have been easier for him, but he couldn't. Dude wore his nerdiness like a Jedi wore his light saber or a Lensman her lens. Couldn't have passed for Normal if he'd wanted to.[6]

6. Where this outsized love of genre jumped off from no one quite seems to know. It might have been a consequence of being Antillean (who more sci-fi than us?) or of living in the DR for the first couple of years of his life and then abruptly wrenchingly relocating to New Jersey—a single green card shifting not only worlds (from Third to First) but centuries (from almost no TV or electricity to plenty of both). After a transition like that I'm guessing only the most extreme scenarios could have satisfied. Maybe it was that in the DR he had watched too much *Spider-Man*, been taken to too many Run Run Shaw kung fu movies, listened to too many of his abuela's spooky stories about el Cuco and la Ciguapa? Maybe it was his first librarian in the U.S., who hooked him on reading, the electricity he felt when he touched that first Danny Dunn book? Maybe it was just the zeitgeist (were not the early seventies the dawn of the Nerd Age?) or the fact that for most of his childhood he had absolutely no friends? Or was it something deeper, something ancestral?

Who can say?

What is clear is that being a reader/fanboy (for lack of a better term)

Oscar was a social introvert who trembled with fear during gym class and watched nerd British shows like *Doctor Who* and *Blake's 7*, and could tell you the difference between a Veritech fighter and a Zentraedi walker, and he used a lot of huge-sounding nerd words like *indefatigable* and *ubiquitous* when talking to niggers who would barely graduate from high school. One of those nerds who was always hiding out in the library, who adored Tolkien and later the Margaret Weis and Tracy Hickman novels (his favorite character was of course Raistlin), and who, as the eighties marched on, de-

helped him get through the rough days of his youth, but it also made him stick out in the mean streets of Paterson even more than he already did. Victimized by the other boys—punches and pushes and wedgies and broken glasses and brand-new books from Scholastic, at a cost of fifty cents each, torn in half before his very eyes. You like books? Now you got two! Har-har! No one, alas, more oppressive than the oppressed. Even his own mother found his preoccupations nutty. Go outside and play! she commanded at least once a day. Pórtate como un muchacho normal.

(Only his sister, a reader too, supporting him. Bringing him books from her own school, which had a better library.)

You really want to know what being an X-Man feels like? Just be a smart bookish boy of color in a contemporary U.S. ghetto. Mamma mia! Like having bat wings or a pair of tentacles growing out of your chest.

Pa' 'fuera! his mother roared. And out he would go, like a boy condemned, to spend a few hours being tormented by the other boys—Please, I want to stay, he would beg his mother, but she shoved him out—You ain't a woman to be staying in the house—one hour, two, until finally he could slip back inside unnoticed, hiding himself in the upstairs closet, where he'd read by the slat of light that razored in from the cracked door. Eventually, his mother rooting him out again: What in carajo is the matter with you?

(And already on scraps of paper, in his composition books, on the backs of his hands, he was beginning to scribble, nothing serious for now, just rough facsimiles of his favorite stories, no sign yet that these half-assed pastiches were to be his Destiny.)

veloped a growing obsession with the End of the World. (No apocalyptic movie or book or game existed that he had not seen or read or played—Wyndham and Christopher and Gamma World were his absolute favorites.) You get the picture. His adolescent nerdliness vaporizing any iota of a chance he had for young love. Everybody else going through the terror and joy of their first crushes, their first dates, their first kisses while Oscar sat in the back of the class, behind his DM's screen, and watched his adolescence stream by. Sucks to be left out of adolescence, sort of like getting locked in the closet on Venus when the sun appears for the first time in a hundred years. It would have been one thing if like some of the nerdboys I'd grown up with he hadn't cared about girls, but alas he was still the passionate enamorao who fell in love easily and deeply. He had secret loves all over town, the kind of curly-haired big-bodied girls who wouldn't have said boo to a loser like him but about whom he could not stop dreaming. His affection—that gravitational mass of love, fear, longing, desire, and lust that he directed at any and every girl in the vicinity without regard to looks, age, or availability—broke his heart each and every day. Despite the fact that he considered it this huge sputtering force, it was actually most like a ghost because no girl ever really seemed to notice it. Occasionally they might shudder or cross their arms when he walked near, but that was about it. He cried often for his love of some girl or another. Cried in the bathroom, where nobody could hear him.

Anywhere else his triple-zero batting average with the ladies might have passed without comment, but this is a Dominican kid we're talking about, in a Dominican family: dude was supposed to have Atomic Level G, was supposed to be pulling in the bitches with both hands. Everybody noticed his lack of game and because they were Dominican everybody talked about it. His tío Rudolfo (only recently released from his last and final bid in the Justice and now living in their house on Main Street) was especially generous in his tutelage. Listen, palomo: you have to grab a muchacha, y metéselo. That will take care of *everything*. Start with a fea. Coje that fea y méteselo! Tío Rudolfo had four kids with three different women so the nigger was without doubt the family's resident méteselo expert.

His mother's only comment? You need to worry about your grades. And in more introspective moments: Just be glad you didn't get my luck, hijo.

What luck? his tío snorted.

Exactly, she said.

His friends Al and Miggs? Dude, you're kinda way fat, you know.

His abuela, La Inca? Hijo, you're the most buenmoso man I know!

Oscar's sister, Lola, was a lot more practical. Now that her crazy years were over—what Dominican girl doesn't have those?—she'd turned into one of those tough Jersey dominicanas, a long-distance runner who drove her own car, had her own checkbook, called men bitches, and would eat a fat cat in front of you without a speck of vergüenza. When she was in fourth grade she'd been attacked by an older acquaintance, and this was common knowledge throughout the family (and by extension a sizable section of Paterson, Union City, and Teaneck), and surviving that urikán of pain, judgment, and bochinche had made her tougher than adamantine. Recently she'd cut her hair short—flipping out her mother yet again—partially I think because when she'd been little her family had let it grow down past her ass, a source of pride, something I'm sure her attacker noticed and admired.

Oscar, Lola warned repeatedly, you're going to die a virgin unless you start *changing*.

Don't you think I know that? Another five years of this and I'll bet you somebody tries to name a church after me.

Cut the hair, lose the glasses, exercise. And get rid of those porn magazines. They're disgusting, they bother Mami, and they'll never get you a date.

Sound counsel that in the end he did not adopt. He tried a couple of times to exercise, leg lifts, sit-ups, walks around the block in the early morning, that sort of thing, but he would notice how everybody else had a girl but him and would despair, plunging right back into eating, *Penthouse*s, designing dungeons, and self-pity.

I seem to be allergic to diligence, and Lola said, Ha. What you're allergic to is *trying*.

It wouldn't have been half bad if Paterson and its surrounding precincts had been like Don Bosco or those seventies feminist sci-fi novels he sometimes read—an all-male-exclusion zone. Paterson, however, was girls the way NYC was girls, Paterson was girls the way Santo Domingo was girls. Paterson had mad girls, and if that wasn't guapas enough for you, well, motherfucker, then roll south and there'd be Newark, Elizabeth, Jersey City, the Oranges, Union City, West New York, Weehawken, Perth Amboy—an urban swath known to niggers everywhere as Negrapolis One. So in effect he saw girls—Hispanophone Caribbean girls—everywhere.

He wasn't safe even in his own house, his sister's girlfriends were always hanging out, permanent guests. When they were around he didn't need no *Penthouse*s. Her girls were not too smart but they were fine as shit: the sort of hot-as-balls Latinas who only dated weight-lifting morenos or Latino cats with guns in their cribs. They were all on the volleyball team together and tall and fit as colts and when they went for runs it was what the track team might have looked like in terrorist heaven. Bergen County's very own cigüapas: la primera was Gladys, who complained endlessly about her chest being too big, that maybe she'd find normal boyfriends if she'd had a smaller pair; Marisol, who'd end up at MIT and *hated* Oscar but whom Oscar liked most of all; Leticia, just off the boat, half Haitian half Dominican, that special blend the Dominican government swears *no existe*, who spoke with the deepest accent, a girl so good she refused to sleep with *three consecutive boyfriends!* It wouldn't have been so bad if these chickies hadn't treated Oscar like some deaf-mute harem guard, ordering him around, having him run their errands, making fun of his games and his looks; to make shit even worse, they blithely went on about the particulars of their sex lives with no regard for him, while he sat in the kitchen, clutching the latest issue of *Dragon*. Hey, he would yell, in case you're wondering there's a male unit in here.

Where? Marisol would say blandly. I don't see one.

And when they talked about how all the Latin guys only seemed to want to date whitegirls, he would offer, *I* like Spanish girls, to which Marisol responded with wide condescension. That's great, Oscar. Only problem is no Spanish girl would date you.

Leave him alone, Leticia said. I think you're cute, Oscar.

Yeah, right, Marisol laughed, rolling her eyes. Now he'll probably write a book about you.

These were Oscar's furies, his personal pantheon, the girls he most dreamed about and most beat off to and who eventually found their way into his little stories. In his dreams he was either saving them from aliens or he was returning to the neighborhood, rich and famous—It's him! The Dominican Stephen King!—and then Marisol would appear, carrying one each of his books for him to sign. Please, Oscar, marry me. Oscar, drolly: I'm sorry, Marisol, I don't marry ignorant bitches. (But then of course he would.) Maritza he still watched from afar, convinced that one day, when the nuclear bombs fell (or the plague broke out or the Tripods invaded) and civilization was wiped out he would end up saving her from a pack of irradiated ghouls and together they'd set out across a ravaged America in search of a better tomorrow. In these apocalyptic daydreams he was always some kind of plátano Doc Savage, a supergenius who combined world-class martial artistry with deadly firearms proficiency. Not bad for a nigger who'd never even shot an air rifle, thrown a punch, or scored higher than a thousand on his SATs.

OSCAR IS BRAVE

Senior year found him bloated, dyspeptic, and, most cruelly, alone in his lack of girlfriend. His two nerdboys, Al and Miggs, had, in the craziest twist of fortune, both succeeded in landing themselves girls that year. Nothing special, skanks really, but girls nonetheless. Al had met his at Menlo Park. She'd come on to *him*, he bragged, and when she informed him, after she sucked his dick of course, that she had a girlfriend *desperate* to meet somebody, Al had dragged Miggs away from his Atari and out to a movie and the rest was, as they say, history. By the end of the week Miggs was getting his too, and only then did Oscar find out about any of it. While they were in his room setting up for another "hair-raising" Champions adventure against the Death-Dealing Destroyers. (Oscar had to retire his famous Aftermath! campaign because nobody else but him was hankering to play in the postapocalyptic ruins of virus-wracked America.) At first, after hearing about the double-bootie coup, Oscar didn't say nothing much. He just rolled his d10's over and over. Said, You guys sure got lucky. It killed him that they hadn't thought to include him in their girl heists; he hated Al for inviting Miggs instead of him and he hated Miggs for getting a girl, period. Al getting a girl Oscar could comprehend; Al (real name Alok) was one of those tall Indian prettyboys who would never have been pegged by anyone as a role-playing nerd. It was Miggs's girl-getting he could not fathom, that astounded him and left him sick with jealousy.

Oscar had always considered Miggs to be an even bigger freak than he was. Acne galore and a retard's laugh and gray fucking teeth from having been given some medicine too young. So is your girlfriend cute? he asked Miggs. He said, Dude, you should see her, she's beautiful. Big fucking tits, Al seconded. That day what little faith Oscar had in the world took an SS-N-17 snipe to the head. When finally he couldn't take it no more he asked, pathetically, What, these girls don't have any other friends?

Al and Miggs traded glances over their character sheets. I don't think so, dude.

And right there he learned something about his friends he'd never known (or at least never admitted to himself). Right there he had an epiphany that echoed through his fat self. He realized his fucked-up comic-book-reading, role-playing-game-loving, no-sports-playing friends were embarrassed by *him*.

Knocked the architecture right out of his legs. He closed the game early, the Exterminators found the Destroyers' hideout right away—That was bogus, Al groused. After he showed them out he locked himself in his room, lay in bed for a couple of stunned hours, then got up, undressed in the bathroom he no longer had to share because his sister was at Rutgers, and examined himself in the mirror. The fat! The miles of stretch marks! The tumescent horribleness of his proportions! He looked straight out of a Daniel Clowes comic book. Or like the fat blackish kid in Beto Hernández's Palomar.

Jesus Christ, he whispered. I'm a Morlock.

The next day at breakfast he asked his mother: Am I ugly?

She sighed. Well, hijo, you certainly don't take after me.

Dominican parents! You got to love them!

Spent a week looking at himself in the mirror, turning every which way, taking stock, not flinching, and decided at last to be like Roberto Durán: No más. That Sunday he went to Chucho's and had the barber shave his Puerto Rican 'fro off. (Wait a minute, Chucho's partner said. *You're* Dominican?) Oscar lost the mustache next, and then the glasses, bought contacts with the money he was making at the lumberyard and tried to polish up what remained of his Dominicanness, tried to be more like his cursing swaggering cousins, if only because he had started to suspect that in their Latin hypermaleness there might be an answer. But he was really too far gone for quick fixes. The next time Al and Miggs saw him he'd been starving himself for three days straight. Miggs said, Dude, what's the matter with *you*?

Changes, Oscar said pseudo-cryptically.

What, are you some album cover now?

He shook his head solemnly. I'm embarking on a new cycle of my life.

Listen to the guy. He already sounds like he's in college.

That summer his mother sent him and his sister to Santo Domingo, and this time he didn't fight it like he had in the recent past. It's not like he had much in the States keeping him. He arrived in Baní with a stack of notebooks and a plan to fill them all up. Since he could no longer be a gamemaster he decided to try his hand at being a real writer. The trip turned out to be something of a turning point for him. Instead of discouraging his writing, chasing him out of the house like his mother used to, his abuela, Nena Inca, let him be. Allowed him to sit in the back of the house as long as he wanted, didn't insist that he should be "out in the world." (She had always been overprotective of him and his sister. Too much bad luck in this family, she sniffed.) Kept the music off and brought him his meals at exactly the same time every day. His sister ran around with her hot Island friends, always jumping out of the house in a bikini and going off to different parts of the Island for overnight trips, but he stayed put. When any family members came looking for him his abuela chased them off with a single imperial sweep of her hand. Can't you see the muchacho's working? What's he doing? his cousins asked, confused. He's being a genius is what, La Inca replied haughtily. Now váyanse. (Later when he thought about it he realized that these very cousins could probably have gotten him laid if only he'd bothered to hang out with them. But you can't regret the life you didn't lead.) In the afternoons, when he couldn't write another word, he'd sit out in front of the house with his abuela and watch the street scene, listen to the raucous exchanges between the neighbors. One evening, at the end of his trip, his abuela confided: Your mother could have been a doctor just like your grandfather was.

What happened?

La Inca shook her head. She was looking at her favorite picture of his mother on her first day at private school, one of those typical serious DR shots. What always happens. Un maldito hombre.

He wrote two books that summer about a young man fighting mutants at the end of the world (neither of them survive). Took crazy amounts of field notes too, names of things he intended to later adapt for science-fictional and fantastic purposes. (Heard about the family curse for like the thousandth time but strangely enough didn't think it worth incorporating into his fiction—I mean, shit, what Latino family doesn't think it's cursed?) When it was time for him and his sister to return to Paterson he was almost sad. Almost. His abuela placed her hand on his head in blessing. Cuídate mucho, mi hijo. Know that in this world there's somebody who will always love you.

At JFK, almost not being recognized by his uncle. Great, his tío said, looking askance at his complexion, now you look Haitian.

After his return he hung out with Miggs and Al, saw movies with them, talked Los Brothers Hernández, Frank Miller, and Alan Moore with them but overall they never regained the friendship they had before Santo Domingo. Oscar listened to their messages on the machine and resisted the urge to run over to their places. Didn't see them but once, twice a week. Focused on his writing. Those were some fucking lonely weeks when all he had were his games, his books, and his words. So now I have a hermit for a son, his mother complained bitterly. At night, unable to sleep, he watched a lot of bad TV, became obsessed with two movies in particular: *Zardoz* (which he'd seen with his uncle before they put him away for the second time) and *Virus* (the Japanese end-of-the-world movie with the hot chick from *Romeo and Juliet*). *Virus* especially he could not watch to the end without crying, the Japanese hero arriving at the South Pole base, having walked from Washington, D.C., down the whole spine of the Andes, for the woman of his dreams. I've been working on my fifth novel, he told the boys when they asked about his absences. It's *amazing*.

See? What did I tell you? Mr. Collegeboy.

In the old days when his so-called friends would hurt him or drag his trust through the mud he always crawled voluntarily back into the abuse, out of fear and loneliness, something he'd always hated himself for, but not this time. If there existed in his high school years any one moment he took pride in it was clearly this one. Even told his sister about it during her next visit. She said, Way to go, O! He'd finally showed some backbone, hence some pride, and although it hurt, it also felt motherfucking *good*.

OSCAR COMES CLOSE

In October, after all his college applications were in (Fairleigh Dickinson, Montclair, Rutgers, Drew, Glassboro State, William Paterson; he also sent an app to NYU, a one-in-a-million shot, and they rejected him so fast he was amazed the shit hadn't come back Pony Express) and winter was settling its pale miserable ass across northern New Jersey, Oscar fell in love with a girl in his SAT prep class. The class was being conducted in one of those "Learning Centers" not far from where he lived, less than a mile, so he'd been walking, a healthy way to lose weight, he thought. He hadn't been expecting to meet anyone, but then he'd seen the beauty in the back row and felt his senses fly out of him. Her name was Ana Obregón, a pretty, loudmouthed gordita who read Henry Miller while she should have been learning to wrestle logic problems. On about their fifth class he noticed her reading *Sexus* and she noticed him noticing, and, leaning over, she showed him a passage and he got an erection like a motherfucker.

You must think I'm weird, right? she said during the break.

You ain't weird, he said. Believe me—I'm the top expert in the state.

Ana was a talker, had beautiful Caribbean-girl eyes, pure anthracite, and was the sort of heavy that almost every Island nigger dug, a body that you just knew would look good in and out of clothes; wasn't shy about her weight, either; she wore tight black stirrup pants like every other girl in the neighborhood and the sexiest underwear she could afford and was a meticulous putter-on of makeup, an intricate bit of multitasking for which Oscar never lost his fascination. She was this peculiar combination of badmash and little girl—even before he'd visited her house he knew she'd have a whole collection of stuffed animals avalanched on her bed—and there was something in the seamlessness with which she switched between these aspects that convinced him that both were masks, that there existed a third Ana, a hidden Ana who determined what mask to throw up for what occasion but who was otherwise obscure and impossible to know. She'd gotten into Miller because her ex-boyfriend, Manny, had given her the books before he joined the army. He used to read passages to her all the time: That made me *so* hot. She'd been thirteen when they started dating, he was twenty-four, a recovering coke addict—Ana talking about these things like they weren't nothing at all.

You were thirteen and your mother *allowed* you to date a septuagenarian?

My parents *loved* Manny, she said. My mom used to cook dinner for him all the time.

He said, That seems highly unorthodox, and later at home he asked his sister, back on winter break, For the sake of argument, would you allow your pubescent daughter to have relations with a twenty-four-year-old male?

I'd kill him first.

He was amazed how relieved he felt to hear that.

Let me guess: You know somebody who's doing this?

He nodded. She sits next to me in SAT class. I think she's orchidaceous.

Lola considered him with her tiger-colored irises. She'd been back a week and it was clear that college-level track was kicking her ass, the sclera in her normally wide manga-eyes were shot through with blood vessels. You know, she said finally, we colored folks talk plenty of shit about loving our children but we really don't. She exhaled. We don't, we don't, we don't.

He tried to put a hand on his sister's shoulder but she shrugged it off. You better go bust out some crunches, Mister.

That's what she called him whenever she was feeling tender or wronged. Mister. Later she'd want to put that on his gravestone but no one would let her, not even me.

Stupid.

AMOR DE PENDEJO

He and Ana in SAT class, he and Ana in the parking lot afterward, he and Ana at the McDonald's, he and Ana become friends. Each day Oscar expected her to be adiós, each day she was still there. They got into the habit of talking on the phone a couple times a week, about nothing really, spinning words out of their everyday; the first time she called *him*, offering him a ride to SAT class; a week later he called her, just to try it. His heart beating so hard he thought he would die but all she did when she picked him up was say, Oscar, listen to the *bullshit* my sister pulled, and off they'd gone, building another one of their word-scrapers. By the fifth time he called he no longer expected the Big Blow-off. She was the only girl outside his family who admitted to having a period, who actually said to him, I'm bleeding like a *hog*, an astounding confidence he turned over and over in his head, sure it meant something, and when he thought about the way she laughed, as though she owned the air around her, his heart thudded inside his chest, a lonely rada. Ana Obregón, unlike every other girl in his secret cosmology, he actually fell for *as* they were getting to know each other. Because her appearance in his life was sudden, because she'd come in under his radar, he didn't have time to raise his usual wall of nonsense or level some wild-ass expectations her way. Maybe he was plain tired after four years of not getting ass, or maybe he'd finally found his zone. Incredibly enough, instead of making an idiot out of himself as one might have expected, given the hard fact that this was the first girl he'd ever had a conversation with, he actually took it a day at a time. He spoke to her plainly and without effort and discovered that his constant self-deprecation pleased her immensely. It was amazing how it was between them; he would say something obvious and uninspired, and she'd say, Oscar, you're really fucking smart. When she said, I *love* men's hands, he spread both of his across his face and said, faux-casual-like, Oh, *really*? It cracked her up.

She never talked about what they were; she only said, Man, I'm glad I got to know you.

And he said, I'm glad I'm me knowing you.

One night while he was listening to New Order and trying to chug through *Clay's Ark*, his sister knocked on his door.

You got a visitor.

I do?

Yup. Lola leaned against his door frame. She'd shaved her head down to the bone, Sinéad-style, and now everybody, including their mother, was convinced she'd turned into a lesbiana.

You might want to clean up a little. She touched his face gently. Shave those pussy hairs.

It was Ana. Standing in his foyer, wearing a full-length leather, her triagueña skin blood-charged from the cold, her face gorgeous with eyeliner, mascara, foundation, lipstick, and blush.

Freezing out, she said. She had her gloves in one hand like a crumpled bouquet.

Hey, was all he managed to say. He could hear his sister upstairs, listening.

What you doing? Ana asked.

Like nothing.

Like let's go to a movie, then.

Like OK, he said.

Upstairs his sister was jumping up and down on his bed, low-screaming, It's a date, it's a date, and then she jumped on his back and nearly toppled them clean through the bedroom window.

So is this some kind of date? he said as he slipped into her car.

She smiled wanly. You could call it that.

Ana drove a Cressida, and instead of taking them to the local theater she headed down to the Amboy Multiplex.

I love this place, she said as she was wrangling for a parking space. My father used to take us here when it was still a drive-in. Did you ever come here back then?

He shook his head. Though I heard they steal plenty of cars here now.

Nobody's stealing *this* baby.

It was so hard to believe what was happening that Oscar really couldn't take it seriously. The whole time the movie—

Manhunter—was on, he kept expecting niggers to jump out with cameras and scream, Surprise! Boy, he said, trying to remain on her map, this is some movie. Ana nodded; she smelled of some perfume he could not name, and when she pressed close the heat off her body was *vertiginous*.

On the ride home Ana complained about having a headache and they didn't speak for a long time. He tried to turn on the radio but she said, No, my head's really killing me. He joked, Would you like some crack? No, Oscar. So he sat back and watched the Hess Building and the rest of Woodbridge slide past through a snarl of overpasses. He was suddenly aware of how tired he was; the nervousness that had raged through him the entire night had exhausted his ass. The longer they went without speaking the more morose he became. It's just a movie, he told himself. It's not like it's a date.

Ana seemed unaccountably sad and she chewed her bottom lip, a real bemba, until most of her lipstick was on her teeth. He was going to make a comment about it but decided not to.

You reading anything good?

Nope, she said. You?

I'm reading *Dune*.

She nodded. I *hate* that book.

They reached the Elizabeth exit, which is what New Jersey is *really* known for, industrial wastes on both sides of the turnpike. He had started holding his breath against those horrible fumes when Ana let loose a scream that threw him into his passenger door. Elizabeth! she shrieked. Close your fucking legs!

Then she looked over at him, tipped back her head, and laughed.

When he returned to the house his sister said, Well?

Well what?

Did you *fuck* her?

Jesus, Lola, he said, blushing.

Don't lie to me.

I do not move so precipitously. He paused and then sighed. In other words, I didn't even get her scarf off.

Sounds a little suspicious. I know you Dominican men. She held up her hands and flexed the fingers in playful menace. Son pulpos.

The next day he woke up feeling like he'd been unshackled from his fat, like he'd been washed clean of his misery, and for a long time he couldn't remember why he felt this way, and then he said her name.

OSCAR IN LOVE

And so now every week they headed out to either a movie or the mall. They talked. He learned that her ex-boyfriend, Manny, used to smack the shit out of her, which was a problem, she confessed, because she liked it when guys were a little rough with her in bed; he learned that her father had died in a car accident when she was a young girl in Macorís, and that her new stepfather didn't care two shits about her but that it didn't matter because once she got into Penn State she didn't ever intend to come back home. In turn he showed her some of his writings and told her about the time he'd gotten struck by a car and put in the hospital and about how his tío used to smack the shit out of him in the old days; he even told her about the crush he had on Maritza Chacón and she screamed, Maritza Chacón? I know that cuero! Oh my God, Oscar, I think even my stepfather slept with her!

Oh, they got close all right, but did they ever kiss in her car? Did he ever put his hands up her skirt? Did he ever thumb her clit? Did she ever push up against him and say his name in a throaty voice? Did he ever stroke her hair while she sucked him off? Did they ever fuck?

Poor Oscar. Without even realizing it he'd fallen into one of those Let's-Be-Friends Vortexes, the bane of nerdboys everywhere. These relationships were love's version of a stay in the stocks, in you go, plenty of misery guaranteed and what you got out of it besides bitterness and heartbreak nobody knows. Perhaps some knowledge of self and of women.

Perhaps.

In April he got his second set of SAT scores back (1020 under the old system) and a week later he learned he was heading to Rutgers New Brunswick. Well, you did it, hijo, his mother said, looking more relieved than was polite. No more selling pencils for me, he agreed. You'll love it, his sister promised him. I know I will. I was meant for college. As for Ana, she was on her way to Penn State, honors program, full ride. And now my stepfather can kiss my ass! It was also in April that her ex-boyfriend, Manny, returned from the army—Ana told him during one of their trips to the Yaohan Mall. His sudden appearance, and Ana's joy over it, shattered the hopes Oscar had cultivated. He's back, Oscar asked, like forever? Ana nodded. Apparently Manny had gotten into trouble again, drugs, but this time, Ana insisted, he'd been set up by these three cocolos, a word he'd never heard her use before, so he figured she'd gotten it from Manny. Poor Manny, she said.

Yeah, poor Manny, Oscar muttered under his breath.

Poor Manny, poor Ana, poor Oscar. Things changed quickly. First off, Ana stopped being home all the time, and Oscar found himself stacking messages on her machine: This is Oscar, a bear is chewing my legs off, please call me; This is Oscar, they want a million dollars or it's over, please call me; This is Oscar, I've just spotted a strange meteorite and I'm going out to investigate. She always got back to him after a couple of days, and was pleasant about it, but still. Then she canceled three Fridays in a row and he had to settle for the clearly reduced berth of Sunday after church. She'd pick him up and they'd drive out to Boulevard East and park and together they'd stare out over the Manhattan skyline. It wasn't an ocean, or a mountain range; it was, at least to Oscar, better, and it inspired their best conversations.

It was during one of those little chats that Ana let slip, God, I'd forgotten how big Manny's cock was.

Like I really need to hear that, he snapped.

I'm sorry, she said hesitantly. I thought we could talk about everything.

Well, it wouldn't be bad if you actually kept Manny's anatomical enormity to yourself.

So we can't talk about everything?

He didn't even bother answering her.

With Manny and his *big cock* around, Oscar was back to dreaming about nuclear annihilation, how through some miraculous accident he'd hear about the attack first and without pausing he'd steal his tío's car, drive it to the stores, stock it full of supplies (maybe shoot a couple of looters en route), and then fetch Ana. What about Manny? she'd wail. There's no time! he'd insist, peeling out, shoot a couple more looters (now slightly mutated), and then repair to the sweaty love den where Ana would quickly succumb to his take-charge genius and his by-then ectomorphic physique. When he was in a better mood he let Ana find Manny hanging from a light fixture in his apartment, his tongue a swollen purple bladder in his mouth, his pants around his ankles. The news of the imminent attack on the TV, a half-literate note pinned to his chest. *I koona taek it*. And then Oscar would comfort Ana with the terse insight, He was too weak for this Hard New World.

So she has a boyfriend? Lola asked him suddenly.

Yes, he said.

You should back off for a little while.

Did he listen? Of course he didn't. Available any time she needed to kvetch. And he even got—joy of joys!—the opportunity to meet the famous Manny, which was about as fun as being called a fag during a school assembly (which had happened). (Twice.) Met him outside Ana's house. He was this intense emaciated guy with marathon-runner limbs and voracious eyes; when they shook hands Oscar was sure the nigger was going to smack him, he acted so surly. Manny was muy bald and completely shaved his head to hide it, had a hoop in each ear and this leathery out-in-the-sun buzzardy look of an old cat straining for youth.

So you're Ana's little friend, Manny said.

That's me, Oscar said in a voice so full of cheerful innocuousness that he could have shot himself for it.

Oscar is a brilliant writer, Ana offered. Even though she had never once asked to read anything he wrote.

He snorted. What would you have to write about?

I'm into the more speculative genres. He knew how absurd he sounded.

The more speculative genres. Manny looked ready to cut a steak off him. You sound mad corny, guy, you know that?

Oscar smiled, hoping somehow an earthquake would demolish all of Paterson.

I just hope you ain't trying to chisel in on my girl, guy.

Oscar said, Ha-ha. Ana flushed red, looked at the ground. A joy.

With Manny around, he was exposed to an entirely new side of Ana. All they talked about now, the little they saw each other, was Manny and the terrible things he did to her. Manny smacked her, Manny kicked her, Manny called her a fat twat, Manny cheated on her, she was sure, with this Cuban chickie from the middle school. So that explains why I couldn't get a date in those days; it was Manny, Oscar joked, but Ana didn't laugh. They couldn't talk ten minutes without Manny beeping her and her having to call him back and assure him she wasn't with anybody else. And one day she arrived at Oscar's house with a bruise on her face and with her blouse torn, and his mother had said: I don't want any trouble here!

What am I going to do? she asked over and over and Oscar always found himself holding her awkwardly and telling her, Well, I think if he's this bad to you, you should break up with him, but she shook her head and said, I know I should, but I can't. I *love* him.

Love. Oscar knew he should have checked out right then. He liked to kid himself that it was only cold anthropological interest that kept him around to see how it would all end, but the truth was he couldn't extricate himself. He was totally and irrevocably in love with Ana. What he used to feel for those girls he'd never really known was nothing compared to the amor he was carrying in his heart for Ana. It had the density of a dwarf-motherfucking-star and at times he was a hundred percent sure it would drive him mad. The only thing that came close was how he felt about his books; only the combined love he had for everything he'd read and everything he hoped to write came even close.

Every Dominican family has stories about crazy loves, about niggers who take love too far, and Oscar's family was no different.

His abuelo, the dead one, had been unyielding about one thing or another (no one ever exactly said) and ended up in prison, first mad, then dead; his abuela Nena Inca had lost her husband six months after they got married. He had drowned on Semana Santa and she never remarried, never touched another man. We'll be together soon enough, Oscar had heard her say.

Your mother, his tía Rubelka had once whispered, was a loca when it came to love. It almost killed her.

And now it seemed that it was Oscar's turn. *Welcome to the family*, his sister said in a dream. *The real family.*

It was obvious what was happening, but what could he do? There was no denying what he felt. Did he lose sleep? Yes. Did he lose important hours of concentration? Yes. Did he stop reading his Andre Norton books and even lose interest in the final issues of *Watchmen*, which were unfolding in the illest way? Yes. Did he start borrowing his tío's car for long rides to the Shore, parking at Sandy Hook, where his mom used to take them before she got sick, back when Oscar hadn't been too fat, before she stopped going to the beach altogether? Yes. Did his youthful unrequited love cause him to lose weight? Unfortunately, this alone it did not provide, and for the life of him he couldn't understand why. When Lola had broken up with Golden Gloves she'd lost almost twenty pounds. What kind of genetic discrimination was this, handed down by what kind of scrub God?

Miraculous things started happening. Once he blacked out while crossing an intersection and woke up with a rugby team gathered around him. Another time Miggs was goofing on him, talking smack about his aspirations to write role-playing games—complicated story, the company Oscar had been hoping to write for, Fantasy Games Unlimited, and which was considering one of his modules for PsiWorld, had recently closed, scuttling all of Oscar's hopes and dreams that he was about to turn into the next Gary Gygax. Well, Miggs said, it looks like *that* didn't work out, and for the first time ever in their relationship Oscar lost his temper and without a word swung on Miggs, connected so hard that homeboy's mouth spouted blood. Jesus Christ, Al said. Calm down! I didn't mean to do it, he said unconvincingly. It was an accident. Mudafuffer, Miggs said. Mudafuffer! He got so bad that one desperate night, after listening to Ana sobbing to him on the phone about Manny's latest bullshit, he said, I have to go to church now, and put down the phone, went to his tío's room (Rudolfo was out at the titty bar), and stole his antique Virginia Dragoon, that oh-so-famous First Nation–exterminating Colt .44, heavier than bad luck and twice as ugly. Stuck its impressive snout down the front of his pants and proceeded to stand in front of Manny's building almost the entire night. Got real friendly with the aluminum siding. Come on, motherfucker, he said calmly. I got a nice eleven-year-old girl for you. He didn't care that he would more than likely be put away forever, or that niggers like him got ass *and* mouth raped in jail, or that if the cops picked him up and found the gun they'd send his tío's ass up the river for parole violation. He didn't care about nada that night. His head contained zero, a perfect vacuum. He saw his entire writing future flash before his eyes; he'd only written one novel worth a damn, about an Australian hunger spirit preying on a group of small-town friends, wouldn't get a chance to write anything better—career over. Luckily for the future of American Letters, Manny did not come home that night.

It was hard to explain. It wasn't just that he thought Ana was his last fucking chance for happiness—this was clearly on his mind—it was also that he'd never ever in all his miserable eighteen years of life experienced anything like he'd felt when he was around that girl. I've waited forever to be in love, he wrote his sister. How many times I thought *this is never going to happen to me.* (When in his second-favorite anime of all time, *Robotech Macross*, Rich Hunter finally hooked up with Lisa, he broke down in front of the TV and cried. Don't tell me they shot the president, his tío called from the back room, where he was quietly snorting you-know-what.) It's like I swallowed a piece of heaven, he wrote to his sister in a letter. You can't imagine how it feels.

Two days later he broke down and confessed to his sister about the gun stuff and she, back on a short laundry visit, flipped out. She got them both on their knees in front of the altar she'd built to their dead abuelo and had him swear on their mother's living soul that he'd never pull anything like that again as long as he lived. She even cried, she was so worried about him.

You need to stop this, Mister.

I know I do, he said. But I don't know if I'm even here, you know?

That night he and his sister both fell asleep on the couch, she first. Lola had just broken up with her boyfriend for like the tenth time, but even Oscar, in his condition, knew they would be back together in no time at all. Sometime before dawn he dreamt about all the girlfriends he'd never had, row upon row upon row upon row, like the extra bodies that the Miraclepeople had in Alan Moore's *Miracleman*. *You can do it*, they said.

He awoke, cold, with a dry throat.

They met at the Japanese mall on Edgewater Road, Yaohan, which he had discovered one day on his long I'm-bored drives and which he now considered part of their landscape, something to tell their children about. It was where he came for his anime tapes and his mecha models. Ordered them both chicken katsu curries and then sat in the large cafeteria with the view of Manhattan, the only gaijin in the whole joint.

You have beautiful breasts, he said as an opener.

Confusion, alarm. Oscar. What's the matter with you?

He looked out through the glass at Manhattan's western flank, looked out like he was some deep nigger. Then he told her.

There were no surprises. Her eyes went soft, she put a hand on his hand, her chair scraped closer, there was a strand of yellow in her teeth. Oscar, she said gently, I *have* a boyfriend.

She drove him home; at the house he thanked her for her time, walked inside, lay in bed.

In June he graduated from Don Bosco. See them at graduation: his mother starting to look thin (the cancer would grab her soon enough), Rudolfo high as shit, only Lola looking her best, beaming, happy. You did it, Mister. You did it. He heard in passing that of everybody in their section of P-town only he and Olga—poor fucked-up Olga—had not attended even one prom. Dude, Miggs joked, maybe you should have asked *her* out.

In September he headed to Rutgers New Brunswick, his

mother gave him a hundred dollars and his first kiss in five years, his tío a box of condoms: Use them all, he said, and then added: On girls. There was the initial euphoria of finding himself alone at college, free of everything, completely on his fucking own, and with it an optimism that here among these thousands of young people he would find someone like him. That, alas, didn't happen. The white kids looked at his black skin and his afro and treated him with inhuman cheeriness. The kids of color, upon hearing him speak and seeing him move his body, shook their heads. You're not Dominican. And he said, over and over again, But I am. Soy dominicano. Dominicano soy. After a spate of parties that led to nothing but being threatened by some drunk whiteboys, and dozens of classes where not a single girl looked at him, he felt the optimism wane, and before he even realized what had happened he had buried himself in what amounted to the college version of what he'd majored in all throughout high school: getting no ass. His happiest moments were genre moments, like when *Akira* was released (1988). Pretty sad. Twice a week he and his sister would dine at the Douglass dining hall; she was a Big Woman on Campus and knew just about everybody with any pigment, had her hand on every protest and every march, but that didn't help his situation any. During their get-togethers she would give him advice and he would nod quietly and afterward would sit at the E bus stop and stare at all the pretty Douglass girls and wonder where he'd gone wrong in his life. He wanted to blame the books, the sci-fi, but he couldn't—he loved them too much. Despite swearing early on to change his nerdly ways, he continued to eat, continued not to exercise, continued to use flash words, and after a couple semesters without any friends but his sister, he joined the university's resident geek organization, RU Gamers, which met in the classrooms beneath Frelinghuysen and boasted an entirely male membership. He had thought college would be better, as far as girls were concerned, but those first years it wasn't.

2

Wildwood

1982–1985

It's never the changes we want that change everything.

This is how it all starts: with your mother calling you into the bathroom. You will remember what you were doing at that precise moment for the rest of your life: You were reading Watership Down *and the rabbits and their does were making their dash for the boat and you didn't want to stop reading, the book has to go back to your brother tomorrow, but then she called you again, louder, her I'm-not-fucking-around voice, and you mumbled irritably, Sí, señora.*

She was standing in front of the medicine cabinet mirror, naked from the waist up, her bra slung about her waist like a torn sail, the scar on her back as vast and inconsolable as a sea. You want to return to your book, to pretend you didn't hear her, but it is too late. Her eyes meet yours, the same big smoky eyes you will have in the future. Ven acá, she commanded. She is frowning at something on one of her breasts. Your mother's breasts are immensities. *One of the wonders of the world. The only ones you've seen that are bigger are in nudie magazines or on really fat ladies.*

They're 35 triple-Ds and the aureoles are as big as saucers and black as pitch and at their edges are fierce hairs that sometimes she plucked and sometimes she didn't. These breasts have always embarrassed you and when you walk in public with her you are always conscious of them. After her face and her hair, her chest is what she is most proud of. Your father could never get enough of them, she always brags. But given the fact that he ran off on her after their third year of marriage, it seemed in the end that he could.

You dread conversations with your mother. Those one-sided dressing-downs. You figured that she has called you in to give you another earful about your diet. Your mom's convinced that if you eat more plátanos you will suddenly acquire her same extraordinary train-wrecking secondary sex characteristics. Even at that age you were nothing if not your mother's daughter. You were twelve years old and already as tall as she was, a long slender-necked ibis of a girl. You had her green eyes (clearer, though) and her straight hair which makes you look more Hindu than Dominican and a behind that the boys haven't been able to stop talking about since the fifth grade and whose appeal you do not yet understand. You have her complexion too, which means you are dark. But for all your similarities, the tides of inheritance have yet to reach your chest. You have only the slightest hint of breast; from most angles you're flat as a board and you're thinking she's going to order you to stop wearing bras again because they're suffocating your potential breasts, discouraging them from popping out of you. You're ready to argue with her to the death because you're as possessive of your bras as you are of the pads you now buy yourself.

But no, she doesn't say a word about eating more plátanos. In-

stead, she takes your right hand and guides you. Your mom is rough in all things but this time she is gentle. You did not think her capable of it.

Do you feel that? she asks in her too-familiar raspy voice.

At first all you feel is the heat of her and the density of the tissue, like a bread that never stopped rising. She kneads your fingers into her. You're as close as you've ever been and your breathing is what you hear.

Don't you feel that?

She turns toward you. Coño, muchacha, stop looking at me and feel.

So you close your eyes and your fingers are pushing down and you're thinking of Helen Keller and how when you were little you wanted to be her except more nun-ish and then suddenly without warning you do feel something. A knot just beneath her skin, tight and secretive as a plot. And at that moment, for reasons you will never quite understand, you are overcome by the feeling, the premonition, that something in your life is about to change. You become light-headed and you can feel a throbbing in your blood, a beat, a rhythm, a drum. Bright lights zoom through you like photon torpedoes, like comets. You don't know how or why you know this thing but that you know it cannot be doubted. It is exhilarating. For as long as you've been alive you've had bruja ways; even your mother will begrudge you that much. Hija de Liborio she called you after you picked your tía's winning numbers for her and you assumed Liborio was a relative. That was before Santo Domingo, before you knew about the Great Power of God.

I feel it, you say, too loudly. Lo siento.

And like that, everything changes. Before the winter is out the *doctors remove that breast you were kneading, along with the ax-illary lymph node. Because of the operations she will have trouble lifting her arm over her head for the rest of her life. Her hair begins to fall out, and one day she pulls it all out herself and puts it inside a plastic bag. You change too. Not right away, but it happens. And it's in that bathroom where it all begins. Where you begin.*

A punk chick. That's what I became. A Siouxsie and the Banshees–loving punk chick. The puertorican kids on the block couldn't stop laughing when they saw my hair, they called me Blacula, and the morenos, they didn't know what to say: they just called me devil-bitch. Yo, devil-bitch, yo, *yo!* My tía Rubelka thought it was some kind of mental illness. Hija, she said while frying pastelitos, maybe you need *help*. But my mother was the worst. It's the last straw, she screamed. The. Last. Straw. But it always was with her. Mornings when I came downstairs she'd be in the kitchen making her coffee in la greca and listening to Radio WADO and when she saw me and my hair she'd get mad all over again, as if during the night she'd forgotten who I was. My mother was one of the tallest women in Paterson, and her anger was just as tall. It pincered you in its long arms, and if you showed any weakness you were finished. Que muchacha tan fea, she said in disgust, splashing the rest of her coffee in the sink. Fea's become my new name. Nothing new, really. She's been saying stuff like that all our lives. My mother would never win any awards, believe me. You could call her an absentee parent: if she wasn't at work she was sleeping, and when she was around it seemed all she did was scream and hit. As kids, me and Oscar were more scared of our mother than we were of the dark or el cuco. She would hit us anywhere, in front of anyone, always free with the chanclas and the correa, but now with her cancer there's not much she can do anymore. The last time she tried to whale on me it was because of my hair, but instead of cringing or running I punched her hand. It was a reflex more than anything, but once it happened I knew I couldn't take it back, not ever, and so I just kept my fist clenched, waiting for whatever came next, for her to attack me with her teeth like she did to this one lady in the Pathmark. But she just stood there shaking, in her stupid wig and her stupid bata, with two huge foam prostheses in her bra, the smell of burning wig all around us. I almost felt sorry for her. This is how you treat your mother? she cried. And if I could have I would have broken the entire length of my life across her face, but instead I screamed back, And this is how you treat your daughter?

Things had been bad between us all year. How could they not have been? She was my Old World Dominican mother and I was her only daughter, the one she had raised up herself with the help of nobody, which meant it was her duty to keep me crushed under her heel. I was fourteen and desperate for my own patch of world that had nothing to do with her. I wanted the life that I used to see when I watched *Big Blue Marble* as a kid, the life that drove me to make pen pals and to take atlases home from school. The life that existed beyond Paterson, beyond my family, beyond Spanish. And as soon as she became sick I saw my chance, and I'm not going to pretend or apologize; I saw my chance and eventually I took it. If you didn't grow up like I did then you don't know and if you don't know it's probably better you don't judge. You don't know the hold our mothers have on us, even the ones that are never around—*especially* the ones that are never around. What it's like to be the perfect Dominican daughter, which is just a nice way of saying a perfect Dominican slave. You don't know what it's like to grow up with a mother who never said a positive thing in her life, not about her children or the world, who was always suspicious, always tearing you down and splitting your dreams straight down the seams. When my first pen pal, Tomoko, stopped writing me after three letters she was the one who laughed: You think someone's going to lose life writing to you? Of course I cried; I was eight and I had already planned that Tomoko and her family would adopt me. My mother of course saw clean into the marrow of those dreams, and laughed. I wouldn't write to you either, she said. She was that kind of mother: who makes you doubt yourself, who would wipe you out if you let her. But I'm not going to pretend either. For a long time I let her say what she wanted about me, and what was worse, for a long time I believed her. I was a fea, I was a worthless, I was an idiota. From ages two to thirteen I believed her and because I believed her I was the perfect hija. I was the one cooking, cleaning, doing the wash, buying groceries, writing letters to the bank to explain why a house payment was going to be late, translating. I had the best grades in my class. I never caused trouble, even when the morenas used to come after me with scissors because of my straight-straight hair. I stayed at home and made sure Oscar was fed and that everything ran right while she was at work. I raised him and I raised me. I was the one. You're my hija, she said, that's what you're supposed to be doing. When that thing happened to me when I was eight and I finally told her what he had done, she told me to shut my mouth and stop crying, and I did exactly that, I shut my mouth and clenched my legs, and my mind, and within a year I couldn't have told you what that neighbor looked like, or even his name. All you do is complain, she said to me. But you have no idea what life really is. Sí, señora. When she told me that I could go on my sixth-grade sleep away to Bear Mountain and I bought a backpack with my own paper-route money and wrote Bobby Santos notes because he was promising to break into my cabin and kiss me in front of everyone I believed her, and when on the morning of the trip she announced that I wasn't going and I said, But you promised, and she said, Muchacha del diablo, I promised you nothing, I didn't throw my backpack at her or pull out my eyes, and when it was Laura Saenz who ended up kissing Bobby Santos, not me, I didn't say anything, either. I just lay in my room with stupid Bear-Bear and sang under my breath, imagining where I would run away to when I grew up. To Japan maybe, where I would track down Tomoko, or to Austria, where my singing would inspire a remake of *The Sound of Music*. All my favorite books from that period were about runaways. *Watership Down*, *The Incredible Journey*, *My Side of the Mountain*, and when Bon Jovi's "Runaway" came out I imagined it was me they were singing about. No one had any idea. I was the tallest, dorkiest girl in the school, the one who dressed up as Wonder Woman every Halloween, the one who never said a word. People saw me in my glasses and my hand-me-down clothes and could not have imagined what I was capable of. And then when I was twelve I got that feeling, the scary witchy one, and before I knew it my mother was sick and the wildness that had been in me all along, that I tried to tamp down with chores and with homework and with promises that once I reached college I would be able to do whatever I pleased, burst out. I couldn't help it. I tried to keep it down but it just flooded through all my quiet spaces. It was a message more than a feeling, a message that tolled like a bell: change, change, change.

It didn't happen overnight. Yes, the wildness was in me, yes it kept my heart beating fast all the long day, yes it danced around me while I walked down the street, yes it let me look boys straight in the face when they stared at me, yes it turned my laugh from a cough into a long wild fever, but I was still scared. How could I not be? I was my mother's daughter. Her hold on me stronger than love. And then one day I was walking home with Karen Cepeda, who at that time was like my friend. Karen did the goth thing really well; she had spiky Robert Smith hair and wore all black and had the skin color of a ghost. Walking with her in Paterson was like walking with the bearded lady. Everybody would stare and it was the scariest thing, and that was, I guess, why I did it.

We were walking down Main and being stared at by everybody and out of nowhere I said, Karen, I want you to cut my hair. As soon as I said it I knew. The feeling in my blood, the rattle, came over me again. Karen raised her eyebrow: What about your mother? You see, it wasn't just me, everybody was scared of Belicia de León.

Fuck her, I said.

Karen looked at me like I was being stupid—I never cursed, but that was something else that was about to change. The next day we locked ourselves in her bathroom and downstairs her father and uncles were bellowing at some soccer game. Well, how do you want it? she asked. I looked at the girl in the mirror for a long time. All I knew was that I didn't want to see her ever again. I put the clippers in Karen's hand, turned them on, and guided her hand until it was all gone.

So now you're punk? Karen asked uncertainly.

Yes, I said.

The next day my mother threw the wig at me. You're going to wear this. You're going to wear it every day. And if I see you without it on I'm going to kill you!

I didn't say a word. I held the wig over the burner.

Don't do it, she swore as the burner clicked. Don't you dare—

It went up in a flash, like gasoline, like a stupid hope, and if I hadn't thrown it in the sink it would have taken my hand. The smell was horrible, like all of the chemicals from all the factories in Elizabeth.

That was when she slapped at me, when I struck her hand and she snatched it back, like I was the fire.

Of course everyone thought I was the worst daughter ever. My tía and our neighbors kept saying, Hija, she's your mother, she's dying, but I wouldn't listen. When I caught her hand a door opened. And I wasn't about to turn my back on it.

But God, how we fought! Sick or not, dying or not, my mother wasn't going to go down easily. She wasn't una pendeja. I'd seen her slap grown men, push white police officers onto their asses, curse a whole group of bochincheras. She had raised me and my brother by herself, she had worked three jobs until she could buy this house we live in, she had survived being abandoned by my father, she had come from Santo Domingo all by herself and as a young girl she claimed to have been beaten, set on fire, left for dead. There was no way she was going to let me go without killing me first. Figurín de mierda, she called me. You think you're someone but you ain't nada. She dug hard, looking for my seams, wanting me to tear like always, but I didn't weaken, I wasn't going to. It was that feeling I had, that my life was waiting for me on the other side, that made me fearless. When she threw away my Smiths and Sisters of Mercy posters—Aquí yo no quiero maricones—I bought replacements. When she threatened to tear up my new clothes, I started keeping them in my locker and at Karen's house. When she told me that I had to quit my job at the Greek diner I explained to my boss that my mother was starting to lose it because of her chemo, so when she called to say I couldn't work there anymore he just handed me the phone and stared out at his customers in embarrassment. When she changed the locks on me—I had started staying out late, going to the Limelight because even though I was fourteen I looked twenty-five—I would knock on Oscar's window and he would let me in, scared because the next day my mother would run around the house screaming, Who the hell let that hija de la gran puta in the house? Who? Who?

And Oscar would be at the breakfast table, stammering, I don't know, Mami, I don't.

Her rage filled the house, flat stale smoke. It got into everything, into our hair and our food, like the fallout they talked to us about in school that would one day drift down soft as snow. My brother didn't know what to do. He stayed in his room, though sometimes he would lamely try to ask me what was going on. Nothing. You can tell me, Lola, he said, and I could only laugh. You need to lose weight, I told him.

In those final weeks I knew better than to walk near my mother. Most of the time she just looked at me with the stink-eye, but sometimes without warning she would grab me by my throat and hang on until I pried her fingers from me. She didn't bother talking to me unless it was to make death threats. When you grow up you'll meet me in a dark alley when you least expect it and then I'll kill you and nobody will know I did it! Literally gloating as she said this.

You're crazy, I told her.

You don't call me crazy, she said, and then she sat down, panting.

It was bad but no one expected what came next. So obvious when you think about it.

All my life I'd been swearing that one day I would just disappear.

And one day I did.

I ran off, dique, because of a boy.

What can I really tell you about him? He was like all boys: beautiful and callow, and like an insect he couldn't sit still. Un blanquito with long hairy legs I met one night at Limelight.

His name was Aldo.

He was nineteen and lived down at the Jersey Shore with his seventy-four-year-old father. In the back of his Oldsmobile on University I pulled my leather skirt up and my fishnet stockings down and the smell of me was everywhere. That was our first date. The spring of my sophomore year we wrote and called each other at least once a day. I even drove down with Karen to visit him in Wildwood (she had a license, I didn't). He lived and worked near the boardwalk, one of three guys who operated the bumper cars, the only one without tattoos. You should stay, he told me that night while Karen walked ahead of us on the beach. Where would I live? I asked and he smiled. With me. Don't lie, I said, but he looked out at the surf. I want you to come, he said seriously.

He asked me three times. I counted, I know.

That summer my brother announced that he was going to dedicate his life to designing role-playing games and my mother was trying to keep a second job, for the first time since her operation. It wasn't working out. She was coming home exhausted, and since I wasn't helping, nothing around the house was getting done. Some weekends my tía Rubelka would help out with the cooking and cleaning and would lecture us both but she had her own family to watch after so most of the time we were on our own. Come, he said on the phone. And then in August Karen left for Slippery Rock. She had graduated from high school a year early. If I don't see Paterson again it will be too soon, she said before she left.

That was the September I cut school six times in my first two weeks. I just couldn't do school anymore. Something inside wouldn't let me. It didn't help that I was reading *The Fountainhead* and had decided that I was Dominique and Aldo was Roark. I'm sure I could have stayed that way forever, too scared to jump, but finally what we'd all been waiting for happened. My mother announced at dinner, quietly: I want you both to listen to me: the doctor is running more tests on me.

Oscar looked like he was going to cry. He put his head down. And my reaction? I looked at her and said: Could you please pass the salt?

These days I don't blame her for smacking me across my face, but right then it was all I needed. We jumped on each other and the table fell and the sancocho spilled all over the floor and Oscar just stood in the corner bellowing, Stop it, stop it, stop it!

Hija de tu maldita madre, she shrieked. And I said: This time I hope you die from it.

For a couple of days the house was a war zone, and then on Friday she let me out of my room and I was allowed to sit next to her on the sofa and watch novelas with her. She was waiting for her blood work to come back but you would never have known her life was in the balance. She watched the TV like it was the only thing that mattered, and whenever one of the characters did something underhanded she would start waving her arms. Someone has to stop her! Can't they see what that puta is up to?

I hate you, I said very quietly, but she didn't hear. Go get me some water, she said. Put an ice cube in it.

That was the last thing I did for her. The next morning I was on the bus bound for the Shore. One bag, two hundred dollars in tips, tío Rudolfo's old knife. I was so scared. I couldn't stop shaking. The whole ride down I was expecting the sky to split open and my mother to reach down and shake me. But it didn't happen. Nobody but the man across the aisle noticed me. You're really beautiful, he said. Like a girl I once knew.

I didn't write them a note. That's how much I hated them. Her.

That night while we lay in Aldo's sweltering kitty-litter-infested room I told him: I want you to do it to me.

He started unbuttoning my pants. Are you sure?

Definitely, I said grimly.

He had a long, thin dick that hurt like hell, but the whole time I just said, Oh yes, Aldo, yes, because that was what I imagined you were supposed to say while you were losing your "virginity" to some boy you thought you loved.

It was like the stupidest thing I ever did. I was miserable. And so bored. But of course I wouldn't admit it. I had run away, so I was happy! Happy! Aldo had neglected to mention all those times he told me to live with him that his father hated him like I hated my mother. Aldo Sr. had been in World War II, and he'd never forgiven the "Japs" for all the friends he had lost. My dad's so full of shit, Aldo said. He never left Fort Dix. I don't think his father said four words to me the whole time I lived with them. He was one mean viejito and even had a padlock around the refrigerator. Stay the hell out of it, he told me. We couldn't even get ice cubes out. Aldo and his dad lived in one of the cheapest little bungalows, and me and Aldo slept in a room where his father kept the cat litter for his two cats and at night we would move it out into the hallway but he always woke up before us and put it back in the room—I told you to leave my crap alone. Which was funny when you think about it. But it wasn't funny then. I got a job selling french fries on the boardwalk, and between the hot oil and the cat piss I couldn't smell anything else. On my days off I would drink with Aldo, or I would sit in the sand dressed in all black and try to write in my journal, which I was sure would form the foundation for a utopian society after we blew ourselves into radioactive kibble. Sometimes other boys would walk up to me and would throw lines at me like, Who fuckin' died? What's with your hair? They would sit down next to me in the sand. You a good-looking girl, you should be in a bikini. Why, so you can rape me? Jesus Christ, one of them said, jumping to his feet, what the hell is wrong with you?

To this day I don't know how I lasted. At the beginning of October I was laid off from the french fry palace; by then most of the boardwalk was closed up and I had nothing to do except hang out at the public library, which was even smaller than my high school one. Aldo had moved on to working with his dad in his garage, which only made them more pissed at each other, and by extension more pissed off at me. When they got home they would drink Schlitz and complain about the Phillies. I guess I should count myself lucky that they didn't just decide to bury the hatchet by gangbanging me. I stayed out as much as I could and waited for the feelings to come back to me, to tell me what I should do next, but I was bone-dry, bereft, no visions whatsoever. I started to think that maybe it was like in the books; as soon as I lost my virginity I lost my power. I got really mad at Aldo after that. You're a drunk, I told him. And an idiot. So what, he shot back. Your pussy smells. Then stay out of it! I will! But of course I was happy! Happy! I kept waiting to run into my family posting up flyers of me on the boardwalk, my mom, the tallest blackest chestiest thing in sight, Oscar looking like the brown blob, my tía Rubelka, maybe even my tío if they could get him off the heroin long enough, but the closest I came to any of that was some flyers someone had put up for a cat they lost. That's white people for you. They lose a cat and it's an all-points bulletin, but we Dominicans, we lose a daughter and we might not even cancel our appointment at the salon.

By November I was so finished. I would sit there with Aldo and his putrid father and the old shows would come on the TV, the ones me and my brother used to watch when we were kids, *Three's Company*, *What's Happening*, *The Jeffersons*, and my disappointment would grind against some organ that was very soft and tender. It was starting to get cold too, and wind just walked right into the bungalow and got under your blankets or jumped in the shower with you. It was awful. I kept having these stupid visions of my brother trying to cook for himself. Don't ask me why. I was the one who cooked for us, the only thing Oscar knew how to make was grilled cheese. I imagined him thin as a reed, wandering around the kitchen, opening cabinets forlornly. I even started dreaming about my mother, except in my dreams she was a little girl, and I mean really little; I could hold her in the palm of my hand and she was always trying to say something. I would put her right up to my ear and I still couldn't hear.

I always hated obvious dreams like that. I still do.

And then Aldo decided to be cute. I knew he was getting unhappy with us but I didn't know exactly how bad it was until one night he had his friends over. His father had gone to Atlantic City and they were all drinking and smoking and telling dumb jokes and suddenly Aldo says: Do you know what Pontiac stands for? Poor Old Nigger Thinks It's A Cadillac. But who was he looking at when he told his punch line? He was looking straight at me.

That night he wanted me, but I pushed his hand away. Don't touch me.

Don't get sore, he said, putting my hand on his cock. It wasn't nothing.

And then he laughed.

So what did I do a couple days later: a really dumb thing. I called home. The first time no one answered. The second time it was Oscar. The de León residence, how may I direct your call? That was my brother for you. This is why everybody in the world hated his guts.

It's me, dumb-ass.

Lola. He was so quiet, and then I realized he was crying. Where *are* you?

You don't want to know. I switched ears, trying to keep my voice casual. How is everybody?

Lola, Mami's going to *kill* you.

Dumb-ass, could you keep your voice down. Mami isn't home, is she?

She's working.

What a surprise, I said. Mami working. On the last minute of the last hour of the last day my mother would be at work. She would be at work when the missiles were in the air.

I guess I must have missed him real bad, or I just wanted to see somebody who knew anything about me, or the cat piss had damaged my common sense because I gave him the address of a coffee shop on the boardwalk and told him to bring some of my clothes and some of my books.

Bring me money too.

He paused. I don't know where Mami keeps it.

You know, Mister. Just bring it.

How much? he asked timidly.

All of it.

That's a lot of money, Lola.

Just bring me the money, Oscar.

OK, OK. He inhaled deeply. Will you at least tell me if you're OK or not?

I'm OK, I said, and that was the only point in the conversation where I almost cried. I kept quiet until I could speak again, and then I asked him how he was going to get down here without our mother finding out.

You know me, he said weakly. I might be a dork but I'm a resourceful dork.

I should have known not to trust anybody whose favorite books as a child were *Encyclopedia Brown*. But I wasn't really thinking; I was so looking forward to seeing him.

By then I had this plan. I was going to convince my brother to run away with me. My plan was that we would go to Dublin. I had met a bunch of Irish guys on the boardwalk and they had sold me on their country. I would become a backup singer for U2, and both Bono and the drummer would fall in love with me, and Oscar could become the Dominican James Joyce. I really believed it would happen too. That's how deluded I was by then.

The next day I walked into the coffee shop, looking brand-new, and he was there, with the bag. Oscar, I said, laughing, you're so fat!

I know, he said, ashamed. I was worried about you.

We embraced for like an hour and then he started crying. Lola, I'm *sorry*.

It's OK, I said, and that's when I looked up and saw my mother and my tía Rubelka and my tío walk into the shop.

Oscar! I screamed but it was too late. My mother already had me in her hands. She looked so thin and worn, almost like a hag, but she was holding on to me like I was her last nickel, and underneath her red wig her green eyes were *furious*. I noticed, absently, that she had dressed up for the occasion. That was typical. Muchacha del diablo, she shrieked. I managed to haul her out of the coffee shop and when she pulled back her hand to smack me I broke free. I ran for it. Behind me I could feel her sprawling, hitting the curb hard with a crack, but I wasn't looking back. No—I was running. In elementary school, whenever we had field day I was always the fastest girl in my grade, took home all the ribbons; they said it wasn't fair because I was so big, but I didn't care. I could even have beat the boys if I'd wanted to, so there was no way my sick mother, my messed-up tío, and my fat brother were going to catch me. I was going to run as fast as my long legs could carry me. I was going to run down the boardwalk, past Aldo's miserable house, out of Wildwood, out of New Jersey, and I wasn't going to stop. I was going to *fly*.

Anyway, that's how it *should* have worked out. But I looked back. I couldn't help it. It's not like I didn't know my Bible, all that pillars-of-salt stuff, but when you're someone's daughter that she raised by herself with no help from nobody, habits die hard. I just wanted to make sure my mom hadn't broken her arm or cracked open her skull. I mean, really, who the hell wants to kill her own mother by accident? That's the only reason I glanced back. She was sprawled on the ground, her wig had fallen out of reach, her poor bald head out in the day like something private and shameful, and she was bawling like a lost calf, Hija, hija. And there I was, wanting to run off into my future. It was right then when I needed that feeling to guide me, but it wasn't anywhere in sight. Only me. In the end I didn't have the ovaries. She was on the ground, bald as a baby, crying, probably a month away from dying, and here I was, her one and only daughter. And there was nothing I could do about it. So I walked back, and when I reached down to help her she clamped on to me with both hands. That was when I realized she hadn't been crying at all. She'd been faking! Her smile was like a lion's.

Ya te tengo, she said, jumping triumphantly to her feet. Te tengo.

And that is how I ended up in Santo Domingo. I guess my mother thought it would be harder for me to run away from an island where I knew no one, and in a way she was right. I'm into my sixth month here and these days I'm just trying to be philosophical about the whole thing. I wasn't like that at first, but in the end I had to let it go. It was like the fight between the egg and the rock, my abuela said. No winning. I'm actually going to school, not that it's going to count when I return to Paterson, but it keeps me busy and out of mischief and around people my own age. You don't need to be around us viejos all day, Abuela says. I have mixed feelings about the school. For one thing, it's improved my Spanish a lot. The —— Academy is a private school, a Carol Morgan wannabe filled with people my tío Carlos Moya calls los hijos de mami y papi. And then there's me. If you think it was tough being a goth in Paterson, try being a Dominican York in one of those private schools back in DR. You will never meet bitchier girls in your whole life. They whisper about me to death. Someone else would have a nervous breakdown, but after Wildwood I'm not so brittle. I don't let it get to me. And the irony of all ironies? I'm on our school's *track* team. I joined because my friend Rosío, the scholarship girl from Los Mina, told me I could win a spot on the team on the length of my legs alone. Those are the pins of a winner, she prophesied. Well, she must have known something I didn't because I'm now our school's top runner in the 400 meters and under. That I have talent at this simple thing never ceases to amaze me. Karen would pass out if she could see me running sprints out behind my school while Coach Cortés screams at us, first in Spanish and then in Catalan. Breathe, breathe, *breathe!* I've got like no fat left on me, and the musculature of my legs impresses everyone, even me. I can't wear shorts anymore without causing traffic jams and the other day when my abuela locked us out of the house she turned to me in frustration and said, Hija, just kick the door open. That pushed a laugh out of both of us.

So much has changed these last months, in my head, my heart. Rosío has me dressing up like a "real Dominican girl." She's the one who fixed my hair and who helps me with my makeup, and sometimes when I see myself in mirrors I don't even know who I am anymore. Not that I'm unhappy or anything. Even if I found a hot-air balloon that would whisk me straight to U2's house, I'm not sure I would take it. (I'm still not talking to my traitor brother, though.) The truth is I'm even thinking of staying one more year. Abuela doesn't want me to ever leave—I'll miss you, she says so simply it can't be anything but true, and my mom has told me I can stay if I want to but that I would be welcome at home too. Tía Rubelka tells me she's hanging tough, my mother, that she's back to two jobs. They send me a picture of the whole family and Abuela frames it and I can't look at them without misting up. My mother's not wearing her fakies in it; she looks so thin I don't even recognize her.

Just know that I would die for you, she told me the last time we talked. And before I could say anything she hung up.

But that's not what I wanted to tell you. It's about that crazy feeling that started this whole mess, the bruja feeling that comes singing out of my bones, that takes hold of me the way blood seizes cotton. The feeling that tells me that everything in my life is about to change. It's come back. Just the other day I woke up from all these dreams and it was there, pulsing inside of me. I imagine this is what it feels like to have a child in you. At first I was scared because I thought it was telling me to run away again, but every time I looked around our house, every time I saw my abuela, the feeling got stronger so I knew this was something different. I was dating a boy by then, a sweet morenito by the name of Max Sánchez, whom I had met in Los Mina while visiting Rosío. He's short but his smile and his snappy dressing make up for a lot. Because I'm from Nueba Yol he talks about how rich he's going to become and I try to explain to him that I don't care about that but he looks at me like I'm crazy. I'm going to get a white Mercedes-Benz, he says. Tú verás. But it's the job he has that I love best, that got me and him started. In Santo Domingo two or three theaters often share the same set of reels for a movie, so when the first theater finishes with the first reel they put it in Max's hands and he rides his motorcycle like crazy to make it to the second theater and then he drives back, waits, picks up the second reel, and so on. If he's held up or gets into an accident the first reel will end and there will be no second reel and the people in the audience will throw bottles. So far he's been blessed, he tells me and kisses his San Miguel medal. Because of me, he brags, one movie becomes three. I'm the man who puts together the pictures. Max's not from "la clase alta," as my abuela would describe it, and if any of the stuck-up bitches in school saw us they would just about die, but I'm fond of him. He holds open doors, he calls me his morena; when he's feeling brave he touches my arm gently and then pulls back.

Anyway, I thought maybe the feeling was about Max and so one day I let him take us to one of the love motels. He was so excited he almost fell off the bed and the first thing he wanted was to look at my ass. I never knew my big ass could be such a star attraction but he kissed it, four, five times, gave me goose bumps with his breath and pronounced it a tesoro. When we were done and he was in the bathroom washing himself I stood in front of the mirror naked and looked at my culo for the first time. A tesoro, I repeated. A treasure.

Well? Rosío asked at school. And I nodded once, quickly, and she grabbed me and laughed and all the girls I hated turned to look but what could they do? Happiness, when it comes, is stronger than all the jerk girls in Santo Domingo combined.

But I was still confused. Because the feeling, it just kept getting stronger and stronger, wouldn't let me sleep, wouldn't give me any peace. I started losing races, which was something I never did.

You ain't so great, are you, gringa, the girls on the other teams hissed at me and I could only hang my head. Coach Cortés was so unhappy he just locked himself in his car and wouldn't say anything to any of us.

The whole thing was driving me crazy, and then one night I came home from being out with Max. He had taken me for a walk along the Malecón—he never had money for anything else—and we had watched the bats zigzagging over the palms and an old ship head into the distance. He talked quietly about moving to the U.S. while I stretched my hamstrings. My abuela was waiting for me at the living room table. Even though she still wears black to mourn the husband she lost when she was young she's one of the most handsome women I've ever known. We have the same jagged lightning-bolt part and the first time I saw her at the airport I didn't want to admit it but I knew that things were going to be OK between us. She stood like she was her own best thing and when she saw me she said, Hija, I have waited for you since the day you left. And then she hugged me and kissed me and said, I'm your abuela, but you can call me La Inca.

Standing over her that night, her part like a crack in her hair, I felt a surge of tenderness. I put my arms around her and that was when I noticed that she was looking at photos. Old photos, the kind I'd never seen in my house. Photos of my mother when she was young and of other people. I picked one up. Mami was standing in front of a Chinese restaurant. Even with the apron on she looked potent, like someone who was going to be someone.

She was very guapa, I said casually.

Abuela snorted. Guapa soy yo. Your mother was a diosa. But so cabeza dura. When she was your age we never got along.

I didn't know that, I said.

She was cabeza dura and I was . . . exigente. But it all turned out for the best, she sighed. We have you and your brother and that's more than anyone could have hoped for, given what came before. She plucked out one photo. This is your mother's father, she offered me the photo. He was my cousin, and—

She was about to say something else and then she stopped.

And that's when it hit with the force of a hurricane. The *feeling*. I stood straight up, the way my mother always wanted me to stand up. My abuela was sitting there, forlorn, trying to cobble together the right words and I could not move or breathe. I felt like I always did at the last seconds of a race, when I was sure that I was going to explode. She was about to say something and I was waiting for whatever she was going to tell me. I was waiting to begin.

3

The Three Heartbreaks
of Belicia Cabral
1955–1962

LOOK AT THE PRINCESS

Before there was an American Story, before Paterson spread before Oscar and Lola like a dream, or the trumpets from the Island of our eviction had even sounded, there was their mother, Hypatía Belicia Cabral:

a girl so tall your leg bones ached just looking at her

so dark it was as if the Creatrix had, in her making, blinked

who, like her yet-to-be-born daughter, would come to exhibit a particularly Jersey malaise—the inextinguishable longing for elsewheres.

UNDER THE SEA

She lived in those days in Baní. Not the frenzied Baní of right now, supported by an endless supply of DoYos who've

laid claim to most of Boston, Providence, New Hampshire.
This was the lovely Baní of times past, beautiful and respectful. A city famed for its resistance to blackness, and it was
here, alas, that the darkest character in our story resided. On
one of the main streets near the central plaza. In a house that
no longer stands. It was here that Beli lived with her mother-
aunt, if not exactly content, then certainly in a state of relative tranquillity. From 1951 on, "hija" and "madre" running
their famous bakery near the Plaza Central and keeping their
fading, airless house in tip-top shape. (Before 1951, our orphaned girl had lived with another foster family, monstrous
people if the rumors are to be believed, a dark period of her
life neither she nor her madre ever referenced. Their very
own página en blanco.)

These were the Beautiful Days. When La Inca would re-
count for Beli her family's illustrious history while they
pounded and wrung dough with bare hands (Your father!
Your mother! Your sisters! Your house!) or when the only talk
between them was the voices on Carlos Moya's radio and the
sound of the butter being applied to Beli's ruined back. Days
of mangoes, days of bread. There are not many surviving
photos from that period but it's not hard to imagine them—
arrayed in front of their immaculate house in Los Pescadores.
Not touching, because it was not their way. Respectability so
dense in la grande that you'd need a blowtorch to cut it, and
a guardedness so Minas Tirith in la pequeña that you'd
need the whole of Mordor to overcome it. Theirs was the life
of the Good People of Sur. Church twice a week, and on
Fridays a stroll through Baní's parque central, where in those

nostalgic Trujillo days stickup kids were nowhere to be seen and the beautiful bands did play. They shared the same sagging bed, and in the morning, while La Inca fished around blindly for her chancletas, Beli would shiver out to the front of the house, and while La Inca brewed her coffee, Beli would lean against the fence and stare. At what? The neighbors? The rising dust? At the world?

Hija, La Inca would call. Hija, come here!

Four, five times until finally La Inca walked over to fetch her, and only then did Beli come.

Why are you shouting? Beli wanted to know, annoyed.

La Inca pushing her back toward the house: Will you listen to this girl! Thinks herself a person when she's not!

Beli, clearly: one of those Oyá-souls, always turning, allergic to tranquilidad. Almost any other Third World girl would have thanked Dios Santísimo for the blessed life she led: after all, she had a madre who didn't beat her, who (out of guilt or inclination) spoiled her rotten, bought her flash clothes and paid her bakery wages, peanuts, I'll admit, but that's more than what ninety-nine percent of other kids in similar situations earned, which was nathan. Our girl had it *made*, and yet it did not feel so in her heart. For reasons she only dimly understood, by the time of our narrative, Beli could no longer abide working at the bakery or being the "daughter" of one of the "most upstanding women in Baní." She could not abide, period. Everything about her present life irked her; she wanted, with all her heart, something *else*. When this dissatisfaction entered her heart she could not recall, would later tell her daughter that it had been with her *all her life*, but who knows if this is true? What exactly it was she wanted was never clear either: her own incredible life, yes, a handsome, wealthy husband, yes, beautiful children, yes, a woman's body, without question. If I had to put it to words I'd say what she wanted, more than anything, was what she'd always wanted throughout her Lost Childhood: to escape. *From what* was easy to enumerate: the bakery, her school, dull-ass Baní, sharing a bed with her madre, the inability to buy the dresses she wanted, having to wait until fifteen to straighten her hair, the impossible expectations of La Inca, the fact that her long-gone parents had died when she was one, the whispers that Trujillo had done it, those first years of her life when she'd been an orphan, the horrible scars from that time, her own despised black skin. But where she wanted to escape *to* she could not tell you. I guess it wouldn't have mattered if she'd been a princess in a high castle or if her dead parents' former estate, the glorious Casa Hatüey, had been miraculously restored from Trujillo's Omega Effect. She would have wanted out.

Every morning the same routine: Hypatía Belicia Cabral, ven acá!

You ven acá, Beli muttered under her breath. You.

Beli had the inchoate longings of nearly every adolescent escapist, of an entire generation, but I ask you: So fucking what? No amount of wishful thinking was changing the cold hard fact that she was a teenage girl living in the Dominican Republic of Rafael Leónidas Trujillo Molina, the Dictatingest Dictator who ever Dictated. This was a country, a society, that had been designed to be virtually escape-proof. Alcatraz of the Antilles. There weren't any Houdini holes in that Plátano Curtain. Options as rare as Tainos and for irascible darkskinned flacas of modest means they were rarer still. (If you want to cast her restlessness in a broader light: she was suffering the same suffocation that was asphyxiating a whole generation of young Dominicans. Twenty-odd years of the Trujillato had guaranteed that. Hers was the generation that would launch the Revolution, but which for the moment was turning blue for want of air. The generation reaching consciousness in a society that lacked any. The generation that despite the consensus that declared change impossible *hankered* for change all the same. At the end of her life, when she was being eaten alive by cancer, Beli would talk about how trapped they all felt. It was like being at the bottom of an ocean, she said. There was no light and a whole ocean crushing down on you. But most people had gotten so used to it they thought it normal, they forgot even that there was a world above.)

But what could she do? Beli was a girl, for fuck's sake; she had no power or beauty (yet) or talent or family that could help her transcend, only La Inca, and La Inca wasn't about to help our girl escape anything. On the contrary, mon frère, La Inca, with her stiff skirts and imperious airs, had as her central goal the planting of Belicia in the provincial soil of Baní and in the inescapable fact of her Family's Glorious Golden Past. The family Beli had never known, whom she had lost early. (Remember, your father was a doctor, a *doctor*, and your mother was a nurse, a *nurse*.) La Inca expected Beli to be the last best hope of her decimated family, expected her to play the key role in a historical rescue mission, but what did she know about her family except the stories she was told ad nauseam? And, ultimately, what did she care? She wasn't a maldita ciguapa, with her feet pointing backward in the past. Her feet pointed forward, she reminded La Inca over and over. Pointed to the future.

Your father was a doctor, La Inca repeated, unperturbed. Your mother was a nurse. They owned the biggest house in La Vega.

Beli did not listen, but at night, when the alizé winds blew in, our girl would groan in her sleep.

LA CHICA DE MI ESCUELA

When Beli was thirteen, La Inca landed her a scholarship at El Redentor, one of the best schools in Baní. On paper it was a pretty solid move. Orphan or not, Beli was the Third and Final Daughter of one of the Cibao's finest families, and a proper education was not only her due, it was her birthright. La Inca also hoped to take some of the heat off Beli's restlessness. A new school with the best people in the valley, she thought, what couldn't this cure? But despite the girl's admirable lineage, Beli herself had not grown up in her parents' upper-class milieu. Had had no kind of breeding until La Inca—her father's favorite cousin—had finally managed to track her down (rescue her, really) and brought her out of the Darkness of those days and into the light of Baní. In these last seven years, meticulous punctilious La Inca had undone a lot of the damage that life in Outer Azua had inflicted, but the girl was still crazy rough around the edges. Had all the upper-class arrogance you could want, but she also had the mouth of a colmado superstar. Would chew anybody out for anything. (Her years in Outer Azua to blame.) Putting her darkskinned media-campesina ass in a tony school where the majority of the pupils were the whiteskinned children of the regime's top ladronazos turned out to be a better idea in theory than in practice. Brilliant doctor father or not, Beli stood out in El Redentor. Given the delicacy of the situation, another girl might have adjusted the polarity of her persona to better fit in, would have kept her head down and survived by ignoring the 10,001 barbs directed at her each day by students and staff alike. Not Beli. She never would admit it (even to herself), but she felt utterly exposed at El Redentor, all those pale eyes gnawing at her duskiness like locusts—and she didn't know how to handle such vulnerability. Did what had always saved her in the past. Was defensive and aggressive and mad overreactive. You said something slightly off-color about her shoes and she brought up the fact that you had a slow eye and danced like a goat with a rock stuck in its ass. Ouch. You would just be playing and homegirl would be coming down on you off the top rope.

Let's just say, by the end of her second quarter Beli could walk down the hall without fear that anyone would crack on her. The downside of this of course was that she was completely alone. (It wasn't like *In the Time of the Butterflies*, where a kindly Mirabal Sister[7] steps up and befriends the poor scholarship student. No Miranda here: everybody shunned her.) Despite the outsized expectations Beli had had on her first days to be Number One in her class and to be crowned prom queen opposite handsome Jack Pujols, Beli quickly found herself exiled beyond the bonewalls of the macroverse itself, flung there by the Ritual of Chüd. She wasn't even lucky enough to be demoted into that lamentable subset—those mega-losers that even the losers pick on. She was beyond that, in Sycorax territory. Her fellow ultra-dalits included: the Boy in the Iron Lung whose servants would wheel him into the corner of the class every morning and who always seemed to be smiling, the idiot, and the Chinese girl whose father owned the largest pulpería in the country and was known, dubiously, as Trujillo's Chino. In her two years at El Redentor, Wei never managed to learn more than a gloss of Spanish, yet despite this obvious impediment she reported dutifully to class every day. In the beginning the other students had scourged her with all the usual anti-Asian nonsense. They cracked on her hair (It's so greasy!), on her eyes (Can you really see through those?), on chopsticks

---

7. The Mirabal Sisters were the Great Martyrs of that period. Patría Mercedes, Minerva Argentina, and María Teresa—three beautiful sisters from Salcedo who resisted Trujillo and were murdered for it. (One of the main reasons why the women from Salcedo have reputations for being so incredibly fierce, don't take shit from nobody, not even a Trujillo.) Their murders and the subsequent public outcry are believed by many to have signaled the official beginning of the end of the Trujillato, the "tipping point," when folks finally decided enough was enough.

(I got some twigs for you!), on language (variations on ching-chong-ese.) The boys especially loved to tug their faces back into bucked-tooth, chinky-eyed rictuses. Charming. Ha-ha. Jokes aplenty.

But once the novelty wore off (she didn't ever respond), the students exiled Wei to the Phantom Zone, and even the cries of *China, China, China* died down eventually.

This was who Beli sat next to her first two years of high school. But even Wei had some choice words for Beli.

You black, she said, fingering Beli's thin forearm. *Black-black.*

Beli tried her hardest but she couldn't spin bomb-grade plutonium from the light-grade uranium of her days. During her Lost Years there had been no education of any kind, and that gap had taken a toll on her neural pathways, such that she could never fully concentrate on the material at hand. It was stubbornness and the expectations of La Inca that kept Belicia lashed to the mast, even though she was miserably alone and her grades were even worse than Wei's. (You would think, La Inca complained, that you could score higher than a china.) The other students bent furiously over their exams while Beli stared at the hurricane whorl at the back of Jack Pujols's crew cut.

Señorita Cabral, are you finished?

No, maestra. And then a forced return to the problem sets, as though she were submerging herself in water against her will.

No one in her barrio could have imagined how much she hated school. La Inca certainly didn't have a clue. Colegio El

Redentor was about a million miles removed from the modest working-class neighborhood where she and La Inca lived. And Beli did everything possible to represent her school as a paradise where she cavorted with the other Immortals, a four-year interval before the final Apotheosis. Took on even more airs: where before, La Inca had to correct her on grammar and against using slang, she now had the best diction and locution in Lower Baní. (She's starting to talk like Cervantes, La Inca bragged to the neighbors. I told you that school would be worth the trouble.) Beli didn't have much in the way of friends—only Dorca, the daughter of the woman who cleaned for La Inca, who owned exactly no pair of shoes and worshipped the ground Beli walked on. For Dorca she put on a show to end all shows. She wore her uniform straight through the day until La Inca forced her to take it off (What do you think, these things were *free*?), and talked unceasingly about her schoolmates, painting each one as her deepest friend and confidante; even the girls who made it their mission to ignore and exclude her from everything, four girls we will call the Squadron Supreme, found themselves rehabilitated in her tales as benevolent older spirits that dropped in on Belicia every now and then to give her invaluable advice on the school and life in general. The Squadron, it turned out, were all very jealous of her relationship with Jack Pujols (who, she reminded Dorca, is my boyfriend) and invariably one member or another of the Squadron fell to weakness and attempted to steal her novio but of course he always rebuked their treacherous advances. I am *appalled*, Jack would say, casting the hussy aside. Especially considering how well Belicia Cabral, daughter of the world-famous surgeon, has treated you. In every version, after a prolonged period of iciness the offending Squadron member would throw herself at Beli's feet and beg forgiveness, which, after tense deliberation, Beli invariably granted. They can't help it that they're weak, she explained to Dorca. Or that Jack is so guapo. What a world she spun! Beli talked of parties and pools and polo games and dinners where bloody steak was heaped onto plates and grapes were as common as tangerines. She in fact, without knowing, was talking about the life she never knew: the life of Casa Hatüey. So astonishing were her descriptions that Dorca often said, I would like to go to school with you one day.

Beli snorted. You must be crazy! You're too stupid!

And Dorca would lower her head. Stare at her own broad feet. Dusty in their chancletas.

La Inca talked about Beli becoming a female doctor (You wouldn't be the first, but you'd be the best!), imagined her hija raising test tubes up to the light, but Beli usually passed her school days dreaming about the various boys around her (she had stopped staring at them openly after one of her teachers had written a letter home to La Inca and La Inca had chastised her, Where do you think you are? A brothel? This is the best school in Baní, muchacha, you're ruining your reputation!), and if not about the boys then about the house she was convinced she would one day own, furnishing it in her mind, room by room by room. Her madre wanted her to bring back Casa Hatüey, a history house, but Beli's house was new and crisp, had no history at all attached to it. In her favorite María Montez daydream, a dashing European of the Jean Pierre Aumont variety (who happened to look exactly like Jack Pujols) would catch sight of her in the bakery and fall madly in love with her and sweep her off to his château in France.[8]

(Wake up, girl! You're going to burn the pan de agua!)

She wasn't the only girl dreaming like this. This jiringonza was in the *air*, it was the dreamshit that they fed girls day and night. It's surprising Beli could think of anything else, what with that heavy rotation of boleros, canciones, and versos spinning in her head, with the *Listín Diario*'s society pages spread before her. Beli at thirteen believed in love like a seventy-year-old widow who's been abandoned by family, husband, children, and fortune believes in God. Belicia was, if it was possible, even more susceptible to the Casanova Wave

8. María Montez, celebrated Dominican actress, moved to the U.S. and made more than twenty-five films between 1940 and 1951, including *Arabian Nights*, *Ali Baba and the Forty Thieves*, *Cobra Woman*, and my personal favorite, *Siren of Atlantis*. Crowned the "Queen of Technicolor" by fans and historians alike. Born María África Gracia Vidal on June 6, 1912, in Barahona, bit her screen name from the famous nineteenth-century courtesan Lola Montez (herself famous for fucking, among others, the part-Haitian Alexandre Dumas). María Montez was the original J. Lo (or whatever smoking caribeña is the number-one eye-crack of your time), the first real international star the DR had. Ended up marrying a Frenchie (sorry, Anacaona) and moving to Paris after World War II. Drowned alone in her bathtub, at the age of thirty-nine. No sign of struggle, no evidence of foul play. Did some photo ops for the Trujillato every now and then, but nothing serious. It should be pointed out that while in France, María proved to be quite the nerd. Wrote three books. Two were published. The third manuscript was lost after her death.

than many of her peers. Our girl was *straight boycrazy*. (To be called boycrazy in a country like Santo Domingo is a singular distinction; it means that you can sustain infatuations that would reduce your average northamericana to cinders.) She stared at the young bravos on the bus, secretly kissed the bread of the buenmosos who frequented the bakery, sang to herself all those beautiful Cuban love songs.

(God save your soul, La Inca grumbled, if you think *boys* are an answer to *anything*.)

But even the boy situation left a lot to be desired. If she'd been interested in the niggers in the barrio our Beli would have had no problems, these cats would have obliged her romantic spirit by jumping her lickety-split. But alas, La Inca's hope that the rarified private airs of Colegio El Redentor would have a salutary effect on the girl's character (like a dozen wet-belt beatings or three months in an unheated convent) had at least in this one aspect borne fruit, for Beli at thirteen only had eyes for the Jack Pujolses of the world. As is usually the case in these situations, the high-class boys she so desired didn't reciprocate her interest—Beli didn't have quite enough of anything to snap these Rubirosas out of their rich-girl reveries.

What a life! Each day turning on its axis slower than a year. She endured school, the bakery, La Inca's suffocating solicitude with a furious jaw. She watched hungrily for visitors from out of town, threw open her arms at the slightest hint of a wind and at night she struggled Jacob-like against the ocean pressing down on her.

KIMOTA!

So what happened?
A boy happened.
Her First.

NÚMERO UNO

Jack Pujols of course: the school's handsomest (read: whitest) boy, a haughty slender melniboién of pure European stock whose cheeks looked like they'd been knapped by a master and whose skin was unflawed by scar, mole, blemish, or hair, his small nipples were the pink perfect ovals of sliced salchicha. His father was a colonel in the Trujillato's beloved air force, a heavy-duty player in Baní (would be instrumental in bombing the capital during the revolution, killing all those helpless civilians, including my poor uncle Venicio), and his mother, a former beauty queen of Venezuelan proportions, now active in the Church, a kisser of cardinal rings and a socorro of orphans. Jack, Eldest Son, Privileged Seed, Hijo Bello, Anointed One, revered by his female family members—and that endless monsoon-rain of praise and indulgence had quickened in him the bamboo of entitlement. He had the physical swagger of a boy twice his size and an unbearable loudmouthed cockiness that he drove into people like a metal spur. In the future he would throw his lot in with the Demon Balaguer[9] and end up ambassador to Panama as his reward, but for the moment he was the school's Apollo, its Mithra. The teachers, the staff, the girls, the boys, all threw petals of adoration beneath his finely arched feet: he was proof positive that God—the Great God absolute! The center and circumference of all democracy!—does not love his children equally.

And how did Beli interact with this insane object of attraction? In a way that is fitting of her bullheaded directness:

9. Although not essential to our tale, per se, Balaguer is essential to the Dominican one, so therefore we must mention him, even though I'd rather piss in his face. The elders say, *Anything uttered for the first time summons a demon*, and when twentieth-century Dominicans first uttered the word *freedom* en masse the demon they summoned was Balaguer. (Known also as the Election Thief—see the 1966 election in the DR—and the Homunculus.) In the days of the Trujillato, Balaguer was just one of El Jefe's more efficient ringwraiths. Much is made of his intelligence (he certainly impressed the Failed Cattle Thief) and of his asceticism (when *he* raped his little girls he kept it real quiet). After Trujillo's death he would take over Project Domo and rule the country from 1960 to 1962, from 1966 to 1978, and again from 1986 to 1996 (by then dude was blind as a bat, a living mummy). During the second period of his rule, known locally as the Twelve Years, he unleashed a wave of violence against the Dominican left, death-squading hundreds and driving thousands more out of the country. It was he who oversaw/initiated the thing we call Diaspora. Considered our national "genius," Joaquín Balaguer was a Negrophobe, an apologist to genocide, an election thief, and a killer of people who wrote better than himself, famously ordering the death of journalist Orlando Martínez. Later, when he wrote his memoirs, he claimed he knew who had done the foul deed (not him, of course) and left a blank page, a página en blanco, in the text to be filled in with the truth upon his death. (Can you say *impunity*?) Balaguer died in 2002. The página is still blanca. Appeared as a sympathetic character in Vargas Llosa's *The Feast of the Goat*. Like most homunculi he did not marry and left no heirs.

she would march down the hallway, books pressed to her pubescent chest, staring down at her feet, and, pretending not to see him, would smash into his hallowed vessel.

Caramb—, he spluttered, wheeling about, and then he'd see it was Belicia, a girl, now stooping over to recover her books, and he bent over too (he was, if nothing, a caballero), his anger diffusing, becoming confusion, irritation. Caramba, Cabral, what are you, a bat? Watch. Where. You're. *Going*.

He had a single worry line creasing his high forehead (his "part," as it became known) and eyes of the deepest cerulean. The Eyes of Atlantis. (Once Beli had overheard him bragging to one of his many female admirers: Oh, these ol' things? I inherited them from my German abuela.)

Come on, Cabral, what's your difficulty?

It's your fault! she swore, meant in more ways than one.

Maybe she'd see better, one of his lieutenants cracked, if it was dark out.

It might as well have been dark out. For all intents and purposes she was invisible to him.

And would have stayed invisible too if the summer of sophomore year she'd not hit the biochemical jackpot, not experienced a Summer of Her Secondary Sex Characteristics, not been transformed utterly (*a terrible beauty has been born*). Where before Beli had been a gangly ibis of a girl, pretty in a typical sort of way, by summer's end she'd become un mujerón total, acquiring that body of hers, that body that made her famous in Baní. Her dead parents' genes on some Roman Polanski shit; like the older sister she had never met, Beli was transformed almost overnight into an underage stunner, and if Trujillo had not been on his last erections he probably would have gunned for her like he'd been rumored to have gunned for her poor dead sister. For the record, that summer our girl caught a cuerpazo so berserk that only a pornographer or a comic-book artist could have designed it with a clear conscience. Every neighborhood has its tetúa, but Beli could have put them all to shame, she was La Tetúa Suprema: her tetas were globes so implausibly titanic they made generous souls pity their bearer and drove every straight male in their vicinity to reevaluate his sorry life. She had the Breasts of Luba (35DDD). And what about that supersonic culo that could tear words right out of niggers' mouths, pull windows from out their motherfucking frames? A culo que jalaba más que una junta de buey. Dios mío! Even your humble Watcher, reviewing her old pictures, is struck by what a fucking babe she was.[10]

Ande el diablo! La Inca exclaimed. Hija, what in the world are you *eating*!

If Beli had been a normal girl, being the neighborhood's most prominent tetúa might have pushed her into shyness, might even have depressed the shit out of her. And at first Beli had both these reactions, and also the feeling that gets delivered to you by the bucket for free during adolescence: *Shame. Sharam. Vergüenza.* She no longer wanted to bathe with La Inca, a huge change to their morning routine. Well,

---

10. My shout-out to Jack Kirby aside, it's hard as a Third Worlder not to feel a certain amount of affinity for Uatu the Watcher; he resides in the hidden Blue Area of the Moon and we DarkZoners reside (to quote Glissant) on *"la face cachée de la Terre"* (Earth's hidden face).

I guess you're grown enough to wash yourself, La Inca said lightly. But you could tell she was hurt. In the close darkness of their washcloset, Beli circled disconsolately around her Novi Orbis, avoiding her hypersensitive nipples at all costs. Now every time she had to head outside, Beli felt like she was stepping into a Danger Room filled with men's laser eyes and women's razor whispers. The blasts of car horns enough to make her fall over herself. She was furious at the world for this newly acquired burden, and furious at herself.

For the first month, that is. Gradually Beli began to see beyond the catcalls and the *Dios mío asesina* and the *y ese tetatorio* and the *que pechonalidad* to the hidden mechanisms that drove these comments. One day on the way back from the bakery, La Inca muttering at her side about that day's receipts, it dawned on Beli: Men liked her! Not only did they like her, they liked her a fucking lot. The proof was the day that one of their customers, the local dentist, slipped her a note with his money, and it said, I want to see you, as simple as that. Beli was terrified, scandalized, and giddy. The dentist had a fat wife who ordered a cake from La Inca almost every month, either for one of her seven children or for her fifty-some cousins (but most likely for her and her alone). She had a wattle and an enormous middle-aged ass that challenged all chairs. Beli mooned over that note like it was a marriage proposal from God's hot son, even though the dentist was bald and paunchier than an OTB regular and had a tracery of fine red veins all over his cheeks. The dentist came in as he always did but now his eyes were always questing, Hello, Señorita Beli! his greeting now fetid with lust and threat, and Beli's heart would beat like nothing she'd ever heard. After two such visits she wrote, on a whim, a little note that said simply, Yes, you can pick me up at the park at tal-and-tal time, and passed it back to him with his change and by hook and crook arranged to be walking with La Inca through the park at the very moment of the assignation. Her heart going like crazy; she didn't know what to expect but she had a wild hope, and just as they were about to leave the park, Beli spotted the dentist sitting in a car that was not his, pretending to read the paper but looking forlornly in her direction. Look, Madre, Beli said loudly, it's the dentist, and La Inca turned and homeboy threw the car frantically into gear and tore out of there before La Inca could even wave. How very strange! La Inca said.

I don't like him, Beli said. He looks at me.

And now it was his wife who came to the bakery to pick up the cakes. Y el dentista? Beli inquired innocently. That one's too lazy to do anything, his wife said with no little exasperation.

Beli, who'd been waiting for something exactly like her body her whole life, was sent *over the moon* by what she now knew. By the undeniable concreteness of her desirability which was, in its own way, Power. Like the accidental discovery of the One Ring. Like stumbling into the wizard Shazam's cave or finding the crashed ship of the Green Lantern! Hypatía Belicia Cabral finally had power and a true sense of self. Started pinching her shoulders back, wearing the tightest clothes she had. Dios mío, La Inca said every time the girl headed out. Why would God give you that burden in this country of all places!

Telling Beli not to flaunt those curves would have been

like asking the persecuted fat kid not to use his recently discovered mutant abilities. With great power comes great responsibility . . . *bullshit*. Our girl ran into the future that her new body represented and never ever looked back.

HUNT THE LIGHT KNIGHT

Now fully, ahem, endowed, Beli returned to El Redentor from summer break to the alarm of faculty and students alike and set out to track down Jack Pujols with the great deliberation of Ahab after you-know-who. (And of all these things the albino boy was the symbol. Wonder ye then at the fiery hunt?) Another girl would have been more subtle, drawn her prey to her, but what did Beli know about process or patience? She threw everything she had at Jack. Batted her eyes so much at him that she almost sprained her eyelids. Put her tremendous chest in his line of sight every chance she got. Adopted a walk that got her yelled at by the teachers but that brought the boys and the male faculty a-running. But Pujols was unmoved, observed her with his deep dolphin eyes and did nothing. After about a week of this, Beli was going out of her mind, she had expected him to fall instantly, and so, one day, out of shameless desperation, she pretended to accidentally leave buttons on her blouse open; she was wearing this lacy bra she stole from Dorca (who had acquired quite a nice chest herself). But before Beli could bring her colossal cleavage to bear—her very own wavemotion gun—Wei, blushing deeply, ran over and buttoned her up.

You showing!

Jack drifting disinterestedly away.

She tried everything, but no dice. Before you know it Beli was back to banging into him in the hall. Cabral, he said with a smile. You have to be more careful.

I love you! she wanted to scream, I want to have all your children! I want to be your woman! But instead she said, *You* be careful.

She was morose. September ended and, alarmingly enough, she had her best month at the school. Academically. English was her number-one subject (how ironic). She learned the names of the fifty states. She could ask for coffee, a bathroom, the time, where the post office was. Her English teacher, a deviant, assured her that her accent was *superb, superb*. The other girls allowed him to touch them, but Beli, now finely attuned to masculine weirdness, and certain that she was worthy only of a prince, sidled out from under his balmy hands.

A teacher asked them to start thinking about the new decade. Where would you like to see yourself, your country, and our glorious president in the coming years? No one understood the question so he had to break it down into two simple parts.

One of her classmates, Mauricio Ledesme, got in serious trouble, so bad that his family had to spirit him out of the country. He was a quiet boy who sat next to one of the Squadron, stewing always in his love for her. Perhaps he thought he'd impress her. (Not that far-fetched, for soon comes the generation whose number-one ass-getting technique will not be to Be Like Mike, but to Be Like Che.) Perhaps he'd just had enough. He wrote in the crabbed handwriting of a future poet-revolutionary: I'd like to see our country be a democracía like the United States. I wish we would stop having dictators. Also I believe that it was Trujillo who killed Galíndez.[11]

11. Much in the news in those days, Jesús de Galíndez was a Basque supernerd and a Columbia University grad student who had written a rather unsettling doctoral dissertation. The topic? Lamentably, unfortunately, sadly: the era of Rafael Leónidas Trujillo Molina. Galíndez, a loyalist in the Spanish Civil War, had firsthand knowledge of the regime; he had taken refuge in Santo Domingo in 1939, occupied high positions therein, and by his departure in 1946 had developed a lethal allergy to the Failed Cattle Thief, could conceive for himself no higher duty than to expose the blight that was his regime. Crassweller describes Galíndez as "a bookish man, a type frequently found among political activists in Latin America . . . the winner of a prize in poetry," what we in the Higher Planes call a Nerd Class 2. But dude was a ferocious leftist, despite the dangers, gallantly toiling on his Trujillo dissertation.

What is it with Dictators and Writers, anyway? Since before the infamous Caesar–Ovid war they've had beef. Like the Fantastic Four and Galactus, like the X-Men and the Brotherhood of Evil Mutants, like the Teen Titans and Deathstroke, Foreman and Ali, Morrison and Crouch, Sammy and Sergio, they seemed destined to be eternally linked in the Halls of Battle. Rushdie claims that tyrants and scribblers are natural antagonists, but I think that's too simple; it lets writers off pretty easy. Dictators, in my opinion, just know competition when they see it. Same with writers. *Like, after all, recognizes like.*

Long story short: upon learning of the dissertation, El Jefe first tried to buy the thing and when that failed he dispatched his chief Nazgul (the sepulchral Felix Bernardino) to NYC and within days Galíndez got gagged, bagged, and dragged to La Capital, and legend has it when he came out of his chloroform nap he found himself naked, dangling from his feet over a cauldron of *boiling oil*, El Jefe standing nearby with a copy of the offending dissertation in hand. (And you thought *your* committee was

That's all it took. The next day both he and the teacher were gone. No one saying nothing.[12]

Beli's essay was far less controversial. *I will be married to a handsome wealthy man. I will also be a doctor with my own hospital that I will name after Trujillo.*

At home she continued to brag to Dorca about her boyfriend, and when Jack Pujols's photo appeared in the

rough.) Who in his right mind could ever have imagined anything so fucking ghastly? I guess El Jefe wanted to host a little tertulia with that poor doomed nerd. And what a tertulia it was, Dios mío! Anyway Galíndez's disappearance caused an uproar in the States, with all fingers pointing to Trujillo, but of course he swore his innocence, and that was what Mauricio was referring to. But take heart: For every phalanx of nerds who die there are always a few who succeed. Not long after that horrific murder, a whole pack of revolutionary nerds ran aground on a sandbar on the southeast coast of Cuba. Yes, it was Fidel and Revolutionary Crew, back for a rematch against Batista. Of the eighty-two revolutionaries who splashed ashore, only twenty-two survived to celebrate the New Year, including one book-loving argentino. A bloodbath, with Batista's forces executing even those who surrendered. But these twenty-two, it would prove, were enough.

12. Reminds me of the sad case of Rafael Yépez: Yépez was a man who in the thirties ran a small prep school in the capital, not far from where I grew up, that catered to the Trujillato's lower-level ladroncitos. One ill-starred day Yépez asked his students to write an essay on the topic of their choice—a broad-minded Betances sort of man was this Yépez—and unsurprisingly, one boy chose to compose a praise song to Trujillo and his wife, Doña María. Yépez made the mistake of suggesting in class that other Dominican women deserved as much praise as Doña María and that in the future, young men like his students would also become great leaders like Trujillo. I think Yépez confused the Santo Domingo he was living in with *another* Santo Domingo. That night the poor schoolteacher, along with his wife, his daughter, and the entire student body were rousted from their beds by military police, brought in closed trucks to the Fortress Ozama, and interrogated. The pupils were eventually released, but no one ever heard of poor Yépez or his wife or his daughter again.

school newspaper she brought it home in triumph. Dorca was so overwhelmed she spent the night in her house, inconsolable, crying and crying. Beli could hear her loud and clear.

And then, in the first days of October, as the pueblo was getting ready to celebrate another Trujillo Birthday, Beli heard a whisper that Jack Pujols had broken up with his girlfriend. (Beli had always known about this girlfriend, who attended another school, but do you think she cared?) She was sure it was just a rumor, didn't need any more hope to torture her. But it turned out to be more than rumor, and more than hope, because not two days later Jack Pujols stopped Beli in the hallway as though he were seeing her for the very first time. Cabral, he whispered, you're *beautiful*. The sharp spice of his cologne like an intoxication. I know I am, she said, her face ablaze with heat. Well, he said, burying a mitt in his perfectly straight hair.

The next thing you know he was giving her rides in his brand-new Mercedes and buying her helados with the knot of dollars he carried in his pocket. Legally, he was too young to drive, but do you think anybody in Santo Domingo stopped a colonel's son for anything? Especially the son of a colonel who was said to be one of Ramfis Trujillo's confidants? [13]

13. By Ramfis Trujillo I mean of course Rafael Leónidas Trujillo Martínez, El Jefe's first son, born while his mother was still married to another man, un cubano. It was only after the cubano refused to accept the boy as blood that Trujillo recognized Ramfis as his own. (Thanks, Dad!) He was the "famous" son that El Jefe made a colonel at the age of four and a brigadier general at the age of nine. (Lil' Fuckface, as he is affectionately known.) As an adult

AMOR!

It wasn't quite the romance she would later make it out to be. A couple of talks, a walk on the beach while the rest of the class was having a picnic, and before she knew it she was sneaking into a closet with him after school and he was slipping it to her something terrible. Let's just say that she finally understood why the other boys had given him the nickname Jack the Ripio; he had what even she knew to be an enormous penis, a Shiva-sized lingam, a destroyer of worlds. (And the whole time she'd thought they'd been calling him Jack the Ripper. Duh!) Later, after she'd been with the Gangster, she would realize how little respect Pujols had for her. But since she had nothing to compare it to at the time she assumed fucking was supposed to feel like she was being run through with a cutlass. The first time she was scared shitless and it hurt bad (4d10), but nothing could obliterate the feeling she had that finally she was on her way,

Ramfis was famed for being a polo player, a fucker of North American actresses (Kim Novak, how could you?), a squabbler with his father, and a frozen-hearted demon with a Humanity Rating of 0 who personally directed the indiscriminate torture-murders of 1959 (the year of the Cuban Invasion) and 1961 (after his father was assassinated, Ramfis personally saw to the horror-torture of the conspirators). (In a secret report filed by the U.S. consul, currently available at the JFK Presidential Library, Ramfis is described as "imbalanced," a young man who during his childhood amused himself by blowing the heads off chickens with a .44 revolver.) Ramfis fled the country after Trujillo's death, lived dissolutely off his father's swag, and ended up dying in a car crash of his own devising in 1969; the other car he hit contained the Duchess of Albuquerque, Teresa Beltrán de Lis, who died instantly; Lil' Fuckface went on murdering right to the end.

the sense of a journey starting, of a first step taken, of the beginning of something big.

Afterward she tried to embrace him, to touch his silken hair, but he shook off her caresses. Hurry up and get dressed. If we get caught my ass will be in the fire.

Which was funny because that's *exactly* how her ass felt.

For about a month they scromfed in various isolated corners of the school until the day a teacher, acting on an anonymous tip from a member of the student body, surprised the undercover couple in flagrante delicto in a broom closet. Just imagine: Beli butt naked, her vast scar like nothing anybody had seen before, and Jack with his pants puddled around his ankles.

The scandal! Remember the time and the place: Baní in the late fifties. Factor in that Jack Pujols was the number-one son of the Blessed B——í clan, one of Baní's most venerable (and filthy-rich) families. Factor in that he'd been caught not with one of his own class (though that might have also been a problem) but with the scholarship girl, una prieta to boot. (The fucking of poor prietas was considered standard operating procedure for elites just as long as it was kept on the do-lo, what is elsewhere called the Strom Thurmond Maneuver.) Pujols of course blamed Beli for everything. Sat in the office of the rector and explained in great detail how she had seduced him. It wasn't me, he insisted. It was her! The real scandal, however, was that Pujols was actually engaged to that girlfriend of his, the half-in-the-grave Rebecca Brito, herself a member of Baní's other powerful family, the R——, and you better believe Jack getting caught in a closet with una prieta kebabbed any future promise of matrimony. (Her family very particular about their Christian reputation.) Pujols's old man was so infuriated/humiliated that he started beating the boy as soon as he laid hands on him and within the week had shipped him off to a military school in Puerto Rico where he would, in the colonel's words, learn the meaning of duty. Beli never saw him again except once in the *Listín Diario* and by then they were both in their forties.

Pujols might have been a bitch-ass rat, but Beli's reaction was one for the history books. Not only was our girl *not* embarrassed by what had happened, even after being shaken down by the rector and the nun and the janitor, a holy triple-team, she absolutely refused to profess her guilt! If she had rotated her head around 360 degrees and vomited green-pea soup it would have caused only slightly less of an uproar. In typical hardheaded Beli fashion, our girl insisted that she'd done nothing wrong, that, in fact, she was well within her rights.

I'm allowed to do anything I want, Beli said stubbornly, with my husband.

Pujols, it seems, had promised Belicia that they would be married as soon as they'd both finished high school, and Beli had believed him, hook, line, and sinker. Hard to square her credulity with the hardnosed no-nonsense femme-matador I'd come to know, but one must remember: she was young and *in love*. Talk about fantasist: the girl sincerely believed that Jack would be true.

The Good Teachers of El Redentor never squeezed anything close to a mea culpa from the girl. She kept shaking her

head, as stubborn as the Laws of the Universe themselves—
No No No No No No No No No No No No No No No No
No No No No No No No No No No No No No No No No
No No No No No No No No No No No No No No No No
No No No No No No No No No No No No No No No No
No No. Not that it mattered in the end. Belicia's tenure at the
school was over, and so were La Inca's dreams of re-creating, in
Beli, her father's genius, his magis (his excellence in all things).

In any other family such a thing would have meant the
beating of Beli to within an inch of her life, beating her
straight into the hospital with no delay, and then once she was
better beating her again and putting her *back* into the hospital, but La Inca was not that kind of parent. La Inca, you see,
was a serious woman, an upstanding woman, one of the best
of her class, but she was incapable of punishing the girl phys-
ically. Call it a hitch in the universe, call it mental illness, but
La Inca just couldn't do it. Not then, not ever. All she could
do was wave her arms in the air and hurl laments. How could
this have happened? La Inca demanded. How? *How?*

He was going to marry me! Beli cried. We were going to
have children!

Are you *insane*? La Inca roared. Hija, have you lost your
mind?

Took a while for shit to calm down—the neighbors loving
the whole thing (I told you that blackie was good for nothing!)—but eventually things did, and only then did La Inca
convoke a special session on our girl's future. First La Inca
gave Beli tongue-lashing number five hundred million and
five, excoriating her poor judgment, her poor morals, her

poor everything, and only when those preliminaries were good and settled did La Inca lay down the law: You are returning to school. Not to El Redentor but somewhere nearly as good. Padre Billini.

And Beli, her eyes still swollen from Jack-loss, laughed. I'm not going back to school. Not ever.

Had she forgotten the suffering that she had endured in her Lost Years in the pursuit of education? The costs? The terrible scars on her back? (*The Burning*.) Perhaps she had, perhaps the prerogatives of this New Age had rendered the vows of the Old irrelevant. However, during those tumultuous post-expulsion weeks, while she'd been writhing in her bed over the loss of her "husband," our girl had been rocked by instances of stupendous turbidity. A first lesson in the fragility of love and the preternatural cowardice of men. And out of this disillusionment and turmoil sprang Beli's first adult oath, one that would follow her into adulthood, to the States and beyond. I will not serve. Never again would she follow any lead other than her own. Not the rector's, not the nuns', not La Inca's, not her poor dead parents'. Only me, she whispered. Me.

This oath did much to rally her. Not long after the back-to-school showdown, Beli put on one of La Inca's dresses (was literally bursting in it) and caught a ride down to the parque central. This was not a huge trip. But, still, for a girl like Beli it was a precursor of things to come.

When she returned to the house in the late afternoon she announced: I have a job! La Inca snorted. I guess the cabarets are always hiring.

It was not a cabaret. Beli might have been a puta major in the cosmology of her neighbors but a cuero she was not. No: she had landed a job as a waitress at a restaurant on the parque. The owner, a stout well-dressed Chinese by the name of Juan Then, had not exactly needed anyone; in fact he didn't know if he needed himself. Business terrible, he lamented. Too much politics. Politics bad for everything but politicians.

No excess money. And already many impossible employees.

But Beli was not willing to be rejected. There's a lot I can do. And pinched her shoulder blades, to emphasize her "assets."

Which for a man any less righteous would have been an open invitation but Juan simply sighed: No obligated be without shame. We try you up. Probationary period. Can't promises build. Political conditions give promises no hospitality.

What's my salary?

Salary! No salary! You a waitress, you tips.

How much are they?

Once again the glumness. It is without certainty.

I don't understand.

His brother José's bloodshot eyes glanced up from the sports section. What my brother is saying is that it all depends.

And here's La Inca shaking her head: A waitress. But, hija, you're a baker's daughter, you don't know the first thing about waitressing!

La Inca assumed that because Beli had of late not shown any enthusiasm for the bakery or school or for cleaning she'd devolved into a zángana. But she'd forgotten that our girl had been a criada in her first life; for half her years she'd know nothing *but* work. La Inca predicted that Beli would call it quits within a couple of months, but Beli never did. On the job our girl, in fact, showed her quality: she was never late, never malingered, worked her sizable ass off. Heck, she *liked* the job. It was not exactly President of the Republic, but for a fourteen-year-old who wanted out of the house, it paid, and kept her in the world while she waited for—for her Glorious Future to materialize.

Eighteen months she worked at the Palacio Peking. (Originally called El Tesoro de ———, in honor of the Admiral's true but never-reached destination, but the Brothers Then had changed it when they learned that the Admiral's name was a fukú! Chinese no like curses, Juan had said.) She would always say she came of age in the restaurant, and in some ways she did. She learned to beat men at dominoes and proved herself so responsible that the Brothers Then could leave her in charge of the cook and the other waitstaff while they slipped out to fish and visit their thick-legged girlfriends. In later years Beli would lament that she had ever lost touch with her "chinos." They were so good to me, she moaned to Oscar and Lola. Nothing like your worthless esponja of a father. Juan, the melancholic gambler, who waxed about Shanghai as though it were a love poem sung by a beautiful woman you love but cannot have. Juan, the shortsighted romantic whose girlfriends robbed him blind and who never mastered Spanish (though in later years when he was living in Skokie, Illinois, he would yell at his Americanized grandchildren in his guttural Spanish, and they laughed at him, thinking it Chinese). Juan, who taught Beli how to play dominoes, and whose only fundamentalism was his bullet-proof optimism: If only Admiral come to our restaurant first, imagine the trouble that could be avoided! Sweating, gentle Juan, who would have lost the restaurant if not for his older brother. José, the enigmatic, who hovered at the periphery with all the menace of a ciclón; José, the bravo, the guapo, his wife and children dead by warlord in the thirties; José, who protected the restaurant and the rooms above with an implacable ferocity. José, whose grief had extracted from his body all softness, idle chatter, and hope. He never seemed to approve of Beli, or any of the other employees, but since she alone wasn't scared of him (I'm almost as tall as you are!), he reciprocated by giving her practical instructions: You want to be a useless woman all your life? Like how to hammer nails, fix electrical outlets, cook chow fun and drive a car, all would come in good use when she became the Empress of Diaspora. (José would acquit himself bravely in the revolution, fighting, I must regretfully report, against the pueblo, and would die in 1976 in Atlanta, cancer of the pancreas, crying out his wife's name, which the nurses confused for more Chinese gobbledy-gook—extra emphasis, in their minds, on the *gook*.)

And then there was Lillian, the other waitress, a squat rice tub, whose rancor against the world turned to glee only when humanity exceeded in its venality, brutality, and mendacity even her own expectations. She didn't take to Beli at first, thought her competition, but eventually would treat Beli more or less with courtesy. She was the first woman our girl met who read the paper. (Her son's bibliomania would remind her al-

ways of Lillian. How's the world keeping? Beli asked her. Jodido, was always her answer.) And Indian Benny, a quiet,
meticulous waiter who had the sad airs of a man long accus-
tomed to the spectacular demolition of dreams. Rumor at the
restaurant had it that Indian Benny was married to a huge,
lusty azuana who regularly put him on the street so that she
could bunk some new sweetmeat. The only time Indian Benny
was known to smile was when he beat José at dominoes—the
two were consummate tile slingers and of course bitter rivals.
He too would fight in the revolution, for the home team, and
it was said that throughout that Summer of Our National Lib-
eration Indian Benny never stopped smiling; even after a Marine sniper cavitated his brains over his entire command he
didn't stop. And what about the cook, Marco Antonio, a one-
legged, no-ear grotesque straight out of Gormenghast? (His
explanation for his appearance: I had an accident.) His bag was
an almost fanatical distrust of cibaeños, whose regional pride,
he was convinced, masked imperial ambitions on a Haitian
level. They want to seize the Republic. I'm telling you, cristiano, they want to start their own country!

The whole day she dealt with hombres of all stripes and it
was here Beli perfected her roughspun salt-of-the-earth
bonhomie. As you might imagine, everybody was in love
with her. (Including her coworkers. But José had warned
them off: Touch her and I'll pull your guts out your culo. You
must be joking, Marco Antonio said in his own defense. I
couldn't climb that mountain even with two legs.) The customers' attention was exhilarating and she in turn gave the
boys something that most men can never get enough of—

ribbing, solicitous mothering from an attractive woman. Still plenty of niggers in Baní, old customers, who remember her with great fondness.

La Inca of course was anguished by Beli's Fall, from princesa to mesera—what is happening to the world? At home the two rarely spoke anymore; La Inca tried to talk, but Beli wouldn't listen, and for her part La Inca filled that silence with prayer, trying to summon a miracle that would transform Beli back into a dutiful daughter. As fate would have it, once Beli had slipped her grasp not even God had enough caracaracol to bring her back. Every now and then La Inca would appear at the restaurant. She'd sit alone, erect as a lectern, all in black, and between sips of tea would watch the girl with a mournful intensity. Perhaps she hoped to shame Beli into returning to Operation Restore House of Cabral, but Beli went about her work with her customary zeal. It must have dismayed La Inca to see how drastically her "daughter" was changing, for Beli, the girl who never used to speak in public, who could be still as Noh, displayed at Palacio Peking a raconteur's gift for palaver that delighted a great many of the all-male clientele. Those of you who have stood at the corner of 142nd and Broadway can guess what it was she spoke: the blunt, irreverent cant of the pueblo that gives all dominicanos cultos nightmares on their 400-thread-count sheets and that La Inca had assumed had perished along with Beli's first life in Outer Azua, but here it was so alive, it was like it had never left: Oye, parigüayo, y qué pasó con esa esposa tuya? Gordo, no me digas que tú todavía tienes hambre?

Eventually there came a moment when she'd pause at La Inca's table: Do you want anything else?

Only that you would return to school, mi'ja.

Sorry. Beli picked up her taza and wiped the table in one perfunctory motion. We stopped serving pendejada last week.

And then La Inca paid her quarter and was gone and a great weight lifted off Beli, proof that she'd done the right thing.

In those eighteen months she learned a great deal about herself. She learned that despite all her dreams to be the most beautiful woman in the world, to have the brothers jumping out of windows in her wake, when Belicia Cabral fell in love she stayed in love. Despite the trove of men, handsome, plain, and ugly, who marched into the restaurant intent on winning her hand in marriage (or at least in fuckage), she never had a thought for anyone but Jack Pujols. Turns out that in her heart our girl was more Penelope than Whore of Babylon. (Of course La Inca, who witnessed the parade of men muddying her doorstep, would not have agreed.) Beli often had dreams where Jack returned from military school, dreams where he'd be waiting for her at the job, spilled out at one of the tables like a beautiful bag of swag, a grin on his magnificent face, his Eyes of Atlantis on her at last, only on her. *I came back for you, mi amor. I came back.*

Our girl learned that even to a chooch like Jack Pujols she was true.

But that didn't mean she recluse herself entirely from the world of men. (For all her "fidelity" she would never be a sister who liked being without male attention.) Even in this rough period, Beli had her princes-in-waiting, brothers willing to brave the barbed-wired minefields of her affections in the hopes that beyond that cruel midden Elysium might await. The poor deluded chumps. The Gangster would have her every which way, but these poor sapos who came before the Gangster, they were lucky to get an abrazo. Let us summon back from the abyss two sapos in particular: the Fiat dealer, bald, white, and smiling, a regular Hipólito Mejía, but suave and cavalier and so enamored of North American baseball that he risked life and limb to listen to games on a contraband shortwave radio. He believed in baseball with the fervor of an adolescent and believed also that in the future Dominicans would storm the Major Leagues and compete with the Mantles and the Marises of the world. Marichal is only the beginning, he predicted, of a reconquista. You're crazy, Beli said, mocking him and his "jueguito." In an inspired stroke of counterprogramming, her other paramour was a student at the UASD—one of those City College types who's been in school eleven years and is always five credits shy of a degree. Student today don't mean na', but in a Latin America whipped into a frenzy by the Fall of Arbenz, by the Stoning of Nixon, by the Guerrillas of the Sierra Maestra, by the endless cynical maneuverings of the Yankee Pig Dogs—in a Latin America already a year and a half into the Decade of the Guerrilla—a student was something else altogether, an agent for change, a vibrating quantum string in the staid Newtonian universe. Such a student was Arquimedes. He also listened to the shortwave, but not for Dodgers scores; what he risked his life for was the news leaking out of Havana, news of the future. Arquimedes was, therefore, *student*, the son of a zapatero and a midwife, a tirapiedra and a quemagoma for life. Being a student wasn't a joke, not with Trujillo and Johnny Abbes[14] scooping up everybody following the foiled Cuban Invasion of 1959. Wasn't a day that passed that his life wasn't in danger, and he had no fixed address, appeared in Beli's day with no warning. Archie (as he was known) had an immacu-

---

14. Johnny Abbes García was one of Trujillo's beloved Morgul Lords. Chief of the dreaded and all-powerful secret police (SIM), Abbes was considered the greatest torturer of the Dominican People ever to have lived. An enthusiast of Chinese torture techniques, Abbes was rumored to have in his employ a dwarf who would crush prisoners' testicles between his teeth. Plotted endlessly against Trujillo's enemies, the killer of many young revolutionaries and students (including the Mirabal Sisters). At Trujillo's behest Abbes organized the plot to assassinate the democratically elected president of Venezuela: Rómulo Betancourt! (Betancourt and T-zillo were old enemies, beefing since the forties, when Trujillo's SIMians tried to inject Betancourt with poison on the streets of Havana.) The second attempt worked no better than the first. The bomb, packed into a green Olds, blew the presidential Cadillac clean out of Caracas, slew the driver and a bystander but failed to kill Betancourt! Now that's *really* gangster! (Venezolanos: Don't ever say we don't have history together. It's not just the novelas that we share or the fact that so many of us flooded your shores to work in the fifties, sixties, seventies, and eighties. Our dictator tried to slay your president!) After Trujillo's death Abbes was named consul to Japan (just to get him out of the country) and ended up working for that other Caribbean nightmare, the Haitian dictator François "Papa Doc" Duvalier. Wasn't nearly as loyal to Papa Doc as he was to Trujillo—after an attempted double-cross Papa Doc shot Abbes and his family and then blew their fucking house up. (I think P. Daddy knew exactly what kind of creature he was dealing with.) No Dominican believes that Abbes died in that blast. He is said to still be out there in the world, waiting for the next coming of El Jefe, when he too will rise from the Shadow.

late head of hair and Héctor Lavoe glasses and the intensity of a South Beach dietician. Reviled the North Americans for their Silent Invasion of the DR and Dominicans for their annexationatist subservience to the North. Guacanagarí has cursed us all! That his most beloved ideologues were a couple of Germans who never met a nigger they liked was beside the point.

Both of these dudes Beli played hard. Visited them at their digs and at the dealership and dished them their daily recommended allowance of noplay. A date couldn't pass without the Fiat dealer *begging* her for a single grope. Just let me touch them with the back of my hand, he mewled, but nearly every time she picked him off in a fielder's choice. Arquimedes, when rebuffed, at least showed some class. He didn't pout or mutter, What the hell am I wasting my money for? He preferred to stay philosophical. The Revolution is not made in a day, he'd say ruefully and then kick back and entertain her with stories about dodging the secret police.

Even to a chooch like Jack Pujols she was true, yes, but eventually she did get over him. A romantic she was, but not a pendeja. When she finally came to, however, things had turned dicey, to say the least. The country was in an uproar; after the failed invasion of 1959 an underground conspiracy of youth had been uncovered and everywhere young people were being arrested and tortured and killed. Politics, Juan spat, staring at all the empty tables, *politics*. José didn't offer comment; he simply cleaned his Smith & Wesson in the privacy of his upstairs room. I don't know if I'll make it out of this one, Arquimedes said in a barefaced attempt to cadge a pity fuck. You'll be fine, Beli snorted, pushing off his embrace. She was right in the end, but he was one of the few who made it through with his balls unfried. (Archie survives into the present, and when I drive through the capital with my man Pedro, I occasionally spot his grill on campaign posters for one of the radical splinter parties whose sole platform is to bring electricity back to the Dominican Republic. Pedro snorts: Ese ladrón no va' pa' ningún la'o.)

In February, Lillian had to quit the job and return to her campo to care for her ailing mother, a señora who, Lillian claimed, had never given a damn for her well-being. But it is the fate of women everywhere to be miserable always, Lillian declared, and then she was gone and only the cheap freebie calendar she liked marking off remained. A week later the Brothers Then hired a replacement. A new girl. Constantina. In her twenties, sunny and amiable, whose cuerpo was all pipa and no culo, a "mujer alegre" (in the parlance of the period). More than once Constantina arrived to lunch straight from a night of partying, smelling of whiskey and stale cigarettes. Muchacha, you wouldn't believe el lío en que me metí anoche. She was disarmingly chill and could curse the black off a crow, and, perhaps recognizing a kindred spirit alone in the world, took an immediate liking to our girl. My hermanita, she called Beli. The most beautiful girl. You're proof that God is Dominican.

Constantina was the person who finally pried the Sad Ballad of Jack Pujols out of her.

Her advice? Forget that hijo de la porra, that comehuevo. Every desgraciado who walks in here is in love with you. You could have the whole maldito world if you wanted.

The world! It was what she desired with her entire heart, but how could she achieve it? She watched the flow of traffic past the parque and did not know.

One day in a burbuja of girlish impulse they finished work early and, taking their earnings to the Spaniards down the street, bought a pair of matching dresses.

Now you look candela, Constantina said approvingly.

So what you going to do now? Beli asked.

A crooked-tooth smile. Me, I'm going to the Hollywood for a dance. I have un buen amigo working in the door and from what I hear there'll be a whole assembly line of rich men with nothing to do but adore me, ay sí. She shivered her hands down the slopes of her hips. Then she stopped the show. Why, does the private-school princess actually want to come along?

Beli thought about it a moment. Thought about La Inca waiting for her at home. Thought about the heartbreak that was beginning to fade in her.

Yes. I want to go.

There it was, the Decision That Changed Everything. Or as she broke it down to Lola in her Last Days: All I wanted was to dance. What I got instead was *esto*, she said, opening her arms to encompass the hospital, her children, her cancer, America.

EL HOLLYWOOD

El Hollywood was Beli's first real club.[15] Imaginate: in those days El Hollywood was the It place to be in Baní, it was Alexander, Café Atlántico, and Jet Set rolled into one. The lights, the opulent décor, the guapos in the fine threads, the women striking their best bird-of-paradise poses, the band upon the stage like a visitation from a world of rhythm, the dancers so caught up in the planting of heel you would have thought they were bidding farewell to death itself—it was all here. Beli might have been out of her league, couldn't order drinks or sit in the high chairs without losing her cheap shoes, but once the music started, well, it didn't matter. A corpulent accountant put his hand out and for the next two hours Beli forgot her awkwardness, her wonderment, her trepidation, and *danced*. Dios mío did she dance! Dancing café out of the sky and exhausting partner after partner. Even the band-leader, a salt-and-pepper veterano from a dozen campaigns throughout Latin America and Miami, shouted her out: La negra está encendida! La negra está encendida indeed! Here at last is her smile: burn it into your memory; you won't see it often. Everybody mistook her for a bailarina cubana from one of the shows and couldn't believe that she was dominicana like them. It can't be, no lo pareces, etc., etc.

And it was in this whirligig of pasos, guapos, and after-

15. A favorite hangout of Trujillo's, my mother tells me when the manuscript is almost complete.

shave that he appeared. She was at the bar, waiting for Tina to return from "a cigarette break." Her dress: wrecked; her perm: kicking; her arches: like they'd been given a starter course in foot binding. He, on the other hand, was the essence of relaxed cool. Here he is, future generation of de Leóns and Cabrals: the man who stole your Founding Mother's heart, who catapulted her and hers into Diaspora. Dressed in a Rat Pack ensemble of black smoking jacket and white pants and not a dot of sweat on him, like he'd been keeping himself in refrigeration. Handsome in that louche potbellied mid-forties Hollywood producer sort of way, with pouched gray eyes that had seen (and didn't miss) much. Eyes that had been scoping Beli for the better part of an hour, and it wasn't like Beli hadn't noticed. The nigger was some kind of baller, everybody in the club was paying tribute to him, and he rocked enough gold to have ransomed Atahualpa.

Let's just say their first contact was not promising. How about I buy you a drink? he said, and when she turned away como una ruda, he grabbed her arm, hard, and said, Where are you going, morena? And that was all it took: a Beli le salío el lobo. First, she didn't like to be touched. Not at all, not ever. Second, she was not a morena (even the car dealer knew better, called her india). And, third, there was that temper of hers. When baller twisted her arm, she went from zero to violence in under .2 seconds. Shrieked: *No. Me. Toques.* Threw her drink, her glass, and then her purse at him—if there had been a baby nearby she would have thrown that too. Then let him have it with a stack of cocktail napkins and almost a hundred plastic olive rapiers, and when those were done dancing on the tile she unleashed one of the great Street Fighter chain attacks of all time. During this unprecedented fusillade of blows the Gangster hunkered down and didn't move except to deflect the stray chop away from his face. When she finished he lifted his head as though out of a fox-hole and put a finger to his lips. You missed a spot, he said solemnly.

Well.

It was nothing but a simple encounter. The fight she had with La Inca upon her return was far more significant—La Inca waiting up for her with a belt in her hand—and when Beli stepped into the house, worn out from dancing, La Inca, lit by the kerosene lamp, lifted the belt in the air and Beli's diamond eyes locked on to her. The primal scene between daughter and mother played out in every country of the world. Go ahead, Madre, Beli said, but La Inca could not do it, her strength leaving her. Hija, if you ever come home late again you'll have to leave this house, and Beli saying, Don't worry, I'll be leaving soon enough. That night La Inca re-fused to get into bed with her, sleeping in her rocking chair, not speaking to her the next day either, going off to work by herself, her disappointment looming above her like a mush-room cloud. No question: it was her madre she should have been worried about, but for the rest of that week Beli found herself instead brooding on the stupidity of that gordo azaroso who (in her words) had ruined her whole night. Al-most every day she found herself recounting the details of the confrontation to both the car dealer and Arquimedes, but with each telling she added further outrages which were not exactly true but seemed accurate in spirit. Un bruto, she called him. Un animal. How dare he try to touch me! As though he were someone, ese poco hombre, ese mamahuevo!

So he hit you? The car dealer was trying to pin her hand down to his leg but failing. Maybe that's what I need to do.

And you'd get exactly what he got, she said.

Arquimedes, who had taken to standing in a closet while she visited him (just in case the secret police burst in), pronounced the Gangster a typical bourgeois type, his voice reaching her through all that fabric that the car dealer had bought her (and which Beli stored at his place). (Is this a *mink* fur? he asked her. Rabbit, she said morosely.)

I should have stabbed him, she said to Constantina.

Muchacha, I think he should have stabbed *you*.

What the hell do you mean?

I'm just saying, you talk about him a whole lot.

No, she said hotly. It's not like that at all.

Then stop talking about him. Tina glanced down at a pretend watch. Five seconds. It must be a record.

She tried to keep him out of her mouth but it was hopeless. Her forearm ached at the oddest of moments and she could feel his hangdog eyes on her everywhere.

The next Friday was a big day at the restaurant; the local chapter of the Dominican Party was having an event and the staff busted their ass from early to late. Beli, who loved the bustle, showed some of her magis for hard work, and even José had to come out of the office to help cook. José awarded the head of the chapter with a bottle of what he claimed was "Chinese rum" but which in fact was Johnnie Walker with the label scraped off. The higher echelons enjoyed their chow fun immensely but their campo underlings poked at the noodles miserably and asked over and over if there was any arroz con habichuelas, of which of course there was none. All in all the event was a success, you never would have guessed there was a dirty war going on, but when the last of the drunks was shuffled onto his feet and ushered into a cab, Beli, feeling not the least bit tired, asked Tina: Can we go back?

Where?

To El Hollywood.

But we have to change—

Don't worry, I brought everything.

And before you know it she was standing over his table.

One of his dinner companions said: Hey, Dionisio, isn't that the girl que te dío una pela last week?

The baller nodded glumly.

His buddy looked her up and down. I hope for your sake she's not back for a rematch. I don't think you'll survive.

What are you waiting for, the baller asked. The bell?

Dance with me. Now it was her turn to grab him and drag him onto the pista.

He might have been a dense slab of tuxedo and thew, but he moved like an enchantment. You came looking for me, didn't you?

Yes, she said, and only then did she know.

I'm glad you didn't lie. I don't like liars. He put his finger under her chin. What's your name?

She tore her head away. My name is Hypatía Belicia Cabral.

No, he said with the gravity of an old-school pimp. Your name is Beautiful.

THE GANGSTER WE'RE
ALL LOOKING FOR

How much Beli knew about the Gangster we will never know. She claims that he only told her he was a businessman. Of course I believed him. How was I supposed to know different?

Well, he certainly was a businessman, but he was also a flunky for the Trujillato, and not a minor one. Don't misunderstand: our boy wasn't no ringwraith, but he wasn't no orc either.

Due partially to Beli's silence on the matter and other folks' lingering unease when it comes to talking about the regime, info on the Gangster is fragmented; I'll give you what I've managed to unearth and the rest will have to wait for the day the páginas en blanco finally speak.

The Gangster was born in Samaná at the dawn of the twenties, the fourth son of a milkman, a bawling, worm-infested brat no one thought would amount to na', an opinion his parents endorsed by turning him out of the house when he was seven. But folks always underestimate what the promise of a lifetime of starvation, powerlessness, and humiliation can provoke in a young person's character. By the time the Gangster was twelve this scrawny, unremarkable boy had shown a resourcefulness and fearlessness beyond his years. His claims that the Failed Cattle Thief had "inspired" him brought him to the attention of the Secret Police, and before you could say SIM-salabím our boy was infiltrating unions and fingering sindicatos left and right. At age fourteen he killed his first "comunista," a favor for the appalling Felix Bernardino,[16] and apparently the hit was so spectacular, so fucking *chunky*, that half the left in Baní immediately abandoned the DR for the relative safety of Nueva York. With the money he earned he bought himself a new suit and four pairs of shoes.

From that point on, the sky was the limit for our young villain. Over the next decade he traveled back and forth to Cuba, dabbled in forgery, theft, extortion, and money laundering—all for the Everlasting Glory of the Trujillato. It was even rumored, never substantiated, that our Gangster was the hammerman who slew Mauricio Báez in Havana in 1950.

16. Felix Wenceslao Bernardino, raised in La Romana, one of Trujillo's most sinister agents, his Witchking of Angmar. Was consul in Cuba when the exiled Dominican labor organizer Mauricio Báez was mysteriously murdered on the streets of Havana. Felix was also rumored to have had a hand in the failed assassination of Dominican exile leader Angel Morales (the assassins burst in on his secretary shaving, mistook the lathered man for Morales, and shot him to pieces). In addition, Felix and his sister, Minerva Bernardino (first woman in the world to be an ambassador before the United Nations), were both in New York City when Jesus de Galíndez mysteriously disappeared on his way home at the Columbus Circle subway station. Talk about *Have Gun, Will Travel*. It was said the power of Trujillo never left him; the fucker died of old age in Santo Domingo, Trujillista to the end, drowning his Haitian workers instead of paying them.

Who can know? It seems a possibility; by then he'd acquired deep contacts in the Havana underworld and clearly had no compunction about slaying motherfuckers. Hard evidence, though, is scarce. That he was a favorite of Johnny Abbes and of Porfirio Rubirosa there can be no denying. He had a special passport from the Palacio, and the rank of major in some branch of the Secret Police.

Skilled our Gangster became in many a perfidy, but where our man truly excelled, where he smashed records and grabbed gold, was in the flesh trade. Then, like now, Santo Domingo was to popóla what Switzerland was to chocolate. And there was something about the binding, selling, and degradation of women that brought out the best in the Gangster; he had an instinct for it, a talent—call him the Caracaracol of Culo. By the time he was twenty-two he was operating his own string of brothels in and around the capital, owned houses and cars in three countries. Never stinted the Jefe on anything, be it money, praise, or a prime cut of culo from Colombia, and so loyal was he to the regime that he once slew a man at a bar simply for pronouncing El Jefe's mother's name wrong. Now here's a man, El Jefe was rumored to have said, who is *capaz*.

The Gangster's devotion did not go unrewarded. By the mid-forties the Gangster was no longer simply a well-paid operator; he was becoming an alguien—in photos he appears in the company of the regime's three witchkings: Johnny Abbes, Joaquín Balaguer, and Felix Bernardino—and while none exists of him and El Jefe, that they broke bread and talked shit cannot be doubted. For it was the Great Eye himself who granted the Gangster authority over a number of the Trujillo family's concessions in Venezuela and Cuba, and under his draconian administration the so-called bang-for-the-buck ratio of Dominican sexworkers trebled. In the forties the Gangster was in his prime; he traveled the entire length of the Americas, from Rosario to Nueva York, in pimpdaddy style, staying at the best hotels, banging the hottest broads (never lost his sureño taste for the morenas, though), dining in four-star restaurants, confabbing with arch-criminals the world over.

An inexhaustible opportunist, he spun deals everywhere he went. Suitcases of dollars accompanied him back and forth from the capital. Life was not always pleasant. Plenty of acts of violence, plenty of beatdowns and knifings. He himself survived any number of gank-attempts, and after each shoot-out, after each drive-by, he always combed his hair and straightened his tie, a dandy's reflex. He was a true gangster, gully to the bone, lived the life all those phony rap acts can only rhyme about.

It was also in this period that his long dalliance with Cuba was formalized. The Gangster might have harbored love for Venezuela and its many long-legged mulatas, and burned for the tall, icy beauties of Argentina, and swooned over México's incomparable brunettes, but it was Cuba that clove his heart, that felt to him like home. If he spent six months out of twelve in Havana I'd call that a conservative estimate, and in honor of his predilections the Secret Police's code name for him was MAX GÓMEZ. So often did he travel to Havana that it was more a case of inevitability than bad luck that on New Year's Eve 1958, the night that Fulgencio Batista sacó piés out of Havana and the whole of Latin America changed, the Gangster was actually partying with Johnny Abbes in Havana, sucking whiskey out of the navels of underage whores, when the guerrillas reached Santa Clara. It was only the timely arrival of one of the Gangster's informants that saved them all. You better leave now or you'll all be hanging from your huevos! In one of the greatest blunders in the history of Dominican intelligence, Johnny Abbes almost didn't make it out of Havana that New Year's Eve; the Dominicans were literally on the last plane smoking, the Gangster's face pressed against the glass, never to return.

When Beli encountered the Gangster, that ignominious midnight flight still haunted him. Beyond the financial attachment, Cuba was an important component to his prestige—to his manhood, really—and our man could still not accept the fact that the country had fallen to a rabble of scurvied students. Some days he was better than others, but whenever the latest news reached him of the revolution's activities he would pull his hair and attack the nearest wall in sight. Not a day passed when he did not fulminate against Batista (That ox! That peasant!) or Castro (The goat-fucking comunista!) or CIA chief Allen Dulles (That effeminate!), who had failed to stop Batista's ill-advised Mother's Day Amnesty that freed Fidel and the other moncadistas to fight another day. If Dulles was right here in front of me I'd shoot him dead, he swore to Beli, and then I'd shoot his mother dead.

Life, it seemed, had struck the Gangster a dolorous blow, and he was uncertain as to how to respond. The future appeared cloudy and there was no doubt he sensed his own mortality and that of Trujillo in the fall of Cuba. Which might explain why, when he met Beli, he jumped on her stat. I mean, what straight middle-aged brother has not attempted to regenerate himself through the alchemy of young pussy. And if what she often said to her daughter was true, Beli had some of the finest pussy around. The sexy isthmus of her waist alone could have launched a thousand yolas, and while the upper-class boys might have had their issues with her, the Gangster was a man of the world, had fucked more prietas than you could count. He didn't care about that shit. What he wanted was to suck Beli's enormous breasts, to fuck her pussy until it was a mango-juice swamp, to spoil her senseless so that Cuba and his failure there disappeared. As the viejos say, clavo saca clavo, and only a girl like Beli could erase the debacle of Cuba from a brother's mind.

At first Beli had her reservations about the Gangster. Her ideal amor had been Jack Pujols, and here was this middle-aged Caliban who dyed his hair and had a thatch of curlies on his back and shoulders. More like a third-base umpire than an Avatar of her Glorious Future. But one should never underestimate what assiduity can accomplish—when assisted by heaping portions of lana and privilege. The Gangster romanced the girl like only middle-aged niggers know how: chipped at her reservation with cool aplomb and unselfconscious cursí-ness. Rained on her head enough flowers to garland Azua, bonfires of roses at the job and her house. (It's romantic, Tina sighed. It's vulgar, La Inca complained.) He escorted her to the most exclusive restaurants of the capital, took her to the clubs that had never tolerated a nonmusician prieto inside their door before (dude was that powerful—to break the injunction against *black*), places like the Hamaca, the Tropicalia (though not, alas, the Country Club, even he didn't have the juice). He flattered her with top-notch muelas (from what I heard he paid a couple of grad-school Cyranos to churn 'em out). Treated her to plays, movies, dances, bought her wardrobes of clothes and pirate chests of jewelry, introduced her to famous celebrities, and once even to Ramfis Trujillo himself—in other words, he exposed her to the fucking world (at least the one circumscribed by the DR), and you'd be surprised how even a hardheaded girl like Beli, committed as she was to an idealized notion of what love was, could find it in her heart to revise her views, if only for the Gangster.

He was a complicated (some would say comical), affable (some would say laughable) man who treated Beli very tenderly and with great consideration, and under him (literally and metaphorically) the education begun at the restaurant was completed. He was un hombre bien social, enjoyed being out and about, seeing and being seen, and that dovetailed nicely with Beli's own dreams. But also un hombre conflicted about his past deeds. On the one hand, he was proud of what he'd accomplished. I made myself, he told Beli, all by myself. I have cars, houses, electricity, clothes, prendas, but when I was a niño I didn't even own a pair of shoes. Not one pair. I had no family. I was an orphan. Do you understand?

She, an orphan herself, understood profoundly.

On the other hand, he was tormented by his crimes. When

he drank too much, and that was often, he would mutter things like, If you only knew the diabluras I've committed, you wouldn't be here right now. And on some nights she would wake up to him crying. I didn't mean to do it! I didn't mean it!

And it was on one of those nights, while she cradled his head and brushed away his tears, that she realized with a start that she loved this Gangster.

Beli in love! Round Two! But unlike what happened with Pujols, this was the real deal: pure uncut unadulterated love, the Holy Grail that would so bedevil her children throughout their lives. Consider that Beli had longed, hungered, for a chance to be *in* love and to be loved back (not very long in real time but a forever by the chronometer of her adolescence). Never had the opportunity in her first lost childhood; and in the intervening years her desire for it had doubled over and doubled over like a katana being forged until finally it was sharper than the truth. With the Gangster our girl finally got her chance. Who is surprised that in the final four months of her relationship with him there would be such an outpouring of affect? As expected: she, the daughter of the Fall, recipient of its heaviest radiations, loved atomically.

As for the Gangster, he normally would have tired right quick of such an intensely adoring plaything, but our Gangster, grounded by the hurricane winds of history, found himself reciprocating. Writing checks with his mouth that his ass could never hope to cover. He promised her that once the troubles with the Communists were over he would take her to Miami and to Havana. I'll buy you a house in both places just so you can know how much I love you!

A house? she whispered. Her hair standing on end. You're lying to me!

I do not lie. How many rooms do you want?

Ten? she said uncertainly.

Ten is nothing. Make it twenty!

The thoughts he put in her head. Someone should have arrested him for it. And believe me, La Inca considered it. He's a panderer, she declaimed. A thief of innocence! There's a pretty solid argument to be made that La Inca was right; the Gangster was simply an old chulo preying on Beli's naïveté. But if you looked at it from, say, a more generous angle you *could* argue that the Gangster adored our girl and that adoration was one of the greatest gifts anybody had ever given her. It felt unbelievably good to Beli, shook her to her core. (*For the first time I actually felt like I owned my skin, like it was me and I was it.*) He made her feel guapa and wanted and safe, and no one had ever done that for her. No one. On their nights together he would pass his hand over her naked body, Narcissus stroking that pool of his, murmuring, Guapa, guapa, over and over again. (He didn't care about the burn scars on her back: It looks like a painting of a ciclón and that's what you are, mi negrita, una tormenta en la madrugada.) The randy old goat could make love to her from sunup to sundown, and it was he who taught her all about her body, her orgasms, her rhythms, who said, You have to be bold, and for that he must be honored, no matter what happened in the end.

This was the affair that once and for all incinerated Beli's reputation in Santo Domingo. No one in Baní knew exactly who the Gangster was and what he did (he kept his shit hush-

hush), but it was enough that he was a man. In the minds of Beli's neighbors, that prieta comparona had finally found her true station in life, as a cuero. Old-timers have told me that during her last months in the DR Beli spent more time inside the love motels than she had in school—an exaggeration, I'm sure, but a sign of how low our girl had fallen in the pueblo's estimation. Beli didn't help matters. Talk about a poor winner: now that she'd vaulted into a higher order of privilege, she strutted around the neighborhood, exulting and heaping steaming piles of contempt on everybody and everything that wasn't the Gangster. Dismissing her barrio as an "infierno" and her neighbors as "brutos" and "cochinos," she bragged about how she would be living in Miami soon, wouldn't have to put up with this un-country much longer. Our girl no longer maintained even a modicum of respectability at home. Stayed out until all hours of the night and permed her hair whenever she wanted. La Inca didn't know what to do with her anymore; all her neighbors advised her to beat the girl into a blood clot (You might even have to kill her, they said regretfully), but La Inca couldn't explain what it had meant to find the burnt girl locked in a chicken coop all those years ago, how that sight had stepped into her and rearranged everything so that now she found she didn't have the strength to raise her hand against the girl. She never stopped trying to talk sense into her, though.

What happened to college?

I don't want to go to college.

So what are you going to do? Be a Gangster's girlfriend your whole life? Your parents, God rest their souls, wanted so much better for you.

I told you not to talk to me about those people. You're the only parents I have.

And look how well you've treated me. Look how well. Maybe people are right, La Inca despaired. Maybe you are cursed.

Beli laughed. You might be cursed, but not me.

Even the chinos had to respond to Beli's change in attitude. We have you go, Juan said.

I don't understand.

He licked his lips and tried again. We have to you go.

You're fired, José said. Please leave your apron on the counter.

The Gangster heard about it and the next day some of his goons paid the Brothers Then a visit and what do you know if our girl wasn't immediately reinstated. It wasn't the same no more, though. The brothers wouldn't talk to her, wouldn't spin no stories about their youth in China and the Philippines. After a couple of days of the silent treatment Beli took the hint and stopped showing up altogether.

And now you don't have a job, La Inca pointed out helpfully.

I don't need a job. He's going to buy me a house.

A man whose own house you yourself have never visited is promising to buy you a house? And you believe him? Oh, hija.

Yessir: our girl believed.

After all, she was in love! The world was coming apart at the seams—Santo Domingo was in the middle of a total meltdown, the Trujillato was tottering, police blockades on every corner—

and even the kids she'd gone to school with, the brightest and the best, were being swept up by the Terror. A girl from El Redentor told her that Jack Pujols's little brother had gotten caught organizing against El Jefe and the colonel's influence could not save the boy from having an eye gouged out with electric shocks. Beli didn't want to hear it. After all, she was in love! In love! She wafted through her day like a woman with a concussion. It's not like she had a number for the Gangster, or even an address (bad sign number one, girls), and he was in the habit of disappearing for days without warning (bad sign number two), and now that Trujillo's war against the world was reaching its bitter crescendo (and now that he had Beli on lock), the days could become weeks, and when he reappeared from "his business" he would smell of cigarettes and old fear and want only to fuck, and afterward he would drink whiskey and mutter to himself by the love-motel window. His hair, Beli noticed, was growing in gray.

She didn't take kindly to these disappearances. They made her look bad in front of La Inca and the neighbors, who were always asking her sweetly, Where's your savior now, Moses? She defended him against every criticism, of course, no brother has had a better advocate, but then took it out on his ass upon his return. Pouted when he appeared with flowers; made him take her to the most expensive restaurants; pestered him around the clock to move her out of her neighborhood; asked him what the hell he'd been doing these past *x* days; talked about the weddings she read about in the *Listín*, and just so you can see that La Inca's doubts were not entirely wasted: wanted to know when he was going to bring her to his house. Hija de la gran puta, would you stop jodiéndome!

We're in the middle of a war here! He stood over her in his wifebeater, waving a pistol. Don't you know what the Communists do to girls like you? They'll hang you up by your beautiful tits. And then they'll cut them off, just like they did to the whores in Cuba!

During one of the Gangster's longer absences, Beli, bored and desperate to escape the schadenfreude in her neighbors' eyes, took it upon herself to ride the Blue Ball Express one last time—in other words, she checked in on her old flames. Ostensibly she wanted to end things in a formal way, but I think she was just feeling down and wanted male attention. Which is fine. But then she made the classic mistake of telling these Dominican hombres about the new love of her life, how happy she was. Sisters: don't ever ever do this. It's about as smart as telling the judge who's about to sentence you that back in the day you finger-fucked his mother. The car dealer, always so gentle, so decorous, threw a whiskey bottle at her, screaming, Why should I be happy for a stupid stinking mona! They were in his apartment on the Malecón—at least he showed you his house, Constantina would later crack—and if he had been a better righty she would have ended up brained, perhaps raped and killed, but his fastball only grazed her and then it was her turn on the mound. She put him away with four sinkers to the head, using the same whiskey bottle he'd thrown at her. Five minutes later, panting and barefoot in a cab, she was pulled over by the Secret Police, tipped off because they'd seen her running and it was only when they questioned her that she realized that she was still holding the bottle and it had bloody hair on one of its edges, the car dealer's straight blond hair.

(*Once they heard what happened they let me go.*)

To his credit, Arquimedes acquitted himself in a more mature fashion. (Maybe because she told him first and had not yet grown flip.) After her confession she heard a "little noise" from the closet where he was hiding and nothing else. Five minutes of silence and then she whispered, I'd better go. (She never saw him again in person, only on the TV, giving speeches, and in later years would wonder if he still thought of her, as she sometimes did of him.)

What have you been up to? the Gangster asked the next time he appeared.

Nothing, she said, throwing her arms around his neck, absolutely nothing.

A month before it all blew up, the Gangster took Beli on a vacation to his old haunts in Samaná. Their first real trip together, a peace offering prompted by a particularly long absence, a promissory note for future trips abroad. For those capitaleños who never leave the 27 de Febrero or who think Güaley is the Center of the Universe: Samaná es una chulería. One of the authors of the King James Bible traveled the Caribbean, and I often think that it was a place like Samaná that was on his mind when he sat down to pen the Eden chapters. For Eden it was, a blessed meridian where mar and sol and green have forged their union and produced a stubborn people that no amount of highfalutin prose can generalize.[17] The Gangster was in high spirits, the war against the subver-

17. In my first draft, Samaná was actually Jarabacoa, but then my girl Leonie, resident expert in all things Domo, pointed out that there are no

sives was going swell, it seemed. (We got 'em on the run, he gloated. Very soon all will be well.)

As for Beli, she remembered that trip as the nicest time she'd ever had in the DR. She would never again hear the name *Samaná* without recalling that final primavera of her youth, the primavera of her perfection, when she was still young and beautiful. Samaná would forever evoke memories of their lovemaking, of the Gangster's rough chin scraping her neck, of the sound of the Mar Caribe romancing those flawless resortless beaches, of the safety she experienced, and the promise.

Three photos from that trip, and in every one she's smiling.

They did all the stuff we Dominicans love to do on our vacations. They ate pescado frito and waded in the río. They walked along the beach and drank rum until the meat behind their eyes throbbed. It was the first time ever that Beli had her own space totally under her control, so while the Gangster dozed restfully in his hamaca she busied herself with playing wife, with creating a preliminary draft of the household they would soon inhabit. Mornings she would subject the cabana to the harshest of scourings and hang boisterous profusions of flowers from every beam and around every window, while her bartering produce and fish from the neighbors resulted in one spectacular meal after another—

---

beaches in Jarabacoa. Beautiful rivers but no beaches. Leonie was also the one who informed me that the perrito (see first paragraphs of chapter one, "GhettoNerd at the End of the World") wasn't popularized until the late eighties, early nineties, but that was one detail I couldn't change, just liked the image too much. Forgive me, historians of popular dance, forgive me!

showing off the skills she acquired during the Lost Years—and the Gangster's satisfaction, the patting of his stomach, the unequivocal praise, the soft emission of gases as he lay in the hamaca, it was music to her ears! (In her mind she became his wife that week in every sense but the legal.)

She and the Gangster even managed to have heart-to-hearts. On the second day, after he showed her his old home, now abandoned and hurricane-ruined, she asked: Do you ever miss having a family?

They were at the only nice restaurant in the city, where El Jefe dined on his visits (they'll still tell you that). You see those people? He pointed toward the bar. All those people have families, you can tell by their faces, they have families that depend on them and that they depend on, and for some of them this is good, and for some of them this is bad. But it all amounts to the same shit because there isn't one of them who is free. They can't do what they want to do or be who they should be. I might have no one in the world, but at least I'm free.

She had never heard anyone say those words. *I'm free* wasn't a popular refrain in the Era of Trujillo. But it struck a chord in her, put La Inca and her neighbors and her still-up-in-the-air life in perspective.

I'm free.

I want to be like you, she told the Gangster days later when they were eating crabs she had cooked in an achiote sauce. He had just been telling her about the nude beaches of Cuba. You would have been the star of the show, he said, pinching her nipple and laughing.

What do you mean, you want to be like me?

I want to be free.

He smiled and chucked her under the chin. Then you will be, mi negra bella.

The next day the protective bubble about their idyll finally burst and the troubles of the real world came rushing in. A motorcycle driven by a hugely overweight policeman arrived at their cabana. Capitán, you're needed in the Palacio, he said from under his chinstrap. More trouble with the subversives, it seems. I'll send a car for you, the Gangster promised. Wait, she said, I'll go with you, not wanting to be left, again, but he either didn't hear or didn't care. Wait, goddamn it, she shouted in frustration. But the motorcycle never slowed. Wait! The ride never materialized either. Fortunately Beli had gotten into the habit of stealing his money while he slept so that she could maintain herself during his absences; otherwise she would have been stranded on that fucking beach. After waiting eight hours like a parigüaya she hoisted her bag (left his shit in the cabana) and marched through the simmering heat like a vengeance on two legs, walked for what felt like half a day, until at last she happened upon a colmado, where a couple of sunstroked campesinos were sharing a warm beer while the colmadero, seated in the only shade in sight, waved the flies from his dulces. When they realized she was standing over them they all scrambled to their feet. By then her anger had drained away and she only wanted to be spared further walking. Do you know anybody who has a car? And by noon she was in a dust-choked Chevy, heading home. You better hold the door, the driver advised, or it might fall off.

Then it falls, she said, her arms firmly crossed.

At one point they passed through one of those godforsaken blisters of a community that frequently afflict the arteries between the major cities, sad assemblages of shacks that seem to have been deposited in situ by a hurricane or other such calamity. The only visible commerce was a single goat carcass hanging unfetchingly from a rope, peeled down to its corded orange musculature, except for the skin of its face, which was still attached, like a funeral mask. He'd been skinned very recently, the flesh was still shivering under the shag of flies. Beli didn't know if it was the heat or the two beers she drank while the colmadero sent for his cousin or the skinned goat or dim memories of her Lost Years, but our girl could have sworn that a man sitting in a rocking chair in front of one of the hovels *had no face* and he waved at her as she passed but before she could confirm it the pueblito vanished into the dust. Did you see something? Her driver sighed, Please I can barely keep my eyes on the road.

Two days after her return the cold had settled in the pit of her stomach like something drowned in there. She didn't know what was wrong; every morning she was vomiting.

It was La Inca who saw it first. Well, you finally did it. You're pregnant.

No I'm not, Beli rasped, wiping the fetid mash from her mouth.

But she was.

REVELATION

When the doctor confirmed La Inca's worst fears Beli let out a cheer. (Young lady, this is not a game, the doctor barked.) She was simultaneously scared shitless *and* out of her mind with happiness. She couldn't sleep for the wonder of it and, after the revelation, became strangely respectful and pliant. (So now you're happy? My God, girl, are you a fool!) For Beli: This was it. The magic she'd been waiting for. She placed her hand on her flat stomach and heard the wedding bells loud and clear, saw in her mind's eye the house that had been promised, that she had dreamed about.

Please don't tell anyone, La Inca begged, but of course she whispered it to her friend Dorca, who put it out on the street. Success, after all, loves a witness, but failure can't exist without one. The bochinche spread through their sector of Baní like wildfire.

The next time the Gangster appeared she had dolled herself up lovely, a brand-new dress, crushed jasmine in her underwear, got her hair done, and even plucked her eyebrows into twin hyphens of alarm. He needed a shave and a haircut, and the hairs curling out of his ears were starting to look like a particularly profitable crop. You smell good enough to eat, he growled, kissing the tender glide of her neck.

Guess what, she said coyly.

He looked up. What?

UPON FURTHER REFLECTION

In her memory he never told her to get rid of it. But later, when she was freezing in basement apartments in the Bronx and working her fingers to the bone, she reflected that he *had* told her exactly that. But like lovergirls everywhere, she had heard only what she wanted to hear.

NAME GAME

I hope it's a son, she said.

I do too, half believing it.

They were lying in bed in a love motel. Above them spun a fan, its blades pursued by a half-dozen flies.

What will his middle name be? she wondered excitedly. It has to be something serious, because he's going to be a doctor, like mi papá. Before he could reply, she said: We'll call him Abelard.

He scowled. What kind of maricón name is that? *If* the baby's a boy we'll call him Manuel. That was my grandfather's name.

I thought you didn't know who your family was.

He pulled from her touch. No me jodas.

Wounded, she reached down to hold her stomach.

TRUTH AND CONSEQUENCES 1

The Gangster had told Beli many things in the course of their relationship, but there was one important item he'd failed to reveal. That he was married.

I'm sure you all guessed that. I mean, he was *dominicano*, after all. But I bet you never would have imagined whom he was married to.

A Trujillo.

TRUTH AND CONSEQUENCES 2

It's true. The Gangster's wife was—drumroll, please—*Trujillo's fucking sister*! Did you really think some street punk from Samaná was going to reach the upper echelons of the Trujillato on hard work alone? Negro, please—this ain't a fucking comic book!

Yes, Trujillo's sister; the one known affectionately as La Fea. They met while the Gangster was carousing in Cuba; she was a bitter tacaña seventeen years his senior. They did a lot of work together in the butt business and before you knew it she had taken a shine to his irresistible joie de vivre. He encouraged it—knew a fantastic opportunity when he saw one—and before the year was out they were cutting the cake and placing the first piece on El Jefe's plate. There are those alive who claim that La Fea had actually been a pro herself in the time before the rise of her brother, but that seems to be more calumny than anything, like saying that Balaguer fathered a dozen illegitimate children and then used the pueblo's money to hush it up—wait, that's true, but probably not the other—shit, who can keep track of what's true and what's false in a country as baká as ours—what is known is that the time before her brother's rise had made her una mujer bien fuerte y bien cruel; she was no pendeja and ate girls like Beli like they were pan de agua—if this was Dickens she'd have to run a brothel—but wait, she *did* run brothels! Well, maybe Dickens would have her run an orphanage. But she was one of those characters only a kleptocracy could have conceived: had hundreds of thousands in the bank and not one yuan of pity in her soul; she cheated everyone she did business with, including her brother, and had already driven two respectable businessmen to early graves by fleecing them to their last mota. She sat in her immense house in La Capital like a shelob in her web, all day handling accounts and ordering around subordinates, and on certain weekend nights she would host tertulias where her "friends" would gather to endure hours of poetry declaimed by her preposterously tone-deaf son (from her first marriage; she and the Gangster didn't have any children). Well, one fine day in May a servant appeared at her door.

Leave it, she said, a pencil in her mouth.

An inhalation. Doña, there's news.

There's always news. Leave it.

An exhale. News about your husband.

IN THE SHADOW OF THE JACARANDA

Two days later Beli was wandering about the parque central in a restless fog. Her hair had seen better days. She was out in the world because she couldn't stand to be at home with La Inca and now that she didn't have a job she didn't have a sanctuary into which to retreat. She was deep in thought, one hand on her belly, the other on her pounding head. She was thinking about the argument she and the Gangster had gotten into earlier in the week. He'd been in one of his foul moods and bellowed, suddenly, that he didn't want to bring a baby into so terrible a world and she had barked that the world wasn't so terrible in Miami and then he had said, grabbing her by the throat, If you're in such a rush to go to Miami, swim. He hadn't tried to contact her since and she was wandering around in the hopes of spotting him. As if he hung around Baní. Her feet were swollen, her head was sending its surplus ache down her neck, and now two huge men with matching pompadours were grabbing her by the arms and propelling her to the center of the parque, where a well-dressed old lady sat on a bench underneath a decrepit jacaranda. White gloves and a coil of pearls about her neck. Scrutinizing Beli with unflinching iguana eyes.

Do you know who I am?

I don't know who in carajo—

Soy Trujillo. I'm also Dionisio's wife. It has reached my ears that you've been telling people that you're going to marry him *and* that you're having his child. Well, I'm here to inform you, mi monita, that you will be doing neither. These two very large and capable officers are going to take you to a doctor, and after he's cleaned out that toto podrido of yours there won't be any baby left to talk about. And then it will be in your best interest that I never see your black cara de culo again because if I do I'll feed you to my dogs myself. But enough talk. It's time for your appointment. Say good-bye now, I don't want you to be late.

Beli might have felt as though the crone had thrown boiling oil on her but she still had the ovaries to spit, Cómeme el culo, you ugly disgusting vieja.

Let's go, Elvis One said, twisting her arm behind her back and, with the help of his partner, dragging her across the park to where a car sat baleful in the sun.

Déjame, she screamed, and when she looked up she saw that there was one more cop sitting in the car, and when he turned toward her she saw that he *didn't have a face*. All the strength fell right out of her.

That's right, tranquila now, the larger one said.

What a sad ending it would have been had not our girl rolled her luck and spotted José Then ambling back from one of his gambling trips, a rolled newspaper under his arm. She tried to say his name, but like in those bad dreams we all have there was no air in her lungs. It wasn't until they tried to force her into the car and her hand brushed the burning chrome of the car that she found her tongue. José, she whispered, please save me.

And then the spell was broken. Shut up! The Elvises struck her in the head and back but it was too late, José Then was running over, and behind him, a miracle, were his brother Juan and the rest of the Palacio Peking crew: Constantina, Marco Antonio, and Indian Benny. The grunts tried to draw their pistols but Beli was all over them, and then José planted his iron next to the biggest one's skull and everybody froze, except, of course, Beli.

You hijos de puta! I'm pregnant! Do you understand! Pregnant! She spun to where the crone had held court, but she had *inexplicably vanished*.

This girl's under arrest, one grunt said sullenly.

No she's not. José tore Beli out of their arms.

You alone her! yelled Juan, a machete in each hand.

Listen, chino, you don't know what you're doing.

This chino knows exactly what he's doing. José cocked the pistol, a noise most dreadful, like a rib breaking. His face was a dead rictus and in it shone everything he had lost. Run, Beli, he said.

And she ran, tears popping out of her eyes, but not before taking one last kick at the grunts.

Mis chinos, she told her daughter, saved my life.

HESITATION

She should have kept running too but she beelined for home instead. Can you believe it? Like everybody in this damn story, she underestimated the depth of the shit she was in.

What's the matter, hija? La Inca said, dropping the frying pan in her hand and holding the girl. You have to tell me.

Beli shook her head, couldn't catch her breath. Latched the door and the windows and then crouched on her bed, a knife in her hand, trembling and weeping, the cold in her stomach like a dead fish. I want Dionisio, she blubbered. I want him now!

What *happened*?

She should have scrammed, I tell you, but she needed to see her Gangster, needed him to explain what was happening. Despite everything that had just transpired she still held out the hope that he would make everything better, that his gruff voice would soothe her heart and stop the animal fear gnawing her guts. Poor Beli. She believed in the Gangster. Was loyal to the end. Which was why a couple hours later, when a neighbor shouted, Oye, Inca, the novio is outside, she bolted out of bed like she'd been shot from a mass driver, blew past La Inca, past caution, ran barefoot to where his car was waiting. In the dark she failed to notice that it wasn't actually his car.

Did you miss us? Elvis One asked, slapping cuffs on her wrist.

She tried to scream but it was too late.

LA INCA, THE DIVINE

After the girl had bolted from the house, and after she was informed by the neighbors that the Secret Police had scooped her up, La Inca knew in her ironclad heart that the girl was funtoosh, that the Doom of the Cabrals had managed to infiltrate her circle at last. Standing on the edge of the neighborhood, rigid as a post, staring hopelessly into the night, she felt herself borne upon a cold tide of despair, as bottomless as our needs. A thousand reasons why it might have happened (starting of course with the accursed Gangster) but none as important as the fact that it had. Stranded out in that growing darkness, without a name, an address, or a relative in the Palacio, La Inca almost succumbed, let herself be lifted from her moorings and carried like a child, like a tangle of seagrape beyond the bright reef of her faith and into the dark reaches. It was in that hour of tribulation, however, that a hand reached out for her and she remembered who she was. Myotís Altagracia Toribio Cabral. One of the Mighty of the Sur. *You must save her*, her husband's spirit said, *or no one else will*.

Shrugging off her weariness, she did what many women of her background would have done. Posted herself beside her portrait of La Virgen de Altagracia and prayed. We postmodern plátanos tend to dismiss the Catholic devotion of our viejas as atavistic, an embarrassing throwback to the olden days, but it's exactly at these moments, when all hope has vanished, when the end draws near, that prayer has dominion.

Let me tell you, True Believers: in the annals of Dominican piety there has never been prayer like this. The rosaries cabling through La Inca's fingers like line flying through a doomed fisherman's hands. And before you could say Holy! Holy! Holy! she was joined by a flock of women, young and old, fierce and mansa, serious and alegre, even those who had previously bagged on the girl and called her whore, arriving without invitation and taking up the prayer without as much as a whisper. Dorca was there, and the wife of the dentist, and many many others. In no time at all the room was filled with the faithful and pulsed with a spirit so dense that it was rumored that the Devil himself had to avoid the Sur for months afterward. La Inca didn't notice. A hurricane could have carried off the entire city and it wouldn't have broken her concentration. Her face veined, her neck corded, the blood roaring in her ears. Too lost, too given over to drawing the girl back from the Abyss was she. So furious and so unrelenting, in fact, was La Inca's pace that more than a few women suffered *shetaat* (spiritual burnout) and collapsed, never again to feel the divine breath of the Todopoderoso on their neck. One woman even lost the ability to determine right from wrong and a few years later became one of Balaguer's chief deputies. By night's end only three of the original circle remained: La Inca of course, her friend and neighbor Momona (who it was said could cure warts and sex an egg just by looking at it), and a plucky seven-year-old whose piety, until then, had been obscured by a penchant for blowing mucus out her nostrils like a man.

To exhaustion and beyond they prayed, to that glittering place where the flesh dies and is born again, where all is agony, and finally, just as La Inca was feeling her spirit begin to loose itself from its earthly pinions, just as the circle began to dissolve—

CHOICE AND CONSEQUENCES

They drove east. In those days the cities hadn't yet metastasized into kaiju, menacing one another with smoking, teeming tendrils of shanties; in those days their limits were a Corbusian dream; the urban dropped off, as precipitous as a beat, one second you were deep in the twentieth century (well, the twentieth century of the Third World) and the next you'd find yourself plunged 180 years into rolling fields of cane. The transition between these states was some real-time machine-type shit. The moon, it has been reported, was full, and the light that rained down cast the leaves of the eucalyptuses into spectral coin.

The world outside so beautiful, but inside the car . . .

They'd been punching her and her right eye had puffed into a malignant slit, her right breast so preposterously swollen that it looked like it would burst, her lip was split and something was wrong with her jaw, she couldn't swallow without causing herself excruciating shocks of pain. She cried out each time they struck her but she did not cry, entiendes? Her fierceness astounds me. She would not give them the pleasure. There was such fear, the sickening blood-draining fear of a drawn pistol, of waking up to find a man standing over your bed, but held, a note sustained indefinitely. Such fear, and yet she refused to show it. How she hated these men. For her whole life she would hate them, never forgive, never forgive, and she would never be able to think of them without succumbing to a vortex of rage. Anyone else would have turned her face from the blows, but Beli offered hers up. And between punches she brought up her knees to comfort her stomach. You'll be OK, she whispered through a broken mouth. You'll live.

Dios mío.

They parked the car on the edge of the road and marched her into the cane. They walked until the cane was roaring so loud around them it sounded as if they were in the middle of a storm. Our girl, she kept flinging her head to get her hair out of her face, could think only about her poor little boy, and that was the sole reason she started to weep.

The large grunt handed his partner a nightstick.

Let's hurry up.

No, Beli said.

How she survived I'll never know. They beat her like she was a slave. Like she was a dog. Let me pass over the actual violence and report instead on the damage inflicted: her clavicle, chickenboned; her right humerus, a triple fracture (she would never again have much strength in that arm); five ribs, broken; left kidney, bruised; liver, bruised; right lung, collapsed; front teeth, blown out. About 167 points of damage in total and it was only sheer accident that these motherfuckers didn't eggshell her cranium, though her head did swell to elephant-man proportions. Was there time for a rape or two? I suspect there was, but we shall never know because it's not something she talked about. All that can be said is that it was the end of language, the end of hope. It was the sort of beating that breaks people, breaks them utterly.

Throughout most of the car ride, and even into the first

stanzas of that wilding, she maintained the fool's hope that her Gangster would save her, would appear out of the darkness with a gun and a reprieve. And when it became clear that no rescue was forthcoming, she fantasized, in the instance of a blackout, that he would visit her at the hospital and there they would be married, he in a suit, she in a body cast, but then that too was revealed to be plepla by the sickening crack of her humerus, and now all that remained was the agony and the foolishness. In a blackout she caught sight of him disappearing on that motorcycle again, felt the tightness in her chest as she screamed for him to wait, wait. Saw for a brief instant La Inca praying in her room—the silence that lay between them now, stronger than love—and in the gloaming of her dwindling strength there yawned a loneliness so total it was beyond death, a loneliness that obliterated all memory, the loneliness of a childhood where she'd not even had her own name. And it was into that loneliness that she was sliding, and it was here that she would dwell forever, alone, black, fea, scratching at the dust with a stick, pretending that the scribble was letters, words, names.

All hope was gone, but then, True Believers, like the Hand of the Ancestors themselves, a miracle. Just as our girl was set to disappear across that event horizon, just as the cold of obliteration was stealing up her legs, she found in herself one last reservoir of strength: her Cabral magis—and all she had to do was realize that once again she'd been tricked, once again she'd been *played*, by the Gangster, by Santo Domingo, by her own dumb needs, to ignite it. Like Superman in *Dark Knight Returns*, who drained from an entire jungle the photonic energy he needed to survive Coldbringer, so did our Beli resolve out of her anger her own survival. In other words, her coraje saved her life.

Like a white light in her. Like a sun.

She came to in the ferocious moonlight. A broken girl, atop broken stalks of cane.

Pain everywhere but alive. Alive.

And now we arrive at the strangest part of our tale. Whether what follows was a figment of Beli's wracked imagination or something else altogether I cannot say. Even your Watcher has his silences, his páginas en blanco. Beyond the Source Wall few have ventured. But no matter what the truth, remember: Dominicans are Caribbean and therefore have an extraordinary tolerance for extreme phenomena. How else could we have survived what we have survived? So as Beli was flitting in and out of life, there appeared at her side a creature that would have been an amiable mongoose if not for its golden lion eyes and the absolute black of its pelt. This one was quite large for its species and placed its intelligent little paws on her chest and stared down at her.

You have to rise.

My baby, Beli wept. Mi hijo precioso.

Hypatía, your baby is dead.

No, no, no, no, no.

It pulled at her unbroken arm. *You have to rise now or you'll never have the son or the daughter.*

What son? she wailed. What daughter?

The ones who await.

It was dark and her legs trembled beneath her like smoke. *You have to follow.*

It rivered into the cane, and Beli, blinking tears, realized she had no idea which way was out. As some of you know, cane-fields are no fucking joke, and even the cleverest of adults can get mazed in their endlessness, only to reappear months later as a cameo of bones. But before Beli lost hope she heard the creature's voice. She (for it had a woman's lilt) was singing! In an accent she could not place: maybe Venezuelan, maybe Colombian. *Sueño, sueño, sueño, como tú te llamas.* She clung unsteadily to the cane, like an anciano clinging to a hammock, and, panting, took her first step, a long dizzy spell, beating back a blackout, and then her next. Precarious progress, because if she fell she knew she would never stand again. Sometimes she saw the creature's chabine eyes flashing through the stalks. *Yo me llamo sueño de la madrugada.* The cane didn't want her to leave, of course; it slashed at her palms, jabbed into her flank and clawed her thighs, and its sweet stench clogged her throat.

Each time she thought she would fall she concentrated on the faces of her promised future—her promised children—and from that obtained the strength she needed to continue. She pulled from strength, from hope, from hate, from her invincible heart, each a different piston driving her forward. Finally, when all were exhausted, when she began to stumble headfirst, heading down like a boxer on his last legs, she stretched her uninjured arm out and what greeted her was not cane but the open world of life. She felt the tarmac under her bare broken feet, and the wind. The wind! But she had only a second to savor it, for just then an unelectrified truck burst out of the darkness in a roar of gears. What a life, she mused, all that lucha only to be run over like a dog. But she wasn't flattened. The driver, who later swore he saw something lion-like in the gloom, with eyes like terrible amber lamps, slammed on the brakes and halted inches from where a naked blood-spattered Beli tottered.

Now check it: the truck held a perico ripiao conjunto, fresh from playing a wedding in Ocoa. Took all the courage they had not to pop the truck in reverse and peel out of there. Cries of, It's a baká, a ciguapa, no, a haitiano! silenced by the lead singer, who shouted, It's a girl! The band members lay Beli among their instruments, swaddled her with their chacabanas, and washed her face with the water they carried for the radiator and for cutting down the klerín. Down the band peered, rubbing their lips and running nervous hands through thinning hair.

What do you think happened?

I think she was attacked.

By a lion, offered the driver.

Maybe she fell out of a car.

It looks like she fell *under* a car.

Trujillo, she whispered.

Aghast, the band looked at one another.

We should leave her.

The guitarrista agreed. She must be a subversive. If they find her with us the police will kill us too.

Put her back on the road, begged the driver. Let the lion finish her.

Silence, and then the lead singer lit a match and held it in the air and in that splinter of light was revealed a blunt-featured woman with the golden eyes of a chabine. We're not leaving her, the lead singer said in a curious cibaeña accent, and only then did Beli understand that she was saved.[18]

FUKÚ VS. ZAFA

There are still many, on and off the Island, who offer Beli's near-fatal beating as irrefutable proof that the House Cabral was indeed victim of a high-level fukú, the local version of House Atreus. Two Trujilíos in one lifetime—what in carajo else could it be? But other heads question that logic, arguing that Beli's survival must be evidence to the contrary. Cursed people, after all, tend not to drag themselves out of canefields with a frightening roster of injuries and then happen to be picked up by a van of sympathetic musicians in the middle of the night who ferry them home without delay to a "mother" with mad connections in the medical community. If these serendipities signify anything, say these heads, it is that our Beli was blessed.

18. The Mongoose, one of the great unstable particles of the Universe and also one of its greatest travelers. Accompanied humanity out of Africa and after a long furlough in India jumped ship to the other India, a.k.a. the Caribbean. Since its earliest appearance in the written record—675 B.C.E., in a nameless scribe's letter to Ashurbanipal's father, Esarhaddon—the Mongoose has proven itself to be an enemy of kingly chariots, chains, and hierarchies. Believed to be an ally of Man. Many Watchers suspect that the Mongoose arrived to our world from another, but to date no evidence of such a migration has been unearthed.

What about the dead son?

The world is full of tragedies enough without niggers having to resort to curses for explanations.

A conclusion La Inca wouldn't have argued with. To her dying day she believed that Beli had met not a curse but God out in that canefield.

I met something, Beli would say, guardedly.

BACK AMONG THE LIVING

Touch and go, I tell you, until the fifth day. And when at last she returned to consciousness she did so *screaming*. Her arm felt like it had been pinched off at the elbow by a grindstone, her head crowned in a burning hoop of brass, her lung like the exploded carcass of a piñata—Jesú Cristo! She started crying almost immediately, but what our girl did not know was that for the last half-week, two of the best doctors in Baní had tended her covertly; friends of La Inca and anti-Trujillo to the core, they set her arm and plastered it, stitched shut the frightening gashes on her scalp (sixty puntos in all), doused her wounds with enough Mercurochrome to disinfect an army, injected her with morphine and against tetanus. Many late nights of worry, but the worst, it seemed, was over. These doctors, with a spiritual assist from La Inca's Bible group, had performed a miracle, and all that remained was the healing. (She is lucky that she is so strong, the doctors said, packing their stethoscopes. The Hand of God is upon her, the prayer leaders confirmed, stowing their Bibles.) But blessed was not what our girl felt. After a couple of minutes of hysterical sobbing, of readjusting to the fact of the bed, to the fact of her life, she lowed out La Inca's name.

From the side of the bed the quiet voice of the Benefactor: Don't talk. Unless it's to thank the Savior for your life.

Mamá, Beli cried. *Mamá.* They killed my bebé, they tried to kill me—

And they did not succeed, La Inca said. Not for lack of trying, though. She put her hand on the girl's forehead.

Now it's time for you to be quiet. For you to be still.

That night was a late-medieval ordeal. Beli alternated from quiet weeping to gusts of rabia so fierce they threatened to throw her out of the bed and reopen her injuries. Like a woman possessed, she drove herself into her mattress, went as rigid as a board, flailed her good arm around, beat her legs, spit and cursed. She wailed—despite a punctured lung and cracked ribs—she wailed inconsolably. *Mamá, me mataron a mi hijo. Estoy sola, estoy sola.*

Sola? La Inca leaned close. Would you like me to call your Gangster?

No, she whispered.

La Inca gazed down at her. I wouldn't call him either.

That night Beli drifted on a vast ocean of loneliness, buffeted by squalls of despair, and during one of her intermittent sleeps she dreamt that she had truly and permanently died and she and her child shared a coffin and when she finally awoke for good, night had broken and out in the street a grade of grief unlike any she'd encountered before was being uncoiled, a cacophony of wails that seemed to have torn free from the cracked soul of humanity itself. Like a funeral song for the entire planet.

Mamá, she gasped, *mamá*.

Mamá!

Tranquilísate, muchacha.

Mamá, is that for me? Am I dying? Dime, mamá.

Ay, hija, no seas ridícula. La Inca put her hands, awkward hyphens, around the girl. Lowered her mouth to her ear: It's Trujillo.

Gunned down, she whispered, the night Beli had been kidnapped.

No one knows anything yet. Except that he's dead.[19]

19. They say he was on his way for some ass that night. Who is surprised? A consummate culocrat to the end. Perhaps on that last night, El Jefe, sprawled in the back of his Bel Air, thought only of the routine pussy that was awaiting him at Estancia Fundación. Perhaps he thought of nothing. Who can know? In any event: there is a black Chevrolet fast approaching, like Death itself, packed to the rim with U.S.-backed assassins of the higher classes, and now both cars are nearing the city limits, where the streetlights end (for modernity indeed has its limits in Santo Domingo), and in the dark distance looms the cattle fairgrounds where seventeen months before some other youth had intended to assassinate him. El Jefe asks his driver, Zacarías, to turn on the radio, but—how appropriate— there is a poetry reading on and off it goes again. Maybe the poetry reminds him of Galíndez.

Maybe not.

The black Chevy flashes its lights innocuously, asking to pass, and Zacarías, thinking it's the Secret Police, obliges by slowing down, and when the cars come abreast, the escopeta wielded by Antonio de la Maza (whose brother—surprise, surprise—was killed in the Galíndez cover-up—which goes to show that you should always be careful when killing nerds, never know who will come after you) goes boo-ya! And now (so goes the legend) El Jefe cries, Coño, me hirieron! The second shotgun

LA INCA, IN DECLINE

It's all true, plataneros. Through the numinous power of prayer La Inca saved the girl's life, laid an A-plus zafa on the Cabral family fukú (but at what cost to herself?). Everybody in the neighborhood will tell you how, shortly after the girl slipped out of the country, La Inca began to diminish, like Galadriel after the temptation of the ring—out of sadness for the girl's failures, some would say, but others would point to that night of Herculean prayer. No matter what your take, it cannot be denied that soon after Beli's departure La Inca's hair began to turn a snowy white, and by the time Lola lived

---

blast hits Zacarías in the shoulder and he almost stops the car, in pain and shock and surprise. Here now the famous exchange: Get the guns, El Jefe says. Vamos a pelear. And Zacarías says: No, Jefe, son mucho, and El Jefe repeats himself: Vamos a pelear. He could have ordered Zacarías to turn the car back to the safety of his capital, but instead he goes out like Tony Montana. Staggers out of the bullet-ridden Bel Air, holding a .38 in his hand. The rest is, of course, history, and if this were a movie you'd have to film it in John Woo slow motion. Shot at twenty-seven times—what a Dominican number—and suffering from four hundred hit points of damage, a mortally wounded Rafael Leónidas Trujillo Molina is said to have taken two steps toward his birthplace, San Cristóbal, for, as we know, all children, whether good or bad, eventually find their way home, but thinking better of it he turned back toward La Capital, to his beloved city, and fell for the last time. Zacarías, who'd had his mid-parietal region creased by a round from a .357, got blown into the grass by the side of the road; miracle of miracles, he would survive to tell the tale of the ajusticiamiento. De la Maza, perhaps thinking of his poor, dead, set-up brother, then took Trujillo's .38 out of his dead hand and shot Trujillo in the face and uttered his now famous words: Este guaraguao ya no comerá más pollito. And then the assassins stashed El Jefe's body—where? In the trunk, of course.

with her she was no longer the Great Power she had been. Yes, she had saved the girl's life, but to what end? Beli was still profoundly vulnerable. At the end of *The Return of the King*, Sauron's evil was taken by "a great wind" and neatly "blown away," with no lasting consequences to our heroes;[20] but Trujillo was too powerful, too toxic a radiation to be dispelled so easily. Even after death his evil *lingered*. Within hours of El Jefe dancing bien pegao with those twenty-seven bullets, his minions ran amok—fulfilling, as it were, his last will and vengeance. A great darkness descended on the Island and for the third time since the rise of Fidel people were being rounded up by Trujillo's son, Ramfis, and a good plenty were sacrificed in the most depraved fashion imaginable, the orgy of terror funeral goods for the father from the son. Even a woman as potent as La Inca, who with the elvish ring of her will had forged within Baní her own personal Lothlórien, knew that she could not protect the girl against a direct assault from the Eye. What was to keep the assassins from

---

And thus passed old Fuckface. And thus passed the Era of Trujillo (sort of).

I've been to the neck of road where he was gunned down many many times. Nothing to report except that the guagua from Haina almost always runs my ass over every time I cross the highway. For a while, I hear, that stretch was the haunt of what El Jefe worried about the most: los maricones.

20. "And as the Captains gazed south to the Land of Mordor, it seemed to them that, black against the pall of cloud, there rose a huge shape of shadow, impenetrable, lightning-crowned, filling all the sky. Enormous it reared above the world, and stretched out towards them a vast threatening hand, terrible but impotent; for even as it leaned over them, a great wind took it, and it was all blown away, and passed; and then a hush fell."

returning to finish what they'd started? After all, they had killed the world-famous Mirabal Sisters,[21] who were of Name; what was to stop them from killing her poor orphaned negrita? La Inca felt the danger palpably, intimately. And perhaps it was the strain of her final prayer, but each time La Inca glanced at the girl she could swear that there was a shadow standing just behind her shoulder which disappeared as soon as you tried to focus on it. A dark horrible shadow that gripped her heart. And it seemed to be growing.

La Inca needed to do *something*, so, not yet recovered from her Hail Mary play, she called upon her ancestors and upon Jesú Cristo for help. Once again she prayed. But on top of that, to show her devotion, she fasted. Pulled a Mother Abigail. Ate nothing but one orange, drank nothing but water. After that last vast expenditure of piety her spirit was in an uproar. She did not know what to do. She had a mind like a mongoose but she was not, in the end, a worldly woman. She spoke to her friends, who argued for sending Beli to the campo. She'll be safe there. She spoke to her priest. You should pray for her.

On the third day, it came to her. She was dreaming that she and her dead husband were on the beach where he had drowned. He was dark again as he always was in summer.

You have to send her away.

But they'll find her in the campo.

You have to send her to Nueva York. I have it on great authority that it is the only way.

---

21. And where were the Mirabal Sisters murdered? In a canefield, of course. And then their bodies were put in a car and a crash was simulated! Talk about two for one!

And then he strutted proudly into the water; she tried to call him back, Please, come back, but he did not listen.

His otherworldly advice was too terrible to consider. Exile to the North! To Nueva York, a city so foreign she herself had never had the ovaries to visit. The girl would be lost to her, and La Inca would have failed her great cause: to heal the wounds of the Fall, to bring House Cabral back from the dead. And who knows what might happen to the girl among the yanquis? In her mind the U.S. was nothing more and nothing less than a país overrun by gangsters, putas, and no-accounts. Its cities swarmed with machines and industry, as thick with sinvergüencería as Santo Domingo was with heat, a cuco shod in iron, exhaling fumes, with the glittering promise of coin deep in the cold lightless shaft of its eyes. How La Inca wrestled with herself those long nights! But which side was Jacob and which side was the Angel? After all, who was to say that the Trujillos would remain in power much longer? Already the necromantic power of El Jefe was waning and in its place could be felt something like a wind. Rumors flew as thick as ciguas, rumors that the Cubans were preparing to invade, that the Marines had been spotted on the horizon. Who could know what tomorrow would bring? Why send her beloved girl away? Why be *hasty*?

La Inca found herself in practically the same predicament Beli's father had found himself in sixteen years earlier, back when the House of Cabral had first come up against the might of the Trujillos. Trying to decide whether to act or to stay still.

Unable to choose, she prayed for further guidance—another

three days without food. Who knows how it might have turned out had not the Elvises come calling? Our Benefactor might have gone out exactly like Mother Abigail. But thankfully the Elvises surprised her as she was sweeping the front of the house. Is your name Myotís Toribio? Their pompadours like the backs of beetles. African muscles encased in pale summer suits, and underneath their jackets the hard, oiled holsters of their firearms did creak.

We want to speak to your daughter, Elvis One growled.

Right now, Elvis Two added.

Por supuesto, she said and when she emerged from the house holding a machete the Elvises retreated to their car, laughing.

Elvis One: We'll be back, vieja.

Elvis Two: Believe us.

Who was that? Beli asked from her bed, her hands clutching at her nonexistent stomach.

No one, La Inca said, putting the machete next to the bed.

The next night, "no one" shot a peephole clean through the front door of the house.

The next couple of nights she and the girl slept under the bed, and a little bit later in the week she told the girl: No matter what happens I want you to remember: your father was a doctor, a *doctor*. And your mother was a nurse.

And finally the words: You should leave.

I want to leave. I hate this place.

The girl by this time could hobble to the latrine under her own power. She was much changed. During the day she would sit by the window in silence, very much like La Inca after her husband drowned. She did not smile, she did not laugh, she talked to no one, not even her friend Dorca. A dark veil had closed over her, like nata over café.

You don't understand, hija. You have to leave *the country*. They'll kill you if you don't.

Beli laughed.

Oh, Beli; not so rashly, not so rashly: What did you know about states or diasporas? What did you know about Nueba Yol or unheated "old law" tenements or children whose self-hate short-circuited their minds? What did you know, madame, about *immigration*? Don't laugh, mi negrita, for your world is about to be changed. Utterly. Yes: a terrible beauty is etc., etc. Take it from me. You laugh because you've been ransacked to the limit of your soul, because your lover betrayed you almost unto death, because your first son was neverborn. You laugh because you have no front teeth and you've sworn never to smile again.

I wish I could say different but I've got it right here on tape. La Inca told you you had to leave the country and you laughed.

End of story.

THE LAST DAYS OF THE REPUBLIC

She would remember little of the final months beyond her anguish and her despair (and her desire to see the Gangster dead). She was in the grips of the Darkness, passed through her days like a shade passes through life. She did not move from the house unless forced; at last they had the relationship La Inca had always longed for, except that they didn't speak. What was there to say? La Inca talked soberly about the trip north, but Beli felt like a good part of her had already disembarked. Santo Domingo was fading. The house, La Inca, the fried yuca she was putting into her mouth were already gone—it was only a matter of allowing the rest of the world to catch up. The only time she felt close to her old sense was when she spotted the Elvises lurking in the neighborhood. She would cry out in mortal fear, but they drove off with smirks on their faces. We'll see you soon. Real soon. At night there were nightmares of the cane, of the Faceless One, but when she awoke from them La Inca was always there. Tranquila, hija. Tranquila.

(Regarding the Elvises: What stayed their hand? Perhaps it was the fear of retribution now that the Trujillato had fallen. Perhaps it was La Inca's power. Perhaps it was that force from the future reaching back to protect the third and final daughter? Who can know?)

La Inca, who I don't think slept a single day during those months. La Inca, who carried a machete with her everywhere. Homegirl was 'bout about it. Knew that when Gondolin falls you don't wait around for the balrogs to tap on your door. You make fucking moves. And make moves she did. Papers were assembled, palms were greased, and permissions secured. In another time it would have been impossible, but with El Jefe dead and the Plátano Curtain shattered all manner of escapes were now possible. La Inca gave Beli photos and letters from the woman she'd be staying with in a place called El Bronx. But none of it reached Beli. She ignored the pictures, left the letters unread, so that when she arrived at Idlewild she would not know who it was she should be looking for. La pobrecita.

Just as the standoff between the Good Neighbor and what remained of Family Trujillo reached the breaking point, Beli was brought before a judge. La Inca made her put ojas de mamón in her shoes so he wouldn't ask too many questions. Homegirl stood through the whole proceedings, numb, drifting. The week before, she and the Gangster had finally managed to meet in one of the first love motels in the capital. The one run by los chinos, about which Luis Díaz sang his famous song. It was not the reunion she had hoped for. Ay, mi pobre negrita, he moaned, stroking her hair. Where once was lightning now there was fat fingers on straight hair. We were betrayed, you and I. Betrayed horribly! She tried to talk about the dead baby but he waved the diminutive ghost away with a flick of his wrist and proceeded to remove her enormous breasts from the vast armature of her bra. We'll have another one, he promised. I'm going to have two, she said quietly. He laughed. We'll have fifty.

The Gangster still had a lot on his mind. He was worried about the fate of the Trujillato, worried that the Cubans were preparing to invade. They shoot people like me in the show trials. I'll be the first person Che looks for.

I'm thinking of going to Nueva York.

She had wanted him to say, No, don't go, or at least to say he would be joining her. But he told her instead about one of his trips to Nueba Yol, a job for the Jefe and how the crab at some *Cuban* restaurant had made him sick. He did not mention his wife, of course, and she did not ask. It would have broken her. Later, when he started coming, she tried to hold on to him, but he wrenched free and came on the dark ruined plain of her back.

Like chalk on a blackboard, the Gangster joked.

She was still thinking about him eighteen days later at the airport.

You don't have to go, La Inca said suddenly, just before the girl stepped into the line. Too late.

I want to.

Her whole life she had tried to be happy, but Santo Domingo . . . FUCKING SANTO DOMINGO had foiled her at every turn. I never want to see it again.

Don't talk that way.

I never want to see it again.

She would be a new person, she vowed. They said no matter how far a mule travels it can never come back a horse, but she would show them all.

Don't leave like this. Toma, for the trip. Dulce de coco.

On the line to passport control she would throw it away but for now she held the jar.

Remember me. La Inca kissed and embraced her. Remember who you are. You are the third and final daughter of the Family Cabral. You are the daughter of a doctor and a nurse.

Last sight of La Inca: waving at her with all her might, crying.

More questions at passport control, and with a last contemptuous flurry of stamps, she was let through. And then the boarding and the preflight chitchat from the natty dude on her right, four rings on his hand—Where are you going? Never-never land, she snapped—and finally the plane, throbbing with engine song, tears itself from the surface of the earth and Beli, not known for her piety, closed her eyes and begged the Lord to protect her.

Poor Beli. Almost until the last she half believed that the Gangster was going to appear and save her. I'm sorry, mi negrita, I'm so sorry, I should never have let you go. (She was still big on dreams of rescue.) She had looked for him everywhere: on the ride to the airport, in the faces of the officials checking passports, even when the plane was boarding, and, finally, for an irrational moment, she thought he would emerge from the cockpit, in a clean-pressed captain's uniform—I tricked you, didn't I? But the Gangster never appeared again in the flesh, only in her dreams. On the plane there were other First Wavers. Many waters waiting to become a river. Here she is, closer now to the mother we will need her to be if we want Oscar and Lola to be born.

She is sixteen and her skin is the darkness before the black, the plum of the day's last light, her breasts like sunsets trapped beneath her skin, but for all her youth and beauty she has a sour distrusting expression that only dissolves under the weight of immense pleasure. Her dreams are spare, lack the propulsion of a mission, her ambition is without traction. Her fiercest hope? That she will find a man. What she doesn't yet know: the cold, the backbreaking drudgery of the factorías, the loneliness of Diaspora, that she will never again live in Santo Domingo, her own heart. What else she doesn't know: that the man next to her would end up being her husband and the father of her two children, that after two years together he would leave her, her third and final heartbreak, and she would never love again.

She awakened just as in her dreams some ciegos were boarding a bus, begging for money, a dream from her Lost Days. The guapo in the seat next to her tapped her elbow.

Señorita, this is not something you'll want to miss.

I've already seen it, she snapped. And then, calming herself, she peered out the window.

It was night and the lights of Nueva York were everywhere.

4

Sentimental Education
1988–1992

It started with me. The year before Oscar fell, I suffered some nuttiness of my own; I got jumped as I was walking home from the Roxy. By this mess of New Brunswick townies. A bunch of fucking morenos. Two a.m., and I was on Joyce Kilmer for no good reason. Alone and on foot. Why? Because I was hard, thought I'd have no problem walking through the thicket of young guns I saw on the corner. Big mistake. Remember the smile on this one dude's face the rest of my fucking life. Only second to his high school ring, which plowed a nice furrow into my cheek (still got the scar). Wish I could say I went down swinging but these cats just laid me out. If it hadn't been for some Samaritan driving by the motherfuckers probably would have killed me. The old guy wanted to take me to Robert Wood Johnson, but I didn't have no medical, and besides, ever since my brother had died of leukemia I hadn't been hot on doctors, so of course I was like: No no no. For having just gotten my ass *kicked* I actually felt pretty good. Until the next day, when I felt like I had died. So dizzy couldn't stand up without puking. My guts feeling like they'd been taken out of me, beaten with mallets, and then reattached with paper clips. It was pretty bad, and of all the friends I had—all my great wonderful friends—only Lola came fucking through. Heard about the beatdown from my boy Melvin and shot over ASAP. Never so happy to see some-one my whole life. Lola, with her big innocent teeth. Lola, who actually *cried* when she saw the state I was in.

She was the one who took care of my sorry ass. Cooked, cleaned, picked up my classwork, got me medicine, even made sure that I showered. In other words, sewed my balls back on, and not any woman can do that for a guy. Believe you me. I could barely stand, my head hurt so bad, but she would wash my back and that was what I remember most about that mess. Her hand on that sponge and that sponge on me. Even though I had a girlfriend, it was Lola who spent those nights with me. Combing her hair out—once, twice, thrice—before folding her long self into bed. No more night-walking, OK, Kung Fu?

At college you're not supposed to care about anything— you're just supposed to fuck around—but believe it or not, I cared about Lola. She was a girl it was easy to care about. Lola like the fucking opposite of the girls I usually macked on: bitch was almost six feet tall and no tetas at all and darker than your darkest grandma. Like two girls in one: the skinni-est upperbody married to a pair of Cadillac hips and an ill donkey. One of those overachiever chicks who run all the or-ganizations in college and wear suits to meetings. Was the president of her sorority, the head of S.A.L.S.A. and co-chair of Take Back the Night. Spoke perfect stuck-up Spanish.

Known each other since pre-fresh weekend, but it wasn't until sophomore year when her mother got sick again that we had our fling. Drive me home, Yunior, was her opening line, and a week later it jumped off. I remember she was wearing a pair of Douglass sweats and a Tribe T-shirt. Took off the ring her boy had given her and then kissed me. Dark eyes never leaving mine.

You have great lips, she said.

How do you forget a girl like that?

Only three fucking nights before she got all guilty about the boyfriend and put an end to it. And when Lola puts an end to something, she puts an end to it *hard*. Even those nights after I got jumped she wouldn't let me steal on her ass for nothing. So you can *sleep* in my bed but you can't sleep *with* me?

Yo soy prieta, Yuni, she said, pero no soy bruta.

Knew exactly what kind of sucio I was. Two days after we broke up saw me hitting on one of her line-sisters and turned her long back to me.

Point is: when her brother lapsed into that killer depression at the end of sophomore year—drank two bottles of 151 because some girl dissed him—almost fucking killing himself and his sick mother in the process, who do you think stepped up?

Me.

Surprised the shit out of Lola when I said I'd live with him the next year. Keep an eye on the fucking dork for you. After the suicide drama nobody in Demarest wanted to room with homeboy, was going to have to spend junior year by himself; no Lola, either, because she was slotted to go abroad to Spain for that year, her big fucking dream finally come true and she was worried shitless about him. Knocked Lola for a loop when I said I'd do it, but it almost killed her dead when I actually did it. Move in with him. In fucking Demarest. Home of all the weirdos and losers and freaks and fem-bots. Me, a guy who could bench 340 pounds, who used to call Demarest Homo Hall like it was nothing. Who never met a little white artist freak he didn't want to smack around. Put in my application for the writing section and by the beginning of September, there we were, me and Oscar. Together.

I liked to play it up as complete philanthropy, but that's not exactly true. Sure I wanted to help Lola out, watch out for her crazy-ass brother (knew he was the only thing she really loved in this world), but I was also taking care of my own damn self. That year I'd pulled what was probably the lowest number in the history of the housing lottery. Was officially the last name on the waiting list, which meant my chances for university housing were zilch to none, which meant that my brokeness was either going to have to live at home or on the street, which meant that Demarest, for all its freakery, and Oscar, for all his unhappiness, didn't seem like so bad an option.

It's not like he was a complete stranger—I mean, he *was* the brother of the girl I'd shadow-fucked. Saw him on campus with her those first couple of years, hard to believe he and Lola were related. (Me Apokolips, he cracked, she New Genesis.) Unlike me, who would have hidden from a Caliban like that, she loved the dork. Invited him to parties and to her rallies. Holding up signs, handing out flyers. Her fat-ass assistant.

To say I'd never in my life met a Dominican like him would be to put it mildly.

Hail, Dog of God, was how he welcomed me my first day in Demarest.

Took a week before I figured out what the hell he meant.

God. Domini. Dog. Canis.

Hail, Dominicanis.

I guess I should have fucking known. Dude used to say he was cursed, used to say this a lot, and if I'd really been old-school Dominican I would have (a) listened to the idiot, and then (b) run the other way. My family are sureños, from Azua, and if we sureños from Azua know anything it's about fucking curses. I mean, Jesus, have you ever seen Azua? My mom wouldn't even have listened, would have just run. She didn't fuck with fukús or guanguas, no way no how. But I wasn't as old-school as I am now, just real fucking dumb, assumed keeping an eye on somebody like Oscar wouldn't be no Herculean chore. I mean, shit, I was a *weight lifter*, picked up bigger fucking piles than him every damn day.

You can start the laugh track anytime you want.

He seemed like the same to me. Still massive—Biggie Smalls minus the smalls—and still lost. Still writing ten, fifteen, twenty pages a day. Still obsessed with his fanboy madness. Do you know what sign fool put up on our dorm door? *Speak, friend, and enter.* In fucking Elvish! (Please don't ask me how I knew this. Please.) When I saw that I said: De León, you gotta be kidding. Elvish?

Actually, he coughed, it's *Sindarin.*

Actually, Melvin said, it's *gay-hay-hay.*

Despite my promises to Lola to watch out, those first couple weeks I didn't have much to do with him. I mean, what can I say? I was busy. What state school player isn't? I had my job and the gym and my boys and my novia and of course I had my slutties.

Out so much that first month that what I saw of O was mostly a big dormant hump crashed out under a sheet. Only thing that kept his nerd ass up late were his role-playing games and his Japanese animation, especially *Akira*, which I think he must have watched at least a thousand times that year. I can't tell you how many nights I came home and caught him parked in front of that movie. I'd bark: You watching this shit again? And Oscar would say, almost as if apologizing for his existence: It's almost over. It's always almost over, I complained. I didn't mind it, though. I liked shit like *Akira*, even if I couldn't always stay awake for it. I'd lay back on my bed while Kaneda screamed *Tetsuo* and the next thing I knew Oscar was standing timidly over me, saying, Yunior, the movie is finis and I would sit up, say, *Fuck!*

Wasn't half as bad as I made it out to be later. For all of his nerdiness, dude was a pretty considerate roommate. I never got stupid little notes from him like the last fucknuts I lived with, and he always paid for his half of shit and if I ever came in during one of his Dungeons & Dragons games he'd relocate to the lounge without even having to be asked. *Akira* I could handle, *Queen of the Demonweb Pits* I could not.

Made my little gestures, of course. A meal once a week. Picked up his writings, five books to date, and tried to read some. Wasn't my cup of tea—*Drop the phaser, Arthurus Prime!*—but even I could tell he had chops. Could write dialogue, crack snappy exposition, keep the narrative moving. Showed him some of my fiction too, all robberies and drug deals and *Fuck you, Nando*, and BLAU! BLAU! BLAU! He gave me four pages of comments for an eight-page story.

Did I try to help him with his girl situation? Share some of my playerly wisdom?

Of course I did. Problem was, when it came to the mujeres my roommate was like no one on the planet. On the one hand, he had the worst case of no-toto-itis I'd ever seen. The last person to even come close was this poor Salvadoran kid I knew in high school who was burned all over his face, couldn't get no girls ever because he looked like the Phantom of the Opera. Well: Oscar had it worse than him. At least Jeffrey could claim an honest medical condition. What could Oscar claim? That it was Sauron's fault? Dude weighed 307 pounds, for fuck's sake! Talked like a *Star Trek* computer! The real irony was that you never met a kid who wanted a girl so fucking bad. I mean, shit, I thought *I* was into females, but no one, and I mean *no one*, was into them the way Oscar was. To him they were the beginning and end, the Alpha and the Omega, the DC and the Marvel. Homes had it *bad*; couldn't so much as see a cute girl without breaking into shakes. Developed crushes out of nothing—must have had at least two dozen high-level ones that first semester alone. Not that any of these shits ever came to anything. How could they? Oscar's idea of G was to talk about role-playing games! How fucking crazy is that? (My favorite was the day on the E bus when he informed some hot morena, If you were in my game I would give you an *eighteen* Charisma!)

I tried to give advice, I really did. Nothing too complicated. Like, Stop hollering at strange girls on the street, and don't bring up the Beyonder any more than necessary. Did he listen? Of course not! Trying to talk sense to Oscar about girls was like trying to throw rocks at Unus the Untouchable. Dude was impenetrable. He'd hear me out and then shrug. Nothing else has any efficacy, I might as well be myself.

But your yourself sucks!

It is, lamentably, all I have.

But my favorite conversation:

Yunior?

What?

Are you awake?

If it's about *Star Trek*—

It's not about *Star Trek*. He coughed. I have heard from a reliable source that no Dominican male has ever died a virgin. You who have experience in these matters—do you think this is true?

I sat up. Dude was peering at me in the dark, dead serious.

O, it's against the laws of nature for a dominicano to die without fucking at least once.

That, he sighed, is what worries me.

So what happens at the beginning of October? What always happens to playboys like me.

I got bopped.

No surprise, given how balls-out I was living. Wasn't just any bop either. My girl Suriyan found out I was messing with one of the hermanas. Players: never never *never* fuck with a bitch named Awilda. Because when she awildas out on your ass you'll know pain for real. The Awilda in question dimed me for fuck knows what reason, actually taped one of my calls to her and before you could say *Oh shit* everybody knew. Homegirl must have played that thing like five hundred times. Second time I'd been caught in two years, a record even for me. Suriyan went absolutely *nuts*. Attacked me on the E bus. The boys laughing and running, and me pretending like I hadn't done anything. Suddenly I was in the dorm a lot. Taking a stab at a story or two. Watching some movies with Oscar. *This Island Earth. Appleseed. Project A.* Casting around for a lifeline.

What I should have done was check myself into Bootie-Rehab. But if you thought I was going to do that, then you don't know Dominican men. Instead of focusing on something hard and useful like, say, my own shit, I focused on something easy and redemptive.

Out of nowhere, and not in the least influenced by my own shitty state—of course not!—I decided that I was going to fix Oscar's life. One night while he was moaning on about his sorry existence I said: Do you really want to change it?

Of course I do, he said, but nothing I've tried has been ameliorative.

I'll change your life.

Really? The look he gave me—still breaks my heart, even after all these years.

Really. You have to listen to me, though.

Oscar scrambled to his feet. Placed his hand over his heart. I swear an oath of obedience, my lord. When do we start?

You'll see.

The next morning, six a.m., I kicked Oscar's bed.

What is it? he cried out.

Nothing much, I said, throwing his sneakers on his stomach. Just the first day of your life.

I really must have been in a dangle over Suriyan—which is why I threw myself something serious into Project Oscar. Those first weeks, while I waited for Suriyan to forgive me, I had fatboy like Master Killer in Shaolin Temple. Was on his ass 24/7. Got him to swear off the walking up to strange girls with his I-love-you craziness. (You're only scaring the poor girls, O.) Got him to start watching his diet and to stop talking crazy negative—*I am ill fated, I am going to perish a virgin, I'm lacking in pulchritude*—at least while I was around, I did. (Positive thoughts, I stressed, positive thoughts, motherfucker!) Even brought him out with me and the boys. Not anything serious— just out for a drink when it was a crowd of us and his monstrousness wouldn't show so much. (The boys hating—What's next? We start inviting out the homeless?)

But my biggest coup of all? I got dude to exercise with me. To fucking *run*.

Goes to show you: O really did look up to me. No one else could have gotten him to do that. The last time he'd tried running had been freshman year, when he'd been fifty pounds lighter. I can't lie: first couple of times I almost laughed, seeing him huffing down George Street, those ashy black knees of his a-shaking. Keeping his head down so he wouldn't have to hear or see all the reactions. Usually just some cackles and a stray *Hey, fat-ass*. The best one I heard? Look, Mom, that guy's taking his planet out for a run.

Don't worry about them jokers, I told him.

No worry, he heaved, *dying*.

Dude was not into it *at all*. As soon as we were through he'd be back at his desk in no time flat. Almost clinging to it. Tried everything he could to weasel out of our runs. Started getting up at five so when I got up he'd already be at his computer, could claim he was in the middle of this amazingly important chapter. Write it later, bitch. After about our fourth run he actually got down on his knees. Please, Yunior, he said, I can't. I snorted. Just go get your fucking shoes.

I knew shit wasn't easy for him. I was callous, but not that callous. I saw how it was. You think people hate a fat person? Try a fat person who's trying to get thin. Brought out the motherfucking balrog in niggers. Sweetest girls you'd ever see would say the vilest shit to him on the street, old ladies would jabber, You're disgusting, *disgusting*, and even Melvin, who'd never shown much in the way of anti-Oscar tendencies, started calling him Jabba the Butt, just because. It was straight-up nuts.

OK, people suck, but what were his options? O had to do

something. Twenty-four/seven at a computer, writing sci-fi monsterpieces, darting out to the Student Center every now and then to play video games, talking about girls but never actually touching one—what kind of life was that? For fuck's sake, we were at Rutgers—Rutgers was just girls everywhere, and there was Oscar, keeping me up at night talking about the Green Lantern. Wondering aloud, If we were orcs, wouldn't we, at a racial level, *imagine* ourselves to look like elves?

Dude had to do *something*.

He did, too.

He quit.

It was a nutty thing really. Four days a week we were running. I put in five miles myself but with him it was just a little every day. Thought he was doing OK, all things considered. Building, you know? And then right in the middle of one of our jogs. Out on George Street, and I looked back over my shoulder, saw that he had stopped. Sweat running down everywhere. Are you having a heart attack? I am not, he said. Then why ain't you running? I've decided to run no more. Why the fuck not? It's not going to work, Yunior. It ain't going to work if you don't want it to work. I know it's not going to work. Come on, Oscar, pick up your goddamn feet. But he shook his head. He tried to squeeze my hand and then walked to the Livingston Ave. stop, took the Double E home. The next morning I prodded him with my foot but he didn't stir.

I will run again no more, he intoned from under his pillow.

I guess I shouldn't have gotten mad. Should have been patient with the herb. But I was *pissed*. Here I was, going the fuck out of my way to help this fucking idiot out, and he was pissing it back in my face. Took this shit real personal.

Three days straight I badgered him about the running and he kept saying, I'd rather not, I'd rather not. For his part he tried to smooth it over. Tried to share his movies and his comic books and to keep up the nerdly banter, tried to go back to how it was before I started the Oscar Redemption Program. But I wasn't having it. Finally dropped the ultimatum. You either run or that's it.

I don't want to do it anymore! I don't! Voice rising.

Stubborn. Like his sister.

Last chance, I said. I was sneakered up and ready to roll, and he was at his desk, pretending not to notice.

He didn't move. I put my hands on him.

Get up!

And that was when he yelled. You leave me alone!

Actually shoved me. I don't think he meant it, but there it was. Both of us astounded. Him trembling, scared sick, me with my fists out, ready to kill. For a second I almost let it go, just a mistake, a mistake, but then I remembered myself.

I pushed him. With both hands. He flew into the wall. Hard.

Dumb, dumb, dumb. Two days later Lola calls from Spain, five o'clock in the morning.

What the fuck is your *problem*, Yunior?

Tired of the whole thing. I said, without thinking, Oh, fuck off, Lola.

Fuck off? The silence of Death. Fuck *you*, Yunior. Don't ever speak to me again.

Say hi to your fiancé for me, I tried to jeer, but she'd already hung up.

Motherfucker, I screamed, throwing the phone into the closet.

And that was that was that was that. The end of our big experiment. He actually did try to apologize a couple of times, in his Oscar way, but I didn't reciprocate. Where before I'd been cool with him, now I just iced him out. No more invitations to dinner or a drink. Acted like roommates act when they're beefing. We were polite and stiff, and where before we would jaw about writing and shit, now I didn't have nothing to say to him. Went back to my own life, back to being the ill sucio. Had this crazy burst of toto-energy. Was being spiteful, I guess. He went back to eating pizzas by the eight-slice and throwing himself kamikaze-style at the girls.

The boys, of course, sensed what was up, that I wasn't protecting the gordo anymore, and swarmed.

I like to think it wasn't *too* bad. The boys didn't slap him around or nothing, didn't steal his shit. But I guess it was pretty heartless any way you slice it. You ever eat toto? Melvin would ask, and Oscar would shake his head, answer decently, no matter how many times Mel asked. Probably the only thing you ain't eaten, right? Harold would say, Tú no eres nada de dominicano, but Oscar would insist unhappily, I am Dominican, I am. It didn't matter what he said. Who the hell, I ask you, had ever met a Domo like him? Halloween he made the mistake of dressing up as Doctor Who, was real proud of his outfit too. When I saw him on Easton, with two other writing-section clowns, I couldn't believe how much he looked like that fat homo Oscar Wilde, and I told him so. You look just like him, which was bad news for Oscar, because Melvin said, Oscar Wao, quién es Oscar Wao, and that was it, all of us started calling him that: Hey, Wao, what you doing? Wao, you want to get your feet off my chair?

And the tragedy? After a couple of weeks dude started *answering* to it.

Fool never got mad when we gave him shit. Just sat there with a confused grin on his face. Made a brother feel bad. A couple times after the others left, I'd say, You know we was just kidding, right, Wao? I know, he said wearily. We cool, I said, thumping him on the shoulder. We cool.

On the days his sister called and I answered the phone I tried to be cheerful, but she wasn't buying. Is my brother there? was all she ever said. Cold as Saturn.

These days I have to ask myself: What made me angrier? That Oscar, the fat loser, quit, or that Oscar, the fat loser, defied me? And I wonder: What hurt him more? That I was never really his friend, or that I pretended to be?

That's all it should have been. Just some fat kid I roomed with my junior year. Nothing more, nothing more. But then Oscar, the dumb-ass, decided to fall in love. And instead of getting him for a year, I got the motherfucker for the rest of my life.

You ever seen that Sargent portrait, *Madame X*? Of course you have. Oscar had that one up on his wall—along with a Robotech poster and the original *Akira* one-sheet, the one with Tetsuo on it and the words NEO TOKYO IS ABOUT TO EXPLODE.

She was drop-dead like that. But she was also fucking crazy.

If you'd lived in Demarest that year, you would have known her: Jenni Muñoz. She was this boricua chick from East Brick City who lived up in the Spanish section. First hard-core goth I'd ever met—in 1990 us niggers were having trouble wrapping our heads around goths, period—but a Puerto Rican goth, that was as strange to us as a black Nazi. Jenni was her real name, but all her little goth buddies called her La Jablesse, and every standard a dude like me had, this diabla short-circuited. Girl was *luminous*. Beautiful jíbara skin, diamond-sharp features, wore her hair in this super-black Egypto-cut, her eyes caked in eyeliner, her lips painted black, had the biggest roundest tits you've ever seen. Every day Halloween for this girl, and on actual Halloween she dressed up as—you guessed it—a dominatrix, had one of the gay guys in the music section on a leash. Never seen a body like that, though. Even I was hot for Jenni first semester, but the one time I'd tried to mack on her at the Douglass Library she laughed at me, and when I said, Don't laugh at me, she asked: Why not?

Fucking bitch.

So, anyway, guess who decided that she was the love of his life? Who fell head over heels for her because he heard her playing Joy Division up in her room and, surprise, he loved Joy Division too? Oscar, of course. At first, dude just stared at her from afar and moaned about her "ineffable perfection." Out of your league, I snarked, but he shrugged, talked to the computer screen: Everybody's out of my league. Didn't think nothing of it until a week later when I caught him putting a move on her in Brower Commons! I was with the boys, listening to them grouse about the Knicks, watching Oscar and La Jablesse on the hot-food line, waiting for the moment she told him off, figured if I'd gotten roasted she was going to *vaporize* his ass. Of course he was full on, doing his usual *Battle of the Planets* routine, talking a mile a minute, sweat running down his face, and homegirl was holding her tray and looking at him askance—not many girls can do askance and keep their cheese fries from plunging off their trays, but this was why niggers were crazy about La Jablesse. She started walking away and Oscar yelled out superloud, We'll talk anon! And she shot back a *Sure*, all larded with sarcasm.

I waved him over. So how'd it go, Romeo?

He looked down at his hands. I think I may be in love.

How can you be in love? You just met the bitch.

Don't call her a bitch, he said darkly.

Yeah, Melvin imitated, don't call her a bitch.

You have to give it to Oscar. He didn't let up. He just kept hitting on her with absolutely no regard for self. In the halls, in front of the bathroom door, in the dining hall, on the buses, dude became *ubiquitous*. Pinned comic books to her door, for Christ's sake.

In my universe, when a dork like Oscar pushes up on a girl like Jenni, he usually gets bounced faster than your tía Daisy's rent checks, but Jenni must have had brain damage or been really into fat loser nerdboys, because by the end of February she was actually treating him all civil and shit. Before I could wrap my brain around that one I saw them hanging out together! In public! I couldn't believe my fucking eyes. And then came the day when I returned from my creative-writing class and found La Jablesse and Oscar sitting in our room. They were just talking, about Alice Walker, but still. Oscar looking like he'd just been asked to join the Jedi Order; Jenni smiling beautiful. And me? I was speechless. Jenni remembered me, all right. Looked at me with her cute smirking eyes and said, You want me to get off your bed? Her Jersey accent enough to knock the guff clean out of me.

Nah, I said. Picked up my gym bag and bolted like a bitch.

When I got back from the weight room Oscar was at his computer—on page a billion of his new novel.

I said, So, what's up with you and Scarypants?

Nothing.

What the hell you two talk about?

Items of little note. Something about his tone made me realize that he knew about her scorching me. The fucker. I said, Well, good luck, Wao. I just hope she doesn't sacrifice you to Beelzebub or anything.

———————

All March they hung out. I tried not to pay attention, but we were all in the same dorm so it was hard not to. Later, Lola would tell me that the two of them even started going to movies together. They saw *Ghost* and this other terrible piece of ass called *Hardware*. Went to Franklin Diner afterward, where Oscar tried his best not to eat for three. I wasn't around for most of this nonsense; I was out chasing the pussy and delivering pool tables and out with the boys on the weekends. Did it kill me that he was spending time with such a fly bitch? Of course it did. I always thought of myself as the Kaneda of our dyad, but here I was playing Tetsuo.

Jenni really put it on for Oscar. Liked to walk arm in arm with him, and hug him every chance she got. Oscar's adoration like the light of a new sun. Being the center of a Universe something that suited her. She read him all her poetry (Thou art the muse of the muses, I heard him say) and showed him her little dumb sketches (which he fucking hung on our door) and told him all about her life (which he dutifully noted in his journal). Living with an aunt because her mom moved to Puerto Rico to be with her new husband when she was seven. Spent from eleven on up making runs into the Village. Lived in a squat the year before she came to college, the Crystal Palace, it was called.

Was I really reading my roommate's journal behind his back? Of course I was.

Oh, but you should have seen the O. He was like I'd never seen him, love the transformer. Started dressing up more, ironing his shirts every morning. Dug this wooden samurai sword out of his closet and in the early morning stood out on the lawn of Demarest, bare-chested, slicing down a billion imaginary foes. Even started running again! Well, jogging. Oh, *now* you can run, I carped, and he saluted me with a brisk upsweep of his hand as he struggled past.

I should have been happy for the Wao. I mean, honestly, who was I to begrudge Oscar a little action? Me, who was fucking with not one, not two, but three fine-ass bitches *at the same time* and that wasn't even counting the side-sluts I scooped at the parties and the clubs; me, who had pussy coming out my ears? But of course I begrudged the mother-fucker. A heart like mine, which never got any kind of affection growing up, is terrible above all things. Was then, is now. Instead of encouraging him, I scowled when I saw him with La Jablesse; instead of sharing my women wisdom I told him to watch himself—in other words I was a player-hater.

Me, the biggest player of them all.

I shouldn't have wasted the energy. Jenni always had boys after her. Oscar only a lull in the action, and one day I saw her out on the Demarest lawn talking to the tall punk kid who used to hang around Demarest, wasn't a resident, crashed with whatever girl would let him. Thin as Lou Reed, and as arrogant. He was showing her a yoga thing and she was laughing. Not two days later I found Oscar in his bed crying. Yo, homes, I said, fingering my weight belt. What the hell is the matter with you?

Leave me alone, he lowed.

Did she diss you? She dissed you, didn't she?

Leave me alone, he yelled. LEAVE. ME. ALONE.

Figured it would be like always. A week of mooning and then back to the writing. The thing that carried him. But it wasn't like always. I knew something was wrong when he stopped writing—Oscar never stopped writing—loved writing the way I loved cheating—just lay in bed and stared at the SDF-1. Ten days of him all fucked up, of him saying shit like, I dream about oblivion like other people dream of good sex, got me a little worried. So I copied his sister's number in Madrid and called her on the sly. Took me like a half-dozen tries and two million *vales* before I got through.

What do you want?

Don't hang up, Lola. It's about Oscar.

She called him that night, asked him what was going on, and of course he told her. Even though I was sitting right there.

Mister, she commanded, you need to let it *go*.

I can't, he whimpered. My heart is overthrown.

You have to, and so on, until at the end of two hours he promised her that he would try.

Come on, Oscar, I said after giving him twenty minutes to stew. Let's go play some video games.

He shook his head, unmoved. I will play Street Fighter no more.

Well? I said to Lola later on the phone.

I don't know, she said. He gets like this sometimes.

What do you want me to do?

Just watch him for me, OK?

Never got the chance. Two weeks later, La Jablesse gave

Oscar the coup de friendship: he walked in on her while she was "entertaining" the punk, caught them both naked, probably covered with blood or something, and before she could even say, Get out, he went berserk. Called her a whore and attacked her walls, tearing down her posters and throwing her books everywhere. I found out because some whitegirl ran up and said, Excuse me, but your stupid roommate is going insane, and I had to bolt upstairs and put him in a headlock. Oscar, I hollered, calm down, calm *down*. Leave me the fuck *alone*, he shrieked, trying to stomp down on my feet.

It was pretty horrible. As for punkboy, apparently dude jumped right out the window and ran all the way to George Street. Buttnaked.

That was Demarest for you. Never a dull fucking moment.

To make a long story short, he had to attend counseling to keep from losing his housing, couldn't go to the second floor for nothing; but now everybody in the dorm thought he was some kind of major psycho. The girls especially stayed away from him. As for La Jablesse, she was graduating that year, so a month later they relocated her to the river dorms and called it even. I didn't really see her again except once while I was on the bus and she was out on the street, walking into Scott Hall with these dominatrix boots.

And that's how our year ended. Him vacated of hope and tapping at the computer, me being asked in the hall how I liked dorming with Mr. Crazyman, and me asking back how their ass would like dorming with my foot? A lame couple of weeks. When it came time to re-up at the dorm, me and O didn't even talk about it. My boys were still stuck in their moms' cribs so I had to take my chances with the lottery again and this time I hit the fucking jackpot, ended up with a single in Frelinghuysen. When I told Oscar that I was leaving Demarest he pulled himself out of his depression long enough to look astounded, like he was expecting something else. I figured—I stammered, but before I could say another word, he said, It's OK, and then, as I was turning away he grabbed my hand and shook it very formally: Sir, it's been an honor.

Oscar, I said.

People asked me, Did you see the signs? Did you? Maybe I did and just didn't want to think about it. Maybe I didn't. What the fuck does it really matter? All I knew was that I'd never seen him more unhappy, but there was a part of me that didn't care. That wanted out of there the same way I had wanted out of my hometown.

On our last night as roommates Oscar housed two bottles of orange Cisco I had bought him. You remember Cisco? Liquid crack, they used to call it. So you know Mr. Lightweight was *fucked up*.

To my virginity! Oscar shouted.

Oscar, cool it, bro. People don't want to hear about all that.

You're right, they just want to *stare* at me.

Come on, tranquilísate.

He slumped. I'm copacetic.

You ain't pathetic.

I said *copacetic*. Everybody, he shook his head, misapprehends me.

All the posters and books were packed and it could have been the first day again if it hadn't been for how unhappy he was. On the real first day he'd been excited, kept calling me by my full name until I told him, It's Yunior, Oscar. Just Yunior.

I guess I knew I should have stayed with him. Should have sat my ass in that chair and told him that shit was going to be cool, but it was our last night and I was fucking tired of him. I wanted to fuck silly this Indian girl I had on Douglass, smoke a joint, and then go to bed.

Fare thee well, he said as I left. Fare thee well!

What he did was this: drank a third bottle of Cisco and then walked unsteadily down to the New Brunswick train station. With its crumbling façade and a long curve of track that shoots high over the Raritan. Even in the middle of the night, doesn't take much to get into the station or to walk out onto the tracks, which is exactly what he did. Stumbled out toward the river, toward Route 18. New Brunswick falling away beneath him until he was seventy-seven feet in the air. Seventy-seven feet precisely. From what he would later recall, he stood on that bridge for a good long time. Watching the streaking lights of the traffic below. Reviewing his miserable life. Wishing he'd been born in a different body. Regretting all the books he would never write. Maybe trying to get himself to reconsider. And then the 4:12 express to Washington blew in the distance. By then he was barely able to stand.

Closed his eyes (or maybe he didn't) and when he opened them there was something straight out of Ursula Le Guin standing by his side. Later, when he would describe it, he would call it the Golden Mongoose, but even he knew that wasn't what it was. It was very placid, very beautiful. Gold-limned eyes that reached through you, not so much in judgment or reproach but for something far scarier. They stared at each other—it serene as a Buddhist, he in total disbelief—and then the whistle blew again and his eyes snapped open (or closed) and it was gone.

Dude had been waiting his whole life for something just like this to happen to him, had always wanted to live in a world of magic and mystery, but instead of taking note of the vision and changing his ways the fuck just shook his swollen head. The train was nearer now, and so, before he could lose his courage, he threw himself down into the darkness.

He had left me a note, of course. (And behind it a letter each for his sister, his mother, and Jenni.) He thanked me for everything. He told me I could have his books, his games, his movies, his special dro's. He told me he was happy to have been friends. He signed off: Your Compañero, Oscar Wao.

If he'd landed on Route 18, as planned, it would have been lights out forever. But in his drunken confusion he must have miscalculated, or maybe, as his mother claims, he was being watched from up on high, because the dude missed 18 proper and landed on the divider! Which should have been fine. Those dividers on 18 are like concrete guillotines. Would have done him lovely. Burst him into intestinal confetti. Except that this one was one of those garden dividers that they plant shrubs on and he hit the freshly tilled loam and not the concrete. Instead of finding himself in nerd heaven—where every nerd gets fifty-eight virgins to role-play with—he woke up in Robert Wood Johnson with two broken legs and a separated shoulder, feeling like, well, he'd jumped off the New Brunswick train bridge.

I was there, of course, with his mother and his thuggish uncle, who took regular bathroom breaks to snort up.

He saw us and what did the idiot do? He turned his head and cried.

His mother tapped him on his good shoulder. You'll be doing a lot more than crying when I get through with you.

A day later Lola arrived from Madrid. Didn't have a chance even to say a word before her mother launched into the standard Dominican welcome. So now you come, now that your brother's dying. If I'd known that's what it would take I would have killed myself a long time ago.

Ignored her, ignored me. Sat next to her brother, took his hand.

Mister, she said, are you OK?

Shook his head: *No.*

It's been a long long time, but when I think of her I still see her at the hospital on that first day, straight from Newark airport, dark rings around her eyes, her hair as tangled as a maenad, and yet she still had taken the time, before appearing, to put on some lipstick and makeup.

I was hoping for some good energy—even at the hospital, trying to get ass—but she blew me up instead. Why didn't you take care of Oscar? she demanded. Why didn't you do it?

Four days later they took him home. And I went back to my life too. Headed home to my lonely mother and to tore-up London Terrace. I guess if I'd been a real pal I would have visited him up in Paterson like every week, but I didn't. What can I tell you? It was fucking summer and I was chasing down a couple of new girls, and besides I had the job. Wasn't enough time, but what there really wasn't enough of was *ganas*. I did manage to call him a couple of times to check up on him. Even that was a lot because I kept expecting his mother or sister to tell me that he was gone. But no, he claimed he was "regenerated." No more suicide attempts for him. He was writing a lot, which was always a good sign. I'm going to be the Dominican Tolkien, he said.

Only once did I drop in, and that was because I was in P-town visiting one of my sucias. Not part of the plan, but then I just spun the wheel, pulled up to a gas station, made the call, and the next thing I knew I was at the house where he had grown up. His mother too sick to come out of her room, and him looking as thin as I'd ever seen him. Suicide suits me, he joked. His room nerdier than him, if that was possible. X-wings and TIE-fighters hanging from the ceilings. Mine and his sister's signatures the only real ones on his last cast (the right leg broken worse than the left); the rest were thoughtful consolations from Robert Heinlein, Isaac Asimov, Frank Herbert, and Samuel Delany. His sister not acknowledging my presence, so I laughed when she walked by the open door, asked loudly: How's la muda doing?

She hates being here, Oscar said.

What's wrong with Paterson? I asked loudly. Hey, muda, what's wrong with Paterson?

Everything, she yelled from down the hall. She was wearing these little running shorts—the sight of her leg muscles jiggling alone made the trip worth making.

Me and Oscar sat in his room for a little bit, not saying much. I stared at all his books and his games. Waited for him to say something; must have known I wasn't going to let it slide.

It was foolish, he said finally. Ill advised.

You could say that twice. What the fuck were you thinking, O?

He shrugged miserably. I didn't know what else to do.

Dude, you don't want to be dead. Take it from me. No-pussy is bad. But dead is like no-pussy times ten.

It went like that for about half an hour. Only one thing sticks out. Right before I headed out, he said: It was the curse that made me do it, you know.

I don't believe in that shit, Oscar. That's our parents' shit.

It's ours too, he said.

Is he going to be OK? I asked Lola on the way out.

I think so, she said. Filling ice-cube trays with faucet water. He says he's going back to Demarest in the spring.

Is that a good idea?

She thought about it a second. That was Lola for you. I do, she said.

You know best. I fished my keys out. So how's the fiancé?

He's fine, she said blandly. Are you and Suriyan still together?

Killed to even hear her name. Not for a long time.

And then we stood there and stared at each other.

In a better world I would have kissed her over the ice trays and that would have been the end of all our troubles. But you know exactly what kind of world we live in. It ain't no fucking Middle-earth. I just nodded my head, said, See you around, Lola, and drove home.

That should have been the end of it, right? Just a memory of some nerd I once knew who tried to kill himself, nothing more, nothing more. But the de Leóns, it turned out, weren't a clan you could just shake off.

Not two weeks into senior year he showed up at my dorm room! To bring over his writings and to ask me about mine! I couldn't believe it. Last I heard he was planning on subbing at his old high school, taking classes over at BCC, but there he was, standing at my door, sheepishly holding a blue folder. Hail and well met, Yunior, he said. Oscar, I said, in disbelief. He had lost even more weight and was trying his best to keep his hair trim and his face shaved. He looked, if you can believe it, good. Still talking Space Opera, though—had just finished with the first of his projected quartet of novels, totally obsessed with it now. May be the death of me, he sighed, and then he caught himself. Sorry. Of course nobody at Demarest wanted to room with him—what a surprise (we all know how tolerant the tolerant are)—so when he returned in the spring he'd have a double to himself, not that it did him any good, he joked.

Demarest won't be the same without your mesomorphic grimness, he said matter-of-factly.

Ha, I said.

You should definitely visit me in Paterson when you have a reprieve. I have a plethora of new Japanimation for your viewing pleasure.

Definitely, bro, I said. Definitely.

I never did go by. I was busy, God's Truth: delivering pool tables, bringing the grades up, getting ready to graduate. And besides, that fall a miracle happened: Suriyan showed up at my door. Looking more beautiful than I ever saw her. I want us to try again. Of course I said yes, and went out and put a cuerno in her that very night. Dios mío! Some niggers couldn't have gotten ass on Judgment Day; me I couldn't not get ass, even when I tried.

My negligence didn't stop O from visiting me every now and then with some new chapter and some new story of a girl he'd spotted on the bus, on the street, or in a class.

Same ole Oscar, I said.

Yes, he said weakly. Same ole me.

Rutgers was always a crazy place, but that last fall it seemed to be especially bugging. In October a bunch of freshman girls I knew on Livingston got busted for dealing coke, four of the quietest gorditas around. Like they say: los que menos corren, vuelan. On Bush, the Lambdas started a fight with the Alphas over some idiocy and for weeks there was talk of a black-Latino war but nothing ever happened, everybody too busy throwing parties and fucking each other to scrap.

That winter I even managed to sit in my dorm room long enough to write a story that wasn't too bad, about the woman who used to live in the patio behind my house in the DR, a woman everybody said was a prostitute but who used to watch me and my brother while my mom and my abuelo were at work. My professor couldn't believe it. I'm impressed. Not a single shooting or stabbing in the whole story. Not that it helped any. I didn't win any of the creative-writing prizes that year. I kinda had been hoping.

And then it was finals, and who of all people do I end up running into? Lola! I almost didn't recognize her because her hair was ill long and because she was wearing these cheap blocky glasses, the kind an alternative whitegirl would wear. Enough silver on her wrists to ransom the royal family and so much leg coming out of her denim skirt it just didn't seem fair. As soon as she saw me she tugged down the skirt, not like it did much good. This was on the E bus; I was on my way back from seeing a girl of zero note and she was heading out to some stupid-ass farewell party for one of her friends. I slopped down next to her and she said, What's up? Her eyes so incredibly big and empty of any guile. Or expectation, for that matter.

How have you been? I asked.

Good. How about you?

Just getting ready for break.

Merry Christmas. And then, just like a de León, she went back to reading her book!

I poked at the book. Introduction to Japanese. What the hell are you studying now? Didn't they throw you out of here already?

I'm teaching English in Japan next year, she said matter-of-factly. It's going to be *amazing*.

Not *I'm thinking about* or *I've applied* but *I am*. Japan? I laughed, a little mean. What the hell is a Dominican going out to Japan for?

You're right, she said, turning the page irritably. Why would *anyone* want to go *anywhere* when they have *New Jersey*?

We let that sit for a sec.

That was a little harsh, I said.

My apologies.

Like I said: it was December. My Indian girl, Lily, was waiting for me back on College Ave., and so was Suriyan. But I wasn't thinking about either of them. I was thinking about the one time I'd seen Lola that year; she'd been reading a book in front of the Henderson Chapel with such concentration I thought she might hurt herself. I'd heard from Oscar that she was living in Edison with some of her girlfriends, working at some office or another, saving money for her next big adventure. That day I'd seen her I'd wanted to say hi but I didn't have the balls, figured she would ig me.

I watched Commercial Ave. slide past and there, in the distance, were the lights of Route 18. That was one of those moments that would always be Rutgers for me. The girls in front giggling about some guy. Her hands on those pages, nails all painted up in cranberry. My own hands like monster crabs. In a couple of months I'd be back in London Terrace if I wasn't careful and she'd be off to Tokyo or Kyoto or wherever she was going. Of all the chicks I'd run up on at Rutgers, of all the chicks I'd run up on ever, Lola was the one I'd never gotten a handle on. So why did it feel like she was the one who knew me best? I thought about Suriyan and how she would never talk to me again. I thought about my own fears of actually being good, because Lola wasn't Suriyan; with her I'd have to be someone I'd never tried to be. We were reaching College Ave. Last chance, so I made like Oscar and said, Have dinner with me, Lola. I promise, I won't try to take your panties off.

Yeah right, she said, almost ripping her page in the turning.

I covered her hand in mine and she gave me this frustrated heart-wrenching look like she was already on her way down with me and didn't, for the life of her, understand why.

It's OK, I said.

No, it's fucking not OK. You're too *short*. But she didn't take her hand away.

We went to her place on Handy and before I could really put a hurt on her she stopped everything, dragged me up from her toto by my ears. Why is this the face I can't seem to forget, even now, after all these years? Tired from working, swollen from lack of sleep, a crazy mixture of ferocity and vulnerability that was and shall ever be Lola.

She looked at me until I couldn't stand it anymore and then she said: Just don't lie to me, Yunior.

I won't, I promised.

Don't laugh. My intentions were pure.

Not much more to tell. Except this:

That spring I moved back in with him. Thought about it all winter. Even at the very end I almost changed my mind. Was waiting by his door in Demarest and despite the fact that I'd been waiting all morning, at the very end I still almost ran off, but then I heard their voices on the stairwell, bringing up his things.

I don't know who was more surprised: Oscar, Lola, or me.

In Oscar's version, I raised my hand and said, *Mellon.* Took him a second to recognize the word.

Mellon, he said finally.

That fall after the Fall was dark (I read in his journal): dark. He was still thinking about doing it but he was afraid. Of his sister mainly, but also of himself. Of the possibility of a miracle, of an invincible summer. Reading and writing and watching TV with his mother. If you try anything stupid, his mother swore, I'll haunt you my whole life. You better believe it.

I do, señora, he reported saying. I do.

Those months he couldn't sleep, and that's how he ended up taking his mother's car out for midnight spins. Every time he pulled out of the house he thought it would be his last. Drove everywhere. Got lost in Camden. Found the neighborhood where I grew up. Drove through New Brunswick just when the clubs were getting out, looking at everybody, his stomach killing him. Even made it down to Wildwood. Looked for the coffee shop where he had saved Lola, but it had closed. Nothing had opened to replace it. One night he picked up a hitchhiker. An immensely pregnant girl. She barely spoke any English. Was a wetback Guatemalan with pits in her cheek. Needed to go to Perth Amboy, and Oscar, our hero, said: No te preocupes. Te traigo.

Que Dios te bendiga, she said. Still looking ready to jump out of a window if need be.

Gave her his number, Just in case, but she never called. He wasn't surprised.

Drove so long and so far on some nights that he would actually fall asleep at the wheel. One second he was thinking about his characters and the next he'd be drifting, a beautiful intoxicating richness, about to go all the way under and then some last alarm would sound.

Lola.

Nothing more exhilarating (he wrote) than saving yourself by the simple act of waking.

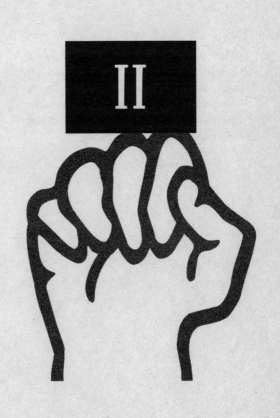

Men are not indispensable. But Trujillo is irreplaceable. For Trujillo is not a man. He is . . . a cosmic force. . . . Those who try to compare him to his ordinary contemporaries are mistaken. He belongs to . . . the category of those born to a special destiny.

La Nación

Of course I tried once more. It was even stupider than the first time. Fourteen months and Abuela announced that it was time for me to return to Paterson, to my mother, I couldn't believe what she was saying. It felt like the deepest of treacheries to me. I wouldn't feel that again until I broke with you.

But I don't want to go! I protested. I want to stay here!

But she wouldn't listen. She held her hands in the air like there was nothing she could do. It's what your mother wants and it's what I want and it's what's right.

But what about me!

I'm sorry, hija.

That's life for you. All the happiness you gather to yourself, it will sweep away like it's nothing. If you ask me I don't think there are any such things as curses. I think there is only life. That's enough.

I wasn't mature. I quit the team. I stopped going to classes and speaking to all my girlfriends, even Rosío. I told Max that we were through and he looked at me like I'd just shot him between the eyes. He tried to stop me from walking away but I screamed at him, like my mother screams, and he dropped his hand like it was dead. I thought I was doing him a favor. Not wanting to hurt him any more than was necessary.

I ended up being really stupid those last weeks. I guess I wanted to disappear more than anything and so I was trying to make it so. I fooled around with someone else, that's how messed up I was. He was the father of one of my classmates. Always after me, even when his daughter was around, so I called him. One thing you can count on in Santo Domingo. Not the lights, not the law.

Sex.

That never goes away.

I didn't bother with the romance. I let him take me to a love motel on our first "date." He was one of those vain politicos, a peledeísta, had his own big air-conditioned jípeta. When I pulled my pants down you never saw anybody so happy.

Until I asked him for two thousand dollars. American, I emphasized.

It's like Abuela says: Every snake always thinks it's biting into a rat until the day it bites into a mongoose.

That was my big puta moment. I knew he had the money, otherwise I wouldn't have asked, and it's not like I was robbing from him. I think we did it like nine times in total, so in my opinion he got a lot more than he gave. Afterward I sat in the motel and drank rum while he snorted from these little bags of coke. He wasn't much of a talker, which was good. He was always pretty ashamed of himself after we fucked and that made me feel great. Complained that this was the money for his daughter's school. Blahblahblah. Steal it from the state, I told him with a smile. I kissed him when he dropped me off at the house only so that I could feel him shrink from me.

I didn't talk to La Inca much those last weeks but she never stopped talking to me. I want you to do well at school. I want you to visit me when you can. I want you to remember where you come from. She prepared everything for my departure. I was too angry to think about her, how sad she would be when I was gone. I was the last person to share her life since my mother. She started closing up the house like she was the one who was leaving.

What? I said. You coming with me?

No, hija. I'm going to my campo for a while.

But you hate the campo!

I have to go there, she explained wearily. If only for a little while.

And then Oscar called, out of the blue. Trying to make up now that I was due back. So you're coming home.

Don't count on it, I said.

Don't do anything precipitous.

Don't do anything precipitous. I laughed. Do you ever hear yourself, Oscar?

He sighed. All the time.

Every morning I would wake up and make sure the money was still under my bed. Two thousand dollars in those days could have taken you anywhere, and of course I was thinking Japan or Goa, which one of the girls at school had told me about. Another island but very beautiful, she assured us. Nothing like Santo Domingo.

And then, finally, she came. She never did anything quiet, my mother. She pulled up in a big black town car, not a normal taxi, and all the kids in the barrio gathered around to see what the show was about. My mother pretending not to notice the crowd. The driver of course was trying to pick her up. She looked thin and worn out and I couldn't believe the taxista.

Leave her alone, I said. Don't you have any shame?

My mother shook her head sadly, looked at La Inca. You didn't teach her anything.

La Inca didn't blink. I taught her as well as I could.

And then the big moment, the one every daughter dreads. My mother looking me over. I'd never been in better shape, never felt more beautiful and desirable in my life, and what does the bitch say?

Coño, pero tú sí eres fea.

Those fourteen months—gone. Like they'd never happened.

Now that I'm a mother myself I realize that she could not have been any different. That's who she was. Like they say: Plátano maduro no se vuelve verde. Even at the end she refused to show me anything close to love. She cried not for me or for herself but only for Oscar. Mi pobre, hijo, she sobbed. Mi pobre, hijo. You always think with your parents that at least at the very end something will change, something will get better. Not for us.

———

I probably would have run. I would have waited until we got back to the States, waited like paja de arroz, burning slow, slow, until they dropped their guard and then one morning I would have disappeared. Like my father disappeared on my mother and was never seen again. Disappeared like everything disappears. Without a trace. I would have lived far away. I would have been happy, I'm sure of it, and I would never have had any children. I would let myself grow dark in the sun, no more hiding from it, let my hair indulge in all its kinks, and she would have passed me on the street and never recognized me. That was the dream I had. But if these years have taught me anything it is this: you can never run away. Not ever. The only way out is in.

And that's what I guess these stories are all about.

Yes, no doubt about it: I would have run. La Inca or not, I would have run.

But then Max died.

I hadn't seen him at all. Not since the day of our breakup. My poor Max, who loved me beyond words. Who said *I'm so lucky* every time we fucked. It was not like we were in the same circles or the same neighborhood. Sometimes when the peledista drove me to the moteles I could swear that I saw Max zipping through the horrendous traffic of the midday, a film reel under his arm (I tried to get him to buy a backpack but he said he liked it his way). My brave Max, who could slip between two bumpers the way a lie can slide between a person's teeth.

What happened was that one day he miscalculated—

heartbroken, I'm sure—and ended up being mashed between a bus bound for the Cibao and one bound for Baní. His skull shattering in a million little pieces, the film unspooling across the entire street.

I only heard about it after they buried him. His sister called me.

He loved you best of all, she sobbed. Best of all.

The curse, some of you will say.

Life, is what I say. Life.

You never saw anybody go so quiet. I gave his mother the money I'd taken from the peledista. His little brother Maxim used it to buy a yola to Puerto Rico and last I heard he was doing good for himself there. He owned a little store and his mother no longer lives in Los Tres Brazos. My toto good for something after all.

I will love you always, my abuela said at the airport. And then she turned away.

It was only when I got on the plane that I started crying. I know this sounds ridiculous but I don't think I really stopped until I met you. I know I didn't stop atoning. The other passengers must have thought I was crazy. I kept expecting my mother to hit me, to call me an idiota, a bruta, a fea, a malcriada, to change seats, but she didn't.

She put her hand on mine and left it there. When the woman in front turned around and said: Tell that girl of yours to be quiet, she said, Tell that culo of yours to stop stinking.

I felt sorriest for the viejo next to us. You could tell he'd been visiting his family. He had on a little fedora and his best pressed chacabana. It's OK, muchacha, he said, patting my back. Santo Domingo will always be there. It was there in the beginning and it will be there at the end.

For God's sake, my mother muttered, and then closed her eyes and went to sleep.

5

Poor Abelard
1944–1946

THE FAMOUS DOCTOR

When the family talks about it at all—which is like never—they always begin in the same place: with Abelard and the Bad Thing he said about Trujillo.[22]

Abelard Luis Cabral was Oscar and Lola's grandfather, a surgeon who had studied in Mexico City in the Lázaro Cárdenas years and in the mid-1940s, before any of us were even born, a man of considerable standing in La Vega. Un hombre muy serio, muy educado y muy bien plantado.

(You can already see where this is headed.)

In those long-ago days—before delincuencia and bank failures, before Diaspora—the Cabrals were numbered among

---

22. There are other beginnings certainly, better ones, to be sure—if you ask me I would have started when the Spaniards "discovered" the New World—or when the U.S. invaded Santo Domingo in 1916—but if this was the opening that the de Leóns chose for themselves, then who am I to question their historiography?

the High of the Land. They were not as filthy-rich or as historically significant as the Ral Cabrals of Santiago, but they
weren't too shabby a cadet branch, either. In La Vega, where
the family had lived since 1791, they were practically royalty, as
much a landmark as La Casa Amarilla and the Río Camú;
neighbors spoke of the fourteen-room house that Abelard's
father had built, Casa Hatüey,[23] a rambling oft-expanded villa
eclectic whose original stone core had been transformed into
Abelard's study, a house bounded by groves of almonds and
dwarf mangos; there was also the modern Art Deco apartment in Santiago, where Abelard often spent his weekends
attending the family businesses; the freshly refurbished stables that could have comfortably billeted a dozen horses; the
horses themselves: six Berbers with skin like vellum; and of
course the five full-time servants (of the rayano variety).
While the rest of the country in that period subsisted on
rocks and scraps of yuca and were host to endless coils of intestinal worms, the Cabrals dined on pastas and sweet Italian
sausages, scraped Jalisco silver on flatware from Beleek. A
surgeon's income was a fine thing but Abelard's portfolio (if

23. Hatüey, in case you've forgotten, was the Taino Ho Chi Minh. When
the Spaniards were committing First Genocide in the Dominican Republic, Hatüey left the Island and canoed to Cuba, looking for reinforcements,
his voyage a precursor to the trip Máximo Gómez would take almost three
hundred years later. Casa Hatüey was named Hatüey because in Times
Past it supposedly had been owned by a descendant of the priest who tried
to baptize Hatüey right before the Spaniards burned him at the stake.
(What Hatüey said on that pyre is a legend in itself: Are there white people in Heaven? Then I'd rather go to Hell.) History, however, has not been
kind to Hatüey. Unless something changes ASAP he will go out like his
camarada Crazy Horse. Coffled to a beer, in a country not his own.

such things existed in those days) was the real source of the family wealth: from his hateful, cantankerous father (now dead) Abelard had inherited a pair of prosperous supermercados in Santiago, a cement factory, and titles to a string of fincas in the Septrionales.

The Cabrals were, as you might have guessed, members of the Fortunate People. Summers they "borrowed" a cousin's cabaña in Puerto Plata and decamped there for a period of no less than three weeks. Abelard's two daughters, Jacquelyn and Astrid, swam and played in the surf (often suffering Mulatto Pigment Degradation Disorder, a.k.a. tans) under the watchful gaze of their mother, who, unable to risk no extra darkness, remained chained to her umbrella's shadow—while their father, when not listening to the news from the War, roamed the shoreline, his face set in tense concentration. He walked barefoot, stripped down to his white shirt and his vest, his pant legs rolled, his demi-afro an avuncular torch, plump with middle age. Sometimes a fragment of a shell or a dying horseshoe crab would catch Abelard's attention and he'd get down on all fours and examine it with a gem-cutter's glass so that to both his delighted daughters, as well as to his appalled wife, he resembled a dog sniffing a turd.

There are still those in the Cibao who remember Abelard, and all will tell you that besides being a brilliant doctor he possessed one of the most remarkable minds in the country: indefatigably curious, alarmingly prodigious, and especially suited for linguistic and computational complexity. The viejo was widely read in Spanish, English, French, Latin, and Greek; a collector of rare books, an advocate of outlandish abstractions, a contributor to the *Journal of Tropical Medicine*, and an amateur ethnographer in the Fernando Ortíz mode. Abelard was, in short, a Brain—not entirely uncommon in the México where he had studied but an exceedingly rare species on the Island of Supreme General Rafael Leónidas Trujillo Molina. He encouraged his daughters to read and prepared them to follow him into the Profession (they could speak French and read Latin before they were nine), and so keen was he about learning that any new piece of knowledge, no matter how arcane or trivial, could send his ass over the Van Allen belt. His parlor, so tastefully wallpapered by his father's second wife, was hangout number one for the local todologos. Discussions would rage for entire evenings, and while Abelard was often frustrated by the poor quality— nothing like at the UNAM—he would not have abandoned these evenings for anything. Often his daughters would bid their father good night only to find him the next morning still engaged in some utterly obscure debate with his friends, eyes red, hair akimbo, woozy but game. They would go to him and he would kiss each in turn, calling them his Brillantes. These youthful intelligences, he often boasted to his friends, will best us all.

The Reign of Trujillo was not the best time to be a lover of Ideas, not the best time to be engaging in parlor debate, to be hosting tertulias, to be doing anything out of the ordinary, but Abelard was nothing if not meticulous. Never allowed contemporary politics (i.e., Trujillo) to be bandied about, kept shit on the abstract plane, allowed anybody who wanted (including members of the Secret Police) to attend his gatherings. Given that you could get lit up for even mispronouncing the Failed Cattle Thief's name, it was a no-brainer, really. As a general practice Abelard tried his best not to think about El Jefe at all, followed sort of the Tao of Dictator Avoidance, which was ironic considering that Abelard was unmatched in maintaining the outward appearance of the enthusiastic Trujillista.[24] Both as an individual and as the executive officer of his medical association he gave unstintingly to the Partido Dominicano; he and his wife, who was his number-one nurse and his best assistant, joined every medical mission that Trujillo organized, no matter how remote the campo; and no one could suppress a guffaw better than Abelard when El Jefe won an election by 103 percent! What enthusiasm from the pueblo! When banquets were held in Trujillo's honor Abelard always drove to Santiago to attend. He arrived early, left late, smiled endlessly, and *didn't say nothing*. Disconnected his intellectual warp engine and operated strictly on impulse power. When the time came, Abelard would shake El Jefe's hand, cover him in the warm effusion of his adoration (if you think the Trujillato was not homoerotic, then, to quote the

---

24. But what was even more ironic was that Abelard had a reputation for being able to keep his head *down* during the worst of the regime's madness—for unseeing, as it were. In 1937, for example, while the Friends of the Dominican Republic were perejiling Haitians and Haitian-Dominicans and Haitian-looking Dominicans to death, while genocide was, in fact, in the making, Abelard kept his head, eyes, and nose safely tucked into his books (let his wife take care of hiding his servants, didn't ask her nothing about it) and when survivors staggered into his surgery with unspeakable machete wounds, he fixed them up as best as he could without making any comments as to the ghastliness of their wounds. Acted like it was any other day.

Priest, *you got another thing coming*), and without further ado
fade back into the shadows (à la Oscar's favorite movie, *Point
Blank*). Kept as far away from El Jefe as possible—he wasn't
under any delusion that he was Trujillo's equal or his buddy or
some kind of necessary individual—after all, niggers who
messed with Him had a habit of ending up with a bad case of
the deads. It didn't hurt that Abelard's family was not totally
in the Jefe's pocket, that his father had cultivated no lands or
negocios in geographic or competitive proximity to the Jefe's
own holding. His Fuckface contact was blessedly limited.[25]

Abelard and the Failed Cattle Thief might have glided
past each other in the Halls of History if not for the fact that
starting in 1944, Abelard, instead of bringing his wife and
daughter to Jefe events, as custom dictated, began to make a
point of leaving them at home. He explained to his friends
that his wife had become "nervous" and that Jacquelyn took
care of her but the real reason for the absences was Trujillo's
notorious rapacity and his daughter Jacquelyn's off-the-hook
looks. Abelard's serious, intellectual oldest daughter was no
longer her tall awkward flaquita self; adolescence had struck

25. He wished that could also have been the case with his Balaguer contact.
In those days the Demon Balaguer had not yet become the Election Thief;
was only Trujillo's Minister of Education—you can see how successful he
was at *that* job—and any chance he got to corner Abelard, he did. He
wanted to talk to Abelard about his *theories*—which were four parts Gob-
ineau, four parts Goddard, and two parts German racial eugenics. The
German theories, he assured Abelard, were all the rage on the Continent.
Abelard nods. I see. (But, you ask, who was the smarter? No comparison.
In a Tables and Ladders match, Abelard, the Cerebro del Cibao, would
have 3D'd the "Genio de Genocidio" in about two seconds flat.)

with a fury, transforming her into a young lady of great beauty. She had caught a serious case of the hips-ass-chest, a condition which during the mid-forties spelled trouble with a capital T to the R to the U to the J to the illo.

Ask any of your elders and they will tell you: Trujillo might have been a Dictator, but he was a Dominican Dictator, which is another way of saying he was the Number-One Bellaco in the Country. Believed that all the toto in the DR was, literally, his. It's a well-documented fact that in Trujillo's DR if you were of a certain class and you put your cute daughter anywhere near El Jefe, within the week she'd be mamando his ripio like an old pro and *there would be nothing you could do about it!* Part of the price of living in Santo Domingo, one of the Island's best-known secrets. So common was the practice, so insatiable Trujillo's appetites, that there were plenty of men in the nation, hombres de calidad y posición, who, believe it or not, offered up their daughters *freely* to the Failed Cattle Thief. Abelard, to his credit, was not one of them; as soon as he realized what was what— after his daughter started stopping traffic on Calle El Sol, after one of his patients looked at his daughter and said, You should be careful with that one—he pulled a Rapunzel on her ass and locked her *in*. It was a Brave Thing, not in keeping with his character, but he'd only had to watch Jacquelyn preparing for school one day, big in body but still a child, goddamn it, still a child, and the Brave Thing became easy.

Hiding your doe-eyed, large-breasted daughter from Trujillo, however, was anything but easy. (Like keeping the Ring from Sauron.) If you think the average Dominican guy's bad,

Trujillo was five thousand times worse. Dude had hundreds of spies whose entire job was to scour the provinces for his next piece of ass; if the procurement of ass had been any more central to the Trujillato the regime would have been the world's first culocracy (and maybe, in fact, it was). In this climate, hoarding your women was tantamount to treason; offenders who didn't cough up the muchachas could easily find themselves enjoying the invigorating charm of an eight-shark bath. Let us be clear: Abelard was taking an enormous risk. It didn't matter that he was upper-class, or that he'd prepared the groundwork well, going as far as having a friend diagnose his wife as manic, then letting the word leak through the elite circles in which he ran. If Trujillo and Company caught wind of his duplicity they'd have him in chains (and Jacquelyn on her back) in two seconds flat. Which was why every time El Jefe shuffled down the welcome line, shaking hands, Abelard expected him to exclaim in that high shrill voice of his, Dr. Abelard Cabral, where is that *delicious* daughter of yours? I've heard so much about her from your *neighbors*. It was enough to make Abelard febrile.

His daughter Jacquelyn of course had absolutely no idea what was at stake. Those were more innocent times, and she was an innocent girl; getting raped by her Illustrious President was the furthest thing from her excellent mind. She of his two daughters had inherited her father's brains. Was studying French religiously because she'd decided to imitate her father and go abroad to study medicine at the Faculté de Médecine de Paris. To France! To become the next Madame Curie! Hit the books night and day, and would practice her French with both her father and with their servant Esteban El Gallo, who'd been born in Haiti and still spoke a pretty good frog.[26] Neither of his daughters had any idea, were as carefree as Hobbits, never guessing the Shadow that loomed on the horizon. On his days off, when he wasn't at the clinic or in his study, writing, Abelard would stand at his rear window and watch his daughters at their silly children's game until his aching heart could stand it no more.

Each morning, before Jackie started her studies, she wrote on a clean piece of paper: *Tarde venientibus ossa.*

To the latecomers are left the bones.

He spoke of these matters to only three people. The first, of course, was his wife, Socorro. Socorro (it must be said here) was a Talent in her own right. A famous beauty from the East (Higüey) and the source of all her daughters' pulchritude, Socorro had looked in her youth like a dark-hued Dejah Thoris (one of the chief reasons Abelard had pursued a girl so beneath his class) and was also one of the finest nurse practitioners he had ever had the honor of working with in Mexico or the Dominican Republic, which, given his estimation of his Mexican colleagues, is no small praise. (The second reason he'd gone after her.) Her workhorse-ness and her encyclopedic knowledge of folk cures and traditional

26. After Trujillo launched the 1937 genocide of Haitian and Haitian-Dominicans, you didn't see that many Haitian types working in the DR. Not until at least the late fifties. Esteban was the exception because (a) he looked so damn Dominican, and (b) during the genocide, Socorro had hidden him inside her daughter Astrid's dollhouse. Spent four days in there, cramped up like a brown-skinned Alice.

remedies made her an indispensable partner in his practice. Her reaction, though, to his Trujillo worries was typical; she was a clever, skilled, hardworking woman who didn't blink when faced with arterial spray hissing from a machete-chopped arm stump, but when it came to more abstract menaces like, say, Trujillo, she stubbornly and willfully refused to acknowledge there might be a problem, all the while dressing Jacqueline in the most suffocating of clothes. Why are you telling people that I'm loca? she demanded.

He spoke of it as well with his mistress, Señora Lydia Abenader, one of the three women who had rejected his marriage offer upon his return from his studies in México; now a widow and his number-one lover, she was the woman his father had wanted him to bag in the first place, and when he'd been unable to close the deal his father had mocked him as a half-man even unto his final days of bilious life (the third reason he'd gone after Socorro).

Last he spoke with his longtime neighbor and friend, Marcus Applegate Román, whom he often had to ferry back and forth from presidential events because Marcus lacked a car. With Marcus it had been a spontaneous outburst, the weight of the problem truly pressing on him; they'd been cruising back to La Vega on one of the old Marine Occupation roads, middle of the night in August, through the black-black farmlands of the Cibao, so hot they had to drive with the windows cranked down, which meant a constant stream of mosquitoes scooting up their nostrils, and out of nowhere Abelard began to talk. Young women have no opportunity to develop unmolested in this country, he complained. Then he gave, as an example, the name of a young woman whom the Jefe had only recently despoiled, a muchacha known to both of them, a graduate of the University of Florida and the daughter of an acquaintance. At first Marcus said nothing; in the darkness of the Packard's interior his face was an absence, a pool of shadow. A worrisome silence. Marcus was no fan of the Jefe, having more than once in Abelard's presence called him un "bruto" y un "imbécil" but that didn't stop Abelard from being suddenly aware of his colossal indiscretion (such was life in those Secret Police days). Finally Abelard said, This doesn't bother you?

Marcus hunched down to light a cigarette, and finally his face reappeared, drawn but familiar. Nothing we can do about it, Abelard.

But imagine you were in similar straits: how would *you* protect yourself?

I'd be sure to have ugly daughters.

Lydia was far more realistic. She'd been seated at her armoire, brushing her Moorish hair. He'd been lying on the bed, naked as well, absently pulling on his rípio. Lydia had said, Send her away to the nuns. Send her to Cuba. My family there will take care of her.

Cuba was Lydia's dream; it was her Mexico. Always talking about moving back there.

But I'd need permission from the state!

Ask for it, then.

But what if El Jefe notices the requests?

Lydia put down her brush with a sharp click. What are the chances of that happening?

You never know, Abelard said defensively. In this country you never know.

His mistress was for Cuba, his wife for house arrest, his best friend said nothing. His own cautiousness told him to await further instructions. And at the end of the year he got them.

At one of the interminable presidential events El Jefe had shaken Abelard's hand, but instead of moving on, he paused—a nightmare come true—held on to his fingers, and said in his shrill voice: You are Dr. Abelard Cabral? Abelard bowed. At your service, Your Excellency. In less than a nanosecond Abelard was drenched in sweat; he knew what was coming next; the Failed Cattle Thief had never spoken more than three words to him his whole life, what else could it be? He dared not glance away from Trujillo's heavily powdered face, but out the corner of his eyes he caught glimpses of the lambesacos, hovering, beginning to realize that an exchange was in the making.

I have seen you here often, Doctor, but lately without your wife. Have you divorced her?

I am still married, Your Enormity. To Socorro Hernández Batista.

That is good to hear, El Jefe said, I was afraid that you might have turned into *un maricón*. Then he turned to the lambesacos and laughed. Oh, Jefe, they screamed, you are *too much*.

It was at this point that another nigger might have, in a fit of cojones, said something to defend his honor, but Abelard was not that nigger. He said nothing.

But of course, El Jefe continued, knuckling a tear from his eye, you are no maricón, for I've heard that you have daughters, Dr. Cabral, una que es muy bella y elegante, no?

Abelard had rehearsed a dozen answers to this question, but his response was pure reflex, came out of nowhere: Yes, Jefe, you are correct, I have two daughters. But to tell you the truth, they're only beautiful if you have a taste for women with mustaches.

For an instant El Jefe had said nothing, and in that twisting silence Abelard could see his daughter being violated in front of him while he was lowered with excruciating slowness into Trujillo's infamous pool of sharks. But then, miracle of miracles, El Jefe had crinkled his porcine face and laughed, Abelard had laughed too, and El Jefe moved on. When Abelard returned home to La Vega late that evening he woke his wife from a deep slumber so that they could both pray and thank the Heavens for their family's salvation. Verbally, Abelard had never been quick on the draw. The inspiration could only have come from the hidden spaces within my soul, he told his wife. From a Numinous Being.

You mean God? his wife pressed.

I mean someone, Abelard said darkly.

AND SO?

For the next three months Abelard waited for the End. Waited for his name to start appearing in the "Foro Popular" section of the paper, thinly veiled criticisms aimed at a certain bone doctor from La Vega—which was often how the regime began the destruction of a respected citizen such as him—with disses about the way your socks and your shirts didn't match; waited for a letter to arrive, demanding a private meeting with the Jefe, waited for his daughter to turn up missing on her trip back to school. Lost nearly twenty pounds during his awful vigil. Began to drink copiously. Nearly killed a patient with a slip of the hand. If his wife hadn't spotted the damage before they stitched, who knows what might have happened? Screamed at his daughters and wife almost every day. Could not get it up much for his mistress. But the rain season turned to hot season and the clinic filled with the hapless, the wounded, the afflicted, and when after four months nothing happened Abelard almost let out a sigh of relief.

Maybe, he wrote on the back of his hairy hand. Maybe.

SANTO DOMINGO CONFIDENTIAL

In some ways living in Santo Domingo during the Trujillato was a lot like being in that famous *Twilight Zone* episode that Oscar loved so much, the one where the monstrous white kid with the godlike powers rules over a town that is completely isolated from the rest of the world, a town called Peaksville. The white kid is vicious and random and all the people in the "community" live in straight terror of him, denouncing and betraying each other at the drop of a hat in order not to be the person he maims or, more ominously, sends to the corn. (After each atrocity he commits—whether it's giving a gopher three heads or banishing a no longer interesting playmate to the corn or raining snow down on the last crops—the horrified people of Peaksville have to say, It was a good thing you did, Anthony. A *good* thing.)

Between 1930 (when the Failed Cattle Thief seized power) and 1961 (the year he got blazed) Santo Domingo was the Caribbean's very own Peaksville, with Trujillo playing the part of Anthony and the rest of us reprising the role of the Man Who Got Turned into Jack-in-the-Box. You might roll your eyes at the comparison, but, friends: it would be hard to exaggerate the power Trujillo exerted over the Dominican people and the shadow of fear he cast throughout the region. Homeboy dominated Santo Domingo like it was his very own private Mordor;[27] not only did he lock the country away from

27. Anthony may have isolated Peaksville with the power of his mind, but Trujillo did the same with the power of his office! Almost as soon as he grabbed the presidency, the Failed Cattle Thief sealed the country away from the rest of the world—a forced isolation that we'll call the Plátano Curtain. As for the country's historically fluid border with Haiti—which was more baká than border—the Failed Cattle Thief became like Dr. Gull in *From Hell*; adopting the creed of the Dionyesian Architects, he aspired to become an architect of history, and through a horrifying ritual of silence and blood, machete and perejil, darkness and denial, inflicted a true border on the countries, a border that exists beyond maps, that is carved directly into the histories and imaginaries of a people. By the middle of T-illo's second decade in "office" the Plátano Curtain had been so successful that when the Allies won World War II the majority of the pueblo didn't even have the remotest idea that it had happened. Those who did know believed the propaganda that Trujillo had played an important role in the overthrow of the Japanese and the Hun. Homeboy could not have had a more private realm had he thrown a forcefield around the island. (After all, who needs

the rest of the world, isolate it behind the Plátano Curtain, he acted like it was his very own plantation, acted like he owned everything and everyone, killed whomever he wanted to kill, sons, brothers, fathers, mothers, took women away from their husbands on their wedding nights and then would brag publicly about "the great honeymoon" he'd had the night before. His Eye was everywhere; he had a Secret Police that out-Stasi'd the Stasi, that kept watch on everyone, even those everyones who lived in *the States*; a security apparatus so ridiculously mongoose that you could say a bad thing about El Jefe at eight-forty in the morning and before the clock struck ten you'd be in the Cuarenta having a cattleprod shoved up your ass. (Who says that we Third World people are inefficient?) It wasn't just Mr. Friday the Thirteenth you had to worry about, either, it was the whole Chivato Nation he helped spawn, for like every Dark Lord worth his Shadow he had the devotion of his people.[28] It was widely believed that at any one time between forty-two and eighty-seven percent of the Dominican population was on the Secret Police's payroll. Your own fucking neighbors could acabar con you just

---

futuristic generators when you have the power of the machete?) Most people argue that El Jefe was trying to keep the world out; some, however, point out that he seemed equally intent on keeping something in.

28. So devoted was the pueblo, in fact, that, as Galíndez recounts in *La Era de Trujillo*, when a graduate student was asked by a panel of examiners to discuss the pre-Columbian culture in the Americas, he replied without hesitation that the most important pre-Columbian culture in the Americas was "the Dominican Republic during the era of Trujillo." Oh, man. But what's more hilarious is that the examiners refused to fail the student, on the grounds that "he had mentioned El Jefe."

because you had something they coveted or because you cut in front of them at the colmado. Mad folks went out in that manner, betrayed by those they considered their panas, by members of their own families, by slips of the tongue. One day you were a law-abiding citizen, cracking nuts on your galería, the next day you were in the Cuarenta, getting *your* nuts cracked. Shit was so tight that many people actually believed that Trujillo had supernatural powers! It was whispered that he did not sleep, did not sweat, that he could see, smell, feel events hundreds of miles away, that he was protected by the most evil fukú on the Island. (You wonder why two generations later our parents are still so damn secretive, why you'll find out your brother ain't your brother only by accident.)

But let's not go completely overboard: Trujillo was certainly formidable, and the regime was like a Caribbean Mordor in many ways, but there were plenty of people who despised El Jefe, who communicated in less-than-veiled ways their contempt, who *resisted*. But Abelard was simply not one of them. Homeboy wasn't like his Mexican colleagues who were always keeping up with what was happening elsewhere in the world, who believed that change was possible. He didn't dream of revolution, didn't care that Trotsky had lived and died not ten blocks from his student pension in Coyoacán; wanted only to tend his wealthy, ailing patients and afterward return to his study without worrying about being shot in the head or thrown to the sharks. Every now and then one of his acquaintances—usually Marcus—would describe for him the latest Trujillo Atrocity: an affluent clan stripped of its properties and sent into exile, an entire family fed piece by piece to the sharks because a son had dared compare Trujillo to Adolf Hitler before a terrified audience of his peers, a suspicious assassination in Bonao of a well-known unionist. Abelard listened to these horrors tensely, and then after an awkward silence would change the subject. He simply didn't wish to dwell on the fates of Unfortunate People, on the goings-on in Peaksville. He didn't want those stories in his house. The way Abelard saw it—his Trujillo philosophy, if you will—he only had to keep his head down, his mouth shut, his pockets open, his daughters hidden for another decade or two. By then, he prophesied, Trujillo would be dead and the Dominican Republic would be a true democracy.

Abelard, it turned out, needed help in the prophecy department. Santo Domingo never became a democracy. He didn't have no couple of decades, either. His luck ran out earlier than anyone expected.

THE BAD THING

Nineteen forty-five should have been a capital year for Abelard and Family. Two of Abelard's articles were published to minor acclaim, one in the prestigious —— and the second in a small journal out of Caracas, and he received complimentary responses from a couple of Continental doctors, very flattering indeed. Business in the supermercados couldn't have been better; the Island was still flush from the war boom and his managers couldn't keep anything on the shelves. The fincas were producing and reaping profits; the worldwide collapse of agricultural prices was still years off. Abelard had a full load of clients, performed a number of tricky surgeries with impeccable skill; his daughters were prospering (Jacquelyn had been accepted at a prestigious boarding school in Le Havre, to begin the following year—her chance to escape); his wife and mistress were pouring on the adoration; even the servants seemed content (not that he ever really spoke to them). All in all, the good doctor should have been immensely satisfied with himself. Should have ended each day with his feet up, un cigarro in the corner of his mouth, and a broad grin creasing his ursine features.

It was—dare we say it?—a *good* life.

Except it wasn't.

In February there was another Presidential Event (for Independence Day!) and this time the invitation was explicit. For Dr. Abelard Luis Cabral *and* wife *and* daughter Jacquelyn. The daughter Jacquelyn part had been underlined by the party's host. Not once, not twice, but three times. Abelard nearly fainted when he saw the damn thing. Slumped back at his desk, his heart pushing up against his esophagus. Stared at the vellum square for almost a whole hour before folding it and placing it inside his shirt pocket. The next morning he visited the host, one of his neighbors. The man was out in his corral, staring balefully as some of his servants were trying to get one of his stallions to stud. When he saw Abelard his face darkened. What the hell do you want from me? The order came straight from the Palacio. When Abelard walked back to his car he tried not to show that he was shaking.

Once again he consulted with Marcus and Lydia. (He

said nothing of the invitation to his wife, not wanting to panic her, and by extension his daughter. Not wanting even to say the words in his own house.)

Where the last time he'd been somewhat rational, this go-around he was fuera de serie, raved like a madman. Waxed indignant to Marcus for nearly an hour about the injustice, about the hopelessness of it all (an amazing amount of circumlocution because he never once directly named who it was he was complaining about). Alternated between impotent rage and pathetic self-pity. In the end his friend had to cover the good doctor's mouth to get a word in edgewise, but Abelard kept talking. It's madness! Sheer madness! I'm the father of my household! I'm the one who says what goes!

What can you do? Marcus said with no little fatalism. Trujillo's the president and you're just a doctor. If he wants your daughter at the party you can do nothing but obey.

But this isn't human!

When has this country ever been human, Abelard? You're the historian. You of all people should know that.

Lydia was even less compassionate. She read the invite and swore a coño under her breath and then she turned on him. I warned you, Abelard. Didn't I tell you to send your daughter abroad while you had the chance? She could have been with my family in Cuba, safe and sound, but now you're jodido. Now He has his Eye on you.

I know, I know, Lydia, but what should I *do*?

Jesú Cristo, Abelard, she said tremulously. What options are there. This is Trujillo you're talking about.

Back home the portrait of Trujillo, which every good citizen had hanging in his house, beamed down on him with insipid, viperous benevolence.

Maybe if the doctor had immediately grabbed his daughters and his wife and smuggled them all aboard a boat in Puerto Plata, or if he'd stolen with them across the border into Haiti, they might have had a chance. The Plátano Curtain was strong but it wasn't that strong. But alas, instead of making his move Abelard fretted and temporized and despaired. He couldn't eat, couldn't sleep, paced the halls of their house all night long and all the weight he regained these last months he immediately lost. (If you think about it, maybe he should have heeded his daughter's philosophy: *Tarde venientibus ossa*.) Every chance he got he spent with his daughters. Jackie, who was her parents' Golden Child, who already had memorized all the streets in the French Quarter and who that year alone had been the object of not four, not five, but twelve marriage proposals. All communicated to Abelard and his wife, of course. Jackie knowing nothing about it. But still. And Astrid, ten years old, who took more after their father in looks and nature; plainer, the jokester, the believer, who played the meanest piano in all of the Cibao and who was her big sister's ally in all things. The sisters wondered about their father's sudden attentiveness: Are you on vacation, Papi? He shook his head sadly. No, I just like spending time with you is all.

What's the matter with you? his wife demanded, but he refused to speak to her. Let me be, mujer.

Things got so bad with him that he even went to church, a first for Abelard (which might have been a really bad idea

since everybody knew the Church at that time was in Trujillo's pocket). He attended confession almost every day and
talked to the priest but he got nothing out of it except to pray
and to hope and to light some fucking stupid candles. He
was going through three bottles of whiskey a day.

His friends in Mexico would have grabbed their rifles and
taken to the interior (at least that's what he thought they
would have done) but he was his father's son in more ways
than he cared to admit. His father, an educated man who had
resisted sending his son to Mexico but who had always
played ball with Trujillo. When in 1937 the army had started
murdering all the Haitians, his father had allowed them to
use his horses, and when he didn't get any of them back he
didn't say nothing to Trujillo. Just chalked it up as the cost of
doing business. Abelard kept drinking and kept fretting,
stopped seeing Lydia, isolated himself in his study, and eventually convinced himself that nothing would happen. It was
only a test. Told his wife and daughter to prepare for the
party. Didn't mention it was a Trujillo party. Made it seem
like nothing was amiss. Hated himself to his core for his
mendacity, but what else could he have done?

Tarde venientibus ossa.

It probably would have gone off without a hitch too, but
Jackie was so excited. Since it was her first big party, who's
surprised that it became something of an event for her? She
went shopping for a dress with her mother, got her hair done
at the salon, bought new shoes, and was even given a pair of
pearl earrings by another of her female relatives. Socorro
helped her daughter with every aspect of the preparation, no

suspicions, but about a week before the party she started having these terrible dreams. She was in her old town, where she'd grown up before her aunt adopted her and put her in nursing school, before she discovered she had the gift of Healing. Staring down that dusty frangipani-lined road that everybody said led to the capital, and in the heat-rippled distance she could see a man approaching, a distant figure who struck in her such dread that she woke up screaming. Abelard leaping out of bed in panic, the girls crying out in their rooms. Had that dream almost every damn night that final week, a countdown clock.

On T-minus-two Lydia urged Abelard to leave with her on a steamer bound for Cuba. She knew the captain, he would hide them, swore it could be done. We'll get your daughters afterward, I promise you.

I can't do that, he said miserably. I can't leave my family.

She returned to combing her hair. They said not another word.

On the afternoon of the party, as Abelard was dolefully tending to the car, he caught sight of his daughter, in her dress, standing in the sala, hunched over another one of her French books, looking absolutely divine, absolutely young, and right then he had one of those epiphanies us lit majors are always forced to talk about. It didn't come in a burst of light or a new color or a sensation in his heart. He just knew. Knew he just couldn't do it. Told his wife to forget about it. Said same to daughter. Ignored their horrified protestations. Jumped in the car, picked up Marcus, and headed to the party.

What about Jacquelyn? Marcus asked.

She's not coming.

Marcus shook his head. Said nothing else.

At the reception line Trujillo again paused before Abelard. Sniffed the air like a cat. And your wife and daughter?

Abelard trembling but holding it together somehow. Already sensing how everything was going to change. My apologies, Your Excellency. They could not attend.

His porcine eyes narrowed. So I see, he said coldly, and then dismissed Abelard with a flick of his wrist.

Not even Marcus would look at him.

CHISTE APOCALYPTUS

Not four weeks after the party, Dr. Abelard Luis Cabral was arrested by the Secret Police. The charge? "Slander and gross calumny against the Person of the President."

If the stories are to be believed, it all had to do with a joke.

One afternoon, so the story goes, shortly after the fateful party, Abelard, who we had better reveal was a short, bearded, heavyset man with surprising physical strength and curious, close-set eyes, drove into Santiago in his old Packard to buy a bureau for his wife (and of course to see his mistress). He was still a mess, and those who saw him that day recall his disheveled appearance. His distraction. The bureau was successfully acquired and lashed haphazardly to the roof of the automobile, but before he could shoot over to Lydia's crib

Abelard was buttonholed by some "buddies" on the street and invited for a few drinks at Club Santiago. Who knows why he went? Maybe to try to keep up appearances, or because every invitation felt like a life-or-death affair. That night at Club Santiago he tried to shake off his sense of imminent doom by talking vigorously about history, medicine, Aristophanes, by getting very very drunk, and when the night wound down he asked the "boys" for assistance in relocating the bureau to the trunk of his Packard. He did not trust the valets, he explained, for they had stupid hands. The muchachos good-naturedly agreed. But while Abelard was fumbling with the keys to open the trunk he stated loudly, I hope there aren't any bodies in here. That he made the foregoing remark is not debated. Abelard conceded as much in his "confession." This trunk-joke in itself caused discomfort among the "boys," who were all too aware of the shadow that the Packard automobile casts on Dominican history. It was the car in which Trujillo had, in his early years, terrorized his first two elections away from the pueblo. During the Hurricane of 1931 the Jefe's henchmen often drove their Packards to the bonfires where the volunteers were burning the dead, and out of their trunks they would pull out "victims of the hurricane." All of whom looked strangely dry and were often clutching opposition party materials. The wind, the henchmen would joke, drove a bullet straight through the head of this one. Har-har!

What followed is still, to this day, hotly disputed. There are those who swear on their mothers that when Abelard finally opened the trunk he poked his head inside and said, Nope, no bodies here. This is what Abelard himself claimed to have said. A poor joke, certainly, but not "slander" or "gross calumny." In Abelard's version of the events, his friends laughed, the bureau was secured, and off he drove to his Santiago apartment, where Lydia was waiting for him (forty-two and still lovely and still worried shitless about his daughter). The court officers and their hidden "witnesses," however, argued that something quite different happened, that when Dr. Abelard Luis Cabral opened the trunk of the Packard, he said, Nope, no bodies here, *Trujillo must have cleaned them out for me.*

End quote.

IN MY HUMBLE OPINION

It sounds like the most unlikely load of jiringonza on this side of the Sierra Madre. But one man's jiringonza is another man's life.

THE FALL

He spent that night with Lydia. It had been a weird time for them. Not ten days earlier Lydia had announced that she was pregnant—I'm going to have your son, she crowed happily. But two days later the son proved to be a false alarm, probably just some indigestion. There was relief—like he needed anything else on his plate, and what if it had been another daughter?—but also disappointment, for Abelard wouldn't have minded a little son, even if the carajito would have been the child of a mistress and born in his darkest hour. He knew that Lydia had been wanting something for some time now, something real that she could claim was theirs and theirs alone. She was forever telling him to leave his wife and move in with her, and while that might have been attractive indeed while they were together in Santiago, the possibility vanished as soon as he set foot back in his house and his two beautiful daughters rushed him. He was a predictable man and liked his predictable comforts, but Lydia never stopped trying to convince him, in a low-intensity way, that love was love and for that reason it should be obeyed. She pretended to be sanguine over the nonappearance of their son—Why would I want to ruin these breasts, she joked—but he could tell she was disheartened. He was too. For these last few days Abelard had been having vague, troubled dreams full of children crying at night, and his father's first house. Left a disquieting stain on his waking hours. Without really thinking about it, he'd not seen Lydia since that night the news turned bad, had gone out drinking in part, I believe, because he feared that the boy's nonbirth might have broken them, but instead he felt for her the old desire, the one that nearly knocked him over the first time they'd met at his cousin Amílcar's birthday, when they'd both been so slender and young and so jam-packed with possibilities.

For once they did not talk about Trujillo.

Can you believe how long it's been? he asked her in amazement during their last Saturday-night tryst.

I can believe it, she said sadly, pulling at the flesh of her stomach. We're clocks, Abelard. Nothing more.

Abelard shook his head. We're more than that. We're marvels, mi amor.

I wish I could stay in this moment, wish I could extend Abelard's happy days, but it's impossible. The next week two atomic eyes opened over civilian centers in Japan and, even though no one knew it yet, the world was then remade. Not two days after the atomic bombs scarred Japan forever, Socorro dreamed that the faceless man was standing over her husband's bed, and she could not scream, could not say anything, and then the next night she dreamed that he was standing over her children too. I've been dreaming, she told her husband, but he waved his hands, dismissing. She began to watch the road in front of their home and burn candles in her room. In Santiago, Abelard is kissing Lydia's hands and she is sighing with pleasure and already we're heading for Victory in the Pacific and for three Secret Police officers in their shiny Chevrolet winding up the road to Abelard's house. Already it's the Fall.

ABELARD IN CHAINS

To say it was the greatest shock in Abelard's life when officers from the Secret Police (it's too early for the SIM but we'll call them SIM anyway) placed him in cuffs and led him to their car would not be an overstatement, if it wasn't for the fact that Abelard was going to spend the next nine years receiving one greatest shock of his life after another. Please, Abelard begged, when he regained his tongue, I must leave my wife a note. Manuel will attend to it, SIMian Número Uno explained, motioning to the largest of the SIMians, who was already glancing about the house. Abelard's last glimpse of his home was of Manuel rifling through his desk with a practiced carelessness.

Abelard had always imagined the SIM to be filled with lowlifes and no-reading reprobates but the two officers who locked him in their car were in fact polite, less like sadistic torturers than vacuum-cleaner salesmen. SIMian Número Uno assured him en route that his "difficulties" were certain to be cleared up. We've seen these cases before, Número Uno explained. Someone has spoken badly of you but they will quickly be revealed for the liars they are. I should hope so, Abelard said, half indignant, half in terror. No te preocupes, said SIMian Número Uno. The Jefe is not in the business of imprisoning the innocent. Número Dos remained silent. His suit was very shabby, and both men, Abelard noticed, reeked of whiskey. He tried to remain calm—fear, as *Dune* teaches us, is the mindkiller—but he could not help himself. He saw his daughters and his wife raped over and over again. He saw his house on fire. If he hadn't emptied his bladder right before the pigs showed up, he would have peed himself right there.

Abelard was driven very quickly to Santiago (everyone he passed on the road made sure to look away at the sight of the VW bug) and taken to the Fortaleza San Luis. The sharp edge of his fear turned knife once they pulled inside that notorious place. Are you sure this is correct? Abelard was so frightened his voice quaked. Don't worry, Doctor, Número Dos said, you are where you belong. He'd been silent so long Abelard had almost forgotten that he could speak. Now it was Número Dos who was smiling and Número Uno who focused his attention out the window.

Once inside those stone walls the polite SIM officers handed him over to a pair of not-so-polite guards who stripped him of his shoes, his wallet, his belt, his wedding band, and then sat him down in a cramped, hot office to fill out some forms. There was a pervasive smell of ripe ass in the air. No officer appeared to explain his case, no one listened to his requests, and when he began to raise his voice about his treatment the guard typing the forms leaned forward and punched him in the face. As easily as you might reach over for a cigarette. The man was wearing a ring and it tore open Abelard's lip something awful. The pain was so sudden, his disbelief so enormous, that Abelard actually asked, through clutched fingers, Why? The guard rocked him again hard, carved a furrow in his forehead. This is how we answer questions around here, the guard said matter-of-factly, bending down to be sure his form was properly aligned in the typewriter. Abelard began to sob, the blood spilling out between his fingers. Which the typing guard just loved; he called in his friends from the other offices. Look at this one! Look at how much he likes to cry!

Before Abelard knew what was happening he was being shoved into a general holding cell that stank of malaria sweat and diarrhea and was crammed with unseemly representatives of what Broca might have called the "criminal class." The guards then proceeded to inform the other prisoners that Abelard was a homosexual and a Communist—That is *untrue!* Abelard protested—but who is going to listen to a gay comunista? Over the next couple of hours Abelard was harassed lovely and most of his clothes were stripped from him. One heavyset cibaeño even demanded his underwear, and when Abelard coughed them up the man pulled them on over his pants. Son muy cómodos, he announced to his friends. Abelard was forced to hunker naked near the shit pots; if he tried to crawl near the dry areas the other prisoners would scream at him—Quédate ahí con la mierda, maricón—and this was how he had to sleep, amidst urine, feces, and flies, and more than once he was awakened by someone tickling his lips with a dried turd. Pre-occupation with sanitation was not high among the Fortalezanos. The deviants didn't allow him to eat, either, stealing his meager allotted portions three days straight. On the fourth day a one-armed pickpocket took pity on him and he was able to eat an entire banana without interruption, even tried to chew up the fibrous peel, he was so famished.

Poor Abelard. It was also on day four that someone from the outside world finally paid him attention. Late in the evening, when everybody else was asleep, a detachment of guards dragged him into a smaller, crudely lit cell. He was strapped down, not unkindly, to a table. From the moment he'd been grabbed he'd not stopped speaking. This is all a misunderstanding please I come from a very respectable family you have to communicate with my wife and my lawyers they will be able to clear this up I cannot believe that I've been treated so despicably I demand that the officer in charge hear my complaints. He couldn't get the words out of his mouth fast enough. It wasn't until he noticed the electrical contraption that the guards were fiddling with in the corner that he fell quiet. Abelard stared at it with a terrible dread, and then, because he suffered from an insatiable urge to taxonomize, asked, What in God's name do you call that?

We call it the pulpo, one of the guards said.

They spent all night showing him how it worked.

It was three days before Socorro could track down her husband and another five days before she received permission from the capital to visit. The visiting room where Socorro awaited her husband seemed to have been fashioned from a latrine. There was only one sputtering kerosene lamp and it looked as though a number of people had taken mountainous shits in the corner. An intentional humiliation that was lost on Socorro; she was too overwrought to notice. After what felt like an hour (again, another señora would have protested, but Socorro bore the shitsmell and the darkness and the no chair stoically), Abelard was brought in handcuffed. He'd been given an undersized shirt and an undersized pair of pants; he was shuffling as though afraid that something in his hands or in his pockets might fall out. Only been inside a week but already he looked frightful. His eyes were blackened; his hands and neck covered in bruises and his torn lip had swollen monstrously, was the color of the meat inside your eye. The night before, he had been interrogated by the guards, and they had beaten him mercilessly with leather truncheons; one of his testicles would be permanently shriveled from the blows.

Poor Socorro. Here was a woman whose lifelong preoccupation had been calamity. Her mother was a mute; her drunk father frittered away the family's middle-class patrimony, one tarea at a time, until their holdings had been reduced to a shack and some chickens and the old man was forced to work other people's land, condemned to a life of constant movement, poor health, and broken hands; it was said that Pa Socorro had never recovered from seeing his own father beaten to death by a neighbor who also happened to be a sergeant in the police. Socorro's childhood had been about missed meals and cousin-clothes, about seeing her father three, four times a year, visits where he didn't talk to anybody; just lay in his room drunk. Socorro became an "anxious" muchacha; for a time she thinned her hair by pulling it, was seventeen when she caught Abelard's eye in a training hospital but didn't start menstruating until a year *after* they were married. Even as an adult, Socorro was in the habit of waking up in the middle of the night in terror, convinced that the house was on fire, would rush from room to room, expecting to be greeted by a carnival of flame. When Abelard read to her from his newspapers she took special interest in earthquakes and fires and floods and cattle stampedes and the sinking of ships. She was the family's first catastrophist, would have made Cuvier proud.

What had she been expecting, while she fiddled with the buttons on her dress, while she shifted the purse on her shoulder and tried not to unbalance her Macy's hat? A mess, un toyo certainly, but not a husband looking nearly destroyed, who shuffled like an old man, whose eyes shone with the sort of fear that is not easily shed. It was worse than she, in all her apocalyptic fervor, had imagined. It was the Fall.

When she placed her hands on Abelard he began to cry very loudly, very shamefully. Tears streamed down his face as he tried to tell her all that had happened to him.

It wasn't long after that visit that Socorro realized that she was pregnant. With Abelard's Third and Final Daughter.

Zafa or Fukú?

You tell me.

There would always be speculation. At the most basic level, did he say it, did he not? (Which is another way of asking: Did he have a hand in his own destruction?) Even the family was divided. La Inca adamant that her cousin had said nothing; it had all been a setup, orchestrated by Abelard's enemies to strip the family of their wealth, their properties, and their businesses. Others were not so sure. He probably *had* said something that night at the club, and unfortunately for him he'd been overheard by the Jefe's agents. No elaborate plot, just drunken stupidity. As for the carnage that followed: que sé yo—just a lot of bad luck.

Most of the folks you speak to prefer the story with a supernatural twist. They believe that not only did Trujillo want Abelard's daughter, but when he couldn't snatch her, out of spite he put a fukú on the family's ass. Which is why all the terrible shit that happened happened.

So which was it? you ask. An accident, a conspiracy, or a

fukú? The only answer I can give you is the least satisfying: you'll have to decide for yourself. What's certain is that nothing's certain. We are trawling in silences here. Trujillo and Company didn't leave a paper trail—they didn't share their German contemporaries' lust for documentation. And it's not like the fukú itself would leave a memoir or anything. The remaining Cabrals ain't much help, either; on all matters related to Abelard's imprisonment and to the subsequent destruction of the clan there is within the family a silence that stands monument to the generations, that sphinxes all attempts at narrative reconstruction. A whisper here and there but nothing more.

Which is to say if you're looking for a full story, I don't have it. Oscar searched for it too, in his last days, and it's not certain whether he found it either.

Let's be honest, though. The rap about The Girl Trujillo Wanted is a pretty common one on the Island.[29] As common as krill. (Not that krill is too common on the Island but you get the drift.) So common that Mario Vargas Llosa didn't have to do much except open his mouth to sift it out of the air. There's

29. Anacaona, a.k.a. the Golden Flower. One of the Founding Mothers of the New World and the most beautiful Indian in the World. (The Mexicans might have their Malinche, but we Dominicans have our Anacaona.) Anacaona was the wife of Caonabo, one of the five caciques who ruled our Island at the time of the "Discovery." In his accounts, Bartolomé de las Casas described her as "a woman of great prudence and authority, very courtly and gracious in her manner of speaking and her gestures." Other witnesses put it more succinctly: the chick was hot and, it would turn out, warrior-brave. When the Euros started going Hannibal Lecter on the

one of these bellaco tales in almost everybody's hometown. It's one of those easy stories because in essence *it explains it all*. Trujillo took your houses, your properties, put your pops and your moms in jail? Well, it was because he wanted to fuck the beautiful daughter of the house! And your family wouldn't let him!

Shit really is perfect. Makes for plenty of fun reading.

But there's another, less-known, variant of the Abelard vs. Trujillo narrative. A secret history that claims that Abelard didn't get in trouble because of his daughter's culo or because of an imprudent joke.

This version contends that he got in trouble because of a book.

(Cue the theremin, please.)

Tainos, they killed Anacaona's husband (which is another story). And like all good warrior-women she tried to rally her people, tried to resist, but the Europeans were the original fukú, no stopping them. Massacre after massacre. Upon being captured, Anacaona tried to parley, saying: "Killing is not honorable, neither does violence redress our honor. Let us build a bridge of love that our enemies may cross, leaving their footprints for all to see." The Spanish weren't trying to build no bridges, though. After a bogus trial they hung brave Anacaona. In Santo Domingo, in the shadow of one of our first churches. The End.

A common story you hear about Anacaona in the DR is that on the eve of her execution she was offered a chance to save herself: all she had to do was marry a Spaniard who was obsessed with her. (See the trend? Trujillo wanted the Mirabal Sisters, and the Spaniard wanted Anacaona.) Offer that choice to a contemporary Island girl and see how fast she fills out that passport application. Anacaona, however, tragically old-school, was reported to have said, Whitemen, kiss my hurricane ass! And that was the end of Anacaona. The Golden Flower. One of the Founding Mothers of the New World and the most beautiful Indian in the World.

Sometime in 1944 (so the story goes), while Abelard was still worried about whether he was in trouble with Trujillo, he started writing a book about—what else?—Trujillo. By 1945 there was already a tradition of ex-officials writing tell-all books about the Trujillo regime. But that apparently was not the kind of book Abelard was writing. His shit, if we are to believe the whispers, was an exposé of the supernatural roots of the Trujillo regime! A book about the Dark Powers of the President, a book in which Abelard argued that the tales the common people told about the president—that he was supernatural, that he was not human—may in some ways have been *true*. That it was possible that Trujillo was, if not in fact, then in principle, a creature from another world!

I only wish I could have read that thing. (I know Oscar did too.) That shit would have been one wild motherfucking ride. Alas, the grimoire in question (so the story goes) was conveniently destroyed after Abelard was arrested. No copies survive. Not his wife or his children knew about its existence, either. Only one of the servants who helped him collect the folktales on the sly, etc., etc. What can I tell you? In Santo Domingo a story is not a story unless it casts a supernatural shadow. It was one of those fictions with a lot of disseminators but no believers. Oscar, as you might imagine, found this version of the Fall very very attractive. Appealed to the deep structures in his nerd brain. Mysterious books, a supernatural, or perhaps alien, dictator who had installed himself on the first Island of the New World and then cut it off from everything else, who could send a curse to destroy his enemies—that was some New Age Lovecraft shit.

The Lost Final Book of Dr. Abelard Luis Cabral. I'm sure that this is nothing more than a figment of our Island's hypertrophied voodoo imagination. And nothing less. The Girl Trujillo Wanted might be trite as far as foundation myths go but at least it's something you can really believe in, no? Something real.

Strange, though, that when all was said and done, Trujillo never went after Jackie, even though he had Abelard in his grasp. He was known to be unpredictable, but still, it's odd, isn't it?

Also strange that none of Abelard's books, not the four he authored or the hundreds he owned, survive. Not in an archive, not in a private collection. Not a one. All of them either lost or destroyed. Every paper he had in his house was confiscated and reportedly burned. You want creepy? Not one single example of his handwriting remains. I mean, OK, Trujillo was thorough. But not one scrap of paper with his handwriting? That was more than thorough. You got to fear a motherfucker or what he's writing to do something like that.

But hey, it's only a story, with no solid evidence, the kind of shit only a nerd could love.

THE SENTENCE

No matter what you believe: in February 1946, Abelard was officially convicted of all charges and sentenced to eighteen years. Eighteen years! Gaunt Abelard dragged from the courtroom before he could say a word. Socorro, immensely pregnant, had to be restrained from attacking the judge. Maybe you'll ask, Why was there was no outcry in the papers, no actions among the civil rights groups, no opposition parties rallying to the cause? Nigger, please: there were no papers, no civil rights groups, no opposition parties; there was only Trujillo. And talk about jurisprudence: Abelard's lawyer got one phone call from the Palacio and promptly dropped the appeal. It's better we say nothing, he advised Socorro. He'll live longer. Say nothing, say everything—it didn't matter. It was the Fall. The fourteen-room house in La Vega, the luxurious apartment in Santiago, the stables in which you could comfortably billet a dozen horses, the two prosperous supermercados and the string of fíncas vanished in the detonation, were all confiscated by the Trujillato and ended up dispersed among the Jefe and his minions, two of whom had been out with Abelard the night he said the Bad Thing. (I could reveal their names but I believe you already know one of them; he was a certain trusted neighbor.) But no disappearance was more total, more ultimate, than Abelard's.

Losing your house and all your properties, that was par for the course with the Trujillato—but the arrest (or if you're more into the fantastic: that book) precipitated an unprecedented downturn in the family fortune. Tripped, at some cosmic level, a lever against the family. Call it a whole lot of bad luck, outstanding karmic debt, or something else. (Fukú?) Whatever it was, the shit started coming at the family something awful and there are some people who would say it's never ever stopped.

FALLOUT

The family claims the first sign was that Abelard's third and final daughter, given the light early on in her father's capsulization, was born black. And not just any kind of black. But *black* black—kongoblack, shangoblack, kaliblack, zapoteblack, rekhablack—and no amount of fancy Dominican racial legerdemain was going to obscure the fact. That's the kind of culture I belong to: people took their child's black complexion as an ill omen.

You want a real first sign?

Not two months after giving birth to the third and final daughter (who was named Hypatía Belicia Cabral), Socorro, perhaps blinded by her grief, by her husband's disappearance, by the fact that all her husband's family had begun avoiding them like, well, a fukú, by postpartum depression, stepped in front of a speeding ammunition truck and was dragged nearly to the front of La Casa Amarilla before the driver realized something was wrong. If she wasn't dead on impact she was certainly dead by the time they pried her body from the truck's axles.

It was the very worst kind of luck, but what could be done? With a dead mom and a dad in prison, with the rest of the family scarce (and I mean Trujillo-scarce), the daughters had to be divvied up among whoever would take them. Jackie got sent to her wealthy godparents in La Capital, while Astrid ended up with relatives in San Juan de la Maguana.

They never saw each other or their father again.

Even those among you who don't believe in fukús of any kind might have wondered what in Creation's name was going on. Shortly after Socorro's horrible accident, Esteban the Gallo, the family's number-one servant, was fatally stabbed outside a cabaret; the attackers were never found. Lydia perished soon after, some say of grief, others of a cancer in her womanly parts. Her body was not found for months. After all, she lived alone.

In 1948, Jackie, the family's Golden Child, was found drowned in her godparents' pool. The pool that had been drained down to its last two feet of water. Up to that point she'd been unflaggingly cheerful, the sort of talkative negra who could have found a positive side to a mustard-gas attack. Despite her traumas, despite the circumstances around her separation from her parents, she disappointed no one, exceeded all expectations. She was number one in her class academically, beating out even the private-school children of the American Colony, so off-the-hook intelligent she made a habit of correcting her teachers' mistakes on exams. She was captain of the debate team, captain of the swim team, and in tennis had no equal, was fucking golden. But never got over the Fall or her role in it, was how people explained it. (Though how odd is it that she was accepted to medical school in France three days before she "killed herself" and from all evidence couldn't wait to be gone from Santo Domingo.)

Her sister, Astrid—we scarcely knew you, babe—wasn't much luckier. In 1951, while praying in a church in San Juan, where she lived with her tíos, a stray bullet flew down the aisle and struck her in the back of the head, killing her instantly. No one knew where the bullet had come from. No one even recalled hearing a weapon discharge.

Of the original family quartet, Abelard lived the longest. Which is ironic since nearly everyone in his circle, including La Inca, believed the government when they announced in 1953 that he was dead. (Why did they do this? Because.) It was only after he died for real that it was revealed that he'd been in Nigüa prison all along. Served fourteen straight years in Trujillo's justice. What a nightmare.[30] A thousand tales I could tell you about Abelard's imprisonment—a thousand tales to wring the salt from your motherfucking *eyes*—but I'm going to spare you the anguish, the torture, the loneliness, and the sickness of those fourteen wasted years, spare you in fact the events and leave you with only the consequences (and you should wonder, rightly, if I've spared you anything).

In 1960, at the height of the clandestine resistance movement against Trujillo, Abelard underwent a particularly

30. Nigüa and El Pozo de Nagua were death camps—Ultamos—considered the worst prisons in the New World. Most niggers who ended up in Nigüa during the Trujillato never left alive, and those who did probably wished they hadn't. The father of one of my friends spent eight years in Nigüa for failing to show proper deference toward the Jefe's father, and he once spoke of a fellow prisoner who made the mistake of complaining to his jailers about a toothache. The guards shoved a gun in his mouth and blew his brains into orbit. I bet it don't hurt now, the guards guffawed. (The one who actually committed the murder was known thereafter as El Dentista.) Nigüa had many famous alumni, including the writer Juan Bosch, who would go on to become Exiled Anti-Trujillista Number One and eventually president of the Dominican Republic. As Juan Isidro Jiménez Grullón said in his book *Una Gestapo en América*, "es mejor tener cien niguas en un pie que un pie en Nigüa."

gruesome procedure. He was manacled to a chair, placed out in the scorching sun, and then a wet rope was cinched cruelly about his forehead. It was called La Corona, a simple but horribly effective torture. At first the rope just grips your skull, but as the sun dries and tightens it, the pain becomes unbearable, would drive you mad. Among the prisoners of the Trujillato few tortures were more feared. Since it neither killed you nor left you alive. Abelard survived it but was never the same. Turned him into a vegetable, The proud flame of his intellect extinguished. For the rest of his short life he existed in an imbecilic stupor, but there were prisoners who remembered moments when he seemed almost lucid, when he would stand in the fields and stare at his hands and weep, as if recalling that there was once a time when he had been more than this. The other prisoners, out of respect, continued to call him El Doctor. It was said he died a couple of days before Trujillo was assassinated. Buried in an unmarked grave somewhere outside of Nigüa. Oscar visited the site on his last days. Nothing to report. Looked like every other scrabby field in Santo Domingo. He burned candles, left flowers, prayed, and went back to his hotel. The government was supposed to have erected a plaque to the dead of Nigüa Prison, but they never did.

THE THIRD AND FINAL DAUGHTER

What about the third and final daughter, Hypatía Belicia Cabral, who was only two months old when her mother died, who never met her father, who was held by her sisters only a few times before they too disappeared, who spent no time inside Casa Hatüey, who was the literal Child of the Apocalypse? What about her? She was not as easy to place as Astrid or Jackie; she was a newborn, after all, and, well, the scuttlebutt around the family has it that as she was so dark no one on Abelard's side of the family would take her. To make matters worse, she was born bakiní—underweight, sickly. She had problems crying, problems nursing, and no one outside the family wanted the darkchild to live. I know it's taboo to make this accusation, but I doubt that anybody inside the family wanted her to live, either. For a couple of weeks it was touch and go, and if it hadn't been for a kindly darkskinned woman named Zoila who gave her some of her own baby's breastmilk and held her for hours a day she probably wouldn't have made it. By the end of her fourth month the baby seemed to be staging a comeback. She was still bakiní central, but she was starting to put on weight, and her crying, which before had sounded like a murmur from the grave, was growing more and more piercing. Zoila (who had become a guardian angel of sorts) stroked the baby's mottled head and declared: Another six months, mi'jita, and you'll be más fuerte que Lílis.

Beli didn't have six months. (Stability was not in our girl's stars, only Change.) Without any warning a group of Socorro's distant relatives showed up and claimed the child, tore her clean out of Zoila's arms (the very same relatives Socorro had happily put behind her when she married Abelard). I suspect these people hadn't actually intended to take care of the girl for any length of time, were only doing it because they expected some monetary reward from the Cabrals, and when no loot was forthcoming, the Fall was total, the brutos passed the girl on to some even more distant relatives on the outskirts of Azua. And here's where the trail gets funky. These people in Azua seemed to be some real wack jobs, what my moms calls salvajes. After only a month of caring for the unhappy infant, the moms of the family disappeared one afternoon with the baby, and when she returned to her village the baby didn't. She told her vecinos that the baby had died. Some people believed her. Beli, after all, had been ailing for a while. The tiniest little negrita on the planet. Fukú, part three. But most folks figured that she had sold the girl to some other family. Back then, as now, the buying and selling of children, common enough.

And that's exactly what happened. Like a character in one of Oscar's fantasy books, the orphan (who may or may not have been the object of a supernatural vendetta) was sold to complete strangers in another part of Azua. That's right—she was sold. Became a criada, a restavek. Lived anonymously among the poorest sectors on the Island, never knowing who her real people were, and subsequently she was lost from sight for a long long time.[31]

31. I lived in Santo Domingo only until I was nine, and even I knew criadas. Two of them lived in the callejón behind our house, and these girls were the most demolished, overworked human beings I'd known at that time. One girl, Sobeida, did all the cooking, all the cleaning, fetched all the water, and took care of two infants for a family of *eight*—and chickie was only seven years old! She never went to school, and if my brother's first girlfriend, Yohana, hadn't taken the time—stolen behind her people's back—to teach her her ABCs, she wouldn't have known nada. Every year I came home from the States, it was the same thing; quiet hardworking

THE BURNING

The next time she appears is in 1955. As a whisper in La Inca's ear.

I think we should be very clear and very honest about La Inca's disposition during the period we have been calling the Fall. Despite some claims that she was living in exile in Puerto Rico during the Fall, La Inca was in fact in Baní, isolated from her family, mourning the death of her husband three years earlier. (Point of clarification for the conspiracy-minded: his death occurred before the Fall, so he was definitely not a victim of it.) Those early years of her mourning had been bad; her hubby the only person she had ever loved, who had ever really loved her, and they'd been married only months before he passed. She was lost in the wilderness of her grief, so when word came down that her cousin Abelard was in Big Trouble with Trujillo, La Inca, to her undying shame, did nothing. She was in such pain. What could she have done? When news reached her of the death of Socorro and the dispersal of the daughters, she still, to her everlasting

---

Sobeida would stop in for a second to say a word to my abuelo and my mother (and also to watch a couple of minutes of a novela) before running off to finish her next chore. (My mother always brought her a gift of cash; the one time she brought her a dress, her "people" were wearing it the next day.) I tried to talk to her, of course—Mr. Community Activist—but she would skitter away from me and my stupid questions. What can you two talk about? my moms demanded. La probrecita can't even write her own name. And then when she was fifteen, one of the callejón idiots knocked her up, and now, my mother tells me, the family has got her kid working for them too, bringing in the water for his mother.

shame, did nothing. Let the rest of the family figure it out. It wasn't until she heard that both Jackie and Astrid had passed that she finally pulled herself out of her malaise long enough to realize that dead husband or no dead husband, mourning or no mourning, she had failed utterly in her responsibility toward her cousin, who had always been kind to her, and who had supported her marriage when the rest of the family did not. This revelation both shamed and mortified La Inca. She got herself cleaned up and went looking for the Third and Final Daughter—but when she got to the family in Azua that had bought the girl, they showed her a little grave, and that was it. She had powerful suspicions about this evil family, about the girl, but since she wasn't a psychic, or a CSI, there was nothing she could do. She had to accept that the girl had perished, and that it was, in part, her fault. One good thing about that shame and that guilt: it blew her out of her mourning. She came back to life. Opened up a string of bakeries. Dedicated herself to serving her customers. Every now and then would dream about the little negrita, the last of her dead cousin's seed. Hi, tía, the girl would say, and La Inca would wake up with a knot in her chest.

And then it was 1955. The Year of the Benefactor. La Inca's bakeries were kicking ass, she had reestablished herself as a presence in her town, when one fine day she heard an astonishing tale. It seems that a little campesina girl living in Outer Azua had tried to attend the new rural school the Trujillato had built out there but her parents, who weren't her parents, didn't want her to attend. The girl, though, was immensely stubborn, and the parents who weren't her parents flipped when the girl kept skipping out on work to attend classes, and in the ensuing brawl the poor muchachita got burned, horribly; the father, who was not her father, splashed a pan of hot oil on her naked back. The burn nearly killing her. (In Santo Domingo good news might travel like thunder, but bad news travels like light.) And the wildest part of the story? Rumor had it that this burned girl was a relative of La Inca!

How could that be possible? La Inca demanded.

Do you remember your cousin who was the doctor up in La Vega? The one who went to prison for saying the Bad Thing about Trujillo? Well, fulano, who knows fulano, who knows fulano, said that that little girl is his daughter!

For two days she didn't want to believe. People were always starting rumors about everything in Santo Domingo. Didn't want to believe that the girl could have survived, could be alive in Outer Azua, of all places![32] For two nights she slept poorly, had to medicate herself with mamajuana,

32. Those of you who know the Island (or are familiar with Kinito Méndez's oeuvre) know exactly the landscape I'm talking about. These are not the campos that your folks rattle on about. These are not the guanábana campos of our dreams. Outer Azua is one of the poorest areas in the DR; it is a wasteland, our own homegrown sertão, resembled the irradiated terrains from those end-of-the-world scenarios that Oscar loved so much—Outer Azua was the Outland, the Badlands, the Cursed Earth, the Forbidden Zone, the Great Wastes, the Desert of Glass, the Burning Lands, the Doben-al, it was Salusa Secundus, it was Ceti Alpha Six, it was Tatooine. Even the residents could have passed for survivors of some not-so-distant holocaust. The poor ones—and it was with these infelices that Beli had lived—often wore rags, walked around barefoot, and lived in homes that looked like they'd been constructed from the detritus of the former world.

and finally, after dreaming of her dead husband and as much to settle her own conscience as anything, La Inca asked her neighbor and number-one dough-kneader, Carlos Moya (the man who had once kneaded her dough, before running off and getting married) to drive her to where this girl was supposed to live. If she is my cousin's daughter I will know her just by looking at her, she announced. Twenty-four hours later La Inca returned with an impossibly tall, impossibly skinny half-dead Belicia in tow, La Inca's mind firmly and permanently set against both campos and their inhabitants. Not only had these savages burned the girl, they proceeded to punish her further by locking her in a chicken coop at night! At first they hadn't wanted to bring her out. She can't be your family, she's a prieta. But La Inca insisted, used the

If you would have dropped Astronaut Taylor amongst these folks he would have fallen to the ground and bellowed, You finally did it! (No, Charlton, it's not the End of the World, it's just Outer Azua.) The only non-thorn non-insect non-lizard life-forms that thrived at these latitudes were the Alcoa mining operations and the region's famous goats (los que brincan las Himalayas y cagan en la bandera de España).

Outer Azua was a dire wasteland indeed. My moms, a contemporary of Belicia, spent a record-breaking fifteen years in Outer Azua. And while her childhood was far nicer than Beli's she nevertheless reports that in the early fifties these precincts were full of smoke, inbreeding, intestinal worms, twelve-year-old brides, and full-on whippings. Families were Glasgow-ghetto huge because, she claims, there was nothing to do after dark and because infant mortality rates were so extreme and calamities so vast you needed a serious supply of reinforcements if you expected your line to continue. A child who *hadn't* escaped a close brush with Death was looked at askance. (My mom survived a rheumatic fever that killed her favorite cousin; by the time her own fever broke and she regained consciousness, my abuelos had already bought the coffin they expected to bury her in.)

Voice on them, and when the girl emerged from the coop, unable to unbend her body because of the burn, La Inca had stared into her wild furious eyes and seen Abelard and Socorro staring back at her. Forget the black skin—it was her. The Third and Final Daughter. Thought lost, now found.

I am your real family, La Inca said forcefully. I am here to save you.

And so, in a heartbeat, by a whisper, were two lives irrevocably changed. La Inca installed Beli in the spare room in her house where her husband had once taken his naps and worked on his carvings. Filed the paperwork to give the girl an identity, called in the doctors. The girl's burns were unbelievably savage. (One hundred and ten hit points minimum.) A monsterglove of festering ruination extending from the back of her neck to the base of her spine. A bomb crater, a world-scar like those of a hibakusha. As soon as she could wear real clothes again, La Inca dressed the girl and had her first real photo taken out in front of the house.

Here she is: Hypatía Belicia Cabral, the Third and Final Daughter. Suspicious, angry, scowling, uncommunicative, a wounded hungering campesina, but with an expression and posture that shouted in bold, gothic letters: DEFIANT. Darkskinned but clearly her family's daughter. Of this there was no doubt. Already taller than Jackie in her prime. Her eyes exactly the same color as those of the father she knew nothing about.

FORGET-ME-NAUT

Of those nine years (and of the Burning) Beli did not speak. It seems that as soon as her days in Outer Azua were over, as soon as she reached Baní, that entire chapter of her life got slopped into those containers in which governments store nuclear waste, triple-sealed by industrial lasers and deposited in the dark, uncharted trenches of her soul. It says a lot about Beli that for *forty years* she never leaked word one about that period of her life: not to her madre, not to her friends, not to her lovers, not to the Gangster, not to her husband. And certainly not to her beloved children, Lola and Oscar. *Forty years.* What little anyone knows about Beli's Azua days comes exclusively from what La Inca heard the day she rescued Beli from her so-called parents. Even today La Inca rarely saying anything more than *Casi la acabaron.*

In fact, I believe that, barring a couple of key moments, Beli never thought about that life again. Embraced the amnesia that was so common throughout the Islands, five parts denial, five parts negative hallucination. Embraced the power of the Untilles. And from it forged herself anew.

SANCTUARY

But enough. What matters is that in Baní, in La Inca's house, Belicia Cabral found Sanctuary. And in La Inca, the mother she never had. Taught the girl to read, write, dress, eat, behave normally. La Inca a finishing school on fast-forward; for here was a woman with a *civilizing mission*, a woman driven by her own colossal feelings of guilt, betrayal, and failure. And Beli, despite all that she'd endured (or perhaps because of it), turned out to be a most apt pupil. Took to La Inca's civilizing procedures like a mongoose to chicken. By the end of Sanctuary's first year, Beli's rough lines had been kneaded out; she might have cursed more, had more of a temper, her movements more aggressive and unrestrained, had the merciless eyes of a falcon, but she had the posture and speech (and arrogance) of una muchacha respetable. And when she wore long sleeves the scar was only visible on her neck (the edge of a larger ruination certainly, but greatly reduced by the cut of the cloth). This was the girl who would travel to the U.S. in 1962, whom Oscar and Lola would never know. La Inca the only one to have seen Beli at her beginnings, when she slept fully dressed and screamed in the middle of the night, who saw her before she constructed a better self, one with Victorian table manners and a disgust of filth and poor people.

Theirs, as you might imagine, was an odd relationship. La Inca never sought to discuss Beli's time in Azua, would never refer to it, or to the Burning. She pretended it didn't exist (the same way she pretended that the poor slobs in her barrio didn't exist when they, in fact, were overrunning the place). Even when she greased the girl's back, every morning and every night, La Inca only said, Siéntese aquí, señorita. It was a silence, a lack of probing, that Beli found most agreeable. (If only the waves of feeling that would occasionally lap her back could be so easily forgotten.) Instead of talking about the Burning, or Outer Azua, La Inca talked to Beli about her lost, forgotten past, about her father, the famous doctor, about her mother, the beautiful nurse, about her sisters Jackie and Astrid, and about that marvelous castle in the Cibao: Casa Hatüey.

They may never have become best friends—Beli too furious, La Inca too correct—but La Inca did give Beli the greatest of gifts, which she would appreciate only much later; one night La Inca produced an old newspaper, pointed to a fotograph: This, she said, is your father and your mother. This, she said, is who you are.

The day they opened their clinic: so young, both of them looking so serious.

For Beli those months truly were her one and only Sanctuary, a world of safety she never thought possible. She had clothes, she had food, she had time, and La Inca never ever yelled at her. Not for nothing, and didn't let anybody else yell at her either. Before La Inca enrolled her in Colegio El Redentor with the richies, Beli attended the dusty, fly-infested public school with children three years younger than her, made no friends (she couldn't have imagined it any other way), and for the first time in her life began to remember her dreams. It was a luxury she'd never dared indulge in, and in the beginning they seemed as powerful as storms. She had the whole variety, from flying to being lost, and even dreamt about the Burning, how her "father's" face had turned blank at the moment he picked up the skillet. In her dreams she was never scared. Would only shake her head. You're gone, she said. No more.

There was a dream, however, that did haunt her. Where she walked alone through a vast, empty house whose roof was being tattooed by rain. Whose house was it? She had not a clue. But she could hear the voices of children in it.

At first year's end, the teacher asked her to come to the board and fill in the date, a privilege that only the "best" children in the class were given. She is a giant at the board and in their minds the children are calling her what they call her in the world: variations on La Prieta Quemada or La Fea Quemada. When Beli sat down the teacher glanced over her scrawl and said, Well done, Señorita Cabral! She would never forget that day, even when she became the Queen of Diaspora.

Well done, Señorita Cabral!

She would never forget. She was nine years, eleven months. It was the Era of Trujillo.

6

Land of the Lost
1992–1995

THE DARK AGE

After graduation Oscar moved back home. Left a virgin, returned one. Took down his childhood posters—*Star Blazers, Captain Harlock*—and tacked up his college ones—*Akira* and *Terminator 2*. Now that Reagan and the Evil Empire had ridden off into never-never land, Oscar didn't dream about the end no more. Only about the Fall. He put away his Aftermath! game and picked up Space Opera.

These were the early Clinton years but the economy was still sucking an eighties cock and he kicked around, doing nada for almost seven months, went back to subbing at Don Bosco whenever one of the teachers got sick. (Oh, the irony!) He started sending his stories and novels out, but no one seemed interested. Still, he kept trying and kept writing. A year later the substituting turned into a full-time job. He could have refused, could have made a "saving throw" against

Torture, but instead he went with the flow. Watched his horizons collapse, told himself it didn't matter.

Had Don Bosco, since last we visited, been miraculously transformed by the spirit of Christian brotherhood? Had the eternal benevolence of the Lord cleansed the students of their vile? Negro, please. Certainly the school struck Oscar as smaller now, and the older brothers all seemed to have acquired the Innsmouth "look" in the past five years, and there were a grip more kids of color—but some things (like white supremacy and people-of-color self-hate) never change: the same charge of gleeful sadism that he remembered from his youth still electrified the halls. And if he'd thought Don Bosco had been the moronic inferno when he was young— try now that he was older and teaching English and history. Jesú Santa María. A nightmare. He wasn't great at teaching. His heart wasn't in it, and boys of all grades and dispositions shitted on him effusively. Students laughed when they spotted him in the halls. Pretended to hide their sandwiches. Asked in the middle of lectures if he ever got laid, and no matter how he responded they guffawed mercilessly. The students, he knew, laughed as much at his embarrassment as at the image they had of him crushing down on some hapless girl. They drew cartoons of said crushings, and Oscar found these on the floor after class, complete with dialogue bubbles. *No, Mr. Oscar, no!* How demoralizing was that? Every day he watched the "cool" kids torture the crap out of the fat, the ugly, the smart, the poor, the dark, the black, the unpopular, the African, the Indian, the Arab, the immigrant, the strange, the feminino, the gay—and in every one of these clashes he saw himself. In the old days it had been the whitekids who had been the chief tormentors, but now it was kids of color who performed the necessaries. Sometimes he tried to reach out to the school's whipping boys, offer them some words of comfort, You are not alone, you know, in this universe, but the last thing a freak wants is a helping hand from another freak. These boys fled from him in terror. In a burst of enthusiasm he attempted to start a science-fiction and fantasy club, posted signs up in the halls, and for two Thursdays in a row he sat in his classroom after school, his favorite books laid out in an attractive pattern, listened to the roar of receding footsteps in the halls, the occasional shout of Beam me up! and Nanoo-Nanoo! outside his door; then, after thirty minutes of nothing he collected his books, locked the room, and walked down those same halls, alone, his footsteps sounding strangely dainty.

His only friend on the staff was another secular, a twenty-nine-year-old alterna-latina named Nataly (yes, she reminded him of Jenni, minus the outrageous pulchritude, minus the smolder). Nataly had spent four years in a mental hospital (nerves, she said) and was an avowed Wiccan. Her boyfriend, Stan the Can, whom she'd met in the nuthouse ("our honeymoon"), worked as an EMS technician, and Nataly told Oscar that the bodies Stan the Can saw splattered on the streets turned him on for some reason. Stan, he said, sounds like a very curious individual. You can say that again, Nataly sighed. Despite Nataly's homeliness and the medicated fog she inhabited, Oscar entertained some pretty strange Harold Lauder fantasies about her. Since she was not hot enough, in his mind, to date openly, he imagined them in one of those twisted bedroom-only relationships. He had these images of walking into her apartment and ordering her to undress and cook grits for him naked. Two seconds later she'd be kneeling on the tile of her kitchen in only an apron, while he remained fully clothed.

From there it only got weirder.

At the end of his first year, Nataly, who used to sneak whiskey during breaks, who introduced him to *Sandman* and *Eightball*, and who borrowed a lot of money from him and never paid it back, transferred to Ridgewood—Yahoo, she said in her usual deadpan, the suburbs—and that was the end of their friendship. He tried calling a couple of times, but her paranoid boyfriend seemed to live with the phone welded to his head, never seemed to give her any of his messages, so he let it fade, let it fade.

Social life? Those first couple of years home he didn't have one. Once a week he drove out to Woodbridge Mall and checked the RPGs at the Game Room, the comic books at Hero's World, the fantasy novels at Waldenbooks. The nerd circuit. Stared at the toothpick-thin blackgirl who worked at the Friendly's, whom he was in love with but with whom he would never speak.

Al and Miggs—hadn't chilled with them in a long time. They'd both dropped out of college, Monmouth and Jersey City State respectively, and both had jobs at the Blockbuster across town. Probably both end up in the same grave.

Maritza he didn't see no more, either. Heard she'd married a Cuban dude, lived in Teaneck, had a kid and everything.

And Olga? Nobody knew exactly. Rumor had it she tried to rob the local Safeway, Dana Plato style—hadn't bothered to wear a mask even though everybody at the supermarket knew her—and there was talk that she was still in Middlesex, wouldn't be getting out until they were all fifty.

No girls who loved him? No girls anywhere in his life?

Not a one. At least at Rutgers there'd been multitudes and an institutional pretense that allowed a mutant like him to approach without causing a panic. In the real world it wasn't that simple. In the real world girls turned away in disgust when he walked past. Changed seats at the cinema, and one woman on the crosstown bus even told him to stop thinking about her! I know what you're up to, she'd hissed. So stop it.

I'm the permanent bachelor, he wrote in a letter to his sister, who had abandoned Japan to come to New York to be with me. There's nothing permanent in the world, his sister wrote back. He pushed his fist into his eye. Wrote: There is in me.

The home life? Didn't kill him but didn't sustain him, either. His moms, thinner, quieter, less afflicted by the craziness of her youth, still the work-golem, still allowed her Peruvian boarders to pack as many relatives as they wanted into the first floors. And tío Rudolfo, Fofo to his friends, had relapsed to some of his hard pre-prison habits. He was on the caballo again, broke into lightning sweats at dinner, had moved into Lola's room, and now Oscar got to listen to him chickenboning his stripper girlfriends almost every single night. Tío, he yelled out once, less bass on the headboard, if you will. On the walls of his room tío Rudolfo hung pictures of his first years in the Bronx, when he'd been sixteen and wearing all the fly Willie Colón pimpshit, before he'd gone off to Vietnam, only Dominican, he claimed, in the whole damned armed forces. And there were pictures of Oscar's mom and dad. Young. Taken in the two years of their relationship.

You loved him, he said to her.

She laughed. Don't talk about what you know nothing about.

On the outside, Oscar simply looked tired, no taller, no fatter, only the skin under his eyes, pouched from years of quiet desperation, had changed. Inside, he was in a world of hurt. He saw black flashes before his eyes. He saw himself falling through the air. He knew what he was turning into. He was turning into the worst kind of human on the planet: an old bitter dork. Saw himself at the Game Room, picking through the miniatures for the rest of his life. He didn't want this future but he couldn't see how it could be avoided, couldn't figure his way out of it.

Fukú.

The Darkness. Some mornings he would wake up and not be able to get out of bed. Like he had a ten-ton weight on his chest. Like he was under acceleration forces. Would have been funny if it didn't hurt his heart so. Had dreams that he was wandering around the evil planet Gordo, searching for parts for his crashed rocketship, but all he encountered were burned-out ruins, each seething with new debilitating forms of radiation. I don't know what's wrong with me, he said to his sister over the phone. I think the word is *crisis* but every time I open my eyes all I see is *meltdown*. This was when he threw students out of class for breathing, when he would tell his mother to fuck off, when he couldn't write a word, when he went into his tío's closet and put the Colt up to his temple, when he thought about the train bridge. The days he lay in bed and thought about his mother fixing him his plate the rest of his life, what he'd heard her say to his tío the other day when she thought he wasn't around, *I don't care, I'm happy he's here*.

Afterward—when he no longer felt like a whipped dog inside, when he could pick up a pen without wanting to cry—he would suffer from overwhelming feelings of guilt. He would apologize to his mother. If there's a goodness part of my brain, it's like somebody had absconded with it. It's OK, hijo, she said. He would take the car and visit Lola. After a year in Brooklyn she was now in Washington Heights, was letting her hair grow, had been pregnant once, a real moment of excitement, but she aborted it because I was cheating on her with some girl. I have returned, he announced when he stepped in the door. She told him it was OK too, would cook for him, and he'd sit with her and smoke her weed tentatively and not understand why he couldn't sustain this feeling of love in his heart forever.

He began to plan a quartet of science-fiction fantasies that would be his crowning achievement. J. R. R. Tolkien meets E. E. "Doc" Smith. He went on long rides. He drove as far as Amish country, would eat alone at a roadside diner, eye the Amish girls, imagine himself in a preacher's suit, sleep in the back of the car, and then drive home.

Sometimes at night he dreamed about the Mongoose.

(And in case you think his life couldn't get any worse: one day he walked into the Game Room and was surprised to discover that overnight the new generation of nerds weren't buying role-playing games anymore. They were obsessed with *Magic* cards! No one had seen it coming. No more characters or campaigns, just endless battles between decks. All the narrative flensed from the game, all the performance, just straight unadorned mechanics. How the fucking kids loved that shit! He tried to give *Magic* a chance, tried to put together a decent deck, but it just wasn't his thing. Lost everything to an eleven-year-old punk and found himself not really caring. First sign that his Age was coming to a close. When the latest nerdery was no longer compelling, when you preferred the old to the new.)

OSCAR TAKES A VACATION

When Oscar had been at Don Bosco nearly three years, his moms asked him what plans he had for the summer. The last couple of years his tío had been spending the better part of July and August in Santo Domingo and this year his mom had decided it was time to go with. I have not seen mi madre in a long long time, she said quietly. I have many promesas to fulfill, so better now than when I'm dead. Oscar hadn't been home in years, not since his abuela's number-one servant, bedridden for months and convinced that the border was about to be reinvaded, had screamed out *Haitians!* and then died, and they'd all gone to the funeral.

It's strange. If he'd said no, nigger would probably still be OK. (If you call being fukú'd, being beyond misery, OK.) But this ain't no Marvel Comics *What if?*—speculation will have to wait—time, as they say, is growing short. That May, Oscar was, for once, in better spirits. A couple of months earlier, after a particularly nasty bout with the Darkness, he'd started another one of his diets and combined it with long lumbering walks around the neighborhood, and guess what? The nigger stuck with it and lost close on twenty pounds! A milagro! He'd finally repaired his ion drive; the evil planet Gordo was pulling him back, but his fifties-style rocket, the *Hijo de Sacrificio*, wouldn't quit. Behold our cosmic explorer: eyes wide, lashed to his acceleration couch, hand over his mutant heart.

He wasn't svelte by any stretch of the imagination, but he wasn't Joseph Conrad's wife no more, either. Earlier in the month he'd even spoken to a bespectacled blackgirl on a bus, said, So, you're into photosynthesis, and she'd actually lowered her issue of *Cell* and said, Yes, I am. So what if he hadn't ever gotten past Earth Sciences or if he hadn't been able to convert that slight communication into a number or a date? So what if he'd gotten off at the next stop and she hadn't, as he had hoped? Homeboy was, for the first time in ten years, feeling resurgent; nothing seemed to bother him, not his students, not the fact that PBS had canceled *Doctor Who*, not his loneliness, not his endless flow of rejection letters; he felt *insuperable*, and Santo Domingo summers . . . well, Santo Domingo summers have their own particular allure, even for one as nerdy as Oscar.

Every summer Santo Domingo slaps the Diaspora engine into reverse, yanks back as many of its expelled children as it can; airports choke with the overdressed; necks and luggage carousels groan under the accumulated weight of that year's cadenas and paquetes, and pilots fear for their planes—overburdened beyond belief—and for themselves; restaurants, bars, clubs, theaters, malecones, beaches, resorts, hotels, moteles, extra rooms, barrios, colonias, campos, ingenios swarm with quisqueyanos from the world over. Like someone had sounded a general reverse evacuation order: Back home, everybody! Back home! From Washington Heights to Roma, from Perth Amboy to Tokyo, from Brijeporr to Amsterdam, from Lawrence to San Juan; this is when basic thermodynamic principle gets modified so that reality can now reflect a final aspect, the picking-up of big-assed girls and the taking of said to moteles; it's one big party; one big party for everybody but the poor, the dark, the jobless, the sick, the Haitian, their children, the bateys, the kids that certain Canadian, American, German, and Italian tourists love to rape—yes, sir, nothing like a Santo Domingo summer. And so for the first time in years Oscar said, My elder spirits have been talking to me, Ma. I think I might accompany you. He was imagining himself in the middle of all that ass-getting, imagining himself in love with an Island girl. (A brother can't be wrong forever, can he?)

So abrupt a change in policy was this that even Lola quizzed him about it. You *never* go to Santo Domingo.

He shrugged. I guess I want to try something new.

THE CONDENSED NOTEBOOK
OF A RETURN TO A NATIVELAND

Family de León flew down to the Island on the fifteenth of June. Oscar scared shitless and excited, but no one was funnier than their mother, who got done up like she was having an audience with King Juan Carlos of Spain himself. If she'd owned a fur she would have worn it, anything to communicate the distance she'd traveled, to emphasize how not like the rest of these dominicanos she was. Oscar, for one, had never seen her looking so dolled-up and elegante. Or acting so comparona. Belicia giving *everybody* a hard time, from the check-in people to the flight attendants, and when they settled into their seats in first class (she was paying) she looked around as if scandalized: These are not gente de calidad!

It was also reported that Oscar drooled on himself and didn't wake up for the meal or the movie, only when the plane touched down and everybody clapped.

What's going on? he demanded, alarmed.

Relax, Mister. That just means we made it.

The beat-you-down heat was the same, and so was the fecund tropical smell that he had never forgotten, that to him was more evocative than any madeleine, and likewise the air pollution and the thousands of motos and cars and dilapidated trucks on the roads and the clusters of peddlers at every traffic light (so dark, he noticed, and his mother said, dismissively, Maldito haitianos) and people walking languidly with nothing to shade them from the sun and the buses that charged past so overflowing with passengers that from the outside they looked like they were making a rush delivery of spare limbs to some far-off war and the general ruination of so many of the buildings as if Santo Domingo was the place that crumbled crippled concrete shells came to die—and the hunger on some of the kids' faces, can't forget that—but also it seemed in many places like a whole new country was materializing atop the ruins of the old one: there were now better roads and nicer vehicles and brand-new luxury air-conditioned buses plying the longer routes to the Cibao and beyond and U.S. fast-food restaurants (Dunkin' Donuts and Burger King) and local ones whose names and logos he did not recognize (Pollos Victorina and El Provocón No. 4) and traffic lights everywhere that nobody seemed to heed. Biggest change of all? A few years back La Inca had moved her entire operation to La Capital—we're getting too big for Baní—and now the family had a new house in Mirador Norte and six bakeries throughout the city's outer zones. We're capitaleños, his cousin, Pedro Pablo (who had picked them up at the airport), announced proudly.

La Inca too had changed since Oscar's last visit. She had always seemed ageless, the family's very own Galadriel, but now he could see that it wasn't true. Nearly all her hair had turned white, and despite her severe unbent carriage, her skin was finely crosshatched with wrinkles and she had to put on glasses to read anything. She was still spry and proud and when she saw him, first time in nearly seven years, she put her hands on his shoulders and said, Mi hijo, you have finally returned to us.

Hi, Abuela. And then, awkwardly: Bendición.

(Nothing more moving, though, than La Inca and his mother. At first saying nothing and then his mother covering her face and breaking down, saying in this little-girl voice: Madre, I'm home. And then the both of them holding each other and crying and Lola joining them and Oscar not knowing what to do so he joined his cousin, Pedro Pablo, who was shuttling all the luggage from the van to the patio de atrás.)

It really was astonishing how much he'd forgotten about the DR: the little lizards that were everywhere, and the roosters in the morning, followed shortly by the cries of the plataneros and the bacalao guy and his tío Carlos Moya, who smashed him up that first night with shots of Brugal and who got all misty at the memories he had of him and his sister.

But what he had forgotten most of all was how incredibly beautiful Dominican women were.

Duh, Lola said.

On the rides he took those first couple of days he almost threw his neck out.

I'm in Heaven, he wrote in his journal.

Heaven? His cousin Pedro Pablo sucked his teeth with exaggerated disdain. Esto aquí es un maldito *infierno*.

EVIDENCE OF A BROTHER'S PAST

In the pictures Lola brought home there are shots of Oscar in the back of the house reading Octavia Butler, shots of Oscar on the Malecón with a bottle of Presidente in his hand, shots of Oscar at the Columbus lighthouse, where half of Villa Duarte used to stand, shots of Oscar with Pedro Pablo in Villa Juana buying spark plugs, shots of Oscar trying on a hat on the Conde, shots of Oscar standing next to a burro in Baní, shots of Oscar next to his sister (she in a string bikini that could have blown your corneas out). You can tell he's trying too. He's smiling a lot, despite the bafflement in his eyes.

He's also, you might notice, not wearing his fatguy coat.

OSCAR GOES NATIVE

After his initial homecoming week, after he'd been taken to a bunch of sights by his cousins, after he'd gotten somewhat used to the scorching weather and the surprise of waking up to the roosters and being called Huáscar by everybody (that was his Dominican name, something else he'd forgotten), after he refused to succumb to that whisper that all long-term immigrants carry inside themselves, the whisper that says *You do not belong*, after he'd gone to about fifty clubs and because he couldn't dance salsa, merengue, or bachata had sat and drunk Presidentes while Lola and his cousins burned holes in the floor, after he'd explained to people a hundred times that he'd been separated from his sister at birth, after he spent a couple of quiet mornings on his own, writing, after he'd given out all his taxi money to beggars and had to call his cousin Pedro Pablo to pick him up, after he'd watched shirtless shoeless seven-year-olds fighting each other for the scraps he'd left on his plate at an outdoor café, after his mother took them all to dinner in the Zona Colonial and the waiters kept looking at their party askance (Watch out, Mom, Lola said, they probably think you're Haitian—La única haitiana aquí eres tú, mi amor, she retorted), after a skeletal vieja grabbed both his hands and begged him for a penny, after his sister had said, You think that's bad, you should see the bateys, after he'd spent a day in Baní (the campo where La Inca had been raised) and he'd taken a dump in a latrine and wiped his ass with a corn cob—now *that's* entertainment, he wrote in his journal—after he'd gotten somewhat used to the surreal whirligig that was life in La Capital—the guaguas, the cops, the mind-boggling poverty, the Dunkin' Donuts, the beggars, the Haitians selling roasted peanuts at the intersections, the mind-boggling poverty, the asshole tourists hogging up all the beaches, the Xica da Silva novelas where homegirl got naked every five seconds that Lola and his female cousins were cracked on, the afternoon walks on the Conde, the mind-boggling poverty, the snarl of streets and rusting zinc shacks that were the barrios populares, the masses of niggers he waded through every day who ran him over if he stood still, the skinny watchmen standing in front of stores with their broke-down shotguns, the music, the raunchy jokes heard on the streets, the mind-boggling poverty, being piledrived into the corner of a concho by the combined weight of four other customers, the music, the new tunnels driving down into the bauxite earth, the signs that banned donkey carts from the same tunnels—after he'd gone to Boca Chica and Villa Mella and eaten so much chicharrones he had to throw up on the side of the road—now *that*, his tío Rudolfo said, is entertainment—after his tío Carlos Moya berated him for having stayed away so long, after his abuela berated him for having stayed away so long, after his cousins berated him for having stayed away so long, after he saw again the unforgettable beauty of the Cibao, after he heard the stories about his mother, after he stopped marveling at the amount of political propaganda plastered up on every spare wall—ladrones, his mother announced, one and all—after the touched-in-the-head tío who'd been tortured during Balaguer's reign came over and got into a heated political argument with Carlos Moya (after which they both got drunk), after he'd caught his first sunburn in Boca Chica, after he'd swum in the Caribbean, after tío Rudolfo had gotten him blasted on mamajuana de marisco, after he'd seen his first Haitians kicked off a guagua because niggers claimed they "smelled," after he'd nearly gone nuts over all the bellezas he saw, after he helped his mother install two new air conditioners and crushed his finger so bad he had dark blood under the nail, after all the gifts they'd brought had been properly distributed, after Lola introduced him to the boyfriend she'd dated as a teenager, now a capitaleño as well, after he'd seen the pictures of Lola in her private-school uniform, a tall muchacha with heartbreak eyes, after he'd brought flowers to his abuela's number-one servant's grave who had taken care of him when he was little, after he had diarrhea so bad his mouth watered before each detonation, after he'd visited all the rinky-dink museums in the capital with his sister, after he stopped being dismayed that everybody called him gordo (and, worse, gringo), after he'd been overcharged for almost everything he wanted to buy, after La Inca prayed over him nearly every morning, after he caught a cold because his abuela set the air conditioner in his room so high, he decided suddenly and without warning to stay on the Island for the rest of the summer with his mother and his tío. Not to go home with Lola. It was a decision that came to him one night on the Malecón, while staring out over the ocean. What do I have waiting for me in Paterson? he wanted to know. He wasn't teaching that summer and he had all his notebooks with him. Sounds like a good idea to me, his sister said. You need some time in the patria. Maybe you'll even find yourself a nice campesina. It felt like the right thing to do. Help clear his head and his heart of the gloom that had filled them these months. His mother was less hot on the idea but La Inca waved her into silence. Hijo, you can stay here all your life. (Though he found it strange that she made him put on a crucifix immediately thereafter.)

So, after Lola flew back to the States (Take good care of yourself, Mister) and the terror and joy of his return had subsided, after he settled down in Abuela's house, the house that Diaspora had built, and tried to figure out what he was going to do with the rest of his summer now that Lola was gone, after his fantasy of an Island girlfriend seemed like a distant joke—Who the fuck had *he* been kidding? He couldn't dance, he didn't have loot, he didn't dress, he wasn't confident, he wasn't handsome, he wasn't from Europe, he wasn't fucking no Island girls—after he spent one week writing and (ironically enough) turned down his male cousins' offer to take him to a whorehouse like fifty times, Oscar fell in love with a semiretired puta.

Her name was Ybón Pimentel. Oscar considered her the start of his *real* life.

LA BEBA

She lived two houses over and, like the de Leóns, was a newcomer to Mirador Norte. (Oscar's moms had bought their house with double shifts at her two jobs. Ybón bought hers with double shifts too, but in a window in Amsterdam.) She was one of those golden mulatas that French-speaking Caribbeans call chabines, that my boys call chicas de oro; she had snarled, apocalyptic hair, copper eyes, and was one whiteskinned relative away from jaba.

At first Oscar thought she was only a visitor, this tiny, slightly paunchy babe who was always high-heeling it out to her Pathfinder. (She didn't have the Nuevo Mundo wannabe American look of the majority of his neighbors.) The two times Oscar bumped into her—during breaks in his writing he would go for walks along the hot, bland cul-de-sacs, or sit at the local café—she smiled at him. And the third time they saw each other—here, folks, is where the miracles begin— she sat at his table and said: What are you reading? At first he didn't know what was happening, and then he realized: *Holy Shit!* A female was talking to *him*. (It was an unprece- dented change in fortune, as though his threadbare Skein of Destiny had accidentally gotten tangled with that of a doper, more fortunate brother.) Turned out Ybón knew his abuela, gave her rides whenever Carlos Moya was out making deliveries. You're the boy in her pictures, she said with a sly smile. I was little, he said defensively. And besides, that was before the war changed me. She didn't laugh. That's probably what it is. Well, I have to go. On went the shades, up went the ass, out went the belleza. Oscar's erection following her like a dowser's wand.

Ybón had attended the UASD a long time ago but she was no college girl, she had lines around her eyes and seemed, to Oscar at least, mad open, mad worldly, had the sort of intense zipper-gravity that hot middle-aged women exude effortlessly. The next time he ran into her in front of her house (he had watched for her), she said, Good morning, Mr. de León, in English. How are you? I am well, he said. And you? She beamed. I am well, thank you. He didn't know what to do with his hands so he laced them behind his back like a gloomy parson. And for a minute there was nothing and she was unlocking her gate and he said, desperately, It is very hot. Ay sí, she said. And I thought it was just my menopause. And then looking over her shoulder at him, curious perhaps at this strange character who was trying not to look at her at all, or recognizing how in crush he was with her and feeling charitable, she said, Come inside. I'll give you a drink.

The casa near empty—his abuela's crib was spare but this was on some next shit—Haven't had the time to move in yet, she said offhandedly—and because there wasn't any furniture besides a kitchen table, a chair, a bureau, a bed, and a TV, they had to sit on the bed. (Oscar peeped the astrology books under the bed and a collection of Paulo Coelho's novels. She followed

his gaze and said with a smile, Paulo Coelho saved my life.)
She gave him a beer, had a double scotch, then for the next six
hours regaled him with tales from her life. You could tell she
hadn't had anyone to talk to in a long time. Oscar reduced to
nodding and trying to laugh when she laughed. The whole
time he was sweating bullets. Wondering if this is when he
should try something. It wasn't until midway through their
chat that it hit Oscar that the job Ybón talked so volubly about
was prostitution. It was *Holy Shit!* the Sequel. Even though
putas were one of Santo Domingo's premier exports, Oscar
had never been in a prostitute's house in his entire life.

Staring out her bedroom window, he saw his abuela
on her front lawn, looking for him. He wanted to raise the
window and call to her but Ybón didn't allow for any
interruptions.

Ybón was an odd odd bird. She might have been talkative,
the sort of easygoing woman a brother can relax around, but
there was something slightly detached about her too; as
though (Oscar's words now) she were some marooned alien
princess who existed partially in another dimension; the sort
of woman who, cool as she was, slips out of your head a little
too quickly, a quality she recognized and was thankful for, as
though she relished the short bursts of attention she provoked
from men, but not anything sustained. She didn't seem to
mind being the girl you called every couple of months at
eleven at night, just to see what she was "up to." As much relationship as she could handle. Reminds me of the morir-vivir
plants we played with as kids, except in reverse.

Her Jedi mindtricks did not, however, work on Oscar.

When it came to girls, the brother had a mind like a yogi. He latched on and stayed latched. By the time he left her house that night and walked home through the Island's million attack mosquitoes he was lost.

(Did it matter that Ybón started mixing Italian in with her Spanish after her fourth drink or that she almost fell flat on her face when she showed him out? Of course not!)

He was in love.

His mother and his abuela met him at the door; excuse the stereotype, but both had their hair in rolos and couldn't believe his sinvergüencería. Do you know that woman's a PUTA? Do you know she bought that house CULEANDO?

For a moment he was overwhelmed by their rage, and then he found his footing and shot back, Do you know her aunt was a JUDGE? Do you know her father worked for the PHONE COMPANY?

You want a woman, I'll get you a good woman, his mother said, peering angrily out the window. But that puta's only going to take your money.

I don't need your help. And she ain't a puta.

La Inca laid one of her Looks of Incredible Power on him. Hijo, obey your mother.

For a moment he almost did. Both women focusing all their energies on him, and then he tasted the beer on his lips and shook his head.

His tío Rudolfo, who was watching the game on the TV, took that moment to call out, in his best Grandpa Simpson voice: Prostitutes ruined my life.

More miracles. The next morning Oscar woke up and despite the tremendous tidings in his heart, despite the fact that he wanted to run over to Ybón's house and shackle himself to her bed, he didn't. He knew he had to cogerlo con take it easy, knew he had to rein in his lunatic heart or he would blow it. Whatever *it* was. Of course the nigger was entertaining mad fantasies inside his head. What do you expect? He was a not-so-fat fatboy who'd never kissed a girl, never even lain in bed with one, and now the world was waving a beautiful puta under his nose. Ybón, he was sure, was the Higher Power's last-ditch attempt to put him back on the proper path of Dominican male-itude. If he blew this, well, it was back to playing Villains and Vigilantes for him. This is it, he told himself. His chance to win. He decided to play the oldest card in the deck. The wait. So for one whole day he moped around the house, tried to write but couldn't, watched a comedy show where black Dominicans in grass skirts put white Dominicans in safari outfits into cannibal cookpots and everybody wondered aloud where their biscocho was. Scary. By noon he had driven Dolores, the thirty-eight-year-old heavily scarred "muchacha" who cooked and cleaned for the family, up a wall.

The next day at one he pulled on a clean chacabana and strolled over to her house. (Well, he sort of trotted.) A red Jeep was parked outside, nose to nose with her Pathfinder. A Policía Nacional plate. He stood in front of her gate while the sun stomped down on him. Felt like a stooge. Of course she was married. Of course she had boyfriends. His optimism, that swollen red giant, collapsed down to an obliterating point of gloom from which there was no escape. Didn't stop him coming back the next day but no one was home, and by the time he saw her again, three days later, he was starting to think that she had warped back to whatever Forerunner world had spawned her. Where were you? he said, trying not to sound as miserable as he felt. I thought maybe you fell in the tub or something. She smiled and gave her ass a little shiver. I was making the patria strong, mi amor.

He had caught her in front of the TV, doing aerobics in a pair of sweatpants and what might have been described as a halter top. It was hard for him not to stare at her body. When she first let him in she'd screamed, Oscar, querido! Come in! Come in!

A NOTE FROM YOUR AUTHOR

I know what Negroes are going to say. Look, he's writing Suburban Tropical now. A puta and she's not an underage snort-addicted mess? Not believable. Should I go down to the Feria and pick me up a more representative model? Would it be better if I turned Ybón into this other puta I know, Jahyra, a friend and a neighbor in Villa Juana, who still lives in one of those old-style pink wooden houses with the zinc roof? Jahyra—your quintessential Caribbean puta, half cute, half not—who'd left home at the age of fifteen and lived in Curazao, Madrid, Amsterdam, and Rome, who also has two kids, who'd gotten an enormous breast job when she was sixteen in Madrid, bigger almost than Luba from *Love and Rockets* (but not as big as Beli), who claimed, proudly, that her aparato had paved half the streets in her mother's hometown. Would it be better if I had Oscar meet Ybón at the World Famous Lavacarro, where Jahyra works six days a week, where a brother can get his head *and* his fenders polished while he waits, talk about convenience? Would this be better? Yes?

But then I'd be lying. I know I've thrown a lot of fantasy and sci-fi in the mix but this is supposed to be a *true* account of the Brief Wondrous Life of Oscar Wao. Can't we believe that an Ybón can exist and that a brother like Oscar might be due a little luck after twenty-three years?

This is your chance. If blue pill, continue. If red pill, return to the Matrix.

THE GIRL FROM SABANA IGLESIA

In their photos, Ybón looks young. It's her smile and the way she perks up her body for every shot as if she's presenting herself to the world, as if she's saying, Ta-da, here I am, take it or leave it. She dressed young too, but she was a solid thirty-six, perfect age for anybody but a stripper. In the close-ups you can see the crow's-feet, and she complained all the time about her little belly, the way her breasts and her ass were starting to lose their firm, which was why, she said, she had to be in the gym five days a week. When you're sixteen a body like this is free; when you're forty—pffft!—it's a full-time occupation. The third time Oscar came over, Ybón doubled up on the scotches again and then took down her photo albums from the closet and showed him all the pictures of herself when she'd been sixteen, seventeen, eighteen, always on a beach, always in an early-eighties bikini, always with big hair, always smiling, always with her arms around some middle-aged eighties yakoub. Looking at those old hairy blancos, Oscar couldn't help but feel hopeful. (Let me guess, he said, these are your uncles?) Each photo had a date and a place at the bottom and this was how he was able to follow Ybón's puta's progress through Italy, Portugal, and Spain. I was so beautiful in those days, she said wistfully. It was true, her smile could have put out a sun, but Oscar didn't think she was any less fine now, the slight declensions in her appearances only seemed to add to her luster (the last bright before the fade) and he told her so.

You're so sweet, mi amor. She knocked back another double and rasped, What's your sign?

How lovesick he became! He stopped writing and began to go over to her house nearly every day, even when he knew she was working, just in case she'd caught ill or decided to quit the profession so she could marry him. The gates of his heart had swung open and he felt light on his feet, he felt weightless, he felt *lithe*. His abuela steady gave him shit, told him that not even God loves a puta. Yeah, his tío laughed, but everybody knows that God *loves* a puto. His tío seemed thrilled that he no longer had a pájaro for a nephew. I can't believe it, he said proudly. The palomo is finally a man. He put Oscar's neck in the NJ State Police–patented niggerkiller lock. When did it happen? I want to play that date as soon as I get home.

Here we go again: Oscar and Ybón at her house, Oscar and
Ybón at the movies, Oscar and Ybón at the beach. Ybón
talked, voluminously, and Oscar slipped some words in too.
Ybón told him about her two sons, Sterling and Perfecto,
who lived with their grandparents in Puerto Rico, whom she
saw only on holidays. (They'd known only her photo and her
money the whole time she'd been in Europe, and when she'd
finally returned to the Island they were little men and she
didn't have the heart to tear them from the only family they'd
ever known. That would have made me roll my eyes, but Oscar bought it hook, line, and sinker.) She told him about the
two abortions she'd had, told him about the time she'd been
jailed in Madrid, told him how hard it was to sell your ass,
asked, Can something be impossible and not impossible at
once? Talked about how if she hadn't studied English at the
UASD she probably would have had it a lot worse. Told him
of a trip she'd taken to Berlin in the company of a rebuilt
Brazilian trannie, a friend, how sometimes the trains would
go so slow you could have plucked a passing flower without
disturbing its neighbors. She told him about her Dominican
boyfriend, the capitán, and her foreign boyfriends: the Italian, the German, and the Canadian, the three benditos, how
they each visited her on different months. You're lucky they
all have families, she said. Or I'd have been *working* this
whole summer. (He wanted to ask her not to talk about any
of these dudes but she would only have laughed. So all he
said was, I could have shown them around Zurza; I hear they
love tourists, and she laughed and told him to play nice.) He,

in turn, talked about the one time he and his dork college buddies had driven up to Wisconsin for a gaming convention, his only big trip, how they had camped out at a Winnebago reservation and drank Pabst with some of the local Indians. He talked about his love for his sister Lola and what had happened to her. He talked about trying to take his own life. This is the only time that Ybón didn't say anything. Instead she poured them both drinks and raised her glass. To life!

They never discussed the amount of time they spent together. Maybe we should get married, he said once, not joking, and she said, I'd make a terrible wife. He was around so often that he even got to see her in a couple of her notorious "moods," when her alien-princess part pushed to the fore and she became very cold and uncommunicative, when she called him an idiot americano for spilling his beer. On these days she opened her door and threw herself in bed and didn't do anything. Hard to be around her but he would say, Hey, I heard Jesus is down at the Plaza Central giving out condoms; he'd convince her to see a movie, the going out and sitting in a theater seemed to put the princess in partial check. Afterward she'd be a little easier; she'd take him to an Italian restaurant and no matter how much her mood had improved she'd insist on drinking herself ridiculous. So bad he'd have to put her in the truck and drive them home through a city he did not know. (Early on he hit on this great scheme: he called Clives, the evangelical taxista his family always used, who would swing by no sweat and lead him home.) When he drove she always put her head in his lap and talked to him, sometimes in Italian, sometimes in Spanish, sometimes about the beatings the women had given each other in prison, sometimes sweet stuff, and having her mouth so close to his nuts was finer than one might imagine.

LA INCA SPEAKS

He didn't meet her on the street like he told you. His cousins, los idiotas, took him to a cabaret and that's where he first saw her. And that's where ella se metió por sus ojos.

YBÓN, AS RECORDED BY OSCAR

I never wanted to come back to Santo Domingo. But after I was let go from jail I had trouble paying back the people I owed, and my mother was sick, and so I just came back.

It was hard at first. Once you've been fuera, Santo Domingo is the smallest place in the world. But if I've learned anything in my travels it's that a person can get used to anything. Even Santo Domingo.

WHAT NEVER CHANGES

Oh, they got close all right, but we have to ask the hard questions again: Did they ever kiss in her Pathfinder? Did he ever put his hands up her supershort skirt? Did she ever push up against him and say his name in a throaty whisper? Did he ever stroke that end-of-the-world tangle that was her hair while she sucked him off? Did they ever fuck?

Of course not. Miracles only go so far. He watched her for the signs, signs that would tell him she loved him. He began to suspect that it might not happen this summer, but already he had plans to come back for Thanksgiving, and then for Christmas. When he told her, she looked at him strangely and said only his name, Oscar, a little sadly.

She liked him, it was obvious, she liked it when he talked his crazy talk, when he stared at a new thing like it might have been from another planet (like the one time she had caught him in the bathroom staring at her soapstone—What the hell is *this* peculiar mineral? he said). It seemed to Oscar that he was one of her few real friends. Outside the boyfriends, foreign and domestic, outside her psychiatrist sister in San Cristóbal and her ailing mother in Sabana Iglesia, her life seemed as spare as her house.

Travel light, was all she ever said about the house when he suggested he buy her a lamp or anything, and he suspected that she would have said the same thing about having more friends. He knew, though, that he wasn't her only visitor. One day he found three discarded condom foils on the floor around her bed, had asked, Are you having trouble with incubuses? She smiled without shame. That's one man who doesn't know the word *quit*.

Poor Oscar. At night he dreamed that his rocketship, the *Hijo de Sacrificio*, was up and off but that it was heading for the Ana Obregón Barrier at the speed of light.

OSCAR AT THE RUBICON

At the beginning of August, Ybón started mentioning her boyfriend, the capitán, a lot more. Seems he'd heard about Oscar and wanted to meet him. He's really jealous, Ybón said rather weakly. Just have him meet me, Oscar said. I make all boyfriends feel better about themselves. I don't know, Ybón said. Maybe we shouldn't spend so much time together. Shouldn't you be looking for a girlfriend?

I got one, he said. She's the girlfriend of my mind.

A jealous Third World cop boyfriend? Maybe we shouldn't spend so much time together? Any other nigger would have pulled a Scooby-Doo double take—Eeuooooorr?— would have thought twice about staying in Santo Domingo another day. Hearing about the capitán only served to depress him, as did the spend-less-time crack. He never stopped to consider the fact that when a Dominican cop says he wants to meet you he ain't exactly talking about bringing you flowers.

One night not long after the condom-foil incident Oscar woke up in his overly air-conditioned room and realized with unusual clarity that he was heading down that road again. The road where he became so nuts over a girl he stopped thinking. The road where very bad things happened. You should stop right now, he told himself. But he knew, with lapidary clarity, that he wasn't going to stop. He loved Ybón. (And love, for this kid, was a geas, something that could not be shaken or denied.) The night before, she'd been so drunk that he had to help her into bed, and the whole time she was saying, God, we have to be careful, Oscar, but as soon as she hit the mattress she started writhing out of her clothes, didn't care that he was there; he tried not to look until she was under her covers but what he did see burned the edges of his eyes. When he turned to leave she sat up, her chest utterly and beautifully naked. Don't go yet. Wait till I'm asleep. He lay down next to her, on top of the sheets, didn't walk home until it was starting to get light out. He'd seen her beautiful chest and knew now that it was far too late to pack up and go home like those little voices were telling him, far too late.

LAST CHANCE

Two days later Oscar found his tío examining the front door. What's the matter? His tío showed him the door and pointed at the concrete-block wall on the other side of the foyer. I think somebody shot at our house last night. He was enraged. Fucking Dominicans. Probably hosed the whole neighborhood down. We're lucky we're alive.

His mother jabbed her finger into the bullet hole. I don't consider this being lucky.

I don't either, La Inca said, staring straight at Oscar.

For a second Oscar felt this strange tugging in the back of his head, what someone else might have called Instinct, but instead of hunkering down and sifting through it he said, We probably didn't hear it because of all our air conditioners, and then he walked over to Ybón's. They were supposed to be going to the Duarte that day.

OSCAR GETS BEAT

In the middle of August Oscar finally met the capitán. But he also got his first kiss ever. So you could say that day changed his life.

Ybón had passed out again (after giving him a long speech about how they had to give each other "space," which he'd listened to with his head down and wondered why she insisted on holding his hand during dinner, then). It was super late and he'd been following Clives in the Pathfinder, the usual routine, when some cops up ahead let Clives pass and then asked Oscar to please step out of the vehicle. It's not my truck, he explained, it's hers. He pointed to the sleeping Ybón. We understand, if you could pull over for a second. He did so, a little worried, but right then Ybón sat up and stared at him with her light eyes. Do you know what I want, Oscar?

I am, he said, too afraid to ask.

I want, she said, moving into position, un beso.

And before he could say anything she was on him.

The first feel of a woman's body pressing against yours—who among us can ever forget that? And that first real kiss—well, to be honest, I've forgotten both of these firsts, but Oscar never would. For a second he was in disbelief. This is it, this is really it! Her lips plush and pliant, and her tongue pushing into his mouth. And then there were lights all around them and he thought I'm going to transcend! Transcendence is miiine! But then he realized that the two plainclothes who had pulled them over—who both looked like they'd been raised on high-G planets, and whom we'll call Solomon Grundy and Gorilla Grod for simplicity's sake—were beaming their flashlights into the car. And who was standing behind them, looking in on the scene inside the car with an expression of sheer murder? Why, the capitán of course. Ybón's boyfriend!

Grod and Grundy yanked him out of the car. And did Ybón fight to keep him in her arms? Did she protest the rude interruption to their making out? Of course not. Homegirl just passed right out again.

The capitán. A skinny forty-something jabao standing near his spotless red Jeep, dressed nice, in slacks and a crisply pressed white button-down, his shoes bright as scarabs. One of those tall, arrogant, acerbically handsome niggers that most of the planet feels inferior to. Also one of those very bad men that not even postmodernism can explain away. He'd been young during the Trujillato, so he never got the chance to run with some real power, wasn't until the North American Invasion that he earned his stripes. Like my father, he supported the U.S. Invaders, and because he was methodical and showed absolutely no mercy to the leftists, he was launched—no, vaulted—into the top ranks of the military police. Was very busy under Demon Balaguer. Shooting at sindicatos from the backseats of cars. Burning down organizers' homes. Smashing in people's faces with crowbars. The Twelve Years were good times for men like him. In 1974 he held an old woman's head underwater until she died (she'd tried to organize some

peasants for land rights in San Juan); in 1977 he played mazel-
tov on a fifteen-year-old boy's throat with the heel of his
Florsheim (another Communist troublemaker, good fucking
riddance). I know this guy well. He has family in Queens and
every Christmas he brings his cousins bottles of Johnnie
Walker Black. His friends call him Fito, and when he was
young he wanted to be a lawyer, but then the calie scene had
pulled him and he forgot about all that lawyering business.

So you're the New Yorker. When Oscar saw the capitán's
eyes he knew he was in deep shit. The capitán, you see, also
had close-set eyes; these, though, were blue and terrible.
(The eyes of Lee Van Cleef!) If it hadn't been for the courage
of his sphincter, Oscar's lunch and his dinner and his breakfast would have whooshed straight out of him.

I didn't do anything, Oscar quailed. Then he blurted out,
I'm an American citizen.

The capitán waved away a mosquito. I'm an American
citizen too. I was naturalized in the city of Buffalo, in the
state of New York.

I bought mine in Miami, Gorilla Grod said. Not me,
Solomon Grundy lamented. I only have my residency.

Please, you have to believe me, I didn't do *anything*.

The capitán smiled. Motherfucker even had First World
teeth. Do you know who I am?

Oscar nodded. He was inexperienced but he wasn't dumb.
You're Ybón's ex-boyfriend.

I'm not her ex-novio, you maldito parigüayo! the capitán
screamed, the cords in his neck standing out like a Krikfalusi
drawing.

She said you were her ex, Oscar insisted.

The capitán grabbed him by the throat.

That's what she said, he whimpered.

Oscar was lucky; if he had looked like my pana, Pedro, the Dominican Superman, or like my boy Benny, who was a model, he probably would have gotten shot right there. But because he was a homely slob, because he really looked like un maldito parigüayo who had never had no luck in his life, the capitán took Gollum-pity on him and only punched him a couple of times. Oscar, who had never been "punched a couple of times" by a military-trained adult, felt like he had just been run over by the entire Steelers backfield circa 1977. Breath knocked out of him so bad he honestly thought he was going to die of asphyxiation. The captain's face appeared over his: If you ever touch my mujer again I'm going to kill you, parigüayo, and Oscar managed to whisper, You're the ex, before Messrs. Grundy and Grod picked him up (with some difficulty), squeezed him back into their Camry, and drove off. Oscar's last sight of Ybón? The capitán dragging her out of the Pathfinder cabin by her hair.

He tried to jump out of the car but Gorilla Grod elbowed him so hard that all the fight jumped clean out of him.

Nighttime in Santo Domingo. A blackout, of course. Even the Lighthouse out for the night.

Where did they take him? Where else. The canefields.

How's that for eternal return? Oscar so bewildered and frightened he pissed himself.

Didn't you grow up around here? Grundy asked his darker-skinned pal.

You stupid dick-sucker, I grew up in Puerto Plata.

Are you sure? You look like you speak a little French to me.

On the ride there Oscar tried to find his voice but couldn't. He was too shook. (In situations like these he had always assumed his secret hero would emerge and snap necks, à la Jim Kelly, but clearly his secret hero was out having some pie.) Everything seemed to be moving so fast. How had this happened? What wrong turn had he taken? He couldn't believe it. He was going to die. He tried to imagine Ybón at the funeral in her nearly see-through black sheath, but couldn't. Saw his mother and La Inca at the grave site. Didn't we tell you? Didn't we tell you? Watched Santo Domingo glide past and felt impossibly alone. How could this be happening? To him? He was boring, he was fat, and he was so very afraid. Thought about his mother, his sister, all the miniatures he hadn't painted yet, and started crying. You need to keep it down, Grundy said, but Oscar couldn't stop, even when he put his hands in his mouth.

They drove for a long time, and then finally, abruptly, they stopped. At the canefields Messrs. Grod and Grundy pulled Oscar out of the car. They opened the trunk but the batteries were dead in the flashlight so they had to drive back to a colmado, buy the batteries, and then drive back. While they argued with the colmado owner about prices, Oscar thought about escaping, thought about jumping out of the car and running down the street, screaming, but he couldn't do it. Fear is the mind killer, he chanted in his head, but he couldn't force himself to act. They had guns! He stared out into the night, hoping that maybe there would be some U.S. Marines out for a stroll, but there was only a lone man sitting in his rocking chair out in front of his ruined house and for a moment Oscar could have sworn the dude had no face, but then the killers got back into the car and drove. Their flashlight newly activated, they walked him into the cane—never had he heard anything so loud and alien, the susurration, the crackling, the flashes of motion underfoot (snake? mongoose?), overhead even the stars, all of them gathered in vainglorious congress. And yet this world seemed strangely familiar to him; he had the overwhelming feeling that he'd been in this very place, a long time ago. It was worse than déjà vu, but before he could focus on it the moment slipped away, drowned by his fear, and then the two men told him to stop and turn around. We have something to give you, they said amiably. Which brought Oscar back to the Real. Please, he shrieked, don't! But instead of the muzzle-flash and the eternal dark, Grod struck him once hard in the head with the butt of his pistol. For a second the pain broke the yoke of his fear and he found the strength to move his legs and was about to turn and run but then they both started whaling on him with their pistols.

It's not clear whether they intended to scare him or kill him. Maybe the capitán had ordered one thing and they did another. Perhaps they did exactly what he asked, or perhaps Oscar just got lucky. Can't say. All I know is, it was the beating to end all beatings. It was the Götterdämmerung of beatdowns, a beatdown so cruel and relentless that even Camden, the City of the Ultimate Beatdown, would have been proud.

(Yes sir, nothing like getting smashed in the face with those patented Pachmayr Presentation Grips.) He *shrieked*, but it didn't stop the beating; he begged, and that didn't stop it, either; he blacked out, but that was no relief; the niggers kicked him in the nuts and perked him right up! He tried to drag himself into the cane, but they pulled him back! It was like one of those nightmare eight-a.m. MLA panels: *endless*. Man, Gorilla Grod said, this kid is making me *sweat*. Most of the time they took turns striking him, but sometimes they got into it together and there were moments Oscar was sure that he was being beaten by three men, not two, that the faceless man from in front of the colmado was joining them. Toward the end, as all life began to slip away, Oscar found himself facing his abuela; she was sitting in her rocking chair, and when she saw him she snarled, What did I tell you about those putas? Didn't I tell you you were going to die?

And then finally Grod jumped down on his head with both his boots and right before it happened Oscar could have sworn that there was a third man with them and he was standing back behind some of the cane but before Oscar could see his face it was Good Night, Sweet Prince, and he felt like he was falling again, falling straight for Route 18, and there was nothing he could do, nothing at all, to stop it.

CLIVES TO THE RESCUE

The only reason he didn't lay out in that rustling endless cane for the rest of his life was because Clives the evangelical taxista had had the guts, and the smarts, and yes, the goodness, to follow the cops on the sly, and when they broke out he turned on his headlights and pulled up to where they'd last been. He didn't have a flashlight and after almost half an hour of stomping around in the dark he was about to abandon the search until the morning. And then he heard someone *singing*. A nice voice too, and Clives, who sang for his congregation, knew the difference. He headed toward the source full speed, and then, just as he was about to part the last stalks a tremendous wind ripped through the cane, nearly blew him off his feet, like the first slap of a hurricane, like the blast an angel might lay down on takeoff, and then, just as quickly as it had kicked up it was gone, leaving behind only the smell of burned cinnamon, and there just behind a couple stalks of cane lay Oscar. Unconscious and bleeding out of both ears and looking like he was one finger tap away from dead. Clives tried his best but he couldn't drag Oscar back to the car alone, so he left him where he was—Just hold on!—drove to a nearby batey, and recruited a couple of Haitian braceros to help him, which took a while because the braceros were afraid to leave the batey lest they get whupped as bad as Oscar by their overseers. Finally Clives prevailed and back they raced to the scene of the crime. This is a big one, one of the braceros cracked. Mucho plátanos, another joked. Mucho mucho plátanos, said a third, and then they heaved him into the backseat. As soon as the door shut, Clives popped his car into gear and was off. Driving fast in the name of the Lord. The Haitians throwing rocks at him because he had promised to give them a ride back to their camp.

CLOSE ENCOUNTERS
OF THE CARIBBEAN KIND

Oscar remembers having a dream where a mongoose was chatting with him. Except the mongoose was the Mongoose.

What will it be, muchacho? it demanded. More or less?

And for a moment he almost said less. So tired, and so much pain—Less! Less! Less!—but then in the back of his head he remembered his family. Lola and his mother and Nena Inca. Remembered how he used to be when he was younger and more optimistic. The lunch box next to his bed, the first thing he saw in the morning. *Planet of the Apes.*

More, he croaked.

——— ——— ———, said the Mongoose, and then the wind swept him back into darkness.

DEAD OR ALIVE

Broken nose, shattered zygomatic arch, crushed seventh cranial nerve, three of his teeth snapped off at the gum, concussion.

But he's still alive, isn't he? his mother demanded.

Yes, the doctors conceded.

Let us pray, La Inca said grimly. She grabbed Beli's hands and lowered her head.

If they noticed the similarities between Past and Present they did not speak of it.

BRIEFING FOR A DESCENT INTO HELL

He was out for three days.

In that time he had the impression of having the most fantastic series of dreams, though by the time he had his first meal, a caldo de pollo, he could not, alas, remember them. All that remained was the image of an Aslan-like figure with golden eyes who kept trying to speak to him but Oscar couldn't hear a word above the blare of the merengue coming from the neighbor's house.

Only later, during his last days, would he actually remember one of those dreams. An old man was standing before him in a ruined bailey, holding up a book for him to read. The old man had a mask on. It took a while for Oscar's eyes to focus, but then he saw that the book was blank.

The book is blank. Those were the words La Inca's servant heard him say just before he broke through the plane of unconsciousness and into the universe of the Real.

ALIVE

That was the end of it. As soon as moms de León got a green light from the doctors she called the airlines. She wasn't no fool; had her own experience with these kinds of things. Put it in the simplest of terms so that even in his addled condition he could understand. You, stupid worthless no-good hijo-de-la-gran-puta, are going home.

No, he said, through demolished lips. He wasn't fooling, either. When he first woke up and realized that he was still alive, he asked for Ybón. I love her, he whispered, and his mother said, Shut up, you! Just shut up!

Why are you screaming at the boy? La Inca demanded.

Because he's an idiot.

The family doctora ruled out epidural hematoma but couldn't guarantee that Oscar didn't have brain trauma. (She was a cop's girlfriend? Tío Rudolfo whistled. I'll vouch for the brain damage.) Send him home right now, the doctora said, but for four days Oscar resisted any attempt to pack him up in a plane, which says a lot about this fat kid's fortitude; he was eating morphine by the handful and his grill was in *agony*, he had an around-the-clock quadruple migraine and couldn't see squat out of his right eye; motherfucker's head was so swole he looked like John Merrick Junior and anytime he attempted to stand, the ground whisked right out from under him. Christ in a handbasket! he thought. So this is what it felt like to get your ass *kicked*. The pain just wouldn't stop rolling, and no matter how hard he tried he could not command it. He swore never to write another fight scene as long as he lived. It wasn't all bad, though; the beating granted him strange insights; he realized, rather unhelpfully, that had he and Ybón not been serious the capitán would probably never have fucked with him. Proof positive that he and Ybón had a relationship. Should I celebrate, he asked the dresser, or should I cry? Other insights? One day while watching his mother tear sheets off the beds it dawned on him that the family curse he'd heard about his whole life might actually be *true*.

Fukú.

He rolled the word experimentally in his mouth. *Fuck you.*

His mother raised her fist in a fury but La Inca intercepted it, their flesh slapping. Are you mad? La Inca said, and Oscar couldn't tell if she was talking to his mother or to him.

As for Ybón, she didn't answer her pager, and the few times he managed to limp to the window he saw that her Pathfinder wasn't there. I love you, he shouted into the street. I love you! Once he made it to her door and buzzed before his tío realized that he was gone and dragged him back inside. At night all Oscar did was lie in bed and suffer, imagining all sorts of horrible *Sucesos*-style endings for Ybón. When his head felt like it was going to explode he tried to reach out to her with his telepathic powers.

And on day three she came. While she sat on the edge of his bed his mother banged pots in the kitchen and said *puta* loud enough for them to hear.

Forgive me if I don't get up, Oscar whispered. I'm having slight difficulties with my cranium.

She was dressed in white, and her hair was still wet from the shower, a tumult of brownish curls. Of course the capitán had beaten the shit out of her too, of course she had two black eyes (he'd also put his .44 Magnum in her vagina and asked her who she *really* loved). And yet there was nothing about her that Oscar wouldn't have gladly kissed. She put her fingers on his hand and told him that she could never be with him again. For some reason Oscar couldn't see her face, it was a blur, she had retreated completely into that other plane of hers. Heard only the sorrow of her breathing. Where was the girl who had noticed him checking out a flaquita the week before and said, half joking, Only a dog likes a bone, Oscar. Where was the girl who had to try on five different outfits before she left the house? He tried to focus his eyes but what he saw was only his love for her.

He held out the pages he'd written. I have so much to talk to you about—

Me and ——— are getting married, she said curtly.

Ybón, he said, trying to form the words, but she was already gone.

Se acabó. His mother and his abuela and his tío delivered the ultimatum and that was that. Oscar didn't look at the ocean or the scenery as they drove to the airport. He was trying to decipher something he'd written the night before, mouthing the words slowly. It's beautiful today, Clives remarked. He looked up with tears in his eyes. Yes, it is.

On the flight over he sat between his tío and his moms. Jesus, Oscar, Rudolfo said nervously. You look like they put a shirt on a turd.

His sister met them at JFK and when she saw his face she cried and didn't stop even when she got back to my apartment. You should see Mister, she sobbed. They tried to *kill* him.

What the fuck, Oscar, I said on the phone. I leave you alone for a couple days and you almost get yourself slabbed?

His voice sounded muffled. I kissed a girl, Yunior. I finally kissed a girl.

But, O, you almost got yourself killed.

It wasn't completely egregious, he said. I still had a few hit points left.

But then, two days later, I saw his face and was like: Holy shit, Oscar. Holy fucking shit.

He shook his head. Bigger game afoot than my appearances.

He wrote out the word for me: *fukú*.

SOME ADVICE

Travel light. She extended her arms to embrace her house, maybe the whole world.

PATERSON, AGAIN

He returned home. He lay in bed, he healed. His mother so infuriated she wouldn't look at him.

He was a complete and utter wreck. Knew he loved her like he'd never loved anyone. Knew what he should be doing—making like a Lola and flying back. Fuck the capitán. Fuck Grundy and Grod. Fuck everybody. Easy to say in the rational day but at night his balls turned to ice water and ran down his fucking legs like piss. Dreamed again and again of the cane, the terrible cane, except now it wasn't him at the receiving end of the beating, but his sister, his mother, heard them shrieking, begging for them to stop, please God *stop*, but instead of racing toward the voices, he *ran away*! Woke up *screaming. Not me. Not me.*

He watched *Virus* for the thousandth time and for the thousandth time teared up when the Japanese scientist finally reached Tierra del Fuego and the love of his life. He read *The Lord of the Rings* for what I'm estimating the millionth time, one of his greatest loves and greatest comforts since he'd first discovered it, back when he was nine and lost and lonely and his favorite librarian had said, Here, try this, and with one suggestion changed his life. Got through almost the whole trilogy, but then the line "and out of Far Harad black men like half-trolls" and he had to stop, his head and heart hurting too much.

Six weeks after the Colossal Beatdown he dreamed about the cane again. But instead of bolting when the cries began, when the bones started breaking, he summoned all the courage he ever had, would ever have, and forced himself to do the one thing he did not want to do, that he could not bear to do.

He listened.

III

This happened in January. Me and Lola were living up in the Heights, separate apartments—this was before the whitekids started their invasion, when you could walk the entire length of Upper Manhattan and see not a single yoga mat. Me and Lola weren't doing that great. Plenty I could tell you, but that's neither here nor there. All you need to know is that if we talked once a week we were lucky, even though we were nominally boyfriend and girlfriend. All my fault, of course. Couldn't keep my rabo in my pants, even though she was the most beautiful fucking girl in the world.

Anyway, I was home that week, no call from the temp agency, when Oscar buzzed me from the street. Hadn't seen his ass in weeks, since the first days of his return. Jesus, Oscar, I said. Come up, come up. I waited for him in the hall and when he stepped out of the elevator I put the mitts on him. How are you, bro? I'm copacetic, he said. We sat down and I broke up a dutch while he filled me in. I'm going back to Don Bosco soon. Word? I said. Word, he said. His face was still fucked up, the left side a little droopy.

You wanna smoke?

I might partake. Just a little, though. I would not want to cloud my faculties.

That last day on our couch he looked like a man at peace with himself. A little distracted but at peace. I would tell Lola that night that it was because he'd finally decided to live, but the truth would turn out to be a little more complicated. You should have seen him. He was so thin, had lost all the weight and was still, still.

What had he been doing? Writing, of course, and reading. Also getting ready to move from Paterson. Wanting to put the past behind him, start a new life. Was trying to decide what he would take with him. Was allowing himself only ten of his books, the core of his canon (his words), was trying to pare it all down to what was necessary. Only what I can carry. It seemed like another odd Oscar thing, until later we would realize it wasn't.

And then after an inhale he said: Please forgive me, Yunior, but I'm here with an ulterior motive. I wish to know if you could do me a favor.

Anything, bro. Just ask it.

He needed money for his security deposit, had a line on an apartment in Brooklyn. I should have thought about it— Oscar never asked anybody for money—but I didn't, fell over myself to give it to him. My guilty conscience.

We smoked the dutch and talked about the problems me and Lola were having. You should never have had carnal relations with that Paraguayan girl, he pointed out. I know, I said, I know.

She loves you.

I know that.

Why do you cheat on her, then?

If I knew that, it wouldn't be a problem.

Maybe you should try to find out.

He stood up.

You ain't going to wait for Lola?

I must be away to Paterson. I have a date.

You're shitting me?

He shook his head, the tricky fuck.

I asked: Is she beautiful?

He smiled. She is.

On Saturday he was gone.

7

The Final Voyage

The last time he flew to Santo Domingo he'd been startled when the applause broke out, but this time he was prepared, and when the plane landed he clapped until his hands stung.

As soon as he hit the airport exit he called Clives and homeboy picked him up an hour later, found him surrounded by taxistas who were trying to pull him into their cabs. Cristiano, Clives said, what are you doing here?

It's the Ancient Powers, Oscar said grimly. They won't leave me alone.

They parked in front of her house and waited almost seven hours before she returned. Clives tried to talk him out of it but he wouldn't listen. Then she pulled up in the Pathfinder. She looked thinner. His heart seized like a bad leg and for a moment he thought about letting the whole thing go, about returning to Bosco and getting on with his miserable life, but then she stooped over, as if the whole world was watching, and that settled it. He winched down the window. Ybón, he said. She stopped, shaded her eyes, and then recognized him. She said his name too. *Oscar*. He popped the door and walked over to where she was standing and embraced her.

Her first words? Mi amor, you have to leave right now.

In the middle of the street he told her how it was. He told her that he was in love with her and that he'd been hurt but now he was all right and if he could just have a week alone with her, one short week, then everything would be fine in him and he would be able to face what he had to face and she said I don't understand and so he said it again, that he loved her more than the Universe and it wasn't something that he could shake so please come away with me for a little while, lend me your strength and then it would be over if she wanted.

Maybe she did love him a little bit. Maybe in her heart of hearts she left the gym bag on the concrete and got in the taxi with him. But she'd known men like the capitán all her life, had been forced to work in Europe one year straight by niggers like that before she could start earning her own money. Knew also that in the DR they called a cop-divorce a bullet. The gym bag was not left on the street.

I'm going to call him, Oscar, she said, misting up a little. So please go before he gets here.

I'm not going anywhere, he said.

Go, she said.

No, he answered.

He let himself into his abuela's house (he still had the key). The capitán showed up an hour later, honked his horn a long time, but Oscar didn't bother to go out. He had gotten

out all of La Inca's photographs, was going through each and
every one. When La Inca returned from the bakery she
found him scribbling at the kitchen table.

Oscar?

Yes, Abuela, he said, not looking up. It's me.

It's hard to explain, he wrote his sister later.

I bet it was.

CURSE OF THE CARIBBEAN

For twenty-seven days he did two things: he researched-
wrote and he chased her. Sat in front of her house, called her
on her beeper, went to the World Famous Riverside, where she
worked, walked to the supermarket whenever he saw her truck
pull out, just in case she was on her way there. Nine times out
of ten she was not. The neighbors, when they saw him on the
curb, shook their heads and said, Look at that loco.

At first it was pure terror for her. She didn't want nothing
to do with him; she wouldn't speak to him, wouldn't acknowledge him, and the first time she saw him at the club
she was so frightened her legs buckled under her. He knew
he was scaring her shitless, but he couldn't help it. By day ten,
though, even terror was too much effort and when he followed her down an aisle or smiled at her at work she would
hiss, Please go home, Oscar.

She was miserable when she saw him, and miserable, she
would tell him later, when she didn't, convinced that he'd

gotten killed. He slipped long passionate letters under her gate, written in English, and the only response he got was when the capitán and his friends called and threatened to chop him to pieces. After each threat he recorded the time and then phoned the embassy and told them that Officer ———— had threatened to kill him, could you please help?

He had hope, because if she really wanted him gone she could have lured him out in the open and let the capitán destroy him. Because if she wanted to she could have had him banned from the Riverside. But she didn't.

Boy, you can dance *good*, he wrote in a letter. In another he laid out the plans he had to marry her and take her back to the States.

She started scribbling back notes and passed them to him at the club, or had them mailed to his house. Please, Oscar, I haven't slept in a week. I don't want you to end up hurt or dead. Go home.

But beautiful girl, above all beautiful girls, he wrote back. This is my home.

Your real home, mi amor.

A person can't have two?

Night nineteen, Ybón rang at the gate, and he put down his pen, knew it was her. She leaned over and unlocked the truck door and when he got in he tried to kiss her but she said, Please, stop it. They drove out toward La Romana, where the capitán didn't have friends supposedly. Nothing new was discussed but he said, I like your new haircut, and she started laughing and crying and said, Really? You don't think it makes me look cheap?

You and cheap do not compute, Ybón.

What could we do? Lola flew down to see him, begged him to come home, told him that he was only going to get Ybón and himself killed; he listened and then said quietly that she didn't understand what was at stake. I understand perfectly, she yelled. No, he said sadly, you don't. His abuela tried to exert her power, tried to use the Voice, but he was no longer the boy she'd known. Something had changed about him. He had gotten some power of his own.

Two weeks into his Final Voyage his mother arrived, and she came loaded for bear. You're coming home, right now. He shook his head. I can't, Mami. She grabbed him and tried to pull, but he was like Unus the Untouchable. Mami, he said softly. You'll hurt yourself.

And you'll kill yourself.

That's not what I'm trying to do.

Did I fly down? Of course I did. With Lola. Nothing brings a couple together quite like catastrophe.

Et tu, Yunior? he said when he saw me.

Nothing worked.

THE LAST DAYS OF OSCAR WAO

How incredibly short are twenty-seven days! One evening the capitán and his friends stalked into the Riverside and Oscar stared at the man for a good ten seconds and then, whole body shaking, he left. Didn't bother to call Clives, jumped in the first taxi he could find. Once in the parking lot of the Riverside he tried again to kiss her and she turned away with her head, not her body. Please don't. He'll kill us.

Twenty-seven days. Wrote on each and every one of them, wrote almost three hundred pages if his letters are to be believed. Almost had it too, he said to me one night on the phone, one of the few calls he made to us. What? I wanted to know. What?

You'll see, was all he would say.

And then the expected happened. One night he and Clives were driving back from the World Famous Riverside and they had to stop at a light and that was where two men got into the cab with them. It was, of course, Gorilla Grod and Solomon Grundy. Good to see you again, Grod said, and then they beat him as best they could, given the limited space inside the cab.

This time Oscar didn't cry when they drove him back to the canefields. Zafra would be here soon, and the cane had grown well and thick and in places you could hear the stalks clack-clack-clacking against each other like triffids and you could hear krïyol voices lost in the night. The smell of the ripening cane was unforgettable, and there was a moon, a beautiful full moon, and Clives begged the men to spare Oscar, but they laughed. You should be worrying, Grod said, about yourself. Oscar laughed a little too through his broken mouth. Don't worry, Clives, he said. They're too late. Grod disagreed. Actually I would say we're just in time. They drove past a bus stop and for a second Oscar imagined he saw his whole family getting on a guagua, even his poor dead abuelo and his poor dead abuela, and who is driving the bus but the

Mongoose, and who is the cobrador but the Man Without a Face, but it was nothing but a final fantasy, gone as soon as he blinked, and when the car stopped, Oscar sent telepathic messages to his mom (I love you, señora), to his tío (Quit, tío, and live), to Lola (I'm so sorry it happened; I will always love you), to all the women he had ever loved—Olga, Maritza, Ana, Jenni, Nataly, and all the other ones whose names he'd never known—and of course to Ybón.[33]

They walked him into the cane and then turned him around. He tried to stand bravely. (Clives they left tied up in the cab and while they had their backs turned he slipped into the cane, and he would be the one who would deliver Oscar to the family.) They looked at Oscar and he looked at them and then he started to speak. The words coming out like they belonged to someone else, his Spanish good for once. He told them that what they were doing was wrong, that they were going to take a great love out of the world. Love was a rare thing, easily confused with a million other things, and if anybody knew this to be true it was him. He told them about Ybón and the way he loved her and how much they had risked and that they'd started to dream the same dreams and say the same words. He told them that it was only because of her love that he'd been able to do the thing that he had done, the thing they could no longer stop, told them if they killed him they would probably feel nothing and their children would probably feel nothing either, not until they were old

33. "No matter how far you travel . . . to whatever reaches of this limitless universe . . . you will never be . . . ALONE!" (The Watcher, *Fantastic Four* #13 May 1963.)

and weak or about to be struck by a car and then they would sense him waiting for them on the other side and over there he wouldn't be no fatboy or dork or kid no girl had ever loved; over there he'd be a hero, an avenger. Because anything you can dream (he put his hand up) you can be.

They waited respectfully for him to finish and then they said, their faces slowly disappearing in the gloom, Listen, we'll let you go if you tell us what *fuego* means in English.

Fire, he blurted out, unable to help himself.

Oscar—

8

The End of the Story

That's pretty much it.

We flew down to claim the body. We arranged the funeral. No one there but us, not even Al and Miggs. Lola crying and crying. A year later their mother's cancer returned and this time it dug in and stayed. I visited her in the hospital with Lola. Six times in all. She would live for another ten months, but by then she'd more or less given up.

I did all I could.

You did enough, Mami, Lola said, but she refused to hear it. Turned her ruined back to us.

I did all I could and it still wasn't enough.

They buried her next to her son, and Lola read a poem she had written, and that was it. Ashes to ashes, dust to dust.

Four times the family hired lawyers but no charges were ever filed. The embassy didn't help and neither did the government. Ybón, I hear, is still living in Mirador Norte, still dancing at the Riverside but La Inca sold the house a year later, moved back to Baní.

Lola swore she would never return to that terrible country. On one of our last nights as novios she said, Ten million Trujillos is all we are.

AS FOR US

I wish I could say it worked out, that Oscar's death brought us together. I was just too much the mess, and after half a year of taking care of her mother Lola had what a lot of females call their Saturn Return. One day she called, asked me where I'd been the night before, and when I didn't have a good excuse, she said, Good-bye, Yunior, please take good care of yourself, and for about a year I scromfed strange girls and alternated between Fuck Lola and these incredibly narcissistic hopes of reconciliation that I did nothing to achieve. And then in August, after I got back from a trip to Santo Domingo, I heard from my mother that Lola had met someone in Miami, which was where she had moved, that she was pregnant and was getting married.

I called her. What the fuck, Lola—

But she hung up.

ON A SUPER FINAL NOTE

Years and years now and I still think about him. The incredible Oscar Wao. I have dreams where he sits on the edge of my bed. We're back at Rutgers, in Demarest, which is where we'll always be, it seems. In this particular dream he's never thin like at the end, always huge. He wants to talk to me, is anxious to jaw, but most of the time I can never say a word and neither can he. So we just sit there quietly.

About five years after he died I started having another kind of dream. About him or someone who looks like him. We're in some kind of ruined bailey that's filled to the rim with old dusty books. He's standing in one of the passages, all mysterious-like, wearing a wrathful mask that hides his face but behind the eyeholes I see a familiar pair of close-set eyes. Dude is holding up a book, waving for me to take a closer look, and I recognize this scene from one of his crazy movies. I want to run from him, and for a long time that's what I do. It takes me a while before I notice that Oscar's hands are seamless and the book's pages are blank.

And that behind his mask his eyes are smiling.

Zafa.

Sometimes, though, I look up at him and he has no face and I wake up screaming.

THE DREAMS

Took ten years to the day, went through more lousy shit than you could imagine, was lost for a good long while—no Lola, no me, no nothing—until finally I woke up next to somebody I didn't give two shits about, my upper lip covered in coke-snot and coke-blood and I said, OK, Wao, OK. You win.

AS FOR ME

These days I live in Perth Amboy, New Jersey, teach composition and creative writing at Middlesex Community College, and even own a house at the top of Elm Street, not far from the steel mill. Not one of the big ones that the bodega owners buy with their earnings, but not too shabby, either. Most of my colleagues think Perth Amboy is a dump, but I beg to differ.

It's not exactly what I dreamed about when I was a kid, the teaching, the living in New Jersey, but I make it work as best as I can. I have a wife I adore and who adores me, a negrita from Salcedo whom I do not deserve, and sometimes we even make vague noises about having children. Every now and then I'm OK with the possibility. I don't run around after girls anymore. Not much, anyway. When I'm not teaching or coaching baseball or going to the gym or hanging out with the wifey I'm at home, writing. These days I write a lot. From can't see in the morning to can't see at night. Learned that from Oscar. I'm a new man, you see, a new man, a new man.

AS FOR US

Believe it or not, we still see each other. She, Cuban Ruben, and their daughter moved back to Paterson a couple of years back, sold the old house, bought a new one, travel everywhere together (at least that's what my mother tells me—Lola, being Lola, still visits her). Every now and then when the stars are aligned I run into her, at rallies, at bookstores we used to chill at, on the streets of NYC. Sometimes Cuban Ruben is with her, sometimes not. Her daughter, though, is always there. Eyes of Oscar. Hair of Hypatía. Her gaze watches everything. A little reader too, if Lola is to be believed. Say hi to Yunior, Lola commands. He was your tío's best friend.

Hi, tío, she says reluctantly.

Tío's *friend*, she corrects.

Hi, tío's *friend*.

Lola's hair is long now and never straightened; she's heavier and less guileless, but she's still the ciguapa of my dreams. Always happy to see me, no bad feelings, entiendes. None at all.

Yunior, how are you?

I'm fine. How are you?

Before all hope died I used to have this stupid dream that shit could be saved, that we would be in bed together like the old times, with the fan on, the smoke from our weed drifting above us, and I'd finally try to say words that could have saved us.

———— ———— ————.

But before I can shape the vowels I wake up. My face is wet, and that's how you know it's never going to come true.

Never, ever.

It ain't too bad, though. During our run-ins we smile, we laugh, we take turns saying her daughter's name.

I never ask if her daughter has started to dream. I never mention our past.

All we ever talk about is Oscar.

It's almost done. Almost over. Only some final things to show you before your Watcher fulfills his cosmic duty and retires at last to the Blue Area of the Moon, not to be heard again until the Last Days.

Behold the girl: the beautiful muchachita: Lola's daughter. Dark and blindingly fast: in her great-grandmother La Inca's words: una jurona. Could have been my daughter if I'd been smart, if I'd been ———. Makes her no less precious. She climbs trees, she rubs her butt against doorjambs, she practices malapalabras when she thinks nobody is listening. Speaks Spanish and English.

Neither Captain Marvel nor Billy Batson, but the lightning.

A happy kid, as far as these things go. Happy!

But on a string around her neck: three azabaches: the one that Oscar wore as a baby, the one that Lola wore as a baby, and the one that Beli was given by La Inca upon reaching Sanctuary. Powerful elder magic. Three barrier shields against the Eye. Backed by a six-mile plinth of prayer. (Lola's not stupid; she made both my mother and La Inca the girl's madrinas.) Powerful wards indeed.

One day, though, the Circle will fail.

As Circles always do.

And for the first time she will hear the word *fukú*.

And she will have a dream of the No Face Man.

Not now, but soon.

If she's her family's daughter—as I suspect she is—one day she will stop being afraid and she will come looking for answers.

Not now, but soon.

One day when I'm least expecting, there will be a knock at my door.

Soy Isis. Hija de Dolores de León.

Holy shit! Come in, chica! Come in!

(I'll notice that she still wears her azabaches, that she has her mother's legs, her uncle's eyes.)

I'll pour her a drink, and the wife will fry up her special pastelitos; I'll ask her about her mother as lightly as I can, and I'll bring out the pictures of the three of us from back in the day, and when it starts getting late I'll take her down to my basement and open the four refrigerators where I store her tío's books, his games, his manuscript, his comic books, his papers—refrigerators the best proof against fire, against earthquake, against almost anything.

A light, a desk, a cot—I've prepared it all.

How many nights will she stay with us?

As many as it takes.

And maybe, just maybe, if she's as smart and as brave as

I'm expecting she'll be, she'll take all we've done and all we've learned and add her own insights and she'll put an end to it.

That is what, on my best days, I hope. What I dream.

And yet there are other days, when I'm downtrodden or morose, when I find myself at my desk late at night, unable to sleep, flipping through (of all things) Oscar's dog-eared copy of *Watchmen*. One of the few things that he took with him on the Final Voyage that we recovered. The original trade. I flip through the book, one of his top three, without question, to the last horrifying chapter: "A Stronger Loving World." To the only panel he's circled. Oscar—who never defaced a book in his life—circled one panel three times in the same emphatic pen he used to write his last letters home. The panel where Adrian Veidt and Dr. Manhattan are having their last convo. After the mutant brain has destroyed New York City; after Dr. Manhattan has murdered Rorschach; after Veidt's plan has succeeded in "saving the world."

Veidt says: "I did the right thing, didn't I? It all worked out in the end."

And Manhattan, before fading from our Universe, replies: "In the end? Nothing ends, Adrian. Nothing ever ends."

The Final Letter

He managed to send mail home before the end. A couple of cards with some breezy platitudes on them. Wrote me one, called me Count Fenring. Recommended the beaches of Azua if I hadn't already visited them. Wrote Lola too; called her My Dear Bene Gesserit Witch.

And then, almost eight months after he died, a package arrived at the house in Paterson. Talk about Dominican Express. Two manuscripts enclosed. One was more chapters of his never-to-be-completed opus, a four-book E. E. "Doc" Smith–esque space opera called *Starscourge*, and the other was a long letter to Lola, the last thing he wrote, apparently, before he was killed. In that letter he talked about his investigations and the new book he was writing, a book that he was sending under another cover. Told her to watch out for a second package. This contains everything I've written on this journey. Everything I think you will need. You'll understand when you read my conclusions. (It's the cure to what ails us, he scribbled in the margins. The Cosmo DNA.)

Only problem was, the fucking thing never arrived! Either got lost in the mail or he was slain before he put it in the mail, or whoever he trusted to deliver it forgot.

Anyway, the package that did arrive had some amazing news. Turns out that toward the end of those twenty-seven days the palomo *did* get Ybón away from La Capital. For one whole weekend they hid out on some beach in Barahona while the capitán was away on "business," and guess what? Ybón actually *kissed* him. Guess what else? Ybón actually *fucked* him. Praise be to Jesus! He reported that he'd liked it, and that Ybón's you-know-what hadn't tasted the way he had expected. She tastes like Heineken, he observed. He wrote that every night Ybón had nightmares that the capitán had found them; once she'd woken up and said in the voice of true fear, Oscar, he's here, really believing he was, and Oscar woke up and threw himself at the capitán, but it turned out only to be a turtleshell the hotel had hung on the wall for decoration. Almost busted my nose! He wrote that Ybón had little hairs coming up to almost her bellybutton and that she crossed her eyes when he entered her but what really got him was not the bam-bam-bam of sex—it was the little intimacies that he'd never in his whole life anticipated, like combing her hair or getting her underwear off a line or watching her walk naked to the bathroom or the way she would suddenly sit on his lap and put her face into his neck. The intimacies like listening to her tell him about being a little girl and him telling her that he'd been a virgin all his life. He wrote that he couldn't believe he'd had to wait for this so goddamn long. (Ybón was the one who suggested calling the wait something else. Yeah, like what? Maybe, she said, you could call it life.) He wrote: So this is what everybody's always talking about! Diablo! If only I'd known. The beauty! The beauty!

ACKNOWLEDGMENTS

I'd like to give thanks to:

the pueblo dominicano. And to Those Who Watch Over Us.

Mi querido abuelo Osterman Sánchez.

Mi madre, Virtudes Díaz, and mis tías Irma and Mercedes.

Mr. and Mrs. El Hamaway (who bought me my first dictionary and signed me up for the Science Fiction Book Club).

Santo Domingo, Villa Juana, Azua, Parlin, Old Bridge, Perth Amboy, Ithaca, Syracuse, Brooklyn, Hunts Point, Harlem, el Distrito Federal de México, Washington Heights, Shimokitazawa, Boston, Cambridge, Roxbury.

Every teacher who gave me kindness, every librarian who gave me books. My students.

ACKNOWLEDGMENTS

Anita Desai (who helped land me the MIT gig: I never thanked you enough, Anita); Julie Grau (whose faith and perseverance brought forth this book); and Nicole Aragi (who in eleven years never once gave up on me, even when I did).

The John Simon Guggenheim Memorial Foundation, the Lila Wallace–Reader's Digest Fund, the Radcliffe Institute for Advanced Study at Harvard University.

Jaime Manrique (for being the first writer to take me serious), David Mura (the jedi master who showed me the way), Francisco Goldman, the Infamous Frankie G (for bringing me to Mexico and being there when it started), Edwidge Danticat (for being mi querida hermana).

Deb Chasman, Eric Gansworth, Juleyka Lantigua, Dr. Janet Lindgren, and Sandra Shagat (for reading it).

Alejandra Frausto, Xanita, Alicia Gonzalez (for México).

Oliver Bidel, Harold del Pino, Victor Díaz, Victoria Lola, Chris Abani, Tony Capellan, Coco Fusco, Silvio Torres-Saillant, Michele Oshima, Soledad Vera, Fabiana Wallis, Ellis Cose, Lee Llambelis, Elisa Cose, Patricia Engel, Shreerekha Pillai (for spinning dark girls beautiful), Lily Oei (for kicking ass), Sean McDonald (for finishing it).

Manny Perez, Alfredo de Villa, Alexis Peña, Farhad Ashgar, Ani Ashgar, Marisol Álcantara, Andrea Greene, Andrew

Simpson, Diem Jones, Francisco Espinosa, Chad Milner, Tony Davis, and Anthony (for building me shelter).

MIT. Riverhead Books. *The New Yorker*. All the schools and institutions that supported me.

The Family: Dana, Maritza, Clifton, and Daniel.

The Hernandez Clan: Rada, Soleil, Debbie, and Reebee.

The Moyer Clan: Peter and Gricel. And Manuel del Villa (Rest in Peace, Son of the Bronx, Son of Brookline, True Hero).

The Benzan Clan: Milagros, Jason, Javier, Tanya, and the twins Mateo y India.

The Sanchez Clan: Ana (for always being there for Eli) and Michael and Kiara (for having her back).

The Piña Clan: Nivia Piña y mi ahijado Sebastian Piña. And for Merengue.

The Ohno Clan: Doctor Tsuneya Ohno, Mrs. Makiko Ohno, Shinya Ohno, and of course Peichen.

Amelia Burns (Brookline and Vineyard Haven), Nefertiti Jaquez (Providence), Fabiano Maisonnave (Campo Grande and São Paulo), and Homero del Pino (who first brought me to Paterson).

ACKNOWLEDGMENTS

The Rodriguez Clan: Luis, Sandra, and my goddaughters Camila and Dalia (I love you both).

The Batista Clan: Pedro, Cesarina, Junior, Elijah y mi ahijada Alondra.

The Bernard–de León Clan: Doña Rosa (mi otra madre), Celines de León (true friend), Rosemary, Kelvin and Kayla, Marvin, Rafael (a.k.a. Rafy), Ariel, and my boy Ramon.

Bertrand Wang, Michiyuki Ohno, Shuya Ohno, Brian O'Halloran, Hisham El Hamaway, for being my brothers at the beginning.

Dennis Benzan, Benny Benzan, Peter Moyer, Héctor Piña: for being my brothers at the end.

And Elizabeth de León: for leading me out of great darkness, and giving me the gift of light.